Oliver Friggieri

LET FAIR WEATHER
BRING ME HOME

Translated from Maltese by
Rose Marie Caruana

AUSTIN MACAULEY
PUBLISHERS LTD.

A CIP catalogue record for this title is available from the British Library.

ISBN 978 1 84963 873 9

www.austinmacauley.com

First Published (2015)
Austin Macauley Publishers Ltd.
25 Canada Square
Canary Wharf
London
E14 5LB

Printed and bound in Great Britain

To Elise and Luca
with all my love

Oliver Friggieri, born in Malta in 1947, is a renowned novelist, poet and scholar whose works have been translated into numerous languages and published throughout the world. He is Professor of Literature at the University of Malta and the winner of various international prizes. His long list of books includes about sixty which have been launched outside his native country. His novel *Children Come By Ship* was launched by Austin Macauley Publishers Ltd in 2013.

Chapter 1

In every corner of the neighbourhood, the measured tones of the smallest bell could be heard spreading out from the top of the steeple, which appeared to spear the sky when seen from below, gathering the villagers together, wherever they happened to be at that moment. Those peals had been ringing out for a long time...one stroke after another...with a precise beat...tolling at short intervals. Not even a hint of error trembled in the air to betray that it was the hand of an elderly man pulling on the rope. The exact regularity was a law unto itself, of heaven and earth. All of this could be read in the sound of the bell, and its echo spread far and wide to penetrate even one's heart and wring out a tear, or to break it, or to make it overflow with joy, but always, always, somehow moving one. Nothing else, no other sound, bar the muted murmuring of the crowd. The bell, although small in size, rang out strongly, enough to drown out any other sound, and nobody ever wanted the neighbourhood to resonate with a stronger voice than this. Nothing else was closer to heaven whenever the villagers were gathered round a cradle or a coffin. It took on the role of the clock, the clock that measured every one of heaven's movements.

In the church, somewhere between the naves, under an arched ceiling with images painted all over it, amid the flickering flames of candles and the fragrance of fresh flowers, the decisive and devout woman's voice sounded like another bell which could not be ignored by all those within earshot. Every word issuing from her mouth was like a precise stroke as well.

"I am Katarina, a decent, respectable woman, as anyone will tell you. I was born in this village ... quite a long time ago ... and it was here that I was christened, here that I was married, and here that I raised my daughter in the secluded shelter of our home. This is where life began for me and it is from here that I wish to leave it. Whenever possible, I don't set foot outside without wearing my *ċulqana*, my long loose cotton gown or my *għonnella*, our traditional hooded cloak. If my dress isn't black underneath the *għonnella*, it will at least be a dark dress. I wear a very long skirt; it brushes the ground as you can see, and it doesn't just hide my ankles but nearly my sandals too. And it's a very wide skirt as well. I've never borrowed a *għonnella* from anybody and have no wish to lend mine. Every time I leave the house, and especially when I set foot inside the church, my hair is always gathered into a bun...or nearly always ... scraped back ... without adornment. This is how I was brought up and have always behaved, and this is how I wish to remain till the very end...

"I am Katarina, Saverju's wife. He's no longer with us, and I hope to God and pray that now he's somewhere up there where you can keep an eye on him from up close. That was his wish. Keep a close watch over him because a leopard never changes its spots. I still worry about him, up to this day. I keep hoping that by now he's calmed down a bit and has softened his attitude. He was such a stubborn man. He used to pray just like I do, slowly, so that his prayers could be heard clearly, and he never looked at anyone whilst praying. He used to think that nothing on Earth was amusing, not even humour itself, and I never ever heard him joke. He was stern because he was certain that all the land was nothing but rock, and people, although made of flesh and blood, were rock hard too. He did not indulge himself, with one exception – he liked to draw on a long reed pipe, even when it was unlit. He would nurse it carefully till it smoked and filled the air around. We would feel suffocated but then he would put it out as soon as he reached the threshold of the church, and he would tip it with its bowl turned down into his shirt pocket. He delighted in placing a mint leaf behind his ear, or a basil leaf. That's what mint and basil leaves were only good for, he thought – for their fragrance. When the fancy took him he would breathe in the leaf's fragrance. Occasionally, he would hold the leaf between his lips, or while away the time twirling it between his fingers as if it was a tiny wind pump...

"I am Katarina, Susanna's mother..."

She stopped speaking for a few heartbeats, lowering her head as if to rest and reflect on what she had to say next. Changing her tone, she took up the recitation once more.

"You know me well, St. Joseph, since I come to visit you so often. Maybe I don't come by every day since there are other niches here in the church, but you frequently find me turning up in front of you. You know me well, don't you?" she said giving a smile and a wink as she addressed the statue. "But I'd like to remind you who I am, all the same, as if you've never seen me before. I don't mean to say that you're forgetful, but so many people pass in front of your eyes, so many faces begging and wanting, everybody in need of something." For a moment, her mouth and eyes took on the visage of a devout person in prayer and then she continued. "And since I feel the time has come for you to hear me out, I want to make sure that you haven't forgotten me. I wouldn't like you to grant my wish and bestow it on someone else, by mistake. We villagers all resemble one another. The sun, burning mercilessly, gives us swarthy skins and the wind rushing in from afar dries up our skin. Look closely at me," she said, slowly lifting up her face as if she was trying to gain attention. She pushed back her veil slightly away from her forehead, being careful not to uncover her head too much, and then she pulled the veil forward again and tightened it at her neck, keeping her hands clasped fast beneath her chin. She let her eyes glance away and lowered her head once more, a token gesture to disclaim any over-familiarity. "You don't remember me this way? I've been coming to pray to you for so long, from the very beginning, and here I am still, ever waiting. I haven't given up. I think that someday you will tell me that my wish has been granted. Sweet St. Joseph, you know what dear wish I pray for. Not for my sake, no, otherwise I'd have been too embarrassed to come in supplication before you … but for my sake too. We are all in the same boat, and we share both our sorrows and our joys. Think back a little on how sad you felt when your little boy was lost … so you must know what I'm going through, and your wife understands as well … maybe more so, if you don't mind me saying it. A mother always remains a mother. But I don't want to keep reminding you."

The peals of the small bell were ringing as usual to remind the populace that it was sunset. It was an old custom, stemming from the time when the villagers noted the sun setting behind the little hills surrounding them, and from then on had set about quickly gathering funds and building a church steeple which they filled with bells. From that time onwards, one of the bells had been assigned this duty, it and no other. As the sun set, the villagers would stop whatever they were doing, call to each other, remove their cap and with one hand would hold it close to their chest and pray, saying a few Hail Mary's in the Latin they knew. This was a special moment, for the women at home and for the men in the fields. For all of them, this moment was not theirs, or only theirs for as much time as it took to have them raise their gaze to the sky and with their words try to penetrate that infinite blue vault over their village ... a very small village ... encompassing only a few streets ... in a square ... surrounded by tracts of agricultural land, worked upon throughout the year, the land that sustained them. The village was by its very nature independent, though it knew not the word. It followed its own direction of thought, sound and solid as foundation blocks, and its bounty from the land was enough to feed every single villager.

But the chimes were not there to ring out uselessly. The sacristan did not mind continuing to ring and ring, one peal after another, until he could be sure in his mind that the call sweeping out from his belfry had reached every corner of the village and everyone had heard it, and that he had nothing on his conscience, he need not reproach himself for anything. He would not be to blame if some villagers ignored that call to prayer and continued working, without pausing to say a prayer.

"It's not my fault! They have to look to their own souls, after all! None of us can work miracles, and the bell isn't going to do that, either!" the sacristan could frequently be heard saying to forestall any misgiving and to set his mind at rest that he had done all that was in his power to do, and more. "I've done my part. I've done so for more years than I can count. Better one peal more than one peal less!" Sometimes he would go to confession afraid that he had rung the bell less than usual and, because of that, some people may not have gone to hear mass. The priest would reassure him but he would remain worried, nonetheless.

Together with the steady tramp of the passing seasons, precise, lasting, that allowed no variation and offered no unwelcome surprises, village life answered to another precise pace – the rhythm voiced by the bells in the steeple. It was the village of bells, and every bell had its own voice which spelt out a different word. Every bell, with its own name and foundry date engraved on it, had a story to tell. Together, the bells formed a family, and all of them needed one another. Their peals during feasts were, more than anything else, a celebration of their togetherness. Only they could voice the glory of a village that had no ambition to seek glory. No person went to extremes if he hailed from this village – neither people who rose to great heights nor those who sank low to the very depths. All the villagers sought the middle road, and the middle road had its own virtue. At different times of the day and night, the solitary sound of the bell would come forth, ringing from up there and settling down unconfined, reaching every corner to prompt the villagers to their duty. A duty that touched even those that had passed away but who were not yet completely dead to the world.

The villagers' dead relatives were in some other place, waiting for the prayers of those who had not forgotten them. In this way the bell would command everybody to pray for the dead as well as for the living. Purgatory was full of villagers, and those who were no longer there had already found a place in Heaven, through the intercession of prayers. It was a church bell that woke you up and put you to sleep, that signalled death and that celebrated feasts. Whether for the dawn mass or for the Paternoster, or for the Angelus in the morning and at noon, the bell was like a mother calling her children during the night and throughout the day.

The church was nearly empty. A few old people lingered here and there in front of some niche or other. Otherwise a deep silence reigned, broken only by the sacristan's devotions, for he never did anything without muttering some usual complaint or repeating some small prayer, hardly less ancient than he. He used to recite some holy verses, each one dedicated to a particular painting of a saint or to a statue and he knew one for all of them, by heart. He did not make a single mistake, not by a word. He would recite the short prayer in front of every picture as he was passing by, and would throw a kiss from afar at every statue. The sacristan never once kissed someone in his life in the land of the living, but he daily covered all the niches with the messages of his mouth. He felt certain that his own work was gathering merit which would count in future, as if they were golden sovereigns of his time, there for the time when he came to close his eyes for the last time. He had no doubt at all that this was one of the advantages his work afforded him, work by which he earned his living down here on Earth and by which he was able to store blessings for his future life after death. He had spent his life close to the altar, amidst the fragrance of incense, inhaling the whiff of red damask and sashes of all colours under the sorrowful gaze of saints always looking out at him from their paintings and statues. All this confirmed him in his belief that he would find an easy path from here to up there. He strongly believed that he would go straight to Heaven from the village, directly, with no time lost in waiting.

Katarina paused in mid-prayer and waited for the strokes of the bell to cease. She could not grumble at their noise because that would give offence to God and to other people. In her books, the least unruly word she could utter, even under her breath, about anything that had to do with the church, would have been a sin. Without wanting to, she started counting the strokes one after another, silently mouthing them, with her lips barely moving. Like all the villagers she felt their measured beat increase her sense of respect and solemnity, and besides, they served to remind her that they were an integral part of her upbringing. Without the village bells, there would be no villagers. Their existence would be null and void. The older the bells became, the more they were renewed.

The last stroke reverberated around the church and silence asserted itself almost with a jolt, and by right.

"That's enough now. That's the last stroke!" the sacristan said to himself as he tied the bell's thick rope to a huge hook which he himself had hammered into the wall of the bell tower many years ago. "That's enough for today. Now it's time for silence! And then, early tomorrow morning I'll make them ring out for prayers to be said for the dear departed souls. *Eternal rest grant unto them, O Lord. Let perpetual light shine upon them ...*"

The heavy tread of the sacristan's footsteps as he climbed down the narrow spiral staircase from the belfry could be heard even inside the church. As usual, the winding stairs made him dizzy but this was one of those tiny little crosses he had to bear each day, endured with hardly an effort on his part though he could never come to like them.

Katarina rolled her eyes at St. Joseph to show him that in the meantime she had neither forgotten him nor had got fed up waiting. She raised her hand to re-arrange her veil. Her hair had to be almost completely covered up, and it would have counted as a sin to leave it uncovered in church. She was in the habit of fixing her veil even when there was no need. Now and then the women in church all had a habit of doing so, as if they managed to change their mood with every gesture, their hand going up and down. Katarina's gaze slowly travelled around her making certain that no one could overhear her from where she sat. Everyone indulged his or her curiosity, it was not merely something let loose in the streets or locked up in houses.

There was only a scattering of old people in the entire church, all far away from her.

"I am Katarina, Susanna's mother!" she continued. "As I was saying, you know what favour I wish you to grant me, not for myself ... though for my sake, too. For my daughter's sake and for that of her son. You know the whole story only too well, I've already recounted it to you, but in my heart I felt I shouldn't ask you to grant me this favour before some time would have passed. I continued to remind you from time to time, lest you'd think I'd changed my mind and wished for something else, but now the time has come ... Just a bit more, St. Joseph, and everything will turn out well. My husband and I always lived decently, from the time when we were still courting..." she told him. With these words a smile could be seen playing around her lips. She raised her face to be certain that St. Joseph could see her better.

After a few moments she glanced around, her gaze sweeping every corner of the church.

~ 0 ~

Katarina and Saverju had first set eyes on each other, close to, at the village market. It was here that most of the villagers met each other every morning, to see the produce that was on offer, haggle over prices, greet each other, gossip about everybody, entertain desires and dreams, smile or scowl, and stop to chat and then leave.

Katarina was an innocent girl; she had no knowledge yet of a young man's love. A young man was a different being, who knew how to talk, was strong, earned money and had many attractive attributes. But above all he was a different being. One day she was out walking with her aunt, staying so close to her that they looked almost as if they were joined together at the hip, arm-in-arm, so as not to get separated in the crowds and lose sight of each other. They were on their way home, their large straw shopping basket full to the brim with that day's shopping. The fresh vegetables gave off a scent which could be smelt some way off. It was one of those rare times when Katarina had not gone out shopping with her mother. She was intent on the shopping basket, but slowly, slowly, several thoughts started intruding, different from usual, and they were pleasing. Often, she had no wish to banish them from her mind and frequently found herself at a loss to know what to make of them. More often than not they confused her. She was not sure that having a flower pot placed on the window ledge really signified that a young maid of marriageable age could be found in that household, waiting for love to come her way. And neither was she certain that if a young man was on the lookout for courtship he would put a flower behind his ear, or wear a red carnation, or knot a red kerchief around his neck. Somewhere, between dreams and the reality of the market place, one could find love. In those days, as soon as a girl became a maid and outgrew her childhood, it was still the custom to have her spend her time embroidering the large sheet her mother would have bought for her, and thus would have to wait for her future to come knocking at her door, all the while embroidering diligently. With needle and thread in hand, eyes lowered down to the cloth, she was expected to come to know and school her own heart, without either haste or delay. Embroidering meant learning to be patient. She was meant to start realizing that she could not walk alone in her youth, but rather was meant to be guided along by older and wiser heads. Above all, she was expected to learn to accept her lot and not ask too many questions.

Up to that day Katarina had never set eyes on such a young man. Being accompanied by her aunt meant that she need not become confused by anything. There was no call for her to blush needlessly, nor to lower her head and gaze down at the ground. Adults knew how to guide the young. Young people could be safely guided through life because life was one whole lesson which adults had already learnt from their forebears.

Life was a one-way street, and everyone had to step forward when it was their turn to do so, time after time.

At that very moment a young man approached them and he addressed Katarina. "May I have a word?" He gazed at her long and respectfully, but impassively, without a smile on his face. He was feeling shy but appeared strong willed and clearly very self-possessed.

Katarina drew back, huddling close to her aunt. She lifted the shopping basket from its large handles and then, holding on to its bottom, pressed it against her chest as if afraid that it was about to be snatched out of her arms. Then she took a few steps forward. She kept her head down but could not help observing the young man and his imprint was a sharp memory that stayed with her. His appearance was pleasing. Truly! The more one could observe a young man from up close the more different he looked. With her thoughts running in that direction that is what struck her.

He was still waiting for her to reply and kept up with her.

"If you want to talk to me you must speak to my father," she told him, pressing herself once more against her aunt. The two of them continued on their way home, at their usual measured pace without looking back. She felt overcome with shyness but at the same time felt a sweet joy that was altogether new to her.

The young man went in search of her father and informed him that he had met his daughter at the market and wanted to court her.

Katarina's father stood straight before him, his hands clasped behind his back, sizing up the young man from head to toe with a penetrating gaze, observing him closely, slightly amused but remaining silent, though not in an intimidating manner. He was not disposed to speak out of turn but neither was he prepared to hold back. These affairs required trust and suspicion, at one and the same time...like a business matter. That very same evening Katarina's father called upon a friend of his, whom he had known since they had been children together, and he asked him to act as a marriage broker.

"You know the entire village...inside out. You know everybody, everyone's parentage. I've got a matter for you to deal with. Are you interested?"

"Yes, I'm interested, but what is it exactly? Don't tell me, to arrange a marriage?"

"Yes, a marriage deal! How did you guess?"

"I've been in this business for quite a while! Everyone comes to me to broker marriages. And since that's why you came to me let me tell you something. Every marriage I've arranged has succeeded. A man and a woman...they met...through my efforts...and I can tell you that they've all lasted, they've all stayed together right till the end. I don't want to boast too much, but that's the way it is. You can ask around and everyone will confirm it. My deals bind people fast together – with a knot!"

"There's no need for me to ask anyone, I know. Where would I find a better marriage broker? There's a lad who's set his sights on my Katarina. See what you can find out about him and his parentage. Let's see what kind of young man he is, what his intentions are and whether he's good marriage material. Make sure that he's a steady boy, not some fly-by-night. If he's the sort to blow hot and cold he can jolly well change direction and clear off at once. I want to make sure he's worthy of my daughter. She's a decent maid. I'll pay you after the marriage service. You can be sure I'll pay up promptly. The lad's name is Saverju," Katarina's father finished telling him.

~ 0 ~

There were many candles burning brightly in front of St. Joseph's niche. Katarina realised that she had not yet lit one herself. She pulled out a coin from her deep skirt pocket and pushed it through the slot of the money box at the side. On the other side of the niche there was another box holding candles, white narrow ones, ready to be chosen by the saint's devotees. Katarina chose one and lit it using the flame of one already burning, placing it in one of the empty spaces left in the rack, spaces waiting to be filled with more newly-lit candles. Their flames, flickering upright, all of them rising with a single slight motion, seemed to be a choir of strong wishful prayers, most probably alike, just as the people of that locality seemed to resemble one another.

"If you grant my prayer St. Joseph, I'll light a much bigger candle than this for you," Katarina continued. "We're decent respectable people who keep our word. Saverju, God forgive him, wasn't a bad man. From the moment he approached me at the market place up to his death, he remained my husband. He spent all his life here, at church, at home, in the fields and nowhere else. He was brought up well, because he came from a decent family, and he never set foot outside the village and didn't know what wickedness was. His whole world revolved around these confines. I am witness to all of this. He wanted to live his life with me in the same way he and I had been brought up. And that is how he wished Susanna to be brought up, not spoilt, and without a lot of empty talk. As long as Susanna lived her life the same way, everything was fine. But when the rules were broken, things couldn't go on being the same for my daughter. And even she herself was changed in our eyes. I felt as if the roof had collapsed on us all, a roof made up of many people, many families, many years. That sheltering roof had been in the making for a very long time. That's what my husband used to say. He had exclaimed in horror 'She's ruined everything! She's destroyed everything we've built up over all this time!' 'No, Saverju, not so!' I had pleaded. 'Everything can be mended!' My words were like straw to a fire...he lost his temper and couldn't even bear to see me; he almost believed I was secretly hand-in-glove with my daughter. Like a bolt out of the blue the roof fell all around us, in a strong and sudden storm that seemed to have arrived too early. But then I started thinking...'I have an idea, Saver, a good one I think,' I ventured to say. 'A good idea? From you? Let's hear this wonderful idea of yours...Go on, spit it out,' he snarled. 'Let us pray to St. Joseph, and we'll see what he has to say,' I said. 'What can St. Joseph possibly say?' he asked me angrily. 'He'll say exactly what I'm saying. He'll side with me. And do you know why? Because I'm not to be moved on this. That's how it always was and that's how it is to this day; and that's how it should remain.' He then fell silent, as if he was mulling it over, and then went on, 'I've taken my decision. But if you want to see what St. Joseph has to say that's fine. Afterwards come and tell me. Mind, keep this all a secret; don't even whisper a word about it to Fr. Grejbel! If you dare to open your mouth I'll soon find out. Don't even think of hoodwinking me!' Those are the very words he said to me," Katarina averred.

There were the usual few old people praying in church, and their mumbled fervent prayers sounded like a muted choir, a sweet choir of singers without any grand pretensions, singing in the way they knew how, with simple words and untutored skill, but from a bottomless heart.

"I'd come before you and laid bare the whole sorry story, St. Joseph! Do you remember?" Katarina went on. "You had advised me to wait and do my part. Your counsel was to let time heal everything and to tell my husband so. 'Is that what St. Joseph had to say?' Saverju had wanted to know the minute I set foot back home. 'Well then, you must leave it all to me. St. Joseph has decided so and I am determined on this. As for you, you must do your part.' I had no idea what was expected of me, and I asked him, 'What am I supposed to do? Susanna is my daughter too!' I was to accompany him and see all that he was going to do as long as – he insisted – as long as we let time pass. I asked him how long did he have in mind and he answered me, 'When the time comes we'll know! We'll know when the time comes! Wait! Only time knows best. This is the law that holds true in the fields.' And so it came to pass. I remained waiting. My husband's death signalled that the time had come. I was able to take everything upon myself. I held the reins from that moment. Now I will leave everything in your hands, St. Joseph. All my strength brought me to this moment but no more! It's as if I've been carrying a sackful of crops, and now look, I'm laying it all down to rest at your feet. Take it!"

There were still some old people in church, praying and praying, ceaselessly.

"The boy is safe and sound. Don't worry, Katarina!" she imagined St. Joseph telling her. The statue of St. Joseph was a very old one, made of wood. He was made to look elderly, his head bent over the figure of Baby Jesus held in his arms, wearing a cloak that came down to the ground, barefoot. In his other hand he held a long stem, with large wide leaves and a pale pink flower. The villagers called this plant 'St. Joseph's staff' or 'St. Joseph's rod' and it flowered every two years. During the month of May his niche would be full of it. Everyone who cultivated it, whether in their garden or field, would bring a bunch of it to lay before his statue.

"I know, St. Joseph. I know where the little boy is to be found, but I don't want him to stay there any more. I want him to be with his mother," Katarina prayed.

"Susanna is looking for him. She's been searching for him for a long time," St. Joseph seemed to be telling her.

"I know, I know all that."

"But if you knew, why didn't you approach her and speak to her? You've spent many years estranged from each other. You never spoke to each other. You never went to see each other. Mother and daughter at odds with one another. But for all that you were still her mother and she was still your daughter."

"Is that what you think, St. Joseph?" she told him, taken aback.

"That's what I think, Katarina."

"That means you've always thought so, right from the start?"

"I always think in the same way, Katarina. Love is always the same."

"Saverju had told me to let time pass. How was I to know how much time had to pass?"

"And time hasn't taught you anything, Katarina?"

"I learnt one thing, at least. And it was Saverju who taught me this lesson. I had to go on praying and wait for change. He knew he would die before me, and he left everything in my hands. Though on his deathbed, he never let a single word pass between his lips to answer Susanna, right up to the end, I knew this was his way of keeping faith with the way he had been brought up. He did not wish to be the one to break this ancient law, but it seemed as if he wanted me to break with the past and take this step. After all, he knew that I was constantly in your confidence. I never hid anything from him; I neither wished to nor could. Susanna had to suffer her punishment, but not forever. That's what I understood."

A little way off, on the other side of the church, the sacristan was looking in her direction in silence. He could not bring himself to interrupt her devotions and ask her to leave so he waited for her to finish. He could see how intent she was from her gestures and the movement of her lips. Occasionally her words became softly audible but not enough to be distinguished. As soon as he saw Katarina making the Sign of the Cross and reaching out her right hand to touch the glass pane of the niche and then bringing it to her lips and kiss it, he concluded that she was about to take her leave. He remained where he was, the candle snuffer in his hand, let a few moments pass and then approached St. Joseph's niche to extinguish the candles burning before it.

As Katarina walked home lost in thought she could not help wondering whether the words she had heard in her head came from St. Joseph or from her late husband. She wished she could believe that those words of comfort came from both of them together. She would have liked to think, too, that this time St. Joseph had touched Saverju's heart, wherever he lay in eternal rest, so that he could agree with her and give her his permission for what she was doing. And Saverju had to yield. Both of them had a part to play, St Joseph in one way and Saverju in another.

Her vow to St. Joseph was like a chest in which she stored all the treasures in her life. She still had to give Susanna a dowry; so far she had not been able to do so. And now she must add to it all these efforts she was making at the saint's feet, and she was certain he would not let her wait in vain. She only needed a final reassurance that she had not left anybody out of her calculations and devotions.

Before she visited St. Joseph again, Katarina picked a bunch of flowers and carried them to the cemetery, walking up to stand in front of her husband's gravestone. "Saverju," she spoke to him, "you are my husband forever, you were my husband before and you still are now. Set your mind at rest about that. I have not looked out for another man. I want you to know what I'm about to do now that the time has finally come, and the power rests with me now. I never made a step without your approval. You are a man. But perhaps my word, at the end of it all, has finally come to mean something. Maybe it's not true that you never listened to what I had to say. It's not true that I counted for nothing. That's not true!" she whimpered. "Tell me that I did count for something too, tell me that I wasn't completely worthless, Saver. I was a woman, from the top of my head to the tips of my toes...Though you didn't know it, didn't even want to, you ended up by yielding to me. You always snapped at me, and I always treated you with sweetness...you behaved in one way and I in another, and finally sweetness won you over. You needn't feel offended because I'm telling you this. And don't be upset if you hear me say these things to people. Let me feel proud about myself, just a little," she pleaded with him, beginning to cry, "even after all this time. I want to cherish every little bit I have left. I, too, need to hold onto something to ease and comfort me, Saver, and for so many years there was never anything to bring me heart's ease. Though I never had the courage to tell you all this before, at least I'm telling you now. Don't feel hurt, Saver; you did your best, in the way you knew how. Now I can look back and understand, more than ever. A woman's heart always keeps waiting and hoping. I've done everything by your leave so far. And I've come here to set my mind at rest that you know everything." She stopped, changed her tone and lightly passed her right hand over the edge of the tombstone. She then raised her hand, shook off the dust and in a firm voice said, "St. Joseph, intercede for him. I'm going now." She placed the bunch of flowers on the grave, made the Sign of the Cross, pulled up her veil with both hands and left the cemetery.

A few days later Katarina woke up very early and said to herself, "Today I'll go to St. Joseph and affirm my vow, word for word. This time I'll go early in the morning, as soon as the bell rings out for the first mass of the day, because that's when my mind feels most fresh, and I'll be able to remember everything, and I'll let him know all that I intend to give in the way of votive thanks if he grants my prayer. Everyone needs somebody to stand by them, and one feels more merciful at the start of a new day." Some minutes later saw her standing at the church door, waiting to be the first one to enter the church.

The sacristan was still raising the heavy bolts from the ground and taking down the cross-bar. That was his first chore in the morning – to open one side of the little door set in the huge doorway, a signal for the old people at the front to enter the church. The main door of the church was only opened wide whenever the village feast came round.

The streets were still silent and hardly anyone could be seen, though it would soon be time to start the day's work.

"You got up early today, Katarina! The first word Our Lord will hear today will be yours," he greeted her. "He hears so many words every day! Wonderful words. At least, I think so since I don't actually know what people are telling him. It's none of my business after all, though I stand as His sentry. What I know for sure is that He needs to have a lot of patience to stand listening to everybody's prayers all day long."

Katarina remained on the doorstep, waiting for the sacristan to move on. He knew everyone and did not hold back from having a word with all those who entered there. He could write a book about all the happenings in the village, and it would end up being a thick volume. He enjoyed repeating that to himself and sometimes would venture to say it also to people, to remind them that everything began and ended in that place, at the centre of the village, in the depths of each heart that entered there to open up and pray for something. Every niche had a long story to tell, and villagers of all ages would gather to pray there. They chanted their hymns, reciting them from memory, taking pleasure in the regular rhythm and words that rhymed at the end. Many a villager had a turn for making up rhyming verses and singing them while at work in the fields, and all villagers recited prayers with an integral rhyme when they got down on their knees before God. Some of them were in the habit of opening their arms wide as soon as they began their prayers, as if they were about to embrace the whole world in their arms, and others used to clasp their palms together and lower their heads till their nose touched their two forefingers. At other times people prayed in silence, in their heart, as if they were holding a conversation with someone in the village square or in a shop or in the market place, spontaneously, with whatever words came to mind. Each prayer would be said once, twice, or even more, to make certain that it would be heard. They prayed unthinkingly, not bothering to reflect what they needed to say, and the words came out as they had been learnt, by word of mouth, from one generation to the next, and no need was ever felt to have them written down. The villagers could not write and continued fast in their belief that there was no need for them to learn. Their every hymn had its beginning somewhere in the fields around the church, or in the hidden places or depths of the Valley, the cradle of an entire village.

Katarina entered the church without saying a word. She dipped her right hand in the font of holy water and raised it to her forehead, passing it slowly, slowly from side to side, till water started dripping down. She bobbed her head and bent her knee slightly in reverence in front of the main altar, said a prayer under her breath and slowly made the Sign of the Cross.

The sacristan did not look more than once at her, but from the corner of his eyes he noticed that she was walking with a walking stick. "Am I seeing right? Does Katarina have a walking stick?" he murmured beneath his breath. He pursed his lips, as if surprised by something quite unexpected, and looked at her once more, surreptitiously. His eyes had not misled him. As far as he knew, that was a man's walking stick. Many old people did not set foot outside their house without one, and on entering the church they would let it rest against the back of a chair or remain leaning on it even when sitting down. They would not trust it out of their sight for even a moment. Their hand had got used to the new strength it gave them. But as for the women, even those who found walking difficult, it was another story and very few ventured outside with one. It smacked too much of something essentially male, and somehow it seemed to detract some quality in a woman's appearance. A woman using a walking stick indicated a woman with uncommon pluck, all the more so since a walking stick denoted a weakness which should not appear in public. Women were not meant to grow old and weak.

Katarina made her way to St. Joseph's niche.

The sacristan tried hard to think of something else to occupy his mind, but curiosity overwhelmed him.

"This is the vow I'd made in front of you, St. Joseph," Katarina began her prayer. "I have no words with which to thank you on behalf of my daughter Susanna and myself. Finally the boy has been returned to us by your grace. Thank you, thank you, thank you. I will never forget your great kindness towards us. I've already told Susanna that we should dress up the boy like you when he comes to church, in the procession during the village feast. I will sew a beautiful garment exactly like yours. I will dress him up as a little St. Joseph! I've set it all out in my mind. In the next few days the votive garment will be ready, you'll see. And before I make him wear it I'll bring it here to show it to you. I've chosen a fine piece of cloth like yours. I bought it a long time ago because I've always had faith that the time would come when I could have it made up. I myself will sew it, and I hope you'll like it. I know you never disregard what people offer up to you. I also promise to bring the boy for early mass and bring him over here to you."

The sacristan remained sitting down on a chair, looking towards the altar, and from time to time sneaking glances at St. Joseph's niche.

"And finally, St. Joseph, I would like you to turn your attention to my husband's soul. A little while before his death he, Saverju that is, turned to me almost in secret and asked me to go on confiding in you," she revealed. "And I understood. Ever since he died my life has changed a lot...I've done everything as it was proper to do so, on my word as a woman. Before I came here I sought his permission. I've done nothing behind his back so he'd have a share in all this too. There, I've done well, haven't I?"

Up to now, so early in the day, only one candle burned brightly in front of the niche.

"Katarina must have lit a candle. Well then, she must be petitioning for something, or perhaps she's already had what she prayed for. Every candle means being granted a huge favour, and nobody will light a candle for no good reason because every candle costs a lot of money, and nobody prays for nothing," the sacristan reasoned in his mind. "But that walking stick...what on earth did she bring it for, so early in the day?"

Katarina slowly raised the walking stick, as if lifting a heavy weight, and was about to lay it down on the edge of the niche, where the candles were placed. She stopped to think for a moment and then searched for a way to open the niche. But she soon realised that it would probably be locked. Looking slightly flustered, she let the stick fall back and turned her head round, looking for assistance.

As soon as he saw her peering round, the sacristan got up from his chair, gestured to her with his hand and walked towards her. This was the moment he had been waiting for. He stopped, waiting for her to speak.

"This was my husband's walking stick, God rest his soul."

"Saverju's walking stick, you say?" the sacristan asked her full of curiosity. "I never saw him walking with it. I seem to remember he always walked on his own two feet. I could be mistaken though, you know. Time passes by quickly..."

"Not for outdoor use, no. He had two of them, one for everyday use and another to use on feast days. And this is it. He didn't like using it too often. It was always kept in the wardrobe. Look what a fine handle it has! It even has a ferrule. His father had bequeathed it to him, and besides being an antique it has good craftsmanship, and it's made out of good quality wood," Katarina elaborated. She thought her mild boasting would cover the confusion she felt at being unable to carry out her word.

"And now you've taken to using it? In memory of Saverju?"

"I use it? Me with a walking stick? No, no, of course not, nothing of the sort," she replied promptly. "I had made a vow to St. Joseph and I want to offer it up. But I don't know how..."

"A vow? That's all? That's nothing. Don't you know what to do? Just let me deal with it, that's what I'm here for," he reassured her, all the while eyeing the walking stick. "It's a handsome piece, truly handsome! That's just the sort of thing to suit such a great saint like St. Joseph. A staff that does him proud, Saverju I mean, it does him honour and reflects well on you too."

"I'm not a rich lady, but one good turn deserves another," she went on. "We should be grateful and reciprocate to whoever does us a good turn."

"Well said, that's how it should be. And such a statue as this deserves that."

"I also told him 'if there's anything else you'd like, St. Joseph, if I can manage it, just tell me. Whatever you wish for, if I have it I'll give it to you.' That's what I vowed."

"There now, that's just as it should be, as it should be," the sacristan repeated.

She understood what he meant to say by his tone of voice. There were some who offered up some paltry commonplace thing after making a vow and having their prayer granted.

The sacristan went nearer to the niche looking closely to see where he could place the walking stick, and he slowly nodded his head. "There's a good place for it. There are still many empty places; that means plenty more vows can be made. All that space needs to be filled up. Look, just look!" he exclaimed gesturing with his hand. "Granted prayers, stored up somewhere above. Closed boxes, ready to be opened up. One day they'll come down here, too. It all depends on how much people pray. If they pray for much, they'll receive much, and if they pray for little...It's been ever so since the dawn of time. You reap what you sow. Yes? Wait here for me a little bit," he continued, "I'll go and get the key to open the niche. I know where it is, I won't leave you here for long, holding that stick. Saverju's walking stick."

"Now it's St. Joseph's staff," she quipped.

"You're right, now it's become even more important," he replied in all seriousness, and went off.

Katarina preened with pleasure at his words. "Goodness knows how many sermons he's heard in his life! And now he himself has come to know how to preach!"

"You can choose a place for it yourself. See where you'd like to put it," he told her as soon as he came back with the key and opened the small door of the niche. "Choose a place where it can be seen clearly, because it's really distinctive and enhances the niche. And everyone will be content, both those up in Heaven and the people down here."

"It really is handsome, isn't it?" Katarina asked him, wanting reassurance.

"It enhances the niche, and, let me tell you, it does you honour!"

As Katarina made her way home she looked at the fields surrounding the village; they looked like open walls standing sentinel over those born and bred within their girth. Fields that offered something special all year round. Some nourished crops for food, and others overflowed with flowers. There were flowers with a sweet fragrance while others had no scent, but all were beautiful to behold. In their midst, one plant grew with a thick and tall stem, and extended wide large leaves. It was a plant which flowered with a pale pink bloom, and it flourished in the month of May.

Chapter 2

The serene silence of that evening seemed too thick and deep to be broken. Not even the clatter of the teaspoon stirring the thick, stewed tea in the teacup could break it. The teaspoon was stirred, rattling the teacup, going round and round, many more times than need be...as if it was a protracted game of patience. It had been raining steadily for a long time, but gently, not heavily. But then it started pouring, growing heavier and heavier, until it was in full spate quite suddenly as if escaping in a torrent from somewhere. Clouds had long been gathering, and darkness had been drawing in for some time, closing in over the whole neighbourhood. Within a short space of time the fields lost their green aspect, and total darkness fell, all of a sudden. The few people remaining outside quickly sought to cover their head somehow and they scuttled back home as fast as they could. A few footsteps could be heard in the street, some slamming of doors, some murmuring, and then nothing; total silence muffled the whole place.

Stroke after stroke, the bell that rang out at sunset reverberated around every street and every alley. That sort of weather seemed to enhance its voice, and draw it affectionately closer to the heart and mind of those long used to hearing it. Bells were part and parcel of each of their lives, accompanying them from the cradle to the grave. The villagers believed that the bell rang out more strongly in bad weather, and it seemed as if it was more attuned to their ears and sounded sweeter than on other evenings. Its strong voice was theirs...a voice that could reach far and wide, because their own had not its reach. The bell that rang out in bad weather also meant a prayer was being said for nothing untoward to happen and to hasten the storm's passing. It was the village of bells. Comfort and pride, grief and joy, all found their essence in each stroke, faithful and firm, which dutifully pealed forth at the right moment.

Even on such an evening as this, everything looked calm when seen through the window left ajar. Silence reigned over the dwellings, the fields were a dark spread, and the streets and alleys glimmered with rain.

Susanna went to the window and closed the inner glazed frames, leaving the shutters open. The rain pelting down made her feel happy. She did not know why it appealed to her, but had never bothered to reason it out. It was a feeling that had grown up with her, she always remembered it so, and it had never left her...The scent of fresh rain...the runnels and smears on the window panes...the water pattering down in measured drumbeats of sound...sometimes running slower and sometimes gathering strength...and above all, the gusts of wind – the sound of strong blustery squalls whistling and blowing and pealing like bells through the chinks in the doorjambs and window frames...She used to enjoy imitating the same sound with her mouth, blowing and blowing with her lips turned into a round circle, an inviting loop calling on the world to look at her, to look upon her with delight. But that was when she was a mere slip of a girl, innocent of any vanity. Her only wish was to enjoy, as much as she could, the rain falling down. It was one of her habits, one of those that grew alongside her without her taking much notice, and these habits suited her still, like a dress for all seasons.

Susanna went back to the table and sat down holding the teacup between both her hands, cupping it, as if it was a wide chalice held lovingly, and cherished as if it was treasured. The tea always tasted good, but mostly when she dunked some *biskuttelli* in it, some sweet-tasting rusks, or when she broke some *galletti* and dropped pieces of them into the cup, watching the fragments of water-biscuits skimming around as if they were little ships which would then swell up and sink to the bottom. All at once she would dip the teaspoon inside the teacup and scoop them up, one by one. Sometimes she threw in pieces of bread as well.

That's what her father used to do. Susanna had spent her whole life watching him from a few paces away, at the same table, in the same room, without one word being spoken between them. Not only was he her father, and a stern one at that, but she was also a girl.

When she was little she used to eat heartily, with a good appetite, but now she knew that a real appetite for something did not come from hunger but from a great desire to remember once more, and become a child again, happy with little things, with anything, even with rain that was there for everyone, with simple food being crumbled in tea, and with anything and everything that came along. Everything was there for her to enjoy, and it was there within her reach, a few paces away from her outstretched arms, just a bit higher up, like the special hideaways her mother used in a cupboard set higher up than was usual, so little Susanna would be unable to reach it, even if she were to get a chair and stand on tip toe on it. Her father's house was full of secrets. Maybe it held money, a few pounds that had been put by, or...

"See now, Wistin, how right we were not to linger outside today? If we had stayed out we would be wet through from head to toe, completely drenched, because...There, can you see? The weather changed all of a sudden. Look how it's pelting down! It's lovely watching the rain but only when you're snug inside watching it from a window, not letting it pour down over your head! Aren't you hearing it?"

"No, I'm not," he answered her in a puling voice.

"You're not hearing it? Well, you know why that is, don't you? It's because I've just closed the window. Shall I open it again so you can hear it?"

"No. I don't want to hear it. And even if you open the window, I won't hear it, all the same!"

"Don't you want to come and sit beside me and have some tea with me? And have a bit of the *biskuttell* or *galletta*? Come and have some like me. Why don't you?"

"No, Mummy. I don't want *biskuttelli*...or *galletti*. I don't like them."

"Aren't you hungry? Or maybe you don't want to eat with me?"

"No, Mummy. I'm not hearing the rain and I'm not hungry either."

"Wistin, Wistin! Are you going to say no to everything I tell you, this evening? Now I'm going to ask you something and mind you say yes this time. Alright?"

"Alright! You can ask me but I don't know if I will say yes. Maybe yes and maybe no, it depends!"

"Well then, hear me out, Wistin, and mind you answer me how I told you to. Do you love your mother?"

Wistin remained silent.

Susanna could hear him in the next room, trying to stifle his laughter. "Wistin, come now, answer me. Do you love your mother? Your mother loves you very much, and did as much as she possibly could for you, and that's why I think you love her too. That's what I think, but I still want to ask you. Do you love your mother?"

"No, I don't love her."

"Wistin! You don't love me! How can that be, all of a sudden?"

Wistin stopped to think for a while. After a few moments he burst out, "I was joking, Mummy. That wasn't true! I was teasing you! Of course I love you!"

"Then I was right. And how much do you love me?"

"A lot, a lot!"

"And a lot, a lot, is how much?" she asked him.

Wistin leapt down from the bed and came forward. "This much, look Mummy, this much!" he exclaimed appearing in the doorway of the dining room. His arms were outstretched, braced, wanting to contain all his love within them. He hugged her to him and she cradled him against her, then lifted him up onto her knees, looked at him long and lovingly, proudly, and then pressed him to her side once more and kissed him fondly over and over again. "I want to kiss you and never stop."

"Ouch, Mummy, you're hurting me!"

"Hurting you! Kisses are hurting you? Don't you know what kisses are made of? Silk. How easily you feel hurt! There now, is the pain gone? Are you still miffed with me, Wistin?"

"I wasn't quarrelling with you, Mummy."

"Well then why did you go to bed earlier than usual? And you left me here all alone. The rain and me, huh! The rain didn't leave me alone, and I kept looking at it and hearing it. That's why the rain falls down too, to keep those who are alone company."

"You and the rain!" Wistin cried in merriment. "As if rain is somebody! The rain isn't anybody."

"Then what is rain, do you think, Wistin?"

"Rain is, rain..." Wistin stammered, and then stopped. "That's true; I don't know what rain is. Water sent down by Baby Jesus. Isn't that what you told me?"

"Baby Jesus is very, very great, boundless, we can't imagine how much. And he has a jug of water, and this jug is huge, and he fills it up with water and pours it over us, and that's how rain falls down, and he has so much water to give us that everywhere becomes wet and the ground drinks it up and everybody drinks and can live. Everybody drinks from Baby Jesus' jug, Wistin."

"And so what is the sea? A big jug, full to the brim? Once you told me that the sea filled up because everybody leaves behind a tear during his life. And another time you said the sea is full of Baby Jesus' tears. When He cries, his tears fall straight down into the sea, and the sea fills up. The sea has been there for a very long time, and slowly, slowly it filled up. Drop by drop. That's what you said, and I don't forget."

Susanna smiled slightly and bowed her head. "Drop by drop, little by little, everything moves forward slowly." She tried to change the subject. "Do you know what I know for sure? The rain, Wistin, is what made us come back home earlier this evening. Isn't that why you were miffed with me, dear heart?"

"We came back when it hadn't started raining yet. You just didn't feel like playing with me any more this evening, didn't you?"

"Wistin, your mother feels what's coming before it happens, and that's why I don't waste time or wait around needlessly..."

"Does that mean you knew it was about to rain? Before any raindrops fell? How did you know? Only Baby Jesus knows what will happen. That's what you said. There weren't any clouds in the sky yet."

The rain grew stronger, and lightning flashed right into the room, and Wistin flinched. Thunder and lightning could be heard, sometimes near and sometimes some way off. Both of them felt apprehensive and drew close to each other. Susanna quickly got up to close the window shutters and latch them securely, and then she went back to Wistin's side.

"Oh, how frightening!" he cried out.

At that very moment they heard the church bells begin to ring out.

"The bells, Mummy!"

"The sacristan is ringing the bells to pray for the storm to end, Wistin. We hear the bells and pray along with him. Don't you know that the sacristan always does that whenever there's a storm?"

"But will the storm pass, Mummy?"

"Pray, just pray, son, our prayers will be answered. It's a long road but it leads to another. Baby Jesus hears all our prayers, even from afar..." she told him as she glanced around. She got up and went to look for the candle blessed at Candlemass which she had put away in the cupboard. She never spent a day inside her house without it. "I'm going to light it. Really I'm supposed to light it behind the window so it can be seen from outside where the storm is raging."

"No, Mummy, no! Don't open the shutters!" Wistin pleaded with her in fright.

"Oh, alright, I won't. You won't see the storm. Only grown-ups should see storms anyhow. There now, there's no need to be afraid." She was just as frightened as he was but was doing her best not to let him realize. She lit the candlemass candle in a corner of the room, and took out two rolls of bread from a drawer in the cupboard and put them on the table.

Wistin stared at her.

"These are rolls baked in honour of the saint. They're not for eating. We'll wet them with water and recite some prayers for the storm to pass quickly. Come, recite after me, Wistin,

Saint Barbara, we look to you and pray,
Let damage and destruction, from us stay away!"

It was cold, and Susanna left the spirit lamp lit, putting a tin can with tea on top to brew. "You won't feel cold anymore," she reassured her son, more to take his mind off the storm. "And tomorrow we'll make *minestra* and some *imbuljuta* too. The thick vegetable soup and dish of boiled chestnuts with chocolate and spices will warm you up, you'll see."

"Mummy, you still haven't told me how you knew it was going to rain," Wistin reminded her.

"It's not just the clouds that give you warning when rain is coming, no, not just clouds. In time, one gets used to life and all it brings. Especially we villagers, far more than other sorts of people, because we know how every blade of grass grows."

"So that's why we didn't go right into the countryside to play today, Mummy? Is that why?"

"Yes, that's another reason why, son. See now, how much your mother takes care of you?"

"But tell me the truth, Mummy! Don't you get fed up playing with me? I like playing children's games. I think you prefer grown-ups' games. And even if you were young, you'd play girls' games. You're not a girl anymore."

"But don't you know that I don't mind playing with you, Wistin? There are games that suit both children like you and grown-ups like me. Can you tell me what sort of games these are?"

Wistin paused to think. His right hand forefinger crept into his mouth, and the fingers on his other hand made involuntary gestures, revealing someone deep in thought.

Susanna removed his finger from his mouth. "Don't do that," she admonished him. "Otherwise you'll end up like that even when you grow up."

"I'm thinking, Mummy, but I don't know. Is it hide-and-seek?"

"No," she denied.

"Whose-the-pat? A race? The castle game? You always play these games with me. And you're a grown-up."

"No, none of these! Guess again. Well, alright , let me tell you...The Kite! The Game of the Kite!"

"The kite? We've never played that game, Mummy. What's that?"

Susanna explained it all to him. "Everyone who has a wish stored up in his heart flies a kite, son. Each wish is like a bird that flies up high, soaring and swooping up above, and slipping far, far away until it cannot be seen any longer, but always with something in its heart that makes it return to earth, to the place from where it left..."

"Back to the nest, Mummy, isn't that what you were going to say?"

"Back to the nest, yes, back to the nest. From all that great height where everything looks small, so very small, the bird keeps thinking it should return back home. Wherever the bird happens to be, its home calls out to it, and it hears its call."

"It seems as if you've started telling me tonight's story, Mummy. If the bad weather is gone tomorrow, can we go out to play?"

"Yes, son, tomorrow we can go early, earlier than usual, to make up for today's lost time. It depends on the weather, though." Susanna always liked to give him some ray of hope, even though she imagined that the dark skies promised stormy weather for days to come.

"And if it rains again, what shall we do?"

"In that case, we'll do the same thing we've done today."

"What tale will you tell me tonight, Mummy? Begin it now."

Susanna kissed him lightly and put him down. She tidied his hair and brushed back a stray lock. She knew that that rogue lock of hair, always getting into his eyes, annoyed him. Wistin wanted her to cut it off but Susanna refused. Seeing it pleased her, and besides, it reminded her of someone. "Tonight's tale! Umm, I haven't thought about it, yet."

"About the kite, Mummy, and the rain, yes, yes please, Mummy, that's what I want for tonight's storytelling," Wistin pleaded with great fervour, in the meantime beginning to gnaw on a *biskuttell* which his mother had left near the tea-cup.

"Oh, very well, alright, but first we must recite the Rosary together. Don't you know that we must recite it every day?"

"Every, every day, Mummy? Why every, every day?"

Susanna looked away from him, her face growing suddenly serious, gazing at nothing and not answering him.

Wistin asked her once more.

"Because when you are given a present you must say thank you. At least once a day. Isn't that what I always tell you to do, Wistin? Make sure you never forget to give thanks. Not only once or twice, but many, many times, until there are no more thanks to give."

"And you give thanks by reciting the Rosary?"

"Yes, Wistin, I give thanks every day."

"You have to, then? Even in bad weather?"

"Yes, I have to, because I made a vow."

"What's a vow?"

Susanna explained it all to him.

"And to whom did you make this vow, Mummy?"

"I made the vow to Her who gave me the gift, son."

"And who is she, the one who gave you the gift, Mummy? And where is this gift, Mummy?"

Susanna fell silent once more and turned her face away from him.

"Answer me, Mummy," he asked her in a long-drawn out drawl, almost as if it was a chant he was about to start singing.

Susanna wished she could change the subject but knew it was no use. His questions never dried up quickly, like the rain falling over the village that spent entire days drizzling down keeping everybody indoors, waiting for it to stop. The rain was still coming down in a steady downpour.

The bells rung by the sacristan had finished pealing, but small bells could be heard in some houses nearby, ringing. Thin peals, modest ones. Many people kept a small bell in the house on purpose: to ring it over and over again while lightning flashed and thunder clapped in the skies.

"I give thanks to Her who gave me the gift. And if I'm reciting the Rosary, then to whom am I talking, Wistin?"

Wistin put his forefinger between his lips again. "To Our Lady, Mummy."

"Very good, son."

"That was a very easy question, Mummy"

"But you were still a bright boy to get it straightaway."

"But the other question is very hard; I don't know the answer, Mummy."

"Leave the other question for now. We'll talk about it another time."

"No, Mummy, I want to know. That gift Our Lady gave you, Mummy, what is it? And where is this gift?"

"It's in this room, Wistin. Look around, what do you see? Take a close look, think about it, and then tell me."

"In this room?" he wondered whilst gazing long and closely at every corner, even raising his head to look at the ceiling. He went to the cupboard and pulled out a chair to stand on so he could reach the drawers and he was about to start opening them. But they were heavy and he gave up and waited. "But there's nothing special in this room, Mummy."

"Certainly there is. Search well. There's a very special gift in here."

Wistin continued looking round the room with renewed interest and greater eagerness than before, looking everywhere and searching and searching.

"You haven't found it yet, Wistin?"

Wistin began to name every single object that caught his eye, and his mother began to smile and tease him, showing him he had not guessed yet. "No, you haven't guessed right, Wistin."

"Well then, you tell me, Mummy. I want to know."

"Let me tell you what we'll do. First we'll recite the Rosary, and then I'll tell you," she decided, hoping he would soon forget all about it.

"No, Mummy, I want you to tell me now, before starting the Rosary, because the Rosary is very long."

"And if I tell you what this gift is, will you believe me?" she asked him without looking at him.

"Of course I'll believe you."

"Try to guess, one last time. Look, let me give you a hint. This gift is right before me now. There, that's an easy question now!"

"Oh no, Mummy, you don't want to tell me! I'm the only thing in front of you."

"Yes, that's right, Wistin. Only you are in front of me. See how clever you are! Now, we'd better begin," she quickly interposed in order to cut him off. She felt her eyes brimming with tears. She hugged him to her one more time, and immediately began the prayer, "Hail Mary, full of grace..."

Wistin did not dare interrupt at first and he continued to pray with her. "So, you're going to keep on praying every day, every, every day, I mean for ever and ever, till you grow up, Mummy?" he interrupted.

"Yes, for ever and ever. But now you must continue the prayer: Holy Mary, Mother of God..."

"And do you always recite the Rosary with those rosary beads? What lovely rosary beads! Was that a gift as well, Mummy?"

Susanna nodded her head to acquiesce, but would not say more than that. Finally she told him, "Let's go to sleep, now."

Wistin went to stand in front of the statue of Our Lady that stood in a corner of the room, drew in a long breath to blow out the red candle that was always lit over there, and then blew it out with all his strength. A puff of smoke rose in the air and, as usual, he looked at it with great interest. The strong smell entered his nostrils and he tried to waft it away by putting up his hand to his nose.

"The story, Mummy," he reminded her as he lay down in his bed, face upwards.

Susanna tucked his blanket under the corners of the mattress, and sat down on the bed next to him. The rain was still pattering against the window panes, and no other noise could be heard. The silence was deeper than usual, the way it always was on rainy days...She began her storytelling. "Once upon a time, there was a little boy who got up early and went outside into the countryside. There were lots of beautiful flowers, and many trees and many fields...and zigzagging these fields were many narrow pathways and the boy went on walking, on and on, until he found himself in a wide-open space. And in that place, wide open to the sky and earth which met and joined together there, he..."

"The kite, Mummy. Weren't you going to tell me a story about the kite?" Wistin interrupted her.

"Of course, of course, that little boy had his kite with him, and now that he'd come to that place, in the middle of the fields, he began to unwind the string rolled around the reel he held in his hand, a big reel, huge, enormous, and it held many lengths of string, and do you know why?"

"So that the kite could fly far, and rise high up in the sky."

"And that's what this boy's kite did. It flew away to a great distance, so far he couldn't see it with his eyes anymore. And he stood there waiting for it for a long time...waiting...and waiting...until suddenly he felt it pulling on the string in his hand again."

"And what had happened, Mummy, for him not to be able to see it with his eyes?"

"It had been swept away by the wind, because that day happened to be quite windy, and the wind likes to carry off everything away. But when the wind changes, a new wind starts to blow and bring everything back again. And the little boy was overjoyed when he saw the kite coming back, closer and closer, slowly, slowly, and he began to wind the string around the reel once more, and the kite swooped ever nearer down until it swirled round a few times in the air and fell a few paces away from his feet. He ran towards it...quickly ran towards it..."

Wistin had his eyes closed, and Susanna thought sleep had finally overcome him. She smiled silently at him and rose quietly from the bed, softly, softly on the tips of her toes. But he realized immediately and opened his eyes.

The dreadful weather was still raging, though not as strongly as it had been.

"Weren't you asleep then?" she asked.

"No, Mummy, I was listening with my eyes closed because that way I can picture your words more clearly in my mind, everything you mention. Go on with the story, Mummy, please. Tell me what happened then..." and Wistin closed his eyes again.

"And then, as he was walking back home, with the kite in his hand, the kite told him..."

"No, Mummy, how can that be? As if a kite can talk! You told me the kite was made of paper..."

"But don't forget, Wistin, this story happened a long, long time ago...when everything was beautiful and good."

"When everything could talk, Mummy?"

"Yes, that's right, at the very beginning. When everybody was friends with everybody else, and so even the children's toys were able to talk to children. And children could speak to them as well."

"And what did that kite say to that boy?"

"It told him, umm, it told him," Susanna hesitated, thinking. She knew her son did not sink into sleep straightaway and so she had to exercise her imagination each and every night to come up with some such story. "It told him, look, some day instead of flying me, I will make you fly instead and I'll take you with me up there, among the clouds, and you'll see your very own village from up high, and you'll see how different it looks. And the boy agreed and said 'yes', and asked it to take him along whenever it pleased."

"And is that what it did?"

"Of course that's what it did..."

"And when? That same day?"

"Yes, right there and then, Wistin. And how come you guessed I was about to say that?"

"'Cause if I was that little boy, that's exactly what I'd have asked it to do, too – to take me up there with it straightaway."

"Don't you want to stay with your mother then, Wistin? Isn't it better in here than up there?"

"Yes, Mummy, but after going about there and looking down on the village from up high, then I'd have asked it to take me back down and bring me back here."

"And what would I have done down here, alone, without you?"

"You'd have waited for me to come back, Mummy."

"And if you wouldn't have come back, what would I have done, huh?"

"No-o-o, Mummy! Don't you know how much I love you? How many times do I have to tell you? I'd have come back for sure, for sure...But then, tell me, what happened? Did the boy and the kite fly up in the air together, up there? You told me that next time it would be the kite that made the boy fly up with it, not the other way round."

"Yes, that's what happened but now, Wistin, it's bedtime and we'd better go to sleep. What do you think? Let's make the Sign of the Cross together and recite the bedtime prayer," she coaxed him taking out his right hand from beneath the bedcovers and raising it to his forehead. "In the name of the Father..."

"In the name of the Father...but aren't you going on with the story?"

"And of the Son..." she went on prompting him.

"And of the Son," he complied.

"And of the Holy Spirit."

No reply came from Wistin. He was already fast asleep, and she threw him a kiss, fearing to wake him if she actually touched him. "Sweet dreams, Wistin, and dream of the kite that takes you far, far away," she whispered silently in his ears. She rose from her son's bed and went into the dining room. She removed the tin can from atop the three-legged spirit-stove and put on the iron to heat instead. With her arms crossed and held against her chest, she waited for it to heat properly.

Through the window panes she could still see the rain sheeting down and that wide expanse of earth, shining and gleaming with water, in the midst of all that thick darkness, enchanted her.

"And were I to tell a story to myself, how would I tell it? Where would I start the tale? Let me see," Susanna mused, nodding and gesturing with her head as if acting onstage and beginning her part. "Susanna's part, let me see how that goes!" She began to move silently, with intense pleasure, and the beauty of her form took shape and shone forth, dazzling, even in the enclosed darkness of that modest dining room. Everywhere counted as the most marvellous backdrop for her. "And where does Fr. Grejbel come into all this? That good and decent man who gives his all to his fellow men? And where do the parts of the Father and the Mother come in? And what of the other characters? I just don't know; the tale would be too complicated to play-act in this way. I'd better tell the tale another way. Well then look here," she continued, in the meantime walking slowly across the room from one side to another and raising her eyes to look round, acknowledging an imaginary audience her imagination had drawn in front of her. She gave a small curtsy to the audience, slightly raising her long skirt from both sides with two fingers of each hand, inclined her head in greeting and smiled, seriously, proudly. "Very well, I may start now. The play begins here. Let me see. Once upon a time there was a maiden, called Susanna, and Susanna met a young man in the Valley, and he loved her very much, but he did not yet know the way of the world, and he was handsome and Susanna loved him in return, and he wanted to show her his love. But it was too soon and the time came when he was taken up away by his kite, and it took him far, far away and took a very long time to come back, but one day it did come back and many years had come and gone."

Susanna went to the window once more and rested her cheek against the glass panes, and she blew on them till the window was all misted over. Then she drew back and with both hands rubbed at it in haste, smearing it all. "Time rots and changes things, but opens closed doors too," she said beneath her breath. "And now, Ladies and Gentlemen, I present to you the young man who loved as he knew how, and then took a very long time to learn how he should love...but love was within him and he didn't know what to do with it. Oh, love...You know, Ladies and Gentlemen, that everything takes time to happen, like the fruit on the trees, the flowers to open, and like the ships that enter harbour and bring children on them, everything needs time...everything waits for its own season, Ladies and Gentlemen, and here he is now...the king of this entire tale...Give him a hand."

It was still raining relentlessly.

As she was playing out this part, she was afraid there would be no applause, and she started looking round as if trying to gauge the audience's reaction. Perfect silence reigned in the room, and the pattering of the rain was the only timepiece that could bring her any comfort. "Applause, please, Ladies and Gentlemen, applause! For now time has passed and it's time, and the storm has passed, though the rain is still coming down heavily." Her thoughts were still on the iron which by now had heated up.

She passed her hand over the glass panes to clean them and stopped to listen. In the distance she could hear the rumblings of thunder...and then she could hear the noise coming nearer. Suddenly, a loud thunderclap burst overhead.

"Mummy...Mummy, I'm frightened, come, Mummy...come, don't leave me alone, Mummy," Wistin implored her from the next room.

"Don't be frightened, son, this is just the same storm. It comes and goes. It will soon pass, you'll see. Don't you know Mother's here, Wistin? Go back to sleep, and go on with that dream where you left off, and soon, you'll see, the storm will have passed," she soothed him.

"Yes, Mummy," she heard him answering her, faintly, in a voice thick with sleep.

"You do know Mother loves you very much, don't you? Do you believe me, Wistin?" she comforted him again, sweetly, her eyes gazing in the distance, beyond the window pane.

"Yes, Mummy," he replied.

With her face turned towards the window she sang, slowly and softly, just audibly enough for Wistin to hear her from his room next door:

Sleep, sleep, dear son, sleep,
In the silk hammock-cradle.
Your mother is Our Lady,
Your father is Baby Jesus.

She stopped to hear if Wistin was still awake and then continued her lullaby, "*Hush-sh-sh! Hush-sh-sh!*"

Wistin whimpered a word she could not make out; it sounded like the fitful muttering of someone half-asleep. His voice came weakly, as if he was on the brink of sleep once more.

"*Hush-sh-sh!*" she sang under her breath. "There now, he's asleep. Oh, Wistin, how I wish I could sing you all those lullabies I couldn't sing to you in the beginning...Yes, that's the right sort of sleep, son, when nothing can disturb and wake you up, not even thunder," she consoled herself. "Learn how to sleep deeply, Wistin, learn how to be strong in both fair weather and bad, because the day is one and they go together, fair weather and bad. You can't have one without the other, otherwise what fun would there be in life? And what stories could we invent and tell, and take seriously? A lovely tale without bad times? A story that only records good times? It doesn't exist! Sleep, Wistin, sleep, and dream a lovely dream, for me."

And as if she suddenly came to herself, acknowledging that she was acting out her part onstage, Susanna continued where she had left off. "Where had I got to? I must remember. Where had I got to?" Her gestures matched her words; seemingly trying to remember something, she rubbed her forehead several times with her right hand, moving it from side to side, and then she raised her eyes and with a clear gaze continued, "Yes, I know at which point I'd got to. I know, I know. Well then let me go on. Ladies and Gentlemen, here he is, the king of my story...give him a hand. He's arrived from a voyage that has taken many years, but he's found the way home. He deserves your appreciation.

His name is Stiefnu!

Once upon a time he had gone out to fly his kite, and he had gone down to the Valley to do it, but he got entangled with it and was taken far, far away and beyond, but in time he came back, and here he is, Stiefnu!"

Susanna laughed soundlessly, blew out the three-legged spirit-stove and took up the iron and wrapped it in a thick cloth, putting it at the foot of Wistin's bed, near his feet. She took up a sack used for fodder and placed it on top of the blanket covering him, reassuring herself he lay snug and warm. She was feeling sleepy and quite content, having no doubt she had a good night's sleep in store. She had promised Wistin that on the morrow they would go into the surrounding fields and spend some long happy hours playing there. She had to hope for fair weather; otherwise Wistin would mope and get bored again. She was ready to do anything to please him and had made many a sacrifice already. She was still looking for work and was only managing to cope on the meagre savings she had put by in a money-box hidden away in a corner in the cupboard. Every coin she did not spend from day to day went into it.

"Good night, Stiefnu," she gave the greeting, "wherever you happen to be, I wish you good night, all the same. And Wistin, though he doesn't know you, wishes you well, too. The two of us are here, you're the only one missing." She hugged her pillow, made the Sign of the Cross once more, and waited for sleep to come. She was certain it would not be long before she would start dreaming. She always longed for dreams that would please her but knew it was not up to her. Dreams, like that kite in the story, look to whatever wind takes their fancy and would roam around only where it pleased them to do so.

Though the window was closed and shuttered, the rapid flashes of lightning still lanced through the chinks. The thunder continued to roar and the forks of lightning kept on flashing into white flames. The candlemass candle had been snuffed out for the night.

Chapter 3

In Arturu's house everything remained the same for years on end, except for his memories. All that had happened within the confines of large rooms were now an endless stream of new pictures in his mind, appearing in his mind's eye as he paced alone from one room to the next, in the meantime facing all that he'd ever lived through before that day when Susanna had first stepped inside that house. He was in a position to make his own decisions, without anybody's help. His life had been changed as soon as Susanna had entered there, and his mother, the Lady of the house, took her on as their servant, on Fr. Grejbel's recommendation. Lady had full faith in that priest. She had asked him to find her a suitable, decent girl to enter their household and be entrusted with its running, everywhere except her late husband's study. Nobody was to enter that room where Arturu's father had died, and none of the books were to be dusted, and everything was to be left as it had been. If nowhere else, at least in that room time stood still.

Katarina came and knocked on the door and he leaned out from the window taking a long look at her. He did not recognize her and she gestured with both her hands raised to her face to try and make him understand that she wanted to speak to him. She told him who she was and that in all that time she had done her best to change matters for the better. Her daughter had endured enough suffering and the time had come for everyone to turn to each other once more.

"That's what I'd like, too," Arturu agreed, "even though, all in all, my life has largely remained the same as before. I admit, Susanna and I had much to stand between us, to keep us at loggerheads with each other, and maybe what did come between us was not our fault."

"No, it was none of your fault, the two of you, Mr. Arturu, Sir," Katarina set his mind at rest. "Both of you were brought up well, you in one way and she, well, permit me to say this, she in another. Both my husband, God rest his soul, and I brought up Susanna within the shelter of our home. Whatever happened, happened because it was meant to happen. Life is full of ups and downs and every place bears its own fruits," she continued.

"No, no, that's not what I meant. I accepted Susanna right from the start. I had known her from a long time before, when she used to keep house the way my mother wanted it kept," Arturu replied.

"The Lady of the house, God rest her soul. I have heard much good said about her. She was generous, a woman of discipline, and did not show her face much outside. That's what people always said about her. I never met her, never laid eyes on her. If I don't see her likeness I won't recognize her as your mother. But her name carries a whiff of fragrance, like the flowers we enjoy in the fields. Here and in the other village too. The villages lie next to each other, and the fragrance passes from one place to another because it belongs to everybody," Katarina continued to speak while her eyes roamed round the room to spy any likeness of her. "Susanna too, Sir, Susanna spoke highly of her, too."

"Susanna spoke of her to you?"

"Not for the first time. Not with any familiarity you understand, and always by a single word, 'Lady'. Susanna always praised her as a woman worthy of respect, proud of your father and very devout. That's what counts, after all."

"And what did Susanna have to say about my father?" Arturu wanted to know.

"Your father? Oh, she only had one word for him, too. And a very good one at that, just as you yourself had said of him, to her. Because, let me tell you, Sir, Susanna remembered every single word you ever spoke to her. One thing I can tell you, now that there's so much water under the bridge, that Susanna remained the same child I had brought up."

"The same? Even at the time we went our separate ways, you mean?"

"Yes, even during that period of time, actually, even more so during that period."

"So whatever happened, she remained the same as you had brought her up, she didn't change."

"It wasn't an easy, comfortable life she led, not by a long chalk!"

"I know, I know, and I'm at fault there...maybe...but time has its own seasons, and the winds of change sweep us up and carry us away. We're not in control. Then, when they abate we look back and wonder 'Just look! We could have hung on to something not to be carried off'". Arturu paused for a moment and then continued, "The wind came from somewhere beyond these parts and swept us away, Susanna and me, both. But there's something else I'd like to ask."

"Ask away, Sir, just ask. I'll answer you as best I can, and honestly. You can trust me. If my husband were alive he would vouch for me. What a shame he never got to know who set his sights on his daughter! But death came a bit early for him. He lived to see only what seemed to go forever against his wishes. And then, when..."

"When, you mean, Susanna and I got married, then..."

"Yes, that's what I meant, that's what I was going to say, but words often don't come to mind promptly."

"After we'd got married and a few years had passed, you thought he'd have changed his mind, and looked upon his daughter with more favour? Is that what you thought?"

"Yes, that's what I had in mind to say, Sir! You have a way with words, because you read books. That's what Susanna says."

"But even all that wasn't enough. After we'd got married, well, umm, Susanna and I lost our baby, we parted and everything came to an end."

Katarina bent her head and he could hear her sobbing.

"I don't want to sadden you. Not everything is lost."

"Is that what you think? How kind you are! Your good upbringing shows through. So you think all is not lost?"

"You told me what Susanna had to say about my mother and father. But you haven't yet said what she thinks about the fact that we got married. That's what I'd really like to know. What does she think that's left for her out of a marriage that took place a long time ago? The rest can wait upon events."

"Her father and I taught her that you only enter into marriage once, Sir. That's what we always thought, and that's how we remained, him and me."

"And what does Susanna think?"

"That's what we think, Sir," declared Katarina, very firmly.

"Yes, yes I understand. But she, what does she think?"

"What do you mean 'she'? She is us and we are her. The same, Sir. We don't know how to read, nor write. We store everything up in our mind, up here," Katarina explained earnestly, raising her right hand to the middle of her forehead. "We don't keep a single piece of paper at home, neither penholders, nor ink, nor even a single book. But we've never forgotten anything, all the same, and even nowadays, there's nothing that slips our mind. We inherited all of this from those who came before us, and we believe wholly in all of it. From one generation to the next. Time has not erased any of it. We don't have anything else, and we are certain it is good. That's how we're made, and our forebears before us. We learn and remember."

"Everything by word of mouth. Everything memorized. And what does Susanna think now, today, about this situation?" Arturu wanted to know.

Katarina hesitated, weighing her words carefully. "Susanna speaks of you still, and is proud of you."

"Are you telling me she hasn't turned to another?"

"No, Sir, there's nobody else."

"You know what I mean."

Katarina bowed her head and quietly insisted, "You only enter into marriage once. She knows this. Whatever happens, she knows it's always been our solemn belief and will remain thus."

"And she? What does she believe?" he reiterated in a voice heightened with emotion.

"Haven't I just told you, Sir? She knows what she's duty-bound to believe."

"And she believes all that she's supposed to believe, huh? In spite of all that's happened?"

"I am doing my utmost to make it so, Sir. I've not exhausted my resources and I intend to expend whatever strength is left in me. I have travelled all along this road, and it's been a long one, full of ups and downs. Just like the footpaths in the fields. Where Fr. Grejbel was brought to a halt, I took up the path."

"And why do you wish things to fall out this way?"

"Because this is the right thing to do, Sir."

"Wasn't this the right thing to do before, in the beginning?"

"In the beginning I counted for nothing. Everything was different."

"And now?"

"Now the clouds are disappearing, Sir. The weather's fine or nearly so."

"Are you telling me there's no hint of a storm brewing?"

"The weather doesn't clear up in a jiffy, Sir. That's what the seasons teach us as we work the fields. They direct our steps, when we should sow the seeds and when we should irrigate the land, and when we should prune shrubs back and wait till harvest time, but not just them...because they too don't march alone. The seasons, I mean. Somebody directs them. No, not just them..."

"Not just them? Then who else?"

Katarina thrust her right hand inside the wide pocket of her skirt and brought out her rosary beads, pressing them against the hand balled into a fist in her lap and remained with her head bowed. Her lips moved slightly as if she was praying.

"Fine, I understand. You've set my mind at rest and made me happy. As soon as you have some news, come again. I'll be on the lookout for you," he escorted her gladly to the front door. At last, after all these years he had got the opportunity to speak face-to-face to Katarina, and the old hopes he had nursed throughout the years of separation heartened him anew.

"Wait! Just wait a bit and don't give up hope, Sir!" Katarina encouraged him. "If it's God's will that the two of you should come together again, well, then that's what will happen. Believe it and you'll see! For us, people of the land, that's what the seasons teach us: to wait. But there's nothing new I can teach you. You can read books."

"No, no, there's still much that you can teach me as well. So, she hasn't put me out of her mind," he still wanted to know.

"She still loves you. Yes, that's what I think and I know the ways of her heart. And as for me, I am praying fervently...and not just praying. Later on you'll understand what I mean." He drew close to shake her hand and she bent her head and wished him goodbye and left, soon turning round the corner.

In the ensuing days and weeks, Arturu's days were long, silent, the same as always.

"Susanna! Susanna! Where are you? Goodness knows where you are at this moment!" Arturu sighed to himself, slumped in an armchair, remembering...

Much time had passed.

"If I could stop time I would," Lady had said to him once, trying to convince him that nothing should be changed in that house unless with her express permission, which was difficult to bring about. "But this is folly, saying these words, even having this wish. If I could, I would wind back time to that day, when the three of us were together, you a small boy and us two adults, not too old, a few years yet from old age...That's where I wished time to stand still, like this house. Do you think this house supersedes us? Look, it hasn't grown old. And as for us, what now? Anyway, I've left your father's study exactly the same way it was. That's one of the ways I feel I mourn him, Arturu, and you must observe this mourning too! Black clothes forever more, and this at the same time – keeping his study untouched. Your father was my husband, and my husband died once, but as for me, I feel he dies every day. I have always thought so, and that's how I've always comported myself. I'm not about to change now, and neither do I wish nor try to. If I change now, everything will come crashing down about me. No."

Lady's words came out decisively.

"In this room my father spent whole hours reading alone, with his spectacles coming half-way down his nose," Arturu had told Susanna once. Time had not managed to change anything in the rooms of that house. Everything was burdened with age and had a story behind it, and everything was a memorial.

"Susanna! Susanna! Are you still as beautiful as you were? Do you still enjoy storytelling? I hope nothing has changed you meanwhile," he murmured to himself.

The entire house, as always, stayed large and still, holding its peace.

Slipping further down in the armchair and nearly sliding off, Arturu let his mind wander back into the past, reliving his former life, alone once more. Everything was simply another large portrait, one of the many scattered around the entire house, paintings of some value, dark, sometimes so dark as to be obscure, that never seemed to age, or change, with thick gilt frames full of ornate motifs. Serious faces, garments from bygone eras...

~ 0~

"Let's make the Sign of the Cross now and say grace, and let's all say it together, without skipping any of the words," Arturu's father directed, and then lowered his head, waited a few moments and then continued, "We can start now."

The three of them made the Sign of the Cross together and then bent their heads over their plates, and Arturu and his mother waited for his father's signal. But his father began to eat straightaway.

"Let's start, let's start. Go on Arturu, you may start eating," Lady fussed, in the meantime bending her own head to her plate and she fiddled with the spoon and then raised her head again to look at her husband.

Her husband gave her a small nod and the meal began.

"Arturu, you're growing up and soon you'll see that your life will be changing in many ways," his father had once begun a conversation. "Nothing around you will remain the same, and neither inside you. You won't hear this said outside our house, or at least I've never heard it said myself. But it's true all the same. However much we might rail against it, we have to admit it. Arturu, in the same way your childhood passed in the way it had to, now the way ahead will reveal new ways and aspects of love...Life is a series of steps, just like the staircase here in our house, and we have to go up the steps one by one, the whole flight, and we can fall and we can also arrive at the top. And what leads us to follow it is called 'love'. It's never too early or too late for such a lesson. I think now is the right moment for it. Better a bit early. I won't be here forever."

"Love, ahh, love! If only you knew what it means, dear heart!" Lady sighed happily.

"I can't say I know everything about it, but I know I've felt it," Arturu's father stated in a firm voice. "And do you know for whom I felt it?" Then he raised his head from his plate and looked at his wife. "For you, my wife, isn't that so? Whatever happens, you will always be my true wife. From so many women around, imagine how many have been born and grown up in all this time, you and you alone, the one...the chosen one, the special one, the beloved. See how life hasn't forgotten you?"

"That's very true, husband," Lady agreed. "And the same goes for me. I gave you everything I could, and I'm not sorry. My honour and happiness all lie here, with you, in your hands. Take care of them up to the very end. Have I ever doubted any of this? Have I ever led you to something you regretted doing? You gave to me in one way, and I returned it in another. We all need one another." She turned to the boy and told him, "Do you understand Arturu? Life is a game..."

"A serious one! A serious game indeed!" exclaimed her husband immediately.

"A very serious game, and sometimes it's so serious that it's not recognized. That's why one must learn its rules. Isn't that what you want to tell Arturu?" his wife interjected.

"A serious thing! Arturu! Your mother and I love each other very much. Ever since we laid eyes on each other something inside us both changed forever. That's what we felt, which is as it should be. We brought before our eyes the amount of men and women who surely exist, times without number, and from all these, your mother and I promised ourselves to each other, forever. And do you know what 'forever' means? From this moment till death. And after death..."

"Even after death!" Lady interrupted him.

"As your mother says, Arturu! Even after death! That's a decision that changes nothing, not even with the change of seasons. Look a bit towards the window, and imagine yourself a tiller of soil, like all the people around us in this village. Even though we three are not the same as they are, at least we are here, in their midst, and we eat what they grow in their fields. They're different from us and we're different from them, but here we all are, in the same place. As for the seasons, well they come and go but the seed must remain there, where it was thrown down, and it must survive on its own, hidden away, underneath, rain or shine, and wait for the right moment to sprout. Seasons come and go but there's something that doesn't change. And do you know what this something is, Arturu?" his father asked.

"Do you know what it is? Come, dear heart, answer your father. What is that something that never changes?" Lady joined in. "Your father knows the answer, and I think I know it too, perhaps, but now it's your turn to say what it is."

Arturu got up from the table so quickly he nearly overturned his chair. He ran from the room into the garden and began to cry. He stayed there for a long time, alone, waiting. Sometimes he screamed with rage and sometimes he was silent picking flowers and tearing off their petals, one by one. What could those two be saying to each other for so long? He heard their raised voices, quarrelling, and then came pockets of silence. He was certain they were arguing about him, both when they were speaking calmly and when they were ranting. He was eager for some attention, and this was his way of trying to gain some, although he had not thought it would cause a fight. He wanted some affectionate attention, some spoiling which only ever came from Lady. He knew already that his father would never change. He frequently asked himself, "Why is Father always so nervous and angry, a man of few words but then loud in speech?" He had become used to his father's ways and character traits, and though he was convinced that his father loved him, Arturu looked for a different kind of love; he expected, without anyone telling him so, a gentler way of loving. Lady loved him in this way, he thought.

When his father had died, his home had undergone some slight changes, but as soon as Lady passed away, it changed completely. Arturu now felt that the whole world had fallen into his lap, a rich inheritance and also the key to have power to rule. No one could interfere and dictate to him anymore, at least, within his house. His new position gave him total command over his household but he was certain he had to make a fresh start. This new beginning had its germination in that same place where the silence of many years had gathered and closed in upon itself – in the study – the room which Lady, with great determination, had wished him never to disturb. She had vacillated for a long time over allowing Susanna to occasionally enter the room to dust the books, and only on condition that Susanna would not move anything from its place, not even the small, black spectacles with the round lenses, left on the desk thickly gathering dust, the accumulated grime and grunge of many years.

Once, as he was rummaging about among his father's books, he found his father's diary, with widely-spaced lines, written up on every alternate line, in an extremely neat hand with large rounded letters. The pages had been penned with an old-style ink-pen that sometimes wrote in thin characters and at other times with very thick strokes that occasionally left large, dark blue ink-blots on the paper. It was a whole copybook, with every page filled up from cover to cover, where no space was left wasted on its yellowed pages. The moment Arturu found this diary was a bit of a shock; he was both pleased and frightened at the same time. He walked towards the light holding it in his hands and turned its pages slowly, as if he was asking for permission from Lady and his father. It was as if he was waiting to hear a clear voice from within, that would speak and reassure him, give him leave to open and read the entire copybook just as if it was another book in there. Every old book was waiting for attention, biding its time.

Half curious and half dutifully, Arturu began to read, and though so many years had drawn a veil over the events described therein, he imagined them unfolding before his eyes, each scene being enacted...

That particular scene which he remembered reading in the diary, began here. The diary jogged his memory and the two of them walked hand-in-hand to help him picture everything once more, after travelling down the path that went back many years...

"All these questions! So heavy and obscure, for goodness' sake! Why are you asking him such questions? What's making you behave like this? Arturu's your son, after all. I cannot feel for him the same way you do. Whatever that is, only you can know. But I still feel this is cruel and let me tell you, I sincerely feel for him, almost more than I can possibly feel for you!" Lady exclaimed to her husband.

"Is that right? Are you sure you know what you're saying, Lady?" her husband shot back.

His wife softened her tone and answered him, "Every word I've ever spoken to you has been said with the utmost certainty, and it's true again now, at this very moment. I could never be weak with you. If I had ever weakened I would have fallen by the wayside and nobody would have noticed, not even you. I had to be a woman of worth, and remain steadfast. Against all odds. Even a woman may hold firm, husband! I learnt how to be resolute from you, and I also recognized that under your hard and steady demeanour, whenever you were standing firm your heart was beating faster than usual. In time, I learnt to understand you. You're not as hard and unwavering as you wish to appear." She stopped speaking and drew near. "Isn't that so?" she gently asked, laying a hand over his heart and tenderly moving it slightly to and fro.

"I've been firm with you as much as with myself. It's a law of nature that we seek to stand firm. Nature itself wants us so, otherwise we'll be swept away by every breeze that blows. And it's also a point of honour with me, a question of self-discipline," her husband declared. "I gave it its first airing many years ago, this code of behaviour. First I tried it out on myself, and at first it was hard, but it soon began to work. And then I applied it as necessary. And it worked there, too, as you know very well."

"You can bring yourself to say this to me because you know how much I love you. We have walked this road together for so long...are we going to lose our way now when we need each other's support more than ever before?" his wife entreated him. "It may have been that winter would not have come by, but by good fortune we made it, too. Autumn did not manage to bowl us over. We're still here. Winter should draw us together more than all the other seasons put together. That's why winter comes along – to remind us that standing alone we are weak and may fall, but by staying together we may survive. And after winter has passed we say 'At least, it didn't just come to give us a hard time.' What do you say? Wasn't it in winter that we felt our love for each other the first time?"

"Don't pay any attention to seasons. They come and go. Actually, they only come to go away again. You only remember them because you're a woman. Your life depends on them. Without them you won't be able to take a single step forward. A woman is a clock, and a clock is in itself a mechanism to measure seasons."

"And so you think you can forget all about seasons, because you're a man?" his wife asked him in derision. "Are you saying that a man can walk without paying attention to a watch? Doesn't he have a straight road in front of him?"

"I can forget all about seasons because I stand firm. You can be resolute as well. In any case, I haven't forgotten what we were saying. Let's continue where we left off," he announced calmly. "Everything must be done at its appointed time and in its proper place, and as it should be, indeed as regular as clockwork. Well then, so..." Arturu's father began to stammer at that point and he raised his right hand and passed it across his brow, in the gesture of someone trying to marshal his thoughts into some sort of order, indeed, to harry them into an exaggeratedly exact line. "I do know how much you love me. And if you love me..."

"Well then...I must love him too, and vice-versa. That's right," his wife reassured him. "Truly life is but a game, and the rules are there, fixed for all time, and when they veer off slightly, they step back into line in no time." She stopped speaking for a few moments and then went on, "I don't want to be bothering you and remind you of something you surely haven't forgotten, but...don't forget, the boy is out there, alone...He's been alone all this while."

"We are all alone, wife, in one way or another. He'll not just be spending a few moments alone but a while. And not a short stint but a long while. You know what a difference that makes. The time you can measure with a timepiece is one thing but the whole of time in which you can sink without trace and not even realize, that's something else altogether."

"True, we, all of us, are alone. At least you have those blessed books for company, always surrounding you in your study, waiting for you to open them up and then speaking to you and then taking their turn to hear you speak to them. At first they may contradict you somewhat but they end by giving in to you. Goodness knows how many journeys you've been through without getting up from that armchair! You have all those books...yes, you!"

"And you, what about you? What do you have? You have...come, come, answer me."

"I have you, husband. Isn't that what you want to say?"

"Very good, that's the right answer. You have me. You have an old book, riddled with bookworm, with rag-eared pages, that's about to close forever. Do you know how many books there are that have never been read, not even by me? Have you any idea how often I use a paper-knife? It's a merciful tool for forgotten books. In any case, the oil-lamp lighting my way along the path is nearing its end, I just know it," her husband came to a halt, his heavy heart heard in the tone of his voice.

"Don't say that, dear heart. The oil-lamp needs to nurse its flame and flicker right till the very end. The merest flame signals light. And the light we see at the end is no less than that which we see in the beginning. Up to the very end, both for you and for me...I need to continue believing that every chink of light is but light. Not because I'm a woman, but because I am me. Every flicker has in it the power of a blaze. I don't know whether this is true or not and I don't want to know. That's what I wish to go on believing. Till I see a flame in there still..."

"Is that what you truly think, wife?"

"That's what I would like to believe, and how I need to think. Everyone looks to his own concerns. Till the very last flicker of flame..."

"That holds true even more for me, and it will be my turn first. My flame is weaker than yours. The oil in my lamp will soon run out. In a house like this, where everything is the same as before, I feel that of all the things here, I'm the only one whose course is run. Our garden still grows green and blossoms with the seasons. The trees always mature, and always grow new leaves. The flowers bloom in season...at the right moment...regular as clockwork. The furniture is always polished to a high gloss, the ancient stones acquire greater beauty with age, and everything in here is more appreciated the more it ages! The venerable age of these objects surrounding us gives them ever greater value." Her husband stopped speaking and then, continued in a sorrowful tone, "And me? The opposite! Everything is falling apart, piece by piece, and I cannot keep up with every bit of me that seems to be crumbling to nothing from one day to the next. If I gather up a fallen piece I feel I'm an object of ridicule. And do you know why? Because I'm a man, master of everything here. What a contradiction!"

"There's still a flickering light, dear heart, and that's still a light of sorts."

"And by the waning light that's left I need to see what I still have to accomplish, wife. Only in this way can being different count."

"The last few flickers of flame. The light that's left. Alright then, till some light is left do all you still need to do. So what else is left to be done? Command me, I'll do it! Don't worry, your every wish will be my pleasure, right up to the end," she cajoled him, her tone halfway between merriment and seriousness.

"That's right. But you're sure, are you, wife? Are you as certain as you were that day, when we danced together, under the dimmed lights of that hall? I can see everything before me as if it was yesterday. There were many people, and many smiles, and more than anything else, lots of curly locks. Ringlets signify wishes, and when they move and stir even more so. With every movement, every wish turns into an invitation. Everything tasted so sweet!"

"Even what had already turned sour?"

"We didn't know how to taste well enough, yet, wife. We were privileged. We created sweetness ourselves. But today we're more intelligent than that."

"That's right, true enough, husband," she set his mind at rest.

"Well then, go and tell the boy to come back inside. Right this minute. Tell him to come and sit at table again and to start eating. He's supposed to know some discipline by now. If he can't stick to some discipline he's not my son. I won't acknowledge him. He was born and bred within it for many a long year. We've said grace and the meal began a long time ago," he spoke decisively, expecting her to do his bidding at once.

His wife took a deep breath controlling her temper, looked at him from beneath her brows and walked towards the door. Then she stopped and turned back to him. She came close and tight-lipped told him, "Husband," and then continued in a softer tone, "Husband, as you say, everything will be done as you say. I, Lady, your wife, will obey! Satisfied now? Within these walls, everything will be as you command. But out there, and you should know this, people are different, aren't they? Their minds work in a different way. Even this village makes up a big world, however small it really is. A time will come when you will have to face this when the village makes its way in here, too. You still refuse to understand this."

"I have understood it, and have done so long ago, wife. I understood it once when I stopped to think and looked ahead beyond the immediate future, far into the future where I could not know what lay in store. And I understood some time later when I began to read books. I understood all this so well that I decided it was not to my liking, and I resist it. I don't want it. The past, the present, what do I care? None of that belongs to me and I have no feeling for it. And so I keep it at bay. I hold nothing in my hands save what I can remember and what I desire – something as unsubstantial as smoke. Look at me, my hands are empty and they are also full of smoke, at one and the same time. Can you just imagine this: visualise me leaving the house and going to the villagers' marketplace, and selling them smoke! Pipe-smoke! Chimney-smoke! Smoke from the stone-oven! Then I would call out like the hawkers do and repeat, "Smoke! Smoke! Cheap smoke! Come and buy some! Come!" He broke off and changed his tone of voice. "There's only one sort of smoke – us. In the depths of your heart you feel exactly the same way I do, wife. And do you know why you feel the same way?"

"Because I love you."

"That's right, Lady! A very simple answer and one that can't be bettered. Times change. We return whence we came and nothing left of us makes a sound, not even the least bit of noise. Maybe just a misty likeness remains, a memory that interests only a few people, and maybe won't even bring a single tear to anyone's eyes. Tears are tricky things. They hoard themselves. But know this, yesterday is like today and tomorrow will be like today too. The sea changes only on the surface. The bottom remains full of the same things – huge fish eating savagely, tearing prey with their teeth, and the more they tear off the more ravenous they become. And this all happens without a single tear being shed, remorselessly. Otherwise the sea itself cannot survive. A cruel law, but there you are. Now you can understand me when I tell you to stand firm."

"And where did you learn all this?" she asked him in some curiosity.

"Sometimes I look out of the window and sometimes I look within. That's how life moves on and in the meantime we can learn something from that." He paused and then addressed her, "You were telling me that you loved me. I know that, but when you're saying something good, it's never enough to hear it many times. Tell me again. I need to hear it said again. Slowly, slowly I'm beginning to forget."

"Dear husband, I love you, I love you, over and over. Set your mind at rest, I love you whatever happens. For those who lie adrift in some wide ocean, whether during a storm or in fair weather, every anchor deserves a kiss. Every anchor that draws near. Every anchor floats on the surface buoyed up by kisses. Did you know that? See, even I can tell you something new, occasionally. Otherwise, what urges the anchor on, to keep up the struggle? A kiss. I'm going to kiss you!" she told him playfully.

"Kiss me? What? Since when did you start wasting kisses on me? Isn't it a sin any longer? Superfluous? Or maybe it's never too late to make up for what was lost? What has been lost remains lost, wife. The clock moves only in one direction. It never repeats unless it breaks down and runs mad. And the clock is the only thing that never runs mad."

"It's a man," she teased him.

"Well then, it's the only man who never runs mad."

"I'm going to kiss you, husband, I truly am! The way I know how and with all my strength, and don't forget my kiss, mine to you, today, here and now," she declared as she bent down to his forehead and lightly, softly, brushed her lips across it.

Her husband grabbed her hand and squeezed it. "Now that you've kissed me," he twinkled at her, "please go and fetch Arturu. Tell him, 'Your father is waiting for you. He can be very patient but his patience is running out, like the oil in the oil-lamp. And his oil-lamp is now very old and...' Tell him that and remind him. 'The meal is waiting for you, too.' If he doesn't want to come, that's fine. You and I will continue eating without him. The meal remains the same, whether we are two at table or three."

"That's what I'll say to him," agreed his wife, and she left the room.

She went out into the garden searching for the little boy. "Arturu, Arturu, where are you?" she called him many times. She could not see him anywhere. "I know you're hiding somewhere, behind a tree or among the shrubs, I know, I know, and I'll soon find you. I'll ask and they'll tell me, I'll search for you and find you. The birds, the plants, the butterflies, the fish in the pond, the clouds, everyone will help me find you. They're all my friends! If you're going to wait longer I'll have to turn to them for help. Here I come! Arturu, don't you know this is part of my life – searching for you whenever you hide even inside? This is a big house and you can even get lost in it, among the trees, up in the branches, oh, I hope you haven't climbed up a tree! Last time when you did that you nearly fell down, remember? Oh dear, if your father should get to know," she prattled on in a loud voice as she paced the garden looking searchingly at the trees to see if there was a branch twitching. "If a branch starts to swing about, well then, I'll say there, that's where he's gone to hide. And if none of the branches move, I will say, he must be hiding among the shrubs. But there's so much greenery here... Where can Arturu be?" She halted in her tracks and called out in a louder voice, "Arturu! Arturu!"

Her husband got up from his chair and leisurely made his way to the window, and he stood there looking out into the garden, waiting.

"Arturu, Arturu! Where are you? Your father's waiting for you, and I'm searching for you. Time is passing. Aren't you hungry?" she called out as she slowly trod the path in the middle of the garden, looking left and right.

"No!" Arturu cried out from somewhere.

"Well then, what do you want?"

"I want you to play with me, Mother."

"Alright, Arturu. What would you like to play? Which game? You tell me because I don't know how to play. Well, definitely not children's games. That's difficult for me. I don't know how to play these games but I'll try."

"Yes you do, Mother, 'cause we're playing right now."

"We're playing games? Right now? While your father is inside waiting for us to eat? Don't forget, he's still in the dining room where we left him a little while ago, before you came outside in the garden."

"We're already playing. Hide-and-seek. I'm hiding and you must come and find me."

"And what do I have to do? Isn't that what I'm doing already? Searching for you! Turning here and there, after every little noise the leaves make. The littlest sound will soon tell me where I can find Arturu. So I'm playing hide-and-seek with you without even knowing it, am I?"

Arturu crept out stealthily from behind a shrub, and realizing that she was coming closer to where he was, he slipped away and hid behind another. But she heard the soft rustle in the leaves as he hid once more and she found him out.

"I saw you, I saw you, Arturu! I'm sure of it!" she cried out.

"But you still haven't won!"

"I still haven't won? And why not? And why should I win, come to that?"

"'Cause that's what the game's all about, Mother. Someone has to win and someone has to lose."

"And you, Arturu, whom do you want to win from the two of us?"

"I love you very much, Mother, but in this game I'd like to be the one to win!"

"That's what I want, too...for you to win! And what do I have to do now to let you win?" she spoke to him, all the while walking on and pretending to look behind every tree and shrub, every hiding-place that offered.

"If I'm going to win, you mustn't find me."

"Pretend I don't know where you are?"

"Yes, pretend you haven't seen me."

"Alright. Look, I'm looking and searching, but I still can't find Arturu. It's no use opening my eyes wide and searching and searching. But where can he be? Birds, did you see someone a little while ago? And you, butterflies, even you haven't seen anyone? Tell me! I'm looking and searching, but all for nothing." She turned round to look back at the house. At the window she could see her husband, waiting. She gave him a slight smile.

He smiled back, and raising his right hand almost imperceptibly gave her a very small wave.

"I don't know where Arturu is. Where is Arturu? I don't know. I must have lost then, and he's won!" Lady cried out loudly.

"I won!" Arturu shouted.

"Yes, you won! The game's over. And now, is Arturu hungry or not? I wonder."

"No, Arturu isn't hungry!" he declared.

"Say that again, Arturu, let me hear you properly."

"Arturu isn't hungry!" the boy yelled again from his hiding place.

Lady did her best to locate his voice. "Now I know you're not hungry..."

"But you don't know where I am, Mother. I'm not going to tell you. I want to stay here."

"Not even if I promise to ask your father to forgive you? I promise to tell him you're a very good boy, and from now on he won't shout at you again."

"Truly, Mother?" he said in a little voice from his hiding place.

"Of course! Truly, darling. And I'll also tell him you won our game of hide-and-seek. I searched for you high and low, among the leaves and branches, in every nook and cranny, everywhere, and I couldn't find you all the same. Don't you believe me?"

"Of course I believe you," he replied happily.

Lady came to a standstill. "Come on then, Arturu, I'm waiting here for you."

"Where are you, Mother? Are you far away, Mother?"

"Far away? I don't know if your mother's far away, darling. I'm here, that's for sure. I've been here for a long time and I'll stay here till the end. Now come out from wherever you are, come to me and we'll go back to your father together."

Arturu came out from the shrubbery walking very slowly towards her. When he was at her side she hugged him to her and taking his hand led him back to the dining room.

"I don't want to eat, I don't want to eat," Arturu wailed.

"Your father loves you, darling."

"Father loves me? You yes, you love me 'cause you speak gently and sweetly to me, but not him. If he loved me he wouldn't shout at me."

"But he shouts at you precisely because he loves you."

"You don't shout at me. So you don't love me?"

"Not everyone's the same, Arturu. People love in different ways. Don't you know that we're not all the same like each other? That's what your father is always saying and I think he's right. You should know this lesson already. He wants only what's best for you. That's why he's telling you so many things, and you should listen to him and learn, and in the end you need to thank him, too," she advised him.

"I don't want to eat. I want to go back where I was," he told her mulishly.

"How come, darling? You want to go back to the Children's Home?"

"Over there they never shouted at me, or spoke with difficult words."

"Your father isn't shouting at you, and neither is he telling you things difficult to understand, darling," she tried to calm him down. "He knows what he's doing. If I can understand him then you can as well. He speaks to you in the way he knows how. That's what everybody does."

"Mother, take me back where I was!" Arturu bawled.

"No, no! What are you saying, darling? This is your home, only here. You must live and grow up here. And can you go back and leave me alone? Come, come on now and we'll continue eating. You'll feel better soon and all you'll remember will be that you won and I lost. Didn't you like the meal I prepared for you?"

The two of them entered the dining room and sat down at the table. Arturu remained sulking, his head down, both hands in his lap, and a frown on his face. At intervals he looked surreptitiously from one side of the table to another, always trying to escape his father's gaze.

"Arturu, son, I love you truly only if I tell you the truth," his father adjured him. "The truth, a little at a time, as much as needs be. Not the whole truth all at once. You don't want me to tell you the truth? Well then, what do you want me to tell you?"

"I want to go out and play with the children in our street," the little boy managed to bring out, hardly daring to raise his head a little and looking at his father through his lashes.

"Let's continue eating, then," his father replied, trying to hide the displeasure on his face and to change the subject quickly, at the same time looking at his wife as if trying to get her to convince the boy to change his mind.

Arturu kept still.

"Eat up, and tell me thank you for having food to eat and for being here. Do you want me to lose all patience with you, and although your father, send you away out on the street to join those naughty boys out there with their tattered clothes, tangled hair, barefoot, roaming the streets of the village, begging for money? So, you want to be part of this village where we are, though we're not part of it? Is that what you want?"

Lady endeavoured to stop her husband's angry torrent of words by raising herself from her chair slightly and opening her arms wide to him.

But her husband was in full flow. "Where do you want to call home? Choose, I'm ordering you to choose, son, choose where you want to stay!"

"Where I was before!" Arturu gulped and ducked his head.

His father rose from the table and taking hold of Arturu's hand pulled him towards the front door. "Very well then, let's go! We'll go right now!" his father barked at him. "Where you were before! That's where you were and want to be and so that's where you can stay, from this very moment. Kindness is lost on those who don't want it, son. A whim! And waste is a sin, a mortal sin. I have no intention of committing a sin because of you. If you're not understanding what I'm saying to you now, don't worry, you will someday. And if you never do understand, know this, life will still go on. Look at other people's fields and work it out for yourself. Life continues on its way alone, without any help from us."

Arturu held back, forcing his feet to stand his ground, trying not to be moved, and he tried to wrench his hand out of his father's grip.

"So you don't want to go back there? You've changed your mind, just like that, so quickly? Then you don't know how to stand firm!" his father roared at him, and then fell silent. "Where you were before?" he continued in an aggrieved tone, briefly describing life in an orphanage. "Just recall a little where you were. You can still remember it. Let me warn you! Never let me hear that word again. Don't you dare mention it to me again. 'Forgive me', that's all you must say. Tell me 'Forgive me', go on!"

A deep silence blanketed the room. Husband and wife looked at the little boy, a very serious look on their face.

"Tell him 'forgive me', Arturu, go on, dear," Lady did her best to pour oil over troubled waters, going up to the little boy and resting her hands on his shoulders. "Say it after me 'for-give-me', as if we're praying, and mind you don't gobble up the words, bit by bit, slowly, slowly...you can't get mixed up and there's no need to be afraid. Forgiveness means love. Isn't that right, Father?" she spoke in a conciliatory tone, turning to face her husband.

Arturu uttered each syllable very slowly, following her lead. "For-give-me" he got out and was silent, remaining with his head down.

"Are you addressing me, Arturu?" his father spoke and his voice was still harsh. "If it's me you're talking to then I need to see you facing me and hear you clearly, and then I can decide what to do."

"To you, of course he's talking to you, Father," his wife quickly interjected.

"Well then, if he's truly talking to me he must raise his head and look at me, please. He must repeat his words from the beginning!" Arturu's father insisted.

"Forgive me," Arturu blurted out rapidly and raised his head a little.

"Very well, I heard you. End of story!" his father told him shortly but beginning to mellow. "Let's put it all behind us now. Let's go on."

"We were talking about love," Lady prompted.

"About love was it, Lady?" her husband spoke in an ironic tone. "I've forgotten what I was saying, in the meantime," he continued more gently. "Love changes from one minute to the next, like the weather. What can I teach you about love, wife? You know as well as I do what it means. What is it? A sultry dance in a dance hall, with powerful lights winking on and off? Lights, all sorts, but mostly red. I wonder why mostly red? With a heavy fug, dense and dark, of cigarette smoke? With one's inner being on fire, the blood drumming a beat in your brain? With the sensuous swaying of the dancers? Wasn't that the love of long ago? Have you forgotten it all, wife? I don't think you've forgotten it and why should you? It's not a bad memory, after all. When time passes, nothing is left except a picture imprinted in your mind. A picture that can be clearly seen sometimes and mistily obscured at other times, according to our mind's weather pattern at the time. We need to make every effort not to let that picture be erased. We don't have anything else left. Do you remember?"

"I remember, of course I remember," she replied. "I wish that time was still around. If I could, I would make it stand still and grab it, like this, so it wouldn't escape me. That's what my hands are for, to snatch at something that time wants to steal from me and make it change. We still had our dreams then, and they were enough for us. We still knew how to wait. Indeed the pleasure we had in life was in the waiting, and that's what we desired."

"And what picture is going to be left in our minds from all this, wife, do you know?"

"What picture is going to be left? From all this?" she asked her husband, full of amazement and rather startled.

"The picture is called Arturu. That's why it must be well made, as much as a picture can possibly be. For your sake and mine."

As soon as he heard his name, the boy lifted up his head gingerly, then went on eating and held his tongue. He was still surly. He continued to scowl and kept his head down as far as he could, as far as his curiosity allowed.

"Do you understand, son?" his father asked him directly.

"I want to go outside," Arturu spoke up.

"You want to go outside? Where? And with whom?" his father questioned him in irritation. "What don't you have here inside the house? Don't you have everything you can wish for, here? When you grow up son, you'll look for love outside these four walls. It will be for love, indeed, that you'll have to leave here. But only for the sake of love. Don't go out when there's no need to do so. As if you're living in a tower with thick walls. Peep out when you need to and then come back quickly inside and close the windows. Lock them. Peace can only be found in here. Those people out there are different. As for the rest, there's everything one could need here. We thought of everything you could possibly need. What else do you want that isn't here?"

"I want to go out. I want to play with other children, like I used to," Arturu repeated stubbornly.

"Like you used to? Don't you want to be happy now? Life isn't worth living if there's no happiness. It's wasted. Don't you know I came into this world before you? Do you think I've never learnt anything in all this time? That all the years that have gone by left me how I was as a child? So you want to roam the village streets? Get out!" his father shouted angrily, but then he paused and then said, "And I won't let you! While I'm still alive, I'll keep you safe in my hands, use all my strength, and the keys to the house will remain in my care. And before I let them go, I will make sure that the woman I will entrust them to will follow in my footsteps. I try to see the whole picture and think in the long term.

That's where my strength lies, son. I am the only one who knows what's best for you. Don't you know about that boy who wanted to go to the forest because he'd heard it was a lovely place?"

"The forest?" Arturu asked him, enchanted with the word.

"The forest, yes, which means the way. Beyond the village, where we don't know what there is except for large, mature trees, which grow older but never die, and darkened shadows. Blackness on blackness. That's what the forest holds. Everything you don't know outside the door. And the boy went to the forest. We don't know who he was. Someone. A little boy, or quite grown-up, someone. He walked and walked until he entered the forest and found himself among many tall trees, and heard the birds sing and was startled by the sounds made by animals hidden from sight, animals he could not recognize, and he heard the soughing of densely-leaved trees all around him. He was full of wonder, enthralled, and his heart filled up with wishes. He became one burning desire himself, from the top of his head to the tips of his toes. Which meant his ruin. Desire is destruction. And then he walked on, and do you know what happened? He never managed to find his way back again. And it was all his own fault!"

"I know this story, Father," Arturu stopped him.

"You know it? They told it to you? Hmm, so they told this story, huh? You mean to say that you know its beginning. I've just started recounting it. But how do you know how it continues? Every story is known by its beginning, but as for how it ends...well, that's a mystery, every ending is different. So let me continue...He began hoping to meet someone who could tell him where he was and where he could go on next. He knocked on the door of the few houses there were. Even houses could be found in this forest. They were closed, these houses, securely locked up with a large key that had many turns of the lock. Houses full of people. But nobody opened their door to him. At last he found himself outside the forest, in an area of vales and rolling hills, and he looked around happily, glad to be there in that wide open space. And then he said to himself, 'I wish I could meet somebody, but there's no one here.' And no one was there, sure enough. And in that wide open space, do you know what he wished for, son?"

Arturu was thinking about his answer. "He wished, umm, let me see, he wished to meet other children so he could play with them, in the forest, or in the vales and dales. That's what I think he wished for. If it was me, that's what I'd want, Father."

"Nothing of the sort, son. Can you see now how every story starts off the same but then continues differently? He wished to find himself within the four walls of his house. Safely back home. And do you know what he had at home? He had some food and a fire to cook it. Nothing else. And in the middle of the forest without end, what do you think he desired? All he wanted was to lock himself up in his own little house. And there he wished to..."

"He wished to find his mother," Arturu promptly interjected.

"Arturu, tell me what he wanted! Did he want his friends, some other children to play with? Or did he want his mother?"

"He wanted his mother, that's what I think."

His father stopped speaking and lowered his head, and then he continued questioning his son. "And if his mother wasn't there, what could he want instead?"

"His friends, the other children, to play with," Arturu reiterated.

"And if there weren't other children to play with?"

"There had to be many other children, Father, with whom he could play. But maybe his father didn't want him to go and play with them."

"And so, if his mother wasn't there, and he couldn't go out to play with the other children, what else did he have?" his father asked him, at the same time glancing at his wife.

"Nothing, Father, he didn't have anything else, then," was Arturu's reply.

Lady looked at her husband and then lowered her head.

"Nothing, son? He truly had nothing? Is that what you think?" his father replied, his voice hoarse, feeling he had lost out. "Now here in this house, you have many more things than he had. You're wishing for much more than you have need of, for now. That's not natural, all that you're wishing for. Let me continue...He fell asleep and began to dream. And what did he dream about?"

Arturu was almost terrified, but remained with his hands in his lap, with bowed head, silent.

"He dreamt his mother and father were by his side, and the time had come for them to leave, and he had to continue on his path alone. He said his goodbyes and went on walking, until the evening drew in and he again wanted to know where his mother and father were, but he heard a voice coming from somewhere telling him, 'Listen, you must realise that they left on a different path that is no longer yours as well, and it's no use trying to find them. Your paths will never cross again. Go on walking straight ahead, always straight on, and you'll arrive someplace. Enjoy whatever path you find yourself on. Along this path you'll come across whatever your heart is searching for. And you need to prove wise to recognize that it will do you good. Your heart will guide you, but your heart can make mistakes, too. Continue walking because the main thing is to leave the forest and go back home.' That's what the voice told him. Do you understand, Arturu? Home is everything, and home means that there's a door that can be locked against the world outside that wants to enter."

"We're not the same kind of people like the others in the village, Arturu. That's what your father is trying to tell you. The streets outside are not for the likes of you. The other children in the street aren't like you," Lady explained.

"The boys or the girls, Mother?"

"Boys and girls, both!" his father snapped at him. "We're different not because we are men or women, but because...I don't know why. The fact remains that we're not the same as them. Make sure you understand this, and keep to it from this very moment, and don't ask too many questions. Don't expect to know the reason for everything. There's no need to know the why and wherefore of truth. Know the truth, and that's all. It's enough to know that. And if even I at my age don't know why, how do you expect to know it? I am nearing the end, and you're just beginning. Our paths are rather far apart from each other."

"I want to go back where I was!" wailed Arturu.

"Do you know where you were, son?"

Arturu was silenced.

"Do you want to go back where you were? Very well, let's go. Come, let's go!" his father exclaimed, getting up to take Arturu's hand to pull him up.

Arturu was terrified and rose from the table and ran to Lady. He burrowed into her lap and she sheltered him with her hands.

"Whenever you want, at whatever moment, we can leave!" his father sternly spoke to him.

"He doesn't really want to go there, Father. He only said that to say something. He's already changed his mind since then. Our mind is like a clock, it moves and changes all the time. Isn't that so, darling? Arturu wants to remain here," Lady tried to placate her husband.

"I want to hear him say it; he can speak and I want him to say it, therefore," his father ordered. "I'm waiting to hear you speak, Arturu. Where do you want to live?"

"Here! I want to stay here," Arturu agreed wretchedly.

"So why did you say that before?"

"He doesn't know what he wants," Lady appeased her husband. "So what should you say to your father?" she turned to her son, gently prompting him.

"Forgive me."

"I forgive you. Yes, I forgive you. But, what's my name, huh? Don't I have a name?"

"Fa...Father."

"So you should tell me..."

"Tell you what? For-give-me, Father...but why?"

His father could not bear it any longer. He rose from the table and made straight for his study; he flung himself into his armchair, put on his spectacles and picked up a book that happened to be lying beside him, riffling through its pages. The next minute he rose again and started pacing his study, but brought himself up short, "Forgive me Arturu, you too need to forgive me."

The extract which Arturu read from his father's diary recounted it so...

"Susanna, Susanna! Where are you? Goodness knows where you are now, at this very moment!" Arturu exclaimed, murmuring to himself, continuing with his memories...

He remembered the years he had spent in an orphanage, brought up with harsh discipline. They used to be woken up early in the morning, every day at the same time, on the stroke of the bell, an ancient one with deep regular strokes which reverberated all around. They used to rise half-heartedly from their bed, get washed and start their day. They were taught to read and write and they had to learn some skill, too. They used to eat the same kind of food, always at the same time, in the refectory, a long, long hall set up with long tables where the plates were dished out one after the other all at the same time, identical plates with an identical helping, the same for everyone. They were content, and also full of desires. The whole day was one entire routine.

Arturu, alone, his thoughts turned to Susanna, went on reading and remembering...

"You'll grow up, Arturu, because as you can see for yourself, time passes for everybody and we don't remain the same as we were," his father had explained to him, giving him a brief glance from beneath his brows. "Childhood is there for us to enjoy when we get old. When we are children, we don't realize we're just children. When we grow older we continue to live with the memory of our childhood. Everything is a memory, from this moment on. It's all that remains and it's nothing but a wish. I, too, was a lad once, a bit older than you, but now I'm old. But I didn't grow old for nothing. In the meantime I had met this woman, Lady, everyone knows her as 'Lady'. I call her wife but people call her 'Lady', and you call her Mother. Wife...Lady...Mother...you choose whichever name you want to call her. It doesn't make a difference, does it? You can see her here, this woman who loves you so much, your mother, my wife. We lived our life together and brought you up without much trouble. You were the whole object of our lives, Arturu, and now it's up to you to nurture our dream, when I'm no longer here, and she will take up the task to lead you till you reach your allotted place." His father stopped speaking and looked to his wife for her approbation.

"Do you understand all that your father is trying to tell you, Arturu?" she joined in. "He knows full well what advice to give you because he's been through it all before you. If you do what he says you won't regret it. I, too, do what he says. He knows best."

Arturu then remembered the times when Lady would go out to attend early mass taking him with her; she would take him by the hand and after returning home she would lock up the house and make him stay inside. The windows were always kept open or ajar during the day, till it was time for the lamp lighter to come along the street when she would do the round of every window in the house to close it. The dim lights in the street corners would set her mind at rest that the street would not be left in total darkness, but at the same time she took it as a signal that it was dark and she had to close all the windows. The lamp lighter, a taciturn man who arrived every evening with his ladder to set it up against each lamp post and light it, for her meant that the evening was drawing in. She frequently leaned out of the window to throw him some small change. Evening meant that all the members of the family would be gathered safe at home; not to adhere to this custom was considered a sin.

"The villagers, Arturu, aren't like us. Though we were born in the same village we're not the same," Lady told him complacently. "There's a gulf of difference between us, going back whole generations and we cannot bridge it by approaching each other, in church during mass, or at the market whilst buying food. Since we're different, we weren't born to be together, though we live in the same village. Make sure you understand all this from now. Tomorrow may be too late for you. I'll have to keep on repeating this to you till the end."

Arturu remembered it all as if it was yesterday...

"Can't I go out to play a bit with the other children in the street, Mother?" he pleaded. "You can be sure I won't go far away. I'll stay only in our street. If they go any further than that I promise you I'll come back, really, I really will."

"Ask your father and see what he says," Lady prevaricated. "If he says yes then you may go out, but if he says no, well then...I think he'll say no, and he'll be right. He thinks in one way, and I happen to think the same. What a coincidence!"

"But can't you say yes or no yourself, Mother?"

"I, give you permission, Arturu? How can I? Your father is the head of the family, and it's only right and proper that he rules the household. Your father. That's how it's supposed to be, and mind you never forget this, even when you grow up, because you will someday and your father and I won't be around, and you'll find you need to hold on to this. All that you're learning today will prove useful tomorrow. Who knows how tomorrow will turn out?"

Arturu was about to run to the study to ask his father.

Lady was quick to hold him back. "No, no, Arturu, wait a moment. Where do you think you're going? Let me go and talk to him. I'm going to tell him that you'd like to go out and play with the village children, and I'll see what he says. He knows what's best for you. Is that alright with you? Wait for me here. Don't go upstairs. He'll be reading and if you go in and interrupt him, you'll startle him. He wants silence, and silence keeps us all together in this house. You're too young to understand what I'm saying. But in time you'll find out. Don't expect to understand everything all at once. It's early days yet, and there's no hurry. Life is long, sometimes too long. You don't know what marriage means, son, and if you want to know a little about it, you have to ask us. We've plenty of time. We started walking on our path before you, many, many years before you, and in circumstances that are hardly understood nowadays. You can't imagine what we had to go through, your father and I, when we met and fell in love and sought to bring you up in the best possible way! Wait here, then, I'll soon be back," she promised.

Arturu remained there, waiting for her.

Lady walked on to the study, gave a few gentle taps on the door, waited a moment and then entered.

"No, no, better not, wife," her husband sounded his concern. "Don't you think it's better not, as well? Where is he getting these ideas from?"

Lady nodded her head in agreement. "They're wishes making an appearance as he grows up. But they're far earlier than our dance hall, don't you think?"

"That's how these affairs begin. Small things will soon give way to bigger things. If you want him to mix with the villagers, let him mix. But if not, you must nip this in the bud, severely. Like this, forcefully! Which means without mercy. And make sure to dig deep for the root cause, in the same way the farmers around us do. They do well to dig up weeds roots and all; if they're bad, they're bad." Her husband spoke to her vehemently, making a swift slashing motion with his right hand as if wielding a hand-scythe. He slowly raised his head from the book, leaving his finger caught between the pages, removed his spectacles and kept hold of them with his right hand, and looked sideways at her. "Maybe it's you who doesn't understand what I'm getting at?"

"Your knowledge is much greater than mine because you read books. After all, whatever I know I learnt either from you or from the time I've spent alone looking out of the window, looking into the distance, beyond our village, waiting for new times to come by. But it seems they're never going to come. I've been waiting for too long now. What else can I do? I waited and waited, stayed at my post, prayed and hoped, gave my heart to the right person, and still, here I am, look, I'm like a hermit."

Her husband raised his head calmly and addressed her, "Is that what you think? Don't you think you're a woman who wants for nothing? Ever since you met me you've found yourself. Where were you before? What did you wish for? And what's happened to you since then? And what would have happened to you had I not danced with you that evening and fallen in love? Remember some more. If you make an effort and close your eyes, you'll find yourself back in that red-lit hall. Those lights, flashing on and off, those people, holding a glass in their hand, and the music being played onstage, everything is still up here," he told her, raising his forefinger to his forehead. "That day was the beginning of today for you. If you were looking for love, can you say you didn't find it in me? I gave you all the love I could, in the way I knew how. More than that you can't expect. After all, you know that for me life had begun much earlier, before I met you."

His wife looked him in the eye and said, "Don't take me wrong. I'm not condemning you. On that occasion, all that I was looking for was a little bit of love. And today, after all this time, I'm not looking for more than that, still. Just a little bit, just enough to last me on my way. The last flame, as long as it flickers to the end. I've always had the same empty plate in my hands, and I've always only begged for the same crumbs to sustain me. Whatever you gave me I've been happy with, welcomed it, and made much of it. Don't you know all this, dear husband?"

"Dear husband? Are you addressing me?"

"Don't you know it's you I'm talking to? There's no one else in the whole world for me, husband. I've loved you ever since that day, my love. I could begin to say that there was one man who was wholly mine."

"Your husband..."

"My husband and at the same time Arturu's father, too! Isn't that what you mean to say? I didn't give you some part of the future, but I gave you my present, wholly, whatever it held and whatever's left. My heart. There's nothing else I can give you of more value than that, not even in some other corner which you think might yield you all your heart's desires. Don't wish for too much."

"I know, I know, we all try to reach as far as we can. I too, found everything in you. The woman who filled my life. But I still have to face the biggest problem – what will happen to all these worldly goods we have? This is the most important question I'd like you to answer. I've amassed all this wealth after many years. Some of it I'd inherited and some I earned through sheer hard work, though I admit, having money in the first place made it easier to earn more. And you looked after it wisely indeed. Thank you very much, wife. But now I'm only concerned about one thing – what's going to happen to all this?"

His wife remained silent. She went to him and he took her hand, still sitting down on his armchair. "The flame flickers on, don't forget. But if you want to discuss the day when it flickers out, and one day it will, well, don't forget I'll be here, still. I'll keep watch over all that belongs to you. Set your mind at rest, you'll have the best possible guard in me. Every lesson you had to give, I've followed to the letter and every thought you've had, I've made it mine. All that belongs to you, I will watch over, day and night, and I know how to stand firm, too!"

"Don't forget that Arturu is waiting for you, below. If you stay too long he'll start thinking the worst," her husband spoke to her somewhat coldly.

"You're right. In marriage, a man and wife depend on what their son thinks."

"You and I salvaged as much as we could from the situation we were in. Up to now, we've managed well enough. Do you want to lose it all now, just when he's starting to grow up? Life is what you make it, but not more than that. The impossible has nothing to do with real life," he spoke decisively.

His wife looked him straight in the eye. "And do you really think we've managed to save all that there was to save? You think there's nothing else to be had? Is our life going to stop now for the two or three of us?"

"I learnt all this by frequently sitting in this armchair, and you've been with me. The whole village calls you 'Lady'," he told her with a smile. "You're a lady because you know how to keep your distance. Remove that, go out into the street, chat with people, go and do your shopping at the market place with everyone else, and from that very day, I promise you, Lady, your whole past will come tumbling down. If you haven't understood this by now, you've understood nothing, wife. You are my wife. And if you call me 'husband', be patient and model your comportment on mine, even if you find it hard to do so. Keep your distance, though there might not be any. Where none exists, it must be created. A small village, a limited space, but a great distance. A craving of the mind. This is what books have taught me. Keep your distance, don't talk, if you've decided to talk say as little as possible, and walk straight, with a firm step, your gaze above people's heads, and don't be afraid. Life is a challenge, even in this tiny village. Soon you'll see how quickly distances grow around you, as if they are sheltering walls. Everything starts with the mind and ends there."

"You mean to say that the key to life is in this room. You can't have learnt all this from the village, dear husband," his wife told him.

"Don't you know where I could have learnt all this, dear wife?"

"From books?"

"A good answer. But not only."

"Well then you must have learnt all this, too, from this very room that has collected all the traditions and customs in which you were born and bred, and which surround you still."

"And I will remain...surrounded by them," he cut her short holding a forefinger straight in front of his face.

"Till the very last flicker of flame, then."

"Till the last flicker."

"Whole centuries of your ancestors are gathered in here, I suppose."

"My ancestors! Yours too. All this belongs to you as well. And even you have entered into this room. All these traditions of mine have long become yours too. In the meantime you've changed. But you know all this. You'd better go now. Arturu is waiting for you."

Lady went downstairs and told Arturu that his father did not want him to go out and play with the children in the street.

It seemed like yesterday, and Arturu had forgotten nothing. From every page of the copybook filled with his father's memories, Arturu set up entire pages of his own, in his mind. He could join up the pieces. The clear handwriting persuaded him to read ever more, and he only had to use a magnifying glass on rare occasions to decipher some illegible word.

He rose from the armchair and put the copybook down on the desk.

"Susanna, Susanna! Where are you? Goodness knows where you are at this moment!" he continued to repeat to himself.

The remaining pages of the copybook were blank.

"It was here that my father stopped writing. He stopped in the middle of a sentence, at the top of a page. How could he write anymore?" Arturu sadly murmured, willing himself to remember more clearly.

It was when his father had fallen ill. He began to mix up words, became confused in his ideas, and more than that, he became forgetful. With a vacant look in his eyes, he turned his gaze here and there but with no fixed purpose. They had become bleary eyes, magnified somewhat by the lenses of his spectacles which he kept half-way down his nose and he spent the entire day sitting down. He never smiled or laughed. He spoke very slowly, as if meting out his words to save the few he had left. His fixed gaze, having stopped on something, was like the minute hand of a watch that had stopped, once and for all.

"Father, Father, how are you?" Arturu asked him one time. He knew his father had completely lost his memory, but he still wanted to try and strike up a conversation, to cherish the least word from him.

"Who am I?"

"No, Father, not who are you but how are you?"

"Who are you? Do I know you? No! I don't know you. Do you live here? And where is here?" his father rambled.

"I'm Arturu, Father."

"Arturu? I'm Arturu?"

"No, Father, I am Arturu."

"You?"

"Yes, Father, I am," Arturu replied with tears in his eyes.

"I've never seen you before," his father answered, his eyes expressionless, gazing vacantly. "I'm certain I've never laid eyes on you! Never before today."

"Tell me, Father, tell me you know I am Arturu," the young man begged.

"Arturu? I don't know anybody called Arturu, I'm sure. I know no one of that name."

"I'm your son."

"My son? No, that can't be."

"And this is my mother, Father."

"Who's this woman?"

"My mother. Look at her closely and you'll recognize her," Arturu told him encouragingly.

"My mother?"

"No, Father, not your mother, but mine."

"Yours? I don't know her. I really want to see my mother," Arturu's father said his voice becoming agitated. "Mother, Mother," he began to mumble bowing his head, with no flicker of emotion kindled in his eyes as they continued to look at emptiness.

Lady caressed her husband's cheeks, but he made no movement whatsoever. Her eyes were full of tears and she did her best not to let him hear her cry.

He had the copybook in his hands.

Arturu continued going over his memories, trying to remember every detail. Right till the very end, Lady used to like calling her husband to come down for his meal, trying to make him mouth something, so that she could hear his voice. That day, it was evening, and she called him once, twice, but he gave no answer. He had just died, the book still in his hand. Arturu remembered telling the whole story to Susanna, years later, and she had remarked on his likeness to the large portrait hanging in the dining room.

It was the season when Arturu opened up his heart to the one love of his life. He remembered the new joy, unlooked for, which Susanna had brought with her, for him.

Chapter 4

The elderly man who was the doorkeeper at the Curia, the Roman Catholic Church's administrative centre, had got up early, as usual. He was known to all and sundry as Doorkeeper. No one knew his name, but that was no great matter, and neither was the fact that his surname was unknown, as well. And no nickname was bestowed on him, either. His face alone was known to all the people of the locality, especially to children for whom the streets were but an extension of their home.

"Door-keeper! How are you, Door-keeper?" the call would be uttered teasingly in a loud sing-song voice by the naughty boys roaming the streets together, as a mob, most times during the day. Passing in front of the Curia they would note whether the door was closed and if not, they would see him standing by, on the threshold. They would see him always on his own, whispering something to himself, standing ramrod straight. He was always dressed neatly in a full suit, complete with jacket and tie, which appeared to restrict him somewhat, because in summer he suffered from hot flushes, whilst in winter he would get the fidgets. His uniform was part and parcel of his job, and this was enough to give him a measure of standing in people's eyes and to command a greater degree of respect.

"Learn some manners and be sensible, foolish boys! Listen to me! Wise up before it's too late! Time flies by without giving notice! You won't be aware when your time is up! Your time – that is, till you start wearing long trousers, that's what I mean. Just you wait a bit and you'll see it won't be long before your mother will make you wear a pair of trousers that brush the ground. You'll become men, then. Young men of course but there you are! The time for foolishness will vanish! And then you won't come by any longer and keep calling out 'Door-keeper! Door-keeper!' in that dreadful way you have. You'll soon become men, and then just come along and see what you have to say for yourselves! We'll see then, huh?" he used to tell them off in a low voice which only his ears could pick up.

Door-keeper! Door-keeper!
Best like this or else you're worse-er!

The boys would cry out as they passed in front of him, jumping and joshing each other and everyone else. They would pick on a word and make it rhyme into a doggerel and go round chanting it till they got fed up of it. Their step was somewhere in-between a hop, a skip and a jump. The street was their home and lair. Some of them would be playing with a hoop, a round object attached in its middle to a long thin piece of tin wire held in their hand, a kind of wheel that the boys would push in front of them, fast or at a run, everywhere they went, but mostly in the middle of the street. Others would be kicking a rag football or a discarded can, or anything else they came across which could be given a good kick. They would sing out the doggerel in the hope of seeing the doorkeeper take offence, even though they would be intent on their games. But games without a dash of teasing were no fun at all. Nicknames were in their heyday, quickly invented and hurled about, and bothering old people was fair game for the boys. The people around would remain onlookers, seemingly glad to come across some unexpected free entertainment in the street.

Door-keeper! Door-keeper!
You are old and we are young-er!

The doorkeeper finally did take offence; he bit his bottom lip not to utter some unruly word, and he came down the front steps and ran after the boys as fast as he could to try and catch them. "If I catch you, you'll see what I can do! Then I won't be Doorkeeper at that big, important door. Even the uniform I'm wearing won't be enough to hold me back...If I catch you, ohh, there won't be anything left of you to tell the tale. I'll pluck you entirely! With these hands of mine, look, I'll soon pluck you! I'll strip away all your cockiness. Today's children are such braggarts!" he shouted, wanting to be heard. He lowered his voice to say to himself, "Who could catch up with you? You're always running around in the streets, shouting, singing and screaming, and never getting tired! You're like a fresh breeze, but as for me, see here, I'm like an old carob tree that cannot be moved even by a hurricane. A carob tree has deep roots, old roots. Ah well, I was just like you once!"

Door-keeper! Door-keeper!
You are here and wifey's home-er!

The doggerel they had made up echoed everywhere. He kept running after them till he gave up any hope of catching anyone. They hid round street corners but he could see neither hide nor hair of them. They fell silent all at once, remaining hidden, crouching down or hugging the wall in order not to be seen, occasionally cautiously peeping round the corner. Their heads could only be glimpsed slightly.

"Where did they go off to hide? Who could possibly control them? I'll tell the bishop all about it when I come face-to-face with him. I'll tell on them! But what elderly man could hope to measure up to them? Everyone advanced in years finds it difficult to run after them. They're like the wind! A breeze, a gust of wind! They can leap away as far and as fast as they want. But as for us? We just shuffle around! Ahh, life was so much better when we were children!" He stopped in his tracks, remained there thinking, and feeling excited at the turn of phrase he had thought of, his face filled with pleasure and with a hint of pride he exclaimed,

Door-keeper! Door-keeper!
Young I was and I was be-tter!

He spoke these words to himself, trying to sing to the same tune the children had chanted just before. "Door-keeper!"

"Door-keeper! Door-keeper!" these loud words uttered by the boys in hiding kept echoing in the streets.

The doorkeeper lowered his head in resignation and turned back, walking at his normal pace back to the Curia's front door. "Wise up! If you don't, do you know what's going to happen to you?" he shouted in as strong a voice as he could manage.

"What will happen to us, Doorkeeper?" they asked him from afar, with one voice, a teasing lilt to it.

"What will happen to you? Guess! Use your heads! Do you have heads to think with or not? That head on your shoulders, what's it doing then, huh? That works just like clockwork. Of course it does, just wind it up. Find the key to its mechanism and turn it round and round, and the clock will start ticking away. Your mind is just like clockwork," he cautioned them, and he paused and then continued, "What will happen to you?...The same thing that's happened to me!"

"And what's happened to you?" came their reply, again as one voice, as one by one they slowly, slowly came out of hiding. They filed into a line in front of him, the hoop at rest at their feet and the footballs in their hands.

"I grew old! Look here, can't you see? Some of my hair has gone white and some has fallen off. Almost all my teeth are loose, they move under my hand whenever I touch them. Ahh! They weren't always like this! They used to be as sound and solid as a rubble wall. My memory isn't what it used to be; I forget bits and there are other bits I can't get rid of. The part I'd like to forget parades clearly in front of my eyes, and that part I'd like to remember, ahh! That's hazy, dim, engulfed in darkness. You'll grow old; you'll all grow old soon enough! But there's still time! You're still brand new! You've just discovered the village, your whole world! Foolish boys!" he maundered on.

The boys remained quiet, listening to him.

"You're just starting life! Just you wait! You won't play with hoops or run after rag balls rolling on the ground, when you grow up. Foolish boys! What do you think life is all about? It's just like one jar for all, and everybody takes a sip in turn, and whether it tastes sweet or bitter is left to chance. Just ask those who've come into this world before you. But there, for now stay just as you are, or else you know what will happen. You'll become just like me. Ah well, in any case, life has always come and gone. When it came by I found a good job and I've spent my time watching it pass by, from here, from the top of these steps in front of this huge door." Then he stopped and raised his hands like a bandmaster does, and he began to sing to them,

Door-keeper! Door-keeper!
Best like this or else you're worse-er!

The boys were cowed looking at him, thunderstruck, waiting on his words.
"Come on then! Come on children! Sing along..."
The children kept quiet.
He kept on singing,

Door-keeper! Door-keeper!
Drops of joy but jar so bi-tter!

The boys sang along for a while but soon lost interest and continued playing their games, gradually moving away. Silence reigned once more in the street.

The doorkeeper had spent his entire life keeping watch at that door, and his work consisted of greeting visitors as soon as they set foot in the doorway and conducting them to one of several large rooms that led to a hall where they could wait till they met with the bishop. He had to be courteous, neatly attired, not effusive, and stand straight.

"I do my best. I don't hold myself so straight because time has made me slightly bent and arthritis has reduced me to a stick, like a vine stalk. But I have to stand up straight and straight I'll stand. Here I am! An order arrives and it will be obeyed! I'm like one of those soldiers or sailors that frequent these parts in the evenings, in search of affection which they haven't found on their ship or back in their country. A soldier standing straight, a doorkeeper like a soldier. I wonder how a soldier that's like a doorkeeper will look!" he mumbled to himself and laughed. His enforced solitude lured him into a solitary game of miming and play-acting, for the long hours he daily spent alone made him invent some activity to while the time away. "How funny! I'm a doorkeeper wanting to behave like a soldier. But for a soldier to become a doorkeeper...well, that's something else altogether! This is how a doorkeeper should behave, look, like me, always alone, waiting, standing guard at a door that's left ajar nearly all year long. A doorkeeper who always looks towards Heaven through his own particular lenses, and keeps checking how close he's come or, Heaven preserve us, if he's going further and further away...I wonder if all this will count in my favour, at the end of the day? Will my soul be saved? I imagine so. I'm not a common doorkeeper. But I can't grumble. I could have been a soldier after all. Hmm, just imagine that! Saluting, singing, standing straight, face forward without moving a muscle, looking into the distance somewhere, wearing a uniform and keeping it clean and tidy...exactly like a soldier. Be that as it may, I'm still the guardian of order. A doorkeeper keeping guard at the door of the tower where all that is sure and certain lies. Poor thing! A doorkeeper must carry a heavy load, heavier than himself. Those children without a care in the world don't have the least idea what it's all about!"

The bishop's quarters were some way off, in a room the doorkeeper knew from its door, always closed, or slightly ajar; a room he never expected to enter himself unless some wildly improbable occasion arose for him to do so. Since he was able to greet everyone respectfully, quietly, as usual with the same genteel formula made up of four words, and since he could see to it that his smart jacket didn't slip off his shoulders, and he had mastered the knack of pinning a respectful smile to his face and keeping it there, he was surely right in assuming that as far as being a good doorkeeper goes, he had no problems. He only had to ask guests the reason for their visit, lead them just inside the doorway, and leave them to wait for the right person to come and deal with them. This is the way the elderly man had spent all his years.

"What a long time has passed! Goodness knows how many people I've conducted in and out of this blessed massive door! And it's grown old together with me! The door and I! If we were to tell each other the story of our lives...Oh, your Excellency, what a lot of stories a simple doorkeeper like me can tell!" he went on talking animatedly to himself. "But I don't know how to write. I've seen many books, and sometimes I've carried them from one place to another as directed, thick volumes, large books, but I've always looked at them distantly. They've never been my concern. I can see them, touch them, open them a bit but only for a look. Oh well, in spite of it all I've still grown old! Time passes by for everyone, and whether with doses of joy or grief, only a tremor in your stomach remains of its passing. You look back with sadness if your time had been troubled – because of the grief it caused you, and you look back with even more sadness if your time had been full of happiness – because the joy has long gone. How funny!"

He had spent his whole life in the shadow of the faded colours of large paintings hung around all the walls, in the corners of a huge palace where he had to tread with bowed head, humbly...without asking any questions; certainly none were expected of him...and with no need for any discussion. The very first lesson had matured and grown old with him, and it was a good lesson – he always had to obey. At the end of the day, this would guarantee the two things he could ever wish for most of all: safeguarding his employment, here on this earth; and saving his soul, in the other world that everybody talked about. The first world was spread all around him. It was a world of gold and silver, close to him and distant at the same time. They were things that belonged to him only insofar as they were his to look at and guard, and to appreciate and admire and praise without wanting to own them. It was a world of beautiful, heavy garments, like that world someone had told him could be found in books, the heavy history tomes, full of old pictures and live bookworms.

"Those books are not your concern!" the priest charged with overseeing the activity in the corridor leading right to the Bishop's room had warned him once. He was the Bishop's pastor but everyone knew him as 'the Priest of the Corridor'. "Those books can make you lose your soul. Careful how you handle them! Wash your hands! They're full of bookworms. Moths are drawn to them! Don't touch them! Don't you even try to read one word in them! And if you touch them, you'll have to leave this place. We will notice immediately, because as soon as you open them you will start to speak and think in a different way. You will only remain here if you concern yourself only with the front door!"

"Just like St. Peter, then!" the doorkeeper had exclaimed.

"What has St. Peter got to do with it? And come to that, do you really dare compare yourself to St. Peter? Or maybe you don't really know who St. Peter was?" the Priest of the Corridor had asked him, outraged.

"But why ever not, Sir? Even St. Peter made mistakes. And he reached his position because of his mistakes, and saved his soul into the bargain, too. I don't know much but the little I know, I know very well indeed. My mother used to tell me I had a good memory. And do you know why? Because once a beggar came knocking at our door and he held out his hands...both of them...straight in front of him...and he asked for alms, and my mother opened the door to give him some money but she didn't have any small change. And she turned to ask me for some and I quickly went to look under my pillow where I kept some money I'd secretly saved, and brought out some coins. And I gave her some which she gave to the beggar. She told me she'd repay me. But she forgot. And I soon reminded her. And she marvelled, 'What a good memory you have, son! You have a sharp mind. I wonder which member of our family you resemble. You'd do well at school!' she'd told me."

"So? What does this signify?" the Priest of the Corridor asked impatiently.

"I'm comparing myself to St. Peter who sinned, and not St. Peter who became a saint. There, is that alright, Sir?" the doorkeeper went on.

"But you want to compare yourself to St. Peter who sinned? The sinner?"

"Sir, please excuse me. If I compare myself to St. Peter the saint I'd be presumptuous. I don't want to appear too forward. And if I compare myself to St. Peter the sinner, I'd be doing something wrong. I don't want to appear as a sinful man, either. Who could possibly wish for something like that? And why do I appear in the wrong? This is where I grew up and was brought up, on this doorstep. Well then, I'm always in the wrong, whatever I do, at least in your eyes, Sir."

"No, no, you're not always in the wrong. A doorkeeper is a very patient man. And patience is a great virtue; there are those who consider it the greatest virtue of all. Job's virtue. We can only save our soul through patience. You can rest assured."

"Job the Doorkeeper...I'm like Job. My wife often says she's like Job because she thinks she has to be very patient with me. I don't know when she finds the time to do so because I spend most of my day in here, stuck to this door. We're a patient couple, Sir."

"A doorkeeper is one who waits. And those who wait are patient."

"Thank you, Sir, thank you. At least you've set my mind at rest now. As for me, I don't want to do anything wrong, not even by speaking. The best thing to do, I think, is not to think about anything. And neither ask questions nor answer any. My duty is only to stand guard at that door, large, heavy, and massive. To see who comes in and who goes out. Why should I go looking for trouble? At my age nothing else should interest me. I should wish for nothing more."

"Very good, that's good. But there's no need to trouble your head with such thoughts. You don't need to try and become a theologian. You're fine just as you are, and you can save yourself all the same, and maybe you're in a better position to do so! Maybe you'll succeed in getting to Heaven before us, and who knows? Maybe you'll find a better place up there than us, too! That's what I think, that's what often happens. Time will tell. But I'd best stop here and be on my way."

"You mean, I can save my soul by taking care of the front door, every single day, don't you, Sir?"

"That's right, and that's good enough for you."

"To see who comes by, ask them what their business here is, say a few more words and sneak a glance at them so as not to be too trusting, and finally let them enter. Just like St. Peter at the gates of Heaven. St. Peter in a good mood!"

"No, that's not quite right," the Priest of the Corridor told him off. "You have to look over anyone who comes, and check if after all they should be allowed in. You can't do it hurriedly if you're going to do it properly, but you can't take your time over it, neither. If you do all this properly, you'll be like..."

"St. Peter. I'm like St. Peter. My wife's going to be so proud of me this evening when I tell her you said so! May I mention your name to her? If I don't mention your name she won't believe me, and my word won't count. I need some recommendation. I'll tell her, 'wife, I'm not saying all this from the top of my head, you know!' Maybe at last she won't keep putting me down as a mere doorkeeper. Now I'll be able to tell her, 'even someone who was called St. Peter was a doorkeeper. St. Peter himself, no less. My colleague! Mind how you talk to me! From now onwards I'm in the company of the most important sort of people.' That's what I'll tell her and from this day onwards she won't be able to contradict me anymore."

"The door keys need to be held by someone. Otherwise, either no one would be able to enter, or anybody could just walk in," the Priest of the Corridor exclaimed. "A doorkeeper is an important man."

"But that's something else. That's your decision, Sir. I don't hold the keys. I'm in charge only of the door, isn't that so?"

"Yes, you're only in charge of the door. Not of the keys. Even if you were to hold them, they would never become yours. They would remain St. Peter's keys. This is something you must never forget."

"And me? Aren't I like St. Peter, always waiting at the door? I'm a doorkeeper, I always was and I always will be a doorkeeper."

"But whatever are we doing, saying all this? We know all this, both you and I. You've been doing this job for many years. Why all these new questions today? New questions are superfluous. The door is in your charge and that's enough for you to know. There's nothing to confuse you. It's a simple job."

"Thank you, Sir, thank you for all that you've told me. I hope Heaven's door is as wide as our Curia door, Sir, otherwise I'm not too sure I'll be able to enter," the elderly man went on. "Once I heard a priest say that Heaven's door is narrow, and not everyone will be able to enter. I remember his words clearly, and though I heard them long ago they still remain fresh and clear in my mind, as if it was yesterday that I heard them. My mind is still sharp."

"How do you know this? Who told you this?"

"I heard it and I never forgot it. These are the words of the Lord, Sir, and therefore they must be right."

"Right. Right. Yes, of course they're right," the Priest of the Corridor nodded assent. "Heaven's door...I wonder now, how narrow can it be? But don't forget, there's St. Peter at the door."

"Which one?"

"The last one, because it was the last one who made up for all he'd done in the past. It's what comes at the end that counts, and not what happens in the beginning. You can be sure of that." The Priest of the Corridor lifted his soutane slightly and went on his way.

On that occasion, that was all that was said between them.

The doorkeeper went back to the main door, and remained there waiting for the day to start in its usual fashion. Different sort of people arrived and passed in front of his eyes. At certain times of the day, beggars would appear, in tatters, lifting door knockers and rapping on doors, all the time chanting their monotonous, long, long cry for charity, "Give alms, Sir, give us alms for charity. For the sake of your dear departed ones, give us something. For their souls' sake. Give us a penny, at least, just a penny, and we'll pray for you and for your kin in the other world." When they stopped their chant they would start mumbling some prayer or other, and sometimes they would stop and companionably grouse together.

The mischievous boys ranging round the streets would often run after them, playfully grabbing at their robes, and repeating their chant behind their backs, "Charity, charity, dum-di-do-dum, dum-di-di." Sometimes the boys would gather up small stones, loose gravel on the ground, and would throw them at the beggars, some of whom would pick up their pace and hurry on as fast as they could because they were afraid whenever they came face-to-face with a mob of children. Some beggars would scream or burst into tears cursing their lot. Others would halt in their tracks and turn to face the mob trying to catch hold of some boy or other, but the children would run away and hide round the street corner, and from there they would begin once more to yell and sing, "Charity, charity, dum-di-do-dum, dum-di-di."

Many of the beggars would be carrying a sack over their shoulder, holding all they possessed in the world. Practically all of them went barefoot, and those among them wearing sandals looked like the petty rich next to their mates, raising eyebrows and not a few envious looks in their direction, besides suspicious stares. The poor vagrants did not enjoy receiving such stares but at the same time they were pathetically grateful for some attention because it would be such a stare that would arouse someone's pity enough to toss a coin to them, into their open palms, or to the ground so that they would run to gather it up. The sound of a coin hitting the ground would arouse a frenzy.

"Give alms, for the sake of the souls of your dear departed, some charity!" they would repeat countless times, as if they were a choir, their gaze lowered to the ground, but still keenly aware of the least movement among the people there.

"Wait a moment! Here you are. These are for you!" the doorkeeper would draw their attention, and they would crowd around him making a grab at whatever he held in his hands. He would dish out whatever stuff he would have been given that day to distribute among the beggars, because this was a daily occurrence, a daily procession to the Curia's main door. Afterwards he would send them on to the Capuchin Friars' Priory. "Go there now. At around noon, the friars prepare a nourishing pot of minestrone soup for you and some fresh bread as well. Go there. They wait for you to come every day. That's where the others gather round. You don't need to come here. The friars are good people, and they love you and won't leave you hungry. Go. A warm plate of soup awaits you."

The beggars, a horde of people with watchful, wary eyes as if frightened of losing what little they had, would heed his words. But the next day they would still turn up. It was a never-ending story, of people doomed to knock on every door they came to, and nobody could change the tale. Some extra importuning was more useful to them than reticence out of misplaced prudence. Most people did not even look at them, much less help them. Beggars were a superfluous sort of people. Wherever a church wall cast its shadow, beggars believed they would find their only shelter there. And they were right. Especially on the doorstep of the Capuchin Friars' Priory. They used to be a sizeable group of beggars, mostly men, who thronged together taking care not to become separated, walking in groups in a secretive fashion, keeping their distance from ordinary folk, unwilling to mingle with them. They helped each other out, as best they could, and at night they would spread out whatever sheets or blankets they had, somewhere close to the harbour, or in the dark, forgotten locality of Taht il-Forka, Lower Gallows Point, and there they would lie down to snatch some sleep. A bit of a sheet and blanket spread on the ground, their sack close by where they could keep an eye on it, and they would drift slowly, slowly into sleep, in the darkness and tranquillity of that locality, far away from the life that ordinary people led.

The arrival of a new ship in port was a source of great expectation for them. "Those people are rich. Money falls from their pocket without them noticing. And then, when they take notice they let the coins fall all the same. They're very kind-hearted." That is what the beggars said to each other. "Those people come from afar, and beyond the Port, what a wide world there is!" The beggars would wait for the sailors to disembark from their ships, and then they would make their approach, rather like a small regiment themselves, and beg for some money, the meanest coin, and they wouldn't leave the sailors alone till they saw them put their hands in the large pockets they had on the sides of the wide trousers they wore, take out a coin and wave it around in the air and then wait for it to hit the ground. A clamour would ensue. The beggars would run towards the coin, fight over it, and someone would then run off triumphantly with it, snatching a glance at it and clamping his fist around it as tightly as possible, putting it into his pocket and moving far away, with his hand deep inside his pocket. From that day onwards, the throng of beggars would not let him be one of their group again, giving him the cold shoulder and making him suffer ugly words and dirty looks, all because of the treasure trove he would have gained. He would have become rich.

"Go, go on now, off you go," the doorkeeper had to repeat nearly everyday to the new beggars that would arrive at the doorstep from early in the morning. "Go on, go, you know who can feed you. But not here, not here, go, go on!"

Two loud raps on the Curia's door startled the Doorkeeper awake. He had been resting for a few minutes on a favourite old chair with a woven rush seat, in the corner of the entrance way. A sweet nap, like the ones little children take, had carried him off but had not altogether cut off his awareness of what was going on around his small world...the world around that door through which people could enter or be left outside, depending on his decision. The keys were not in his keeping, he mused, but the door certainly was. And what importance do keys hold without a door? The elderly man could count on his own little, but important, consolations. This was something he could boast about when every evening he went back home and he would tell his wife all that had taken place that day. Taking his wages home was expected, but he was also expected to bring back accounts of all that he had seen, heard and imagined. He knew that the money he earned had to be spent, and that without it in his pocket he had no business going home, but he also knew that, at least, the memories of his stories would remain and he would be able to boast about his job. The elderly man felt the need to boast that, though he himself was unimportant, he daily met and dealt with important people, and that he worked in a large palace. The keys were there somewhere in his wide, capacious pocket. They were almost too big for the space he had for them.

"Have you brought the keys with you this evening?" his wife often taunted him as soon as she saw him entering the house.

"Those aren't in my charge, wife," he would calmly reply.

"Make sure you bring your wages home with you; don't you dare set foot inside the house empty-handed! But that only serves us in this world. See if you can sneak the keys because with those we'll gain the other world as well."

"Wife, stop this nonsense!"

His wife mocked him everyday but then always boasted about his job. He never let on that occasionally he nodded off and enjoyed a thoroughly sweet nap whilst he was supposed to be keeping watch at the door.

Two other loud knocks on the door startled him anew and this time he stood up with a jerk from the rickety chair he refused to throw away. "I'm coming, I'm coming...wait...what a hurry you're in!" he grumbled under his breath as he advanced on the door. "It's not as if you're knocking on Heaven's door. I'm not St. Peter, when all's said and done. A mild-mannered, simple, poor man, that's who I am. Who did you think I was to open this huge great door just like that...in the blink of an eye? Wait a moment, wait, I'm not St. Peter. A colleague of his, true enough, but no more than that. Can't I even have forty winks? There's no fixed time when you can enjoy a sweet nap. It feels wonderful whenever it comes, and it's always welcome."

Not a soul could be seen in the long wide corridor that led to the main door. The doorkeeper rubbed the sleep out of his eyes, patted his sparse hair into place, straightened his waistcoat, and began walking, squaring his shoulders as he did so, with a seemly pace suited to the occasion.

Another two raps made him start, once more.

"I'm coming, my goodness, I'm coming! Did you imagine I was St. Peter? I've told you three times already I'm not. What's the big hurry? You're certainly in a tearing rush!" the doorkeeper kept grousing to himself, as he lifted and drew back the heavy bolt and lifted the cross-bar, and then opened the door a crack. "Let's see who's making all this racket."

In front of him stood a youth who was the picture of health, staring back at him intently. The young man looked on the point of uttering something but then remained silent.

"You're certainly not a beggar. You don't have the appearance of one. Beggars are easily recognized, and not just from the clothes they wear, if you can call their miserable rags clothes! Well then, you haven't come round asking for alms. What do you want? What's happened to you? Tell me, tell me," the doorkeeper told him impatiently. "I'm a busy man."

"I would like to speak to the Bishop."

The doorkeeper was astounded; he drew back and the expression on his face changed in an instant. He shook his head and brought it closer towards the young man, as if doubting what his ears had heard. His eyes grew hard, like two black marbles, hard and round and unmoving. He transfixed the young man with his gaze, and slowly, slowly let his eyes travel down from the top of the youth's head down to his toes. The doorkeeper scrutinized every square inch of the youth...his haircut ... shirt ... waistcoat ...the shape of his hands...trousers...the stance he took...his sandals. There was nothing there to give him pause, but such a request was too much.

The young man waited, apparently feeling no need to explain himself further or to repeat his request.

"Speak to the Bishop?" the doorkeeper repeated after a moment in a shocked voice. "Speak to the Bishop...you?"

"Yes, I would like to speak to the Bishop. People speak to other people, I hear them say. I need to tell him something."

"You? Not even I, who've spent all my life in here, can speak to the Bishop just like that, at a moment's notice. Just look at you! Here you are turning up one fine day, looking as if you have all the right in the world to do so, and yet where have you sprung from?" the doorkeeper rebuffed him, at the same time drawing near to observe him more closely. "Not that I want to pry, but, but, where are you from, actually? Do you live far away? Just look at you, wanting to speak to the Bishop just like that, at a moment's notice. As if! As if!" the doorkeeper exclaimed almost angrily. "Look here, my man, go on your way and learn some wisdom, and you can leave from the same door that you entered. There's only one door in front of you. Never mind now. The same wind that blew you in can whisk you out again, and no harm done." The doorkeeper walked back to the main door and gestured for the young man to leave. He stopped at the door and waited, striking a pose that had patience written all over it.

The young man remained where he was, unmoving.

"What do you mean by standing there? Come on now, here's where you came in and this is where you have to go away. I'm in charge of the door. Goodbye, good day to you and hope to see you another time! Well, not really hope to see you another time, it's just something polite we say, but if you please...I want to close the door behind you now. I opened it and I must close it. That's my job. You made me miss a delightful nap, my fine young man!"

"I'm telling you, I need to talk to him," the youth insisted.

"And what am I to tell them, if I go in there? There, can you see where? Right in there! I would have to go in and ask to speak with the masters and tell them, 'Look here, Sirs. I have some news for you. There's a young man at the door. I don't know where he comes from, or who he is, but he wants to speak to the Bishop.' And they would tell me, 'As if, how disgraceful!' Can you just imagine how small I'd feel if they told me off? If they said such words to me, after all these years? Just imagine a bit and put yourself in my place, young man, for you're still a youth and these things wouldn't occur to you. Maybe your mind is still untroubled and carefree, isn't that so, son? You're still young! Now don't take it personally, but let me tell you I'm an old man and I know how I've gone through life and what the world is like. You're still discovering it."

A smile spread itself across the young man's features and then he seemed to start laughing, all the time looking affectionately at the elderly man spouting all those words which he seemed to know by heart and which fell from his lips as if they were part and parcel of his job.

"You smile and dare to laugh at me, what cheek! A doorkeeper who's seen everything! You should at least show some respect for my age, if not for my uniform. Not even my uniform impresses you? Then why do you think I wear it? Don't you know that I'm talking to you with long years of experience behind me?"

"No, no, Sir..."

"And you call me Sir, as well. Can't you see I'm no rich gentleman, and if I'd been I wouldn't be here now, at my job guarding this massive door, and waiting for the hours to pass, and snatching forty winks whenever I can?"

"I called you 'Sir' out of respect," the young man replied.

"Ah, that's alright then."

"I would like to speak to him. It's very important. Go and tell him, 'There's someone here to see you to tell you something important. And it cannot wait any longer'. Tell him exactly what I'm telling you."

"Oh then! Well, since you insist...I'm not made of stone. I'll go. I'm going to deliver your message. Not to him, but to someone else who'll tell him. Wait here a bit."

"It's up to you how you go about it, it's in your hands. The important thing is that he gets to know that I have something urgent to tell him."

The doorkeeper complained under his breath and got up, taking a few steps. Then he halted in his tracks and turned round to ask, "And who shall I say you are? You know how these things are done! They're going to ask me, 'Very well, someone's here who wants to speak to the Bishop. But who is he? Where does he come from?'" He stopped talking and in a different tone of voice asked, "What's your name?"

"Stiefnu."

"Stiefnu. Hmm, nice name that. St. Stephen was an important saint. Who knows, perhaps when he learns your name, the Bishop will see you. I don't know that he will, mind; I'm not promising anything, not a single thing, because it doesn't depend on me. If I were the Bishop, imagine me, huh...can you imagine me? Anyway, if I were, I would leave this door wide open all the time. And hard luck on the doorkeeper, like me, who'd be in charge."

"And you'd have accepted to talk to me straightaway, I think, without any beating around the bush. It would've been better if you were the Bishop, see, 'cause you wouldn't have made such a big fuss. That means you're being more difficult today than you'd have been then!"

"You win, young man. You've won me over. You young men today! Hmm," he went on taking a closer look at his face, curiosity etched on his brow, "hmm, can you read and write, is that it? Let me go then and you wait here."

After a while, Stiefnu stood up and wandered around. Everything he saw struck him, the large paintings full of dark figures, the high ceilings, various pieces of sculpture scattered around, the columns, the tiled floor decorated with complicated designs and many whorls, and, above all, the silence. He walked on tip-toes and peeped into rooms where the door had been left open. He looked in every corner in astonishment, as if he was a little boy discovering a new world. Suddenly he heard footsteps coming his way and startled, he returned to his seat taking up the same position as before, as if he had not moved from the place where the elderly man had told him to stay put.

"Wait a little there. Just wait a bit," the doorkeeper said to him as soon as he stood before him in a voice full of authority but without facing him directly. "There's a good chance you'll get your wish. Maybe yes...anyway maybe, because they're the ones to decide, not me. Though that includes me, too. I'm only in charge of the door. But whoever comes in only does so because I would've let him in. Who will know if I close the door and not hear anyone? Or take a nap and let everything slide? I have to take some merit, too. What d'you think? I'm not a mere nothing!"

A few minutes later the Priest of the Corridor made an appearance, an elderly man like the doorkeeper, and approaching the young man he asked him, "Are you Stiefnu?"

The doorkeeper bowed his head coming to the conclusion that he had to leave them and move away.

"What do you want to speak to the Bishop about?" the Priest of the Corridor enquired.

"That's between him and me, Sir."

"But, you know, before you can speak to him you must tell us what your business with him is all about. Otherwise, otherwise..."

"Otherwise, otherwise, no, I won't be allowed to speak to him. That's what you mean, don't you?"

The Priest of the Corridor moved his head in assent. "That's right, that's exactly right, you won't speak to him," he answered the young man shortly. His voice was firm but a certain hesitation betrayed the fact that he was not entirely convinced of his own words. He coughed, as if to clear his throat, and stopped to wait for the young man to speak.

The youth grasped the situation and immediately took advantage of the situation. "Very well, I won't speak to him. I've done my part and the responsibility isn't mine any longer." He quickly stepped to the door and went out.

The Priest of the Corridor looked dumbfounded and he went to have a look outside. He stopped on the threshold seeing the young man hurrying away. His feelings were mixed, between anger and concern, but he sought to control himself and speak in his usual manner. "Hmm," he murmured disapprovingly, turning his head back to look meaningfully at the doorkeeper.

The doorkeeper had arrived at the door and he understood what was expected of him without any words passing between them. He went out and followed Stiefnu till he came to the street corner, and then called out to him, "Young man, ho there, young man!"

Stiefnu turned back and entered the Curia together with the doorkeeper. The doorkeeper first accompanied him and then left to go into a different room. He was used to playing his part and then taking his leave. In this way, besides patience he had also acquired a reputation for being discreet.

The Priest of the Corridor met the youth a few paces inside the doorway, one hand resting on the cross-bar that had been left to dangle down. "Responsibility, did you say?"

"Yes, I said responsibility."

"That's a very serious word. You know it's very serious. We carry it on our shoulders, it fills our heart and we either fly or fall down to the ground with it. Do you know what you're saying?"

"Yes, I know, Sir."

"And when do you want to speak to him? Have you come a great distance?"

"Distance doesn't count. I don't mind distances. I'm used to walking and running, and when it's necessary, I have to fly too. Circumstances have taught me to row in every kind of current, Sir."

"You mean you're not in a hurry to speak to him."

"Oh yes I am."

"And does it have to be today? Can't you wait?"

"No, not today..."

"At least, at least, not today." The Priest of the Corridor drew in a long breath, in appreciation of this prudent behaviour.

"I would like to speak to him this very instant!"

"You seem quite decided, young man. This very instant, huh?" The Priest of the Corridor appeared to find this answer, full and arrogant, as quite enough. There didn't seem to be a way of thwarting this young man with words. But then he went on. "This very instant, you said. And why does it have to be this very instant?"

"Because this is the moment I felt I should take this step. I don't want to give myself the least excuse to withdraw."

"This step? What step is this?"

The youth remained silent, and his look plainly said he would not say another word. He put his hands in his pockets, shook his head and looked down at the floor.

The Priest of the Corridor understood and he too bowed his head, as if acknowledging defeat. "Wait here for a bit, then. Wait, just wait. I'm going and then I'll come back. I'll bring you an answer, that's certain," he told him and left.

The doorkeeper's heavy tread began tapping on the floor tiles along the corridor. As soon as he appeared he looked the youth in the face and told him, "Apparently you've succeeded, haven't you, you scamp. Young people succeed where old people like us have hardly begun. Ah, how cheeky you all are! How times change! It seems he's going to let you in to speak to the Bishop."

"Yes, it seems he's letting me in."

The glint in the doorkeeper's eyes seemed to be saying that one should not give up easily at the first setback life deals out. Then he took himself off. He had no wish to be found standing there, in the middle of the room, when the priest returned.

"He'll speak to you. You can come with me, now," the Priest of the Corridor reappeared and summoned Stiefnu.

The youth stood up and followed him. It was a long way off and he walked with bowed head, one step after another trying to make the least noise possible. It seemed a greater distance than it actually was. This time, his curiosity did not get the better of him, because he was feeling far too overwhelmed with shyness, and he did not spare a glance here and there to look at the paintings and all the rest. He knew very well that he was entering a place the like of which he had never set eyes on before, and that it was a far cry from the village environs, starting with the small church near where he had grown up, to his house and that of his family as well as the humble dwellings of the other villagers.

As they were walking down the corridor, the Priest of the Corridor turned his face to check that the youth was still at his heels. Then he gestured to him and ushered him inside the Bishop's room, leaving the door ajar.

"I would never have guessed that behind these thick walls there's so much," Stiefnu said to himself. As yet there was no one in the room. "A massive door, high walls and a lofty ceiling. I don't know how I should speak to him now, when he comes. Where am I going to start?" He tried to remember a few words, then he made up some sentences and spoke them to himself under his breath, nodding his head and gesturing with both hands. He was wholly engrossed in looking at the door, expecting it to open wider with each passing moment, and then he suddenly let both his hands fall and put them behind his back. He remained standing up, gazing around him.

The Bishop came soon after. He closed the door and approached the young man. "You may sit down," he invited Stiefnu, glancing lightly at him and extending his right hand in a welcoming manner. "You wished to see me, urgently, I was told."

"Yes, your Excellency."

"You're called Stiefnu, I'm told."

"Yes, your Excellency."

"Very well, you may begin," the Bishop spoke as he walked over to his armchair and sat down.

Stiefnu hesitated. "I don't know where to begin. It's a long story..."

"A long story? There's nothing long or short in the eyes of God. Never fear, for God everything is here and now. Begin from this moment. After all, that's when you wanted to speak to me. Right now. Look, tell me where you are at this moment, where you feel you are at. Right now. Right here and now. It's easy to begin and it will be even easier to continue. I'll help you."

"At the moment I feel that something urged me to come and talk to you. I can't tell anyone else all that I'm about to tell you. It's useless telling somebody else. I've been waiting many years for this to happen to me, and this moment has now arrived ...right now. That's why I couldn't wait any longer."

"Then you did well, and I want to encourage you to speak up. Go on; say what you have to say, Stiefnu."

"Your Excellency, Fr. Grejbel is innocent," the young man spoke with difficulty, stammering and then falling silent.

"Fr. Grejbel?" the Bishop repeated in astonishment, seeming to address himself, as if thinking aloud would jog his memory and bring all the sad and sorry details dredged up from the past right in front of his eyes. "Innocent? Fr. Grejbel, the priest who..."

"The priest who helped Susanna, that young woman who'd fallen pregnant, when still unmarried...and whose mother and father didn't want her to keep the baby...and had taken the newborn away from her as soon as he was born...giving it to someone else to bring up...and she remained for many years without setting eyes on him. She could turn to no one in her plight. She had neither a roof over her head nor a job. And Fr. Grejbel let her sleep at his house and found her a job. And...he rescued her from certain death. If it hadn't been for him, your Excellency..."

"If it hadn't been for him..." the Bishop interrupted, "what would have happened?"

"Then today Susanna would...God only knows."

"True, God only knows, but what do you think?"

"I think that only God knows."

"And do you think that Fr. Grejbel did well?"

"He did well, everything, from beginning to end."

"Everything? Do you know what this word means?"

"Yes, your Excellency, everything."

"And why do you think he did the right thing?"

"Because he risked everything and everyone took against him. Susanna's mother and father. Everybody. Including all the villagers...

"And who else, Stiefnu? Come, come, go on, tell me. Who else took against him? You're saying everyone was up in arms about his actions."

Stiefnu bowed his head and fell silent. He was on the point of tears but he clenched his fists and succeeded in holding them back. He had learnt to master himself facing the sun and winds, thinking he needed to be much harder than his heart would allow. Tears signified weakness, he thought, and he would not show himself a weak man by letting his tears fall.

"Everybody?" the Bishop asked him, getting up to start pacing about the room slowly.

"Everybody, yes, everybody."

"You mean, you're saying..."

"Even you, your Excellency."

The Bishop drew back, as if he was offended by unexpected words. "Even me? Yes, even me, because my duty called for that position. Everyone did his duty, after all. We, all of us, have different positions to uphold and these might call for us to behave differently. But," he asked hesitantly, "why are you bringing up all this?"

"Maybe I'm the only one amongst you all, who didn't do his duty, your Excellency."

"Amongst us all? Us? Who are we?"

"Amongst you all, and me too."

"You? But who are you? I should have asked you right at the beginning to tell me who you are, before we began talking about people. All I know is that your name is Stiefnu, and that's not enough."

"I'm the father of Susanna's baby, your Excellency. Now I'm certain that I should never have left Susanna to fend on her own. If I'd stayed none of this would have happened."

The Bishop made an effort to conceal all that he felt. He did not want to let on how much that piece of news had staggered him. After a few moments of silence he asked Stiefnu, "And may I ask...what happened?"

"You know all that happened, your Excellency."

"But other things happened that I know nothing about, Stiefnu."

"There's nothing much to add. There was a time when Susanna and I became lovers, in the Valley, and then..."

"I can imagine what happened, but what then?"

"We separated. I left her in the lurch almost immediately. Fr. Grejbel found her a job with a rich and decent lady. Then she married somebody, but then..."

"Very well, the story continues. And now, here in this place, after all this time, what else is left to be done?"

Stiefnu stopped to think for a few moments, took heart and began. "Your Excellency, I would like to ask for Fr. Grejbel's return. He doesn't deserve to remain exiled from here. Really and truly he deserves a reward for all that he did. I don't know what can be done, I don't have a clue how these things are managed, but I know for certain he shouldn't be left to shoulder the blame for something he didn't do, and really he shouldn't be blamed at all because all that he did was to risk himself for someone else's sake."

"For someone else's sake?"

"For me, first and foremost. Without even knowing me. And also for my son."

"And the villagers? What do you have to say about what happened to the villagers? And for their souls, their peace of mind?" the Bishop asked him in a graver tone than before. "Maybe I shouldn't be discussing all this with you. But what am I to do in such a situation?"

"The villagers, your Excellency, I think the villagers had never seen what they heard about from the altar happen before their very eyes. And when it did happen they got confused. Just as when once the crowd became confused and started shouting 'Crucify him! Crucify him!' What little I learnt once, when I was a little boy, I still remember today, and I know what it means."

The Bishop was greatly struck by these words and he stared with admiration at Stiefnu. "And if that's so, Stiefnu, then who is Fr. Grejbel? Who is he according to you?"

"Don't you know who he is, your Excellency?"

"You mean to say that Fr. Grejbel passed through his crucifixion. We, all of us crucified him, and he was without blame."

Stiefnu lifted his head with a serious smile on his face, showing he had understood.

"And so, who am I? What part have I taken in this drama?"

Stiefnu knew the answer to that question but lacked the courage to express it.

"Pilate, isn't that what you're thinking? That I am Pontius Pilate? I asked what was the truth of it all, but perhaps I didn't expect a simple answer. Neither was I very patient, waiting to hear it. I was up against time. And there was the crowd...all of it convinced of the truth of the matter. And the voice of the people is the voice of God...or isn't it?"

"Your Excellency, if this is the case, then the drama must end with what came after the Crucifixion. The Resurrection..."

"I can tell you know the doctrine well, Stiefnu. Who taught it to you?"

"Can't you guess who taught it to us, your Excellency?"

"The Resurrection. After the Crucifixion, there comes the Resurrection," stammered the Bishop, almost as if he was speaking to himself, alone. "You mean to say..."

"I mean – the resurrection...Fr. Grejbel's resurrection, your Excellency."

"Don't forget, Stiefnu, the Resurrection happened after three days. It requires its own time."

"Your Excellency, Fr. Grejbel has been absent from here for years on end."

"Very well, let's stop here for today. I am very glad to have met you and that we talked together. Continue in the good direction you've taken up, and don't look back. Think only of what's ahead."

Stiefnu stood up, realizing his time was up and he had to leave, but he was reluctant to depart unless the words he had come here to hear, were spoken. "And Fr. Grejbel, your Excellency..."

"Don't worry your head over what doesn't concern you, Stiefnu. You need only think about what's ahead of you."

"But how can I? When I look ahead I don't see anything...nothing but one thing only. Always just one thing."

"You can pray and you will succeed."

"And if I pray and still don't succeed, your Excellency?"

"You cannot pray and then not succeed, Stiefnu. Our prayers soon reach God's heart. Pray, and then wait and see."

"And people's heart, how can that be reached?"

"People's heart! Hmm," the Bishop came to a standstill. "That can also be reached if people pray. Prayer opens every door."

Stiefnu brought to mind the massive door he had walked through to enter that place. He got up, took leave of the Bishop and went out.

As he gazed at the young man on his way out, the Bishop left the room too. His steps beat a loud tattoo on the floor tiles of that long and wide corridor.

Stiefnu stopped and involuntarily looked back.

"I myself told you to look ahead and not to look back. But you do well to look back at this moment," the Bishop smiled slightly at him. "Listen to me, think well about what I'm going to say and answer me with care. I'm going to pass on a heavy responsibility, but you won't have to carry it alone. Listen to me," he repeated, coming closer and laying his right hand straight on Stiefnu's shoulder. "When we were talking we mentioned the crowd. What does the crowd say about Fr. Grejbel? What do you think the crowd would say if..."

"If he comes back? I'm part of the crowd, your Excellency, and I've always followed the crowd's thinking. As I did yesterday and still do today...which means that I too, once accused a man whom I consider a saint today, who, I firmly believe, did all he did because he is a saint."

"A saint? That's a very strong word, Stiefnu."

"It is a strong word but I think it's precise. I don't know another word to describe it better."

"And so you think it's his saintliness that destroyed him?"

"I don't know what usually happens in the case of saintliness, your Excellency, but in this case that's what happened. I have no more doubts about it."

"Doubts. You had some doubts, then?"

"The day I went down the Valley with that young woman, I didn't remain the same person, your Excellency, and it took me a long time to soften my heart. Fr. Grejbel, as you said, always kept looking ahead."

"And do you think he never looked back?"

"Maybe for him, looking ahead and looking back mean the same thing. He always walked along the one and only way."

"And the crowd? I was talking about the villagers."

"The villagers will be happy, more than ever before, and they will thank you for it and, more than anything else, they will be free of the burden that has been weighing them down for many a long year, your Excellency."

The Bishop took his leave, gave Stiefnu his blessing and went back to his room. He sat down heavily on his armchair and laced his hands together, closing his eyes at the same time. Sometime before, Susanna's mother had also told him the very same thing. Everything was clear to him now, as if a ray of sunshine was suddenly illuminating him, shining like a beam from the big window in front of him. It was set high up in the wall, where you could not reach up properly to look outside, not even if you stood on tip-toes. But the light it let in was like a long line angling straight down from up high to make its presence felt in all the room.

He rose and went to the window. It only came down to the level of his shoulders. At least he could open it to hear the day's bustling noises. He remained standing up in front of it, imagining the street which he knew so very well but could not see. The boys' voices had reached that area again.

Door-keeper! Door-keeper!
You are old and we are young-er!

With hands held down straight at his sides, the doorkeeper stood on the doorstep at the main door, waiting for the day to pass. As usual, he whiled away the time talking to himself, scolding the children from afar without making his voice heard, and whistling a tune from his youth. The melody was a popular one, often sung by sailors and soldiers, full of sentiments of love. Which is why he did not dare whistle too loudly. He could be clearly heard from a few rooms away.

Chapter 5

"Don't forget, Mummy, you'd promised to continue the story when I was on the point of sleeping... " Wistin wheedled.

"I know, I know, you little scamp! I realized you weren't asleep," Susanna smiled down at her son.

"We'd got to the part where the kite was telling the boy that instead of letting him fly it as he usually liked to do, it wished to make him fly. Now Mummy, I know that kites don't talk, but in this story the kite could talk because in olden times kites could talk and it was only afterwards that they couldn't anymore. Isn't that what you told me, Mummy?" Wistin went on, expecting his mother to join in.

"A long time ago, a very long time ago, when everywhere was surrounded by trees and flowers, and there were rivers and mountains, long, long ago, toys could talk. And the kite enjoyed talking to the little boy in this story," Susanna went on. "Wouldn't you like to live in such a world, Wistin?"

"I already know that part, Mummy, because you've already told it to me. I remember it all. Shall I tell it to you?"

"No, no," quickly answered Susanna, wanting to get on with things. "If you want to recount it once more, do you know what we should do? This evening, instead of me telling you a story, you tell me one."

"Uff, Mummy, that's not fair on me..."

"I forgot to tell you, Wistin, but long, long ago, it wasn't the mothers who did the storytelling for their children, it was the children who told stories to their mothers. The children would tell a story and the mothers would listen."

"That's not true! How can that be? How do you know?"

"Because I was there!" his mother said with a serious smile.

"That's not true, Mummy! You weren't there!"

"And where were you?"

"I was still with Baby Jesus."

"Even I was still with Baby Jesus. Don't you believe me?"

"Yes, I believe you, Mummy. Well then you too were there, with Baby Jesus, but somewhere where I couldn't see you!"

"In the same house, Wistin. Baby Jesus' large house, where everybody is gathered to meet each other. We would be waiting, all of us waiting, to meet the others."

"A large house? Yes, yes, I remember that, a very large house. But how come we didn't meet each other? Why didn't I see you? We were in the same house!"

Susanna thought he was so sweet talking in that fashion and she didn't contradict him. "There were ever so many people, son, from every age and from every country, all gathered there together, without knowing how they had got there and not knowing a soul. But everybody was waiting, quietly, patiently, without asking questions, everybody waiting."

"Waiting? What for, Mummy?"

"Don't you know what everybody was waiting for, Wistin?"

"Let me think a bit, Mummy..." he answered her, putting his forefinger in his mouth. "Everybody was waiting for his turn to come here."

"Come here? And where is here?"

"The village, Mummy!"

"Yes, the village. And from where?"

"From Heaven, Mummy!"

Susanna began to wonder and ask herself where he could have learnt all these things. Her mother had taught him many things, and she herself had done so, too, but she was certain that there were some things he had known beforehand, before she saw him for the first time and took him away with her. She was glad that although she had not set eyes on him since he was born, at least he had fallen into good hands who had loved him and told him wonderful things, and now it was up to her to continue telling him such things. She kept her gaze on him as he chattered on happily. "From Heaven, you said, Wistin...You came from Heaven."

"From Heaven, Mummy. There's only one road, from Heaven, direct to the village. We came from Heaven. I know for sure, that's what they told me. I remember everything. They used to tell us that we came from there, and then, once, as we were walking, we got lost in the wood, among many tall, hardy trees. And then there were kind people who let us wait at their place, till the day arrived when we could leave. And that's what happened, Mummy. We were many children, waiting to leave Heaven..."

"And did you wait for a very long time, Wistin?"

"They used to tell us that a ship had just arrived and many people had gone aboard, and there was no place left for us, and we would have to wait a little while longer. But when were we going to leave? That's what we used to ask them. And they used to answer, 'Don't worry, wait. Wait. Other ships are due to arrive and they will take you to the village.' Empty ships would dock, take on children on board and leave. They would let as many children as possible embark, and would not leave with a single empty space. They would tell us this every day, every day. From Heaven straight to the village. I never saw these ships, but everybody used to say that they were somewhere outside from where we lived. Somebody once peeped out of the window in secret, when Baby Jesus was asleep, and he saw them, and then he told everybody."

"And where were you all?" Susanna asked with a catch in her voice and tears in her eyes.

"Haven't I just told you, Mummy? We were in Heaven."

"Were you happy?"

"We were very happy, Mummy. Women dressed all in white used to look after us. They wore a long, long dress, much longer than yours, and it didn't have any pockets, and their head was covered, and they would stand up straight and walk with bowed head. Sometimes they raised their hands to their face, as if they were about to pray, even when they were walking. They woke us up in the morning and put us to bed always at the same time. They worked hard. They had huge rosary beads, much bigger than yours, hanging around their waist and we would play about with these and tug and pull the kind women from these beads. They would smile, but not much."

"They didn't smile much, Wistin?"

"No, not much, because remember Mummy, we were in Heaven."

"And people don't smile in Heaven?"

Wistin stopped to think it through. "Yes, they did smile, yes, just not much. Baby Jesus was there."

"But doesn't Baby Jesus smile, Wistin? He's kind-hearted. Isn't that so?"

"Yes, Baby Jesus is very kind-hearted. But he doesn't smile a lot. I think He would actually be crying, sometimes with happiness and sometimes with sadness, but He wouldn't want anyone to see Him and not everybody would realize."

"Baby Jesus used to cry?"

"He used to have tears sliding down His cheeks, and His eyes would be red-rimmed, because there were many little children who remained unwanted by anyone. That means a ship would come and take everyone on board but they would remain there..."

"In Heaven...," Susanna finished the sentence herself, with great interest.

"In Heaven. It was a lovely house because there were many games to play but, Mummy, everyone wanted to go down and live in the village, all the same. They used to say it had always been like that, from the time before, and everybody shared that wish."

"I understand you better now, Wistin. What a lovely story this is!"

"But this isn't a story, Mummy. You said that you too had been in Heaven waiting to come down here."

"It seems like a fairy-tale..."

"But it isn't, Mummy. Baby Jesus is for real, and I have seen Him. I saw Him smile and I saw Him cry. I saw Him sleep and I saw Him wait. But He remains there. He never leaves Heaven, because otherwise Heaven has to close down, because it's His house. And I think He's there still. Waiting. Always the same story, a long time ago, yesterday and the day before yesterday, and today, as well."

"How do you know all this, Wistin?"

"That's what they told us, Mummy, and I believe them."

"Why do you believe them, Wistin?"

"Because they were so very kind..."

"Women dressed all in white, from top to bottom."

"How do you know, Mummy?"

"I too saw them once, son."

"When you were still in Heaven, Mummy?"

Susanna didn't reply but lowered her head and waited for him to change the subject.

"Now you must tell me some new part of the story. Go on, Mummy, go on," Wistin importuned her, taking hold of her skirt and almost losing himself in its folds. He put his hand inside one of her pockets, curious to see what he would bring up.

"But not now, it's not time. We only tell stories when it's getting dark, or before we go to sleep. It's just like when we light a candle in the morning. It doesn't give off any light. But when we light it in the evening, yes. Light can shine only in darkness."

"Oh no, Mummy, we can tell stories at any time of the day, even now if you want. That's what they used to teach us in Heaven. They told us stories all day long. Whenever we felt like it."

"But I can't think of anything at the moment, son, I don't know how to continue the story I began to tell you."

"Do you make up the story in your own head, then, Mummy? They aren't real stories, then? You said they were, once. I haven't forgotten. I remember everything you tell me. I remember your words more than I do whatever they used to tell me, before."

"You know what, Wistin? One day we'll buy a kite and we'll go and fly it together, there, in the middle of the fields, where it can roam and climb up high without us losing sight of it. A kite needs wide, open spaces, and it will always stay near, even if it looks far away. Yes, that's what we'll do one fine day," Susanna spoke decisively.

"Oh no, Mummy! Not one fine day..."

"Don't you want that? Well then, when?"

"Now, today, let's go, Mummy. Buy me one. I want to fly a kite, Mummy, and I want you with me, and like that it won't get lost or fly so far away that I won't see it anymore."

"You want it today?"

"Yes, today, Mummy, before you go on with the story tonight. Look, here's what we'll do – don't go on with the story now, because it's still early, and buy me a kite instead of the storytelling."

Susanna and Wistin set off to the market where there were many stallholders, all shouting out their special cry or chant to sell their fruit and vegetables and other ware. Standing straight with their eyes roving everywhere, they were men of all ages behind a plank of wood that served as a table to display their wares. Some of them shouted and some others spoke quietly, inviting shoppers to their stall with a whispered word, a smile that was part and parcel of their skill in enticing shoppers to make a purchase. Every stallholder kept to his usual place, no one ever set up his stall in place of another's, and their day's luck would be somewhere about that place. They didn't only talk to prospective buyers but also amongst themselves, especially when the crowds thinned and fell to a trickle. Sometimes they grumbled and sometimes they boasted about their particular display, but always on the watch against pilfering. Other sellers sold their vegetables from two reed baskets, generally very large ones to accommodate as many vegetables as they could. The baskets would be attached to each other with a strip of leather or a length of rope which the seller would wear across a shoulder; one basket dangling behind his back and the other dangling in front of his chest. These hawkers would come with the hope of selling their vegetables to housewives who would want to make the popular thick *minestra* soup or *kawlata* stew. They never brought anything larger than a cauliflower or an eggplant to market, but they offered a vast variety of vegetables which women used for their cooking pots. The itinerant vegetable sellers would find a place to suit them and stop there for a while letting people gather round, or else they would trek from street to street and approach knots of people themselves.

"Vegetables for your cooking pots! Marjoram, small marrows, turnips, cucumbers, lettuce! Whatever you want!" the vegetable seller would cry, enticing housewives by promising a bunch of fresh parsley with every sale. "Everything is cheap, everything is full of goodness, and there's free parsley for you!" Every time he was asked for something, the hawker would dip his hand in one of his large baskets and bring out the desired vegetable. All the produce was crammed in the basket but he would know where everything was. Every hawker carried around all that the day was worth in there.

Some hawkers had a horse-cart and others a hand-cart. The one who sold cheeselets came round with two buckets, one on his head and the other held in the crook of his arm. There were hawkers selling fish, *bigilla* bean paté and also bread. Very young vendors would carry two baskets full of oranges and lemons while the one selling peanuts would carry a large basket and he would put it down on the ground whenever he saw people looking as if they were tempted to buy. He would dip the wooden cup-measure in it and fill it with peanuts, cramming them in with his hand to show his largesse, and sometimes he would add one or two other peanuts, too, for free. As soon as he would see people thronging around he would take up his shout, 'Broad beans and peanuts...chickpeas and peanuts...roasted peanuts!' There was one hawker who always settled on the same spot, at the end of the street. He came with a horse-drawn cart loaded up with goods: kettles; tin containers; jugs; brooms; tin buckets; basins. He never did a brisk business at the market proper because the women would be intent on buying fresh produce for the meals they would want to prepare, but over there in that spot they would get to know he was around, and then he would do the rounds of the streets, covering the entire village. The clatter and noise of his goods would announce his arrival to everybody, to the people going about barefoot, men and young boys wearing a cap, and women wearing their cheap everyday woollen *ghonnella*. And there would be cats and dogs everywhere, darting here and there to catch their supper...Every morning, the street was just like a feast.

Whoever was absent from the crowd was at work somewhere else, not far away. Men walking behind the plough being pulled by an ox or mule. Or threshing corn in a rhythmic waggle that was a dance in itself. Women weaving on the loom or making lace. Or hanging up clothes to dry on the roof or in the balcony or on lengths of wood attached to doorways or house walls...Everybody played their part in that self-sufficient world of theirs, needing no help from outside.

Although a humble village affair, the market displayed the fruits of the villagers' work, in the fields and farms a few paces away. There were some women helping their husbands sell their produce, and some children were learning the trade because soon they would be doing the selling themselves. They would be taking up their fathers' trade. The distinctive hawkers' cries, chants, doggerels, loud-voiced patter – everything was part of the whole picture, full of movement and colour. Men and women, all were moving to and fro, in the same tiny street. Occasionally a woman wearing the *ċulqana*, the loose, long cotton gown, would pass by carrying a full sack on her head. Women wearing a long cloth wound around their head to support a heavy burden could also be seen, scurrying along carrying some large pottery jar or a reed basket. One could only wonder at the skill employed to carry such burdens without faltering. They would take pains not to bump into anybody. And if someone did cannon into them, a quarrel would ensue. Every woman could make the journey home almost without once having to raise her hand to her head, even momentarily. This was all part of the natural spectacle to be had at the market, and every woman drew all eyes to her as she passed by. Her fleshy sides could still be discerned with every step she took, clearly outlined under the one or two skirts that endeavoured to blanket them from view. The women's husbands, in the manner of a ferret, jealously guarded them against any lingering glance sent their way.

Housewives, with their children milling around them, were walking along in search of whatever they needed, looking produce over and handling it before buying, haggling over prices and asking for discounts. For the benefit of those who could read, prices were written up in very large figures on bits of paper. Those who were unlettered relied on their memory. Every villager had a good memory. The price of goods remained the same and so was remembered with ease. Every woman used to lug around a *ġewlaq*, a large straw shopping basket, filling it to the brim before returning home to begin that day's cooking. Even when they stopped to chat and exchange gossip, housewives still had their cooking pot in mind for it had to be ready by a certain time, everyday - at around noon. The strokes of the church bell would ring out, one stroke after another with a measured gap in between, and a prayer would be said before the meal began.

Every hawker had his own particular cry, a string of words in the form of a chant, directing housewives who needed their goods. The women made their way to them accordingly for besides recognizing sellers from their particular cry, each woman felt that that cry, ages-old, required a certain loyalty in return. Each and every woman felt that she should not give her custom to someone else, on a spurious whim. Everyone would notice and then, soon enough, she would start having dirty looks cast her way, and that would be very unpleasant indeed.

Suddenly, sweet music could be heard approaching. Clashing noises like castanets make, thin notes from small bells and harmonious playing of a piano mixed together to bring forth sweet melodies of popular tunes. It all made a loud noise which could be heard all along the street. A song, or an aria from an opera or operetta, or a waltz or a mazurka. All these melodies could never be heard in the village unless a man came by with a huge music-box carried on a cart and led by a donkey. The hawkers welcomed him because the music drew crowds of people who would stop and listen for a while, and maybe they would be tempted to buy more goods.

"That's a barrel-organ, look, look, Wistin!" Susanna pointed out excitedly.

The man with the barrel-organ brought the donkey to a halt, and he went to turn the wheel which wound up the music-box. And the box began to play, one melody after another – some of them well-known and some less so – all of them simple catchy tunes.

People stopped all around him, spellbound.

"What shall I play for you, my friends? Listen to this lovely music I have here – it can melt your heart! Listen, listen! Have you ever heard the like? Open your ears to it and let yourselves dream! Dreams, yes dreams! Is there anything more wonderful?" he began addressing the crowd in a loud voice, continuing to turn the wheel in the meantime. "I have many beautiful songs for you, one more beautiful than the other. Come close, come and listen! Enjoy it while you can 'cause I rarely come here. I won't be coming tomorrow. Hmm, you know music can't be enjoyed every day. Tomorrow I have to visit another village, and then I'll be going somewhere else, too. My music is enjoyed in every place I go. You have no idea how long I've been travelling from one place to another. You can ask that donkey there! We're always together, that jenny and I. We carry with us some musical notes to offer them gladly to whoever wants to hear them. There's no pathway we haven't trekked across or Madamesquare we haven't visited. Don't you believe me? And wherever we go, the people come, crowd around and are bewitched. Today it's your turn! This is quite an event, my friends, an event! Make the most of it!" he called out encouragingly.

The barrel-organ was adorned with a set of statues which turned in time to the music, on and on without stopping. They turned and twirled, calmly. Each one was in a kind of little niche, glued from the bottom, from the middle, and set into a small, round pedestal.

"Look, look, Mummy!" Wistin exclaimed in excitement to his mother.

"Those little statues have started turning and dancing in time with the music, now," Susanna told her son. "And when the music stops, they'll stop as well. The man will play the music and they will be glad, all at once and will obey him and dance. Every time he tells them to. They are always in total accord with each other. Everything moves precisely, step by step."

"But those aren't real people, Mummy," Wistin answered her in a serious tone. "They're too tiny to be real."

"It's only a pretence that they're real, Wistin. But just imagine if they were real men and women!"

"If they were real they'd have become dizzy, Mummy, because if you keep turning round and round you end up feeling dizzy. But I prefer them like this, more than if they were real."

They were wooden figurines, painted in bright colours, two men and two women, fashioned like country folk with a serious smile etched on their face, their heads bent to one side, their hands raised and their feet made to move slightly, to simulate dancing. They looked happy and content. Every inch of the music-box's surface was carved with elaborate designs. No one could look at it without feeling curious. There was nothing remotely like it in the village except for the stone sculptures that decorated every corner in the church. The whole point of the barrel-organ was not merely to gratify one's ears but also to draw all eyes to it.

The organ-grinder began doing the rounds with a small platter in his hands and people dug into their pocket or shopping basket to give him a coin. The sound of a coin hitting the tin drew people's eyes and the man openly showed his appreciation, seeming to count the day's takings in his head. Sometimes, as soon as he saw their interest flagging, he would strike up a pose, as if he was about to start dancing. "Come on now, my friends, give something, for me and my jenny. A little something – good, good! And if you want to give more – why, that's better still! A little something is good, and a lot is better...We all need one another! The more you give me, the more music I'll play for you. I haven't played all that I have! And I can play the music you've already heard, too, if that's what you want. You can never have enough of my music and hearing it once is never enough. More than that, the more you hear it, the more it moves you and sounds sweeter still! Sweeter and sweeter!"

It was not just the crowd in the street who welcomed his arrival. The music coming from the barrel-organ made people inside their houses open their windows and peer out or come out onto their balcony. They remained there, listening. Some of them threw down coins to the organ-grinder and he removed his cap and gave it a flourish in their direction, rather like an actor on stage acknowledging the applause from his audience, and he bent his head in search of the coins, looking to where he would have heard them fall and swiftly gathering them up from the ground. Other people would also be tempted to give him something.

"How lovely!" the people cried, smiling at one another. "What lovely music he plays! It all comes out of that box! I wonder what there is inside it? You can hardly believe all that music comes from inside there!"

The organ-grinder played some more melodies but when people started trickling away, he took up the reins left looped near the jenny's mouth and moved forward to make the donkey start walking. And the two of them left the market.

Wistin remained bewitched, but his mind was still thinking about something else. "The kite, Mummy, don't forget the kite. I want a kite, Mummy," he kept on insisting, tugging impatiently at his mother's skirts.

"Yes, we'll go and buy one, soon. But just wait a while. We can't buy it from here. You can only buy things to eat here. Hadn't you noticed?"

Wistin was pacified and waited patiently. When Susanna had bought all she needed in the way of foodstuffs, they left the street and made their way into an alley approaching the shop that sold kites. It was a small shop, crammed from top to bottom and from wall to wall with things, and it was a shop that had been familiar to her throughout her childhood and youth; it was far older than her. She had not set foot inside it much; it had been more like a little kingdom reserved only for boys.

"I make all these myself, don't worry. Choose whichever one takes your fancy. I have them in all colours and in all sizes. You'll find out soon enough how such a good quality kite can climb up high, and nothing will bring it down! One more beautiful than the other!" the shopkeeper enthused, carefully unearthing one kite after another to show them. They were fragile and took up a lot of space in the shop. He was eager to sell them off.

Wistin became enraptured straightaway and could hardly say a word.

"The kite must be for you, little one, isn't that so?" the shopkeeper smiled down at the boy and then nodded his head at Susanna and turned his smile on her.

"Yes, it's for him, of course! It's for him!" she replied.

"But you can fly it yourself, too, you know!" he told Susanna. "Some people like flying kites even when they're grown up. You can never tell. It's such a sweet pastime. It appeals to everyone, young and old, to people of all ages. Wouldn't you like to fly it too, Missus? Look at them and choose one! Just don't touch them, please! They're very delicate. The paper doesn't rip easily with the wind but in people's hands, yes, it tears very quickly."

In the meantime, other people had entered the shop and the shopkeeper's attention was diverted to these newcomers, away from Susanna and Wistin.

"Choose one, Wistin. They're all so beautiful! Don't set your heart on any of the large ones because you'll find it too difficult to hold."

"Oh no, Mummy, that doesn't matter. In case, fly it with me. And that way it can serve me till I grow up," he spoke his thoughts.

"When you grow up you'll want to fly a different kite, son. And don't forget, the kite is made with paper and that will soon tear."

"Madame, you're right, this kite is made with paper. What else? But set your mind at rest that it will serve you as long as you'll look after it well. That paper can withstand a lot of tear and wear!" the shopkeeper quickly interrupted, wanting to boast in the others' hearing. He knew very well that children easily give in to temptation by seeing what other children have and half his sales were made up of such impulse buying, dependant on children's wishes. It was enough for him to see children looking at his shop for him to start boasting about his goods in a loud voice. Children were easily tempted by what they saw. "Look here! This is such a good quality kite! This is made from firm reed strips!" he continued, inviting Susanna to touch it. "Firm! Look how straight the centre strip is! And how perfectly arched in a half-circle the bow spar is! Look, the bow is firmly tied with string. It's just like a rainbow lacking nothing, isn't it? And look at its tail, just see what a fine figure it cuts! I have tails made of paper strips or paper loops, take your pick. A quality kite, Madame! In fine form, I mean, it won't bend this way or that. Or distort its shape and swing every which way. It's perfectly balanced on both sides!"

Wistin was full of amazement, gazing round with open mouth. Susanna too, was quite amazed hearing all this.

The shopkeeper was pleased to see them so attentive. "Do you want to see how well-balanced it is? Let me hold it on my forefinger from its spine, in the centre. See if it inclines one way or the other, or remains straight! Incredible, huh?! It's just like a pair of scales, with two pans on each side, exact and equal. This means I don't have to tighten up the bow bit of the frame anymore."

"And how do I fly it, Mummy?"

"I'm going to tell you, let me tell you in a minute, little one, but first let me finish," interjected the shopkeeper. "Your mother would like to know, and you too, and this way you'll both learn. We can decorate a kite with tassels too, like a pair of earrings. And do you know what these tassels are? They're little pieces of paper stuck to the bow-part. Everything is stuck fast, can you see, with glue made from flour. And look at the fringe, how pretty it is, with its multi-coloured thin and long edges! This kite can also be used to beat others in a fight! Some boys do it, I know, but that's none of my business. I don't want to see any fights, because quarrels only make me lose custom. Look, the kite comes complete with the string. And if you want it totally complete and ready for flying, here's the reel as well, to spool the string better. You can fly it either using string on the reel or twine."

"There, are you happy now, Wistin?" Susanna asked her son.

"Oh and by the way, before I forget, Madame. When the kite doesn't rise, see from which direction the wind is blowing, and run as fast as you can against it. If it's blowing from here, look, run towards it from the opposite direction. And then, as soon as you see it taking wind in its sail, give it a tweak, yank it as much as needs be, you can even tug it hard, always holding firmly on to the reel of string or twine...And then you'll see it fly up and up..." the shopkeeper twittered on excitedly, slowly lifting his gaze towards the ceiling as if following a kite's progress, looking as if he'd turned back into a young boy. "And that's it! A kite that can serve you for a long time to come, that's it!"

"Yes, it can last for long, that's true, unless it's blown away by the wind..." Susanna was amused by the shopkeeper, giving him a half-smile, serious and courteous.

"Hmm, the wind doesn't blow away just kites, Madame! When it turns blustery, it blows even us away! Its nature is in its very name."

"Have you decided on one, Wistin?" Susanna turned to her son.

"This one, Mummy," he quickly replied and was about to reach for it to take it.

"Gently, little one, have a care, or else it will tear in a jiffy," the shopkeeper quickly interposed himself. "Don't forget, paper tears quickly, and this kite paper is very thin. Tissue paper, that's what we call it. Remember this and learn it well. There's nothing better than learning. Tissue paper. You chose the green. You've chosen well, little one. Do you know what the colour green is?"

"It's a nice colour, and I like it," Wistin replied.

"Green is the colour of hope. The colour for children like you, who are just starting life. Not for me, look; I'm already past my prime. Still, while I'm around I might as well sell kites...and other stuff too. I sell all sorts of things. You're welcome to have a look around. Everything is for sale, whatever you see here is for sale," the shopkeeper invited them.

Wistin opened his eyes wide, as wide as wide can be, and looked around, wishing hard. The shopkeeper looked eagle-eyed at him, waiting for him to choose something so that his mother would have to dig into her pocket and pay for it.

Susanna took the kite in one hand and paid up with her other.

"Buy me that cart and that horse, Mummy," her son was prompt to ask.

"Hmm, I thought he would fall for something in the twinkling of an eye," Susanna gently groused.

"It doesn't cost much, Madame, not that toy. A wooden horse and cart, stuck together, and he can take it outside to play holding it from a piece of string. One toy, but with two parts. It's cheap. Fancy buying it for him? It's handmade.

Come to that, most stuff in here is handmade. That means it's genuine, and will last. It will last much longer than the kite, as you can imagine," the shopkeeper eagerly tried to clinch another sale and he would have continued in this drift if Susanna had not cut him off by asking the price and then promptly paying up.

Susanna and Wistin left the shop together and walked home. Wistin immediately set his new toy on the ground and holding its string, walked with his head turned back to watch it roll along the street behind him, seeing the horse move forward in a straight line, its eyes pointing ahead, and the cart being pulled behind it. Susanna's hands were full; a heavy shopping basket in one hand and the kite in the other. But she still had a care for her son and she ordered him to hold onto the basket handles with his left hand and to drag the toy behind him with his right.

"When are we going to go and fly the kite, Mummy? Today, Mummy?" Wistin asked her as soon as they arrived home.

Susanna took out all her shopping and spread the items on the dining room table, looking at them in satisfaction.

"Tell me, Mummy, are we going today?"

"It must be a bit windy, son, or else the kite won't rise. It will stay on the ground, or else it will lift itself slightly, weave about a bit and come down again."

"What a lot you know about kites, Mummy! Did you fly kites when you were little?"

"No, Wistin, I never flew kites but I knew someone who used to fly a kite from the roof of their house or from the village square or from the fields."

"You used to know someone, Mummy?"

"Yes, son."

"A man or a woman, Mummy? I think it was a man, wasn't it? Men usually fly kites."

Susanna did not answer, calmly continuing to sort and put away the things she had bought in the cupboard.

"Tell me, Mummy. A man?"

"What do you think, Wistin?"

"I think it was a man."

"Clever boy! Now see where you're going to put it away and don't forget you also have the horse and cart."

"What was the man's name, Mummy?"

Again she did not answer him, and beneath her breath she said to herself, "I'll tell you one day, and then I'll get you to meet him, too. But not yet. It's too soon."

"Too soon?" her son asked. "Why is that, Mummy?"

Susanna stayed stubbornly silent.

"Mummy, talk to me!" Wistin cried in a loud voice.

"Tell you what, shall I begin telling you a story, Wistin? As you were speaking I thought of many things I could say in today's story."

"Oh no, Mummy, I think it would come out better this evening as usual, before we sleep. The more thoughts you have the better, 'cause then it will be longer, and stories are nicer when they take a long time to come to an end. And then, after the story, tell me that man's name."

"But how can I remember all that, son? It's either one thing or another!"

"Don't worry, I'll remind you myself."

"And by this evening I'll have forgotten it."

That evening, as usual, after reciting the Rosary together, Wistin waited expectantly for his mother to begin telling him a story. He got into bed but did not want to lie down as he usually did.

"I want to sit up, with my head on a pillow."

"Why, son?"

"I hear you better like this. And today it's not stormy. There's no lightning and thunder."

"But you usually like to lie down."

"Don't worry; if I begin to feel sleepy I'll lie down. Go on, Mummy, begin."

"Once upon a time there was a little boy..."

"Who had a kite that wanted to make him fly. Do you remember how the story continues?" he asked her.

"There was a boy who had a kite that wanted to make him fly," she faithfully repeated. "It happened a very long time ago, when kites could talk, and when children could understand them. And that's what happened. It let him onto its back and the two of them went off..."

"Up there, in the sky, among the clouds," he chipped in.

"Among the clouds. It told him it wished to take him far away, where a good man lived, close to the sky, who loved everybody. 'Hold on tight,' the kite told the boy. 'Be careful or else you'll fall down, back into the people's village, down there. In the village we're coming to in a moment, you'll see people walking by underneath us and they'll look the same, all of them tiny, but they're not really all the same. Each heart is different, belonging to a different person. Can you see them?' it asked him. 'Yes, I see them, but not very well. They're too far away. Except for one of them; he's very big next to them. Why is he so very big, that man among them?' the little boy asked the kite. 'Because his heart is bigger than all of theirs put together. That's why he's so big,' it told him. 'There he is, look, dressed all in black, from head to toe.' But the boy was thinking of something else."

"What was he thinking of, up there, Mummy? Wasn't he happy flying up so high in the sky, seeing the world from far away?" Wistin interrupted his mother making her pause.

"He was thinking fearfully about how he was going to come down here."

"But wasn't he on the kite?"

"Yes, but the kite could rip and tear at any moment, and it could go somewhere else by mistake and take him down to another village, one he didn't know, far, far away from where he lived."

"And how does the story end, Mummy?"

"The story is a very long one, son, and it doesn't finish tonight. Then, the two of them went on flying high up in the sky, and the village began vanishing ever so slowly beneath them, and the kite asked him if he wanted to stay up there a while longer... 'Do you want us to go down?' it asked. 'It's late and our folk are expecting us back...'" Susanna continued, and then she stopped at that juncture, realizing that Wistin had fallen asleep. "They're expecting us back, my darling," she repeated below her breath, when the little boy was unable to hear her. She gently raised him without letting him slip out of the bed, pushed away the pillow behind his back to let it lie beneath his head, and laid him down. He remained with his eyes closed, and she was certain he was fast asleep. She was glad because she did not feel like making up more of the story.

"And that man, Mummy, what was his name?" Wistin got out in the voice of a little boy who was more asleep than awake.

"In that time, son, that man didn't have a name," she said under her breath. "It was a very long time ago when people had no names." Then she tip-toed out of the room and went to the kitchen to make herself a cup of tea. She never went to bed without taking a cup of tea with her. It was an old habit, formed in her childhood, and it was even older than that because she could remember her family had always had that habit. She stared at the cup full to the brim, and she imagined she was back in her youth, seeing it all pass in front of her eyes.

It was on one such evening that she had knocked on the door of the small house belonging to Fr. Grejbel, and the priest had soon opened the door and welcomed her inside, telling her many wonderful things. She had opened her heart to him, telling him that she had just been thrown out of her parents' house. She had had to leave immediately. She was with child but Fr. Grejbel had continued talking to her and made her take heart. He was unlike any other man. It was then that she had found out what a very kind man he was, and why he was bigger than the entire village, him alone. He lived in a humble house, on his own.

She stood up, imitating him, as if she was acting his part on stage. "I too am on my own," Fr. Grejbel said to her, "even I have nobody. Courage, my child! I will help you." She felt profoundly relieved to have found a sheltering arm in him. Then she told him she had nowhere to sleep that night. And he immediately soothed her fears, "Never fear! Tonight you'll be sleeping here!" And she had been taken aback, "Sleep here? How can I? What would people think and say?" Susanna continued playacting, getting up and moving about the room in the manner of that young woman.

"Susanna was beautiful, that's what people always said," Susanna went on, "but this wasn't enough, neither for her lover who left her half-way through her pregnancy, nor for her mother and father. Her father was a stern man, hard and unforgiving. He would never change his mind once it was made up and he thought up a plan to let his daughter give birth and not keep the baby. That was the best thing and the right thing to do, he firmly believed," Susanna continued spinning out the story to herself, standing straight against the table, speaking decisively. "But Fr. Grejbel remained at her side from that day onwards, and he didn't leave her in the lurch. It was almost as if he forgot about the rest of the village because of her. Then he helped her get married and supported her in her married life. Well anyway, it's a long story and there's no need to go into all the details tonight, Ladies and Gentlemen! The important thing is one thing only – Fr. Grejbel gave her everything, he gave himself no less, to save her. Was he duty–bound to do so or was it far and above the call of duty? Did he do the right thing? Of course he did, because that young woman had a need beyond that of all the other people put together. But people didn't see it that way and they didn't rest till they had hounded and uprooted him and sent him away from them."

Susanna came to a sudden stop for a breather, going back to her seat at the table with her cup of tea steaming in front of her. The whole sorry tale, tortuous and long-drawn out, was right there, written on the surface of that dark drink, shimmering in the dim light pervading the room, as on any other commonplace night, but mostly like that one night when her whole life was changed forever. As she gazed at her tea, all desire to drink it left her. She was afraid of disturbing that tea, afraid that the whole story would somehow swirl away. But how could that be? She remained there worrying and brooding for a long time, and her drowsiness vanished. No sound stirred the silence, not even the snores from her son sleeping in the next room could be heard. Only the barking of a dog in the street broke it perhaps, or the mewling of a cat. Every quarter of an hour, a few strokes of the church clock would sound, firm but modest.

"How strange," she said to herself, raising her gaze from the teacup. "Since I found Wistin I had to learn to spin some tales. I never knew how to tell stories before I had to. I invent some tale or other, one every day, and it has to make him go to sleep. The past is just like a story, because it exists and at the same time it doesn't any more. Isn't that what Fr. Grejbel used to say? I wonder where he is at this very moment! He was such a good man; he must still be one. No, he must have become even better over time! Just like wine, it becomes better if it's good and worse if it's bad. That's what father used to say, God rest his soul, as he was having a drink after his meal. My father never did take to Fr. Grejbel much. Not much! Actually he couldn't stand the sight of him! But he did what he thought was best. I don't want to do Fr. Grejbel less than justice. He was the one who taught me to forgive. But besides forgiveness, what other lesson have I learnt that didn't come from him?"

Slowly, slowly, she felt drowsiness steal over her. She did not want to sleep because she wanted to relive and tell her tale, telling stories to herself. At the same time she wanted to sleep in order to dream. To dream a wonderful dream.

"What would I like to dream about?" she asked herself. Then she stood up, looking straight at the window giving on to the street, one hand holding firmly to the table. "I would like to dream because I wish to announce," she went on, taking up the role once more, "that many of my dreams have come true. Only one great wish is left, as large as a man's heart. I wish for Fr. Grejbel's return, to see him enter the village he loved so much, to dream of seeing him held high on the shoulders of those same villagers who sent him away. I long so much for this wish to come true, Ladies and Gentlemen! This is a good dream and I expect it to happen. And when he returns I will tell you, in a loud voice, 'Ladies and Gentlemen, please stand up! Look at him! Look closely! This is what a man of God looks like!' That's my dream!"

And now she could not hold back her tears anymore. She wiped her eyes on her sleeve and raised the cup to her lips. She had a sip and then returned the cup to the table. The tea had gone cold and the desire to drink it had gone. It was as if it had become a duty to spend some time alone, every day, before she went to bed, with a full cup of tea in front of her. It was a habit, one of the many customs that had been around since before she had been born, accompanying her throughout her childhood and left to her as some sort of inheritance. Customs and habits, she pondered, were as dense as carob trees, as ancient as carob trees. The neighbourhood was full of these trees. The village elders used to say that those trees had sprouted and grown in the mists of time and would remain till the end of time. That was another tale, as ancient as themselves.

Chapter 6

In the wine-tavern at the edge of the village, the usual small group of men were drinking the last of their red wine for that day. They never missed this daily rendezvous, from about sunset till the streets turned as quiet as the grave and the night would have drawn in, and everybody would be safe at home behind locked doors. That was how life in this neighbourhood had passed by for hundreds of years, and that is how it remained and would stay. Nobody in the village had ever railed against being born somewhere and spending the rest of his life there, finally giving up his place to someone else, bidding goodbye and going to the other side of the village, taking up residence in a place full of crosses and candles and flowers, without ever returning.

Everything was well planned and time proved it all right. The village provided all one's needs from the first breath one took to the last. The vines in the vicinity grew luscious grapes, every bunch full of plump grapes which the villagers made into wine, a drink that would not be traded for another by the men. It was their salvation when they felt like lost souls, and it was their dream when they felt like wishful thinking, and they would embark on a long and colourful litany, of everything their life was not, and everything it would now never be. They would find relief in describing their great wishes, always the same and ever new. That drink would turn every day into a feast day, maybe even at any time of the day, and summer or winter, rain or shine, that drop of wine wrought miracles. The village had need of its fantasies, too, and it was fantasy that kept that tavern ticking.

Only men frequented the wine tavern; it would have caused a big scandal if a woman had taken a fancy to set foot across its threshold. The house, the market and the fields were considered a woman's place, and so were the streets around her house.

"It would be a miracle if the rumours going round were true. Nothing less than a miracle, and I don't know of anyone praying for such a thing. Miracles do happen. But they only come from Heaven above. Just like rain! Hmm, I wonder, have you ever thought how rain falls from above? And where is it stored, hidden away?" Ġwakkin pondered aloud, in the manner of someone who has made a big discovery and is very proud of the fact.

"In the clouds, don't you know?" Ġamri answered him with a taunt.

"But when there are no clouds, where is it?"

"A miracle! You were talking about miracles...why have you gone on to clouds?"

"Because they both fall from up there, Ġamri. I'm not mixing things up, and I know what I'm saying. I haven't drunk all that much, yet," Ġwakkin defended himself. "I know where I've saved up every drop I've drunk, and it obeys my every word. Set your mind at rest that I know what I'm talking about."

"Well then, help yourself a little bit and help yourself to some more wine to wet your whistle and you'll see how things will become clear in your mind, like cloudless skies after a downpour," Ġamri mocked him once more. "Help your mind and your mind will help you!"

"Stop making a joke about it! Who knows, maybe, like they say, time makes you forget. Yes, it makes you forget because the mind gets tired and changes, and gets old, too," grumbled Ġwakkin. "Just look at us, what time has turned us into! Oh time! Oh time! Oh time! How capricious you are!"

"Oh time! Oh time!" Ġamri pounced on these words, wanting to tease and make fun of Ġwakkin. "You're not going to start making up rhymes about time tonight, are you? Don't wake up people who've gone to bed already! Keep your doggerel for some other time."

"No, no, I'm not about to start singing some għana. I'm not starting on some traditional singing but just saying a few words about time. Time makes you forget, but change? No and no! What's happened has happened, it's over."

"And what's happened, after all? Isn't life on this world one big wheel?" Kieli piped up. "Our people, who've come before us, used to live in these same houses in these same squares and alleyways, giving birth, bringing up children, getting ill and dying, there, just like us, and they've lived many years and now it's our turn. Can you see, my friends? Today we are here. And are we any different from them? And how can we be any different? And why should we be any different, come to that? Are we going to let them down now, now that they're resting on that other side?" he asked, turning his head and with his hand gesturing towards the side of the village where the cemetery lay. "Tell me, use your heads, and if your mind fails you, oil it a bit. The coloured oil Baskal provides, always from the same blessed barrel. You know what I'm saying." Kieli paused and then went on, "And those that will come after us, how will they be?"

"Oh, our friend here knows what he's saying!" Ġamri chimed in. "Now he knows what to say either because the wine he's drunk is stirring his mind and filling it with all sorts of thoughts, or else because he's got an inbuilt knack for public speaking! Let's applaud him, friends, because he truly speaks beautifully! He knows how to find the right word without even looking for it, I think. And so, he must be a very able speaker! Another carafe if you please, landlord! It's my round this time! Alright? Happy now, Gentlemen?"

Each one of them sported bleary eyes and bright red faces. They sat in the wine tavern round tables with their palms open on the surface, each one seeming to wait for the world to change for the better with each glass he downed. What they lacked in real life they expected to find in drink inside that tavern. Their thirst was never slaked, and with every carafe they imbibed, they required another one, then another and yet another. Many a long year had they gone through, many enough for them to realize that they could not make it through the day unless a full glass of wine awaited them in the evening. Maybe life, of itself, was not sufficient? Their evening drink made them sleep soundly at night, and gave them the necessary impetus to rise and work another day. Their entire thinking about life lay stored in the wine.

"Gentlemen! Did you hear how our friend here just called us? Gentlemen! And since when have we become well-heeled gentlemen? The well-heeled aren't here," Ġwakkin made himself heard once again.

"Gentlemen! – I called you that because it suits you. Just imagine for a moment that we're watching some piece of playacting in our village square, or in the street, or in an alley. Every place is good enough to hold some play or other. Isn't that what the actor in a theatre calls you? He would say 'Ladies and Gentlemen, my dear and most welcome Ladies and Gentlemen!' And for just one moment I want to be that actor," Ġamri said in a rush, getting to his feet and raising his glass and slapping a noisy kiss on it, so loudly that it echoed around the whole tavern. "Oh, how much I love you! I'm truly nothing without you! Oh wonderful dear love of mine!" he tipsily spoke to his full glass, pressed to his lips.

"Ġamri knows how to kiss," Ġwakkin laughed. "It looks to me as if this isn't the first kiss he's given. We could hear it from here. It was so loud and it echoed so much that it sounded like the strokes of the large bell. And large bells don't rumble like that from the very first. It takes time to develop its deep sound. It takes a long time to learn."

The others joined in the laughter but then fell silent waiting for him to continue.

"Don't confuse me, and leave those stupidities alone now, Gentlemen! Some seriousness, if you please! I was telling you that I'm like an actor," Ġamri took up his speech once more. "And you too are actors, you know; don't be offended. But I'm a bit more of an actor than you. Everyone looks after his own, isn't that right? And don't I deserve it, anyway? I am an actor and so are you all. I can draw on as many words as I please; they're all stored here, in me...I call them up and out they come. And I have stories aplenty, too, and if I forget them, you can continue with the storytelling. Above everything else, I have you as an audience What else do I need?" Then he paused and looked at the landlord, the owner of the wine tavern. "And you Baskal, our fine landlord, what say you? You're like that man who directs the play from backstage. Together we form the village theatre company. Glass after glass, the words come tumbling out, out of our minds, and our story goes on. Without wine, our brain doesn't work properly, and without some tale or other the day takes too long to pass by. What's there to do, otherwise? Life is long and the village is always asleep. Yes, yes, there's nothing better than a long sleep!"

"What's there to do?" Baskal interrupted Ġamri's flow. "Just ask me! Have you ever seen me rest, take a break? I have no idea how I've spent all these years, always under this very roof. Have you ever seen me take a nap? Wine needs looking after, you know, it's the master, and it needs most attention when people aren't around."

"Now see here, Baskal, understand. Village life is just too long, and I don't know if city life is long as well," Ġamri went on. "In the city...Do you know how they spend their time in the city? Saying idiotic things. Take this for example! They say that things fall to the ground because there is a magnet there...There's a magnet in the ground."

"A magnet?" exclaimed the others, full of astonishment.

"Yes, a big magnet, hidden there," Ġamri affirmed.

"And where is it hidden?"

"In the ground itself. Underneath."

All of them looked down at the ground, starting to tap their feet. They stayed perfectly still and silent, wanting to hear the sound they made clearly.

"Then, under this tavern I have a magnet?" Baskal asked in disbelief. "I've been here all these years and I never realized! Are you sure?"

"Dig, dig, Baskal! Go on! Why don't you start digging?" Ġwakkin interjected. "And when you find it, keep it. Or exchange it for money. Go to the market and sell it!"

"And there's more, besides. Listen! If we throw things up in the air, what do they do?" Ġamri asked them.

The others were silent looking at him with great attention.

"What do they do, huh? What do you think they do, friends?" he asked them again. "Don't you know? Have you lost your voices? After all, how much can this poor mind take? Well then, let me tell you. Those things fall straight down to the ground."

"But we knew that, we knew it. Even children know that," the others began repeating the same thing to each other.

"You're trying to make fun of us tonight, Ġamri, or are you just joking?" Baskal told him off, feeling a little offended. "We don't know how to read, that's true, but our minds still work properly."

"And now it will work even better, listen! Once upon a time there was a man walking in the countryside, and he stopped to rest under a tree. And as he lay there, in the shade, do you know what happened? All of a sudden, imagine this...boom...imagine this...an apple fell right in front of him! A lovely luscious apple! I don't know whether it was a Golden Delicious or a Red Delicious or an Imperial or a Gala or some other variety," Ġamri went on. "And what did this man do, this man who was in his prime and who found himself all of a sudden faced with this incredible thing – an apple? Think! What do you think he did?"

"He ate it," decided Ġwakkin. "A fresh, lovely apple, and free to boot. And with a glass of wine, why, then I would cut it up into pieces and put them in the wine and it would all go down a treat!"

"He ate it, skin and all," was Kieli's guess.

"No. Nothing of the sort," Ġamri answered them. "He didn't eat it. And do you know why? He wasn't hungry. This man was renowned for his great learning."

"But don't men of learning eat apples then?" Kieli wanted to know.

"He was wise," Ġamri continued, his voice betraying the slight irritation he felt though he tried to ignore Kieli. "In the city that's what they say about him."

"Well then, he must have eaten it, for sure," the others chorused together.

"No, he didn't eat it. He kept staring at it, staring and thinking, and finally he concluded that the apple had fallen down to the ground because there's something there that attracts things to it, it had to be so," Ġamri declared.

"An apple magnet!" Ġwakkin concluded.

"What incredible things they come up with, nowadays!" Baskal expressed his amazement.

"Well, then he wasn't wise, that's for sure. How idiotic! That was just stupid!" Kieli declared roundly, denigrating the whole affair.

"And you've never heard it said that a ton of feathers is as heavy as a ton of iron?" Ġamri tried to make himself heard again. "Are feathers as heavy as iron, then?"

"In the city, umm, who knows what you can find in the city? And who knows what lies beyond our village?" Kieli wondered. "They say that over there people are different, even though they are born in the same way we are..."

"Different? How different? Better than us, you mean?" Ġwakkin was prompt to interrupt.

"Listen to this," Kieli broke in. "Once, my wife, God grant her the joys of Heaven! God save her soul and look after her wherever she is now...This is my wife, look, wait a minute," he stammered, putting his hand in his inside pocket under his waistcoat, and fumbling, brought out some papers. "See here, see, where's her photo? It has to be here. Oh, here it is, this is her!" he declared as he raised the photo for them to see it.

The others drew slightly nearer to him, full of curiosity, wanting to see it from up close, but Kieli did not let them come too close. He kissed the photo hurriedly and made haste to return it to his inside pocket. Spreading his right hand across his chest, he looked reassured that the photo was safely back in place.

There was a long pregnant pause inside the tavern, and utter silence. Even the glasses were left abandoned on the table.

"She was a pretty woman and very kind, but now there's nothing left of her except remembrance in my mind, nowhere else," Kieli continued. "I don't even have any tears left to mourn her, but I loved her dearly and it seems like yesterday that I saw her for the first time. I don't remember where we were. I only know that she struck me, you know, umm, I can't describe what I felt, and I didn't rest till I found out who she was and..."

"And then, Kieli? And then, what?" Ġwakkin teased him.

"And then?" the rest joined in loudly, mockingly.

"And then? Rain and thunder God knows when! Isn't that what we say?" Ġwakkin broke in once more.

"And truly rain and thunder followed, my friends. That's it, rain and thunder," Kieli went on in a changed voice, with a catch in his voice and as if he felt tired all of a sudden. He coughed twice, bowed his head, was silent for a few moments and was soon heard crying softly. He tried as hard as he could to stifle his sobs and appear as if he was not weeping.

The others were dumbstruck. They would have liked him to continue but lacked the courage to tell him. But their silence spoke for them and Kieli realized that they wanted him to go on with his personal tale.

"And then, Gentlemen...Once, my wife, now I remember, that's what I was about to tell you, once she asked me to take her to town. I wasn't pleased. It's quite a long way off and it's not for the likes of us. And at one point she wanted me to take her inside a café, and we had a drink. Some drink! I could see that all she was interested in was the café owner. She gave him a long look as soon as we went in, and he gazed back at her in return. She lowered her head then and blushed, and he flushed too, and it was clear there was something between them." He stopped all at once, as if he was embarrassing himself. "I don't know,

96

I really don't know after all, why I started on this subject, tonight. This was uncalled for, simply uncalled for..."

"Go on, Kieli, go on," the others encouraged him.

"Oh alright, I'll go on. When a story starts, it should continue, after all. He was the first man she had ever loved, a long time before, before she'd met me anyway, and she'd never forgotten him. He couldn't leave from there and she refused to leave this village. She left him for me. She used to tell me that she'd never loved anyone but me..."

"But, then why did she want you to take her back to town?" Baskal asked perplexed.

"As soon as we got back home we had a furious quarrel. I felt really hurt. But then she said something. Usually she was a woman of few words but she told me, 'Kieli, I wanted to be sure; after all this time I wanted to make certain that nothing of that first love remained except a memory.' And this reminder could only be a memory if she saw that man again, there, in front of her eyes, and she could reassure herself, saying, 'I love Kieli.' It's as if she wanted to rub out the past like that. That's what the town means to me, trouble."

"Now look here, Kieli, you must know that people talk and make friends with others and she did nothing wrong if she met that townie before she'd met you and fell in love with him," Ġwakkin reasoned with Kieli. "Then, as time went on she came to love you. That's life, incidents that follow on each other, choices, one after another."

"That's right, that's it exactly," the others chorused as one.

"Choices, one after another, Kieli," Ġwakkin repeated. "The street we walk isn't the same for everyone. Take me, do you think I didn't want to meet some young woman and have a lasting relationship? My mother was always urging me to do so, telling me off as if I was still a little boy clinging to her skirts. 'Ġwakkin, son, when are you going to set your sights on some decent girl, who will love you and who knows how to cook and clean and sew? There are many young women in our village who are sweet and decent, who'll make excellent housewives. They all attend church and you can see them there, one behind the other. Or at the market when they go shopping and in their heart they would be wishing to find some young man like yourself. Or looking out of their window, waiting for some bachelor to pass by. Or else you can send a message to a girl you fancy by way of the parish priest or another priest. Why is it that only you don't have any luck? For Heaven's sake! Let me tell you, I won't be around forever!' She was always going on and on about it, every day, and I was really fed up."

"Nobody lives forever, not even married people!" Kieli answered him.

"But then, I mean, umm, I don't want to pry but, do you mean to say that you've never courted a girl? Never?" Ġamri asked him in astonishment.

Ġwakkin blushed, bowed his head and gripped the wine glass cupped between his hands tighter. He nodded assent and raised the glass but then lowered it to the table and pushed it roughly away from him, almost to the table's edge. He opened his hands wide on the table's surface as if smoothing down a tablecloth, and stopped halfway. "Gentlemen," he said, "I wished to court a woman someday, and I would have liked my mother to get her wish, too.

But it wasn't to be, God willed it so. But let me say this. A woman pleases me because it's only natural, because there's nothing more beautiful than a woman, but for me women were to be seen at a distance, as if they were figurines placed in a display cabinet, little statuettes of lovely women with curls coming halfway down their forehead, wearing a tiny pair of silver earrings and a necklace, and with a wide dress, all flowers and colours rioting together...Beautiful, so beautiful that they look unreal. A figurine in a display cabinet, like one of those you find in town. Isn't that what a woman is?"

"Ġwakkin, you can't say you're a total innocent!" Kieli teased him.

"Not an innocent, no, certainly no innocent!" the others joined in the fun.

"You're pulling my leg, I know, I know. But don't run away with the idea that I didn't wish to go to some Carnival Ball, or in a bar, and don't think I never wanted to speak to one or other of the young women as they were leaving church. But, umm, well, it just never happened!"

"Not even during one of the feasts in the village, when the band would be marching past, or at the band club? You never came face to face with some pretty girl?" Ġamri asked, openly inquisitive.

"Ġwakkin, it's never too late. Live your life right to the end. And if you don't manage to bring it off yourself, someone else can help you out. Someone could put in a good word for you. That's how it is in life and that's what friends are for," Kieli suggested helpfully. "At least that way you'd have got something out of life, before old age catches up with you and you'd have nothing left. Plunge your hand into the display cabinet, you too!"

"Oh come on, Kieli, don't forget, we're past our prime now, it's downhill all the way, and no saint will intercede for me," Ġwakkin grumbled.

"But that's not what the proverb says. The proverb says the opposite," Kieli corrected him.

"When you're going downhill, expect to trip and fall," Ġwakkin insisted morosely. "An awful fall! When you're going downhill every wheel turns and no-one can stop even one of them!"

"And what about going uphill? What's an uphill journey like, then?" Kieli calmly spoke up, convinced he was in the right of it.

"Going uphill? Uphill..."Ġwakkin stuttered to a halt.

"If you're going uphill, my friend, the same thing that happened to me will happen to you. Let me tell you this tale now, Gentlemen!" Ġamri began, getting to his feet to stand up straight, his face raised high. He patted his waistcoat into place, passed his left hand gently through his hair as if making sure he looked as attractive as possible, and with his other hand raised his glass. "A toast to Love, Gentlemen! A toast to Womankind, full of dreams and desires, eager, proud, sleeping little but dreaming much, and always waiting for Prince Charming, day and night, waiting for him to come riding by on a..."

"Horse," the others promptly supplied the word, together with one voice as if they were children, happy to have learnt something new.

"No, no!" Ġamri answered in a teasing drawl. "Riding on a...come on, Gentlemen, let's see which one of you will guess right!"

"On a donkey, I bet!" Ġwakkin eagerly said.

"Not that either!"

"On a camel!" was Kieli's contribution.

"Neither!"

"Oh, why don't you tell us, then! You're taking your time! We're going to get old by the time this fine prince of yours arrives. And anyway, don't you know there aren't any princes in the village?" Baskal scoffed.

"Well then let me tell you. A woman's dream lover comes riding by on a big balloon, a huge one, Gentlemen. And do you know what that balloon is?" Ġamri posed his question with the palms of his hands fully open.

"How can we know what this special balloon of yours is? What does it mean?" Kieli wanted to know.

"What a palaver! What on earth is this balloon?" Ġwakkin broke in. "Anyway, I can't say much about this...I've not ridden balloons. I've seen them burst, of course, and truth to say it was fun seeing them burst with a bang, but I've never ridden a single one, no Sir!"

"Oh come on, what is this balloon? Spit it out!" they chorused as one.

"Imagine a balloon! Go on, imagine!"

"Yes, yes, we're imagining it!" they cried together, as if they were a choir of little boys, half serious and half joking.

"Imagine it some more, go on, just a bit more!" Ġamri encouraged them.

"We can't! Can't you see we're doing our best to imagine it? How much more do you expect our poor minds to work?" they answered him in the same tone of voice as before. They all said something or other.

"Look here; let's have an end to it. You don't know, do you, Gentlemen?"

"No, we don't know!" they answered somewhat miffed as they looked blankly at each other.

"You don't know? Well, neither do I!" he answered and burst out laughing.

"What! You don't know either?" they complained but laughing at the same time.

"And do you know why?" Ġamri piped up again. "Because I was betrothed several times, and every time I changed my mind. Either because she was a townie or because she was a country girl. Because she was too serious or because she was too fond of laughter. Because she was fair or because she was swarthy... because of one thing or because of the opposite! And that was it, I couldn't choose! Gentlemen, I broke it off every time and remained single! I ask myself what should I have done to this very day," he freely confessed.

"You sat on the fence, stopping at the cross-roads, then," Kieli observed.

"And I remained there, at the cross-roads," Ġamri confirmed. "That's where I still am, between wishing yes and wishing no, wanting to go on and wanting to stay. My mother too, if she were still alive, would tell me the same thing Ġwakkin's mother said. I can still picture each one of those girls in my mind, as if they were colourful paintings, all the faces of those I loved. One of them had long hair that came down below her waist, all curls, with a coloured bow on each side of her head. She smiled easily and never took that smile off her face. Another always wore a hat with a long, narrow ribbon dangling down at the side. Once she started talking she never knew when to stop and nobody could contradict her. Another girl always wore lace. She was taciturn and serious. And then there was one who liked to wear a cap with a long, straight feather stuck on the front. She liked to joke. Then there was one who wore her hair with a fringe hanging over her face. She was always laughing. And I remember those dainty earrings, and that necklace with a pendant in the shape of a cross, and those long skirts brushing the ground...Oh! And those soft hands, and that walk with swinging hips...and all those big dreams...and all those beautiful words...and that singing...One of them liked singing arias from operas she remembered. Another was mad about modern songs. And yet another only liked operettas...And the other one? Oh yes, she liked singing the traditional songs her mother liked...All of them used to boast that they sang with the window open, while they were washing clothes or cooking, to be heard by the neighbours. Singing meant they were happy besides showing off their beautiful voices."

"You don't see them around anymore, Ġamri?" Ġwakkin asked him in astonishment.

"Oh-ho! You're not thinking of getting on with one of them, are you, Ġwakkin?" Kieli interjected, wanting to poke fun at Ġwakkin.

"No, I don't see them anymore. But dream of them? Yes, I do. They've all gone their separate ways, and after all, none of them were from our village," Ġamri answered Ġwakkin, ignoring Kieli.

"You had a wandering eye, it seems," Baskal commented. "And as they say in town, the ground has a magnet and it pulls everything down to it. And they also say that the world is a very big place. Well then, the world must have a far larger magnet than ours."

"That's true, the world is very big indeed," the others repeated solemnly together. "That's what they say."

"That's what they say," Baskal took exception to this. "But you can't trust what they say. The whole truth is gathered here in these streets around us, because these are certain and true."

"And now, Gentlemen, the tale comes to an end. Stand up and let's drink to...To whom? Let's see now!" Ġamri exclaimed. "To us all! We all walked on our allotted paths and now we've all arrived here!"

"Here...at Baskal's wine tavern!" Ġwakkin capped Ġamri's words.

"Stand up, all of you. To our good health, Gentlemen!" Ġamri chivvied them on once more.

"To our good health!" the others obediently said the toast, getting to their feet, somewhat reluctantly but still quite amused. And they drained their glass.

"And that's it...my dear and most esteemed Gentlemen...much appreciated members of the public...this most famous...most sought after theatrical company of our dearest village...is finishing its spectacular drama...tonight...on this historic night...right here...in Baskal's wine tavern with genuine drink!" Ġamri declaimed in a loud voice full of mockery and seriousness. Both his voice and body movements betrayed his drunken state.

The others were in the same state.

"Applause! Gentlemen, some applause, if you please! Don't we deserve some applause? For ourselves! What does it cost? Not even a carafe of red wine," Ġamri spoke in the tone of one addressing a huge crowd, as if he was the head of a theatrical company, onstage.

All the others began clapping. They kept it up and the applause became a long-drawn out affair, growing ever louder. They remained with their gaze fixed on each other till their clapping melded into one noise, repeated without any variation, and it seemed as if they did not know when to stop, and they kept clapping with the tempo getting slower and slower.

At that moment, Luqa appeared in the doorway. He was one of the regulars and he was about to enter as usual but he was quite taken aback, looking at them in amazement, as if he could not believe his eyes. "What's happened here?" he said under his breath.

"Applause! Some applause from you too, Luqa! Right now! Come, show us you know how to clap when the need arises!" Ġamri ordered. "What does it cost?"

Luqa remained rooted to the spot, standing straight, flabbergasted. The others did not give him a chance to speak.

"Ġamri's right! Quick, for the spectacle is over now. You were late, it's your fault, but you still need to clap. Actually, look, the next round must be on you!" Kieli told him.

"If you don't clap!" Ġamri informed him, wagging his forefinger at him. "That's the condition!"

"And if I clap?" Luqa asked.

"Oh, if you clap...if you clap, that's another thing," Ġamri went on in a kindly voice. "You'll have become one of us, a part of the play. We might even consider giving you a free full glass of wine! Let's see...And Baskal may fill it up more than usual, too. A special offer! Usually the glass isn't filled to the brim. But today he can tip the jug more generously, what say you? It belongs to him but we can all repay him by drinking more than usual. We all need one another."

"In that case, with all my heart...with all my heart, my friends!" Luqa said to them beginning to clap on his own because the others had stopped and had clasped their glass once more. He became embarrassed and let his hands fall down slowly to his sides.

"From today onwards, make sure to call us 'Gentlemen', not 'my friends'!" Ġwakkin informed him.

"Pour a carafe for them, and here's the money, look, coins on top of each other!" Luqa shouted out the order, approaching the counter.

"We'll drink to your good health, Luqa!" Ġamri said expansively.

Baskal began to pour the wine into glasses again.

"You want to toast me, tonight?" Luqa was prompt to ask. "Of course not!"

"Why not?" the others asked him in astonishment.

"We'll toast Fr. Grejbel! Let's drink to his good health, tonight. That would be fitting. Am I not right, my friends? Umm..no, no...not friends, I should say Gentlemen! That's what you've become and that's how I'll be calling you now," Luqa declared happily.

In a flash, they all fell silent, lowering their glass slowly onto the table, looking towards each other befuddled and bewildered, as if they had not heard properly, and they remained like that, waiting for all to be made clear. A deep silence fell over the tavern. They grimaced and carefully sat down with a loud jolt, as one. It was as if they had rehearsed it before: the way they sat down in a single movement; the way they spread their fingers across the table surface; and the way they looked at their hands. Each one faced ten fingers splayed out straight, right in front of his eyes.

"Fr. – Grej – bel's – good – health," Luqa gave the toast, drawling out each syllable slowly, chanting it as if it was a popular ditty, known to all.

His words echoed and reverberated in perfect silence.

Baskal was the first to raise his head and break the silence that was beginning to unnerve him. "Drink to Fr. Grejbel's good health? Tonight? After all this time? Have you learnt some part of a play, by any chance, and you've come here to act it out, in front of us?" he asked in amazement.

"That's it, that's it," the others were quick to agree. "You're right. This is something we can act out."

"Where on earth did this idea of yours spring from, tonight? It's not a bad idea as such, and there's a tale behind it, but..." Baskal continued in a doubting tone. "But!" he finished on a warning note.

"Haven't you heard the news, yet, Gentlemen?" Luqa enquired.

"What news? Do you have another story for us, you too? That's how we've spent this evening: telling stories," Kieli spoke in an ironic voice. "Each story brought on another. That's how we spend our life here, and you know all this just as well, but tonight you came here late. We make fun of it – life – by telling stories about it! When we were little children we used to hear stories before we went to sleep, and when we grew older we began creating stories ourselves, the way we knew how, good or bad. And now that we've piled on the years, what else is left for us to do? See if we still remember them. Our memories aren't what they used to be. This poor mind...but every story is a part, and all the stories together make up one long tale." He stopped there and looking at Luqa spoke in a decisive tone. "Your story is the only part that's missing. Come on, tell us a story, you too must tell us something. Think! Remember! Imagine!"

"You want to hear a story? Very well, here it is. Fr. Grejbel is coming back!" Luqa announced.

"Fr. Grejbel is coming back?" they asked him in amazement, together with one voice.

"If you're going to keep this up, I, that is, the landlord, absolute owner under this roof, that we've just found out also has a big magnet under the ground," Baskal spoke up in a serious tone, "I, the landlord, have to order you to either not drink another single drop or else to start paying for all the drinks I pour from now on. Decide!"

Ġamri, too, was not disposed to believe Luqa. "I have some news for you, my most esteemed Gentlemen!" he said as he stood up straight, a suitably baleful look on his face, and with an unnatural seriousness. "The village theatrical company has the great pleasure to announce Luqa's new drama, a truly original play, brilliant, which means it shines, full of fantasy, created entirely by his incredibly fertile mind for this historic night. Laughter and tears, expectations and surprises, natural costumes and scenery, all in colour, a play that appeals to everyone. A play where fantasy verges on the impossible. You tell me, my ever most esteemed Gentlemen," Ġamri declaimed, melodramatically, "what more can you ask for?"

"Truly, Gentlemen! Fr. Grejbel is coming back! Go and ask around. The whole village knows," Luqa assured them.

"Well then, let's drink to him," Ġwakkin said, indifferently, slowly, as one resigned on hearing news that did not move him at all.

"Let's drink to him, then, let's toast him," the others complied, resigned as well.

~ 0~

A few days later, Fr. Grejbel returned from that faraway place he had been sent to many years before. Some villagers went down to the harbour to wait for him to disembark. They went, riding on their beasts, dressed in their best clothes to mark the occasion, as they did during the village feast. They began to cheer and wave as soon as the ship was sighted on the horizon, and the cheers grew louder when the ship approached the quay and finally berthed.

"There he is, look folks! There he is!" the people began shouting.

Fr. Grejbel waved to them from where he stood. Coming down the gangplank between the ship and the quay, he nearly tripped over his soutane. That often happened to him and once, it had happened as he was getting out of a *karozzin*, stumbling over its high step. He remembered it well, and at that moment, everything passed clearly before his eyes, as never before. He loved his soutane, and he never appeared in front of people without it, not even when he was at home receiving unexpected visitors, villagers who wanted to have a word with him. It would all be buttoned up right up to the top button at his collar, even if he was in his room.

However, though he'd grown old wearing it over the years, he had never got used to it. It was not the first time he nearly tripped over it going up the altar steps. He never fell down but the fear of doing so never left him.

"Dear me! How embarrassing if I trip over it! That's why you must always pay attention, mind your every step, Fr. Grejbel," he constantly used to say to himself, devoutly, nervously. And now that he was returning to his native land, these ancient words began to echo once more in his inner ear. He used to hear the words coming from within, as if it was the voice of conscience speaking. "Be careful with each step you take, mind the slightest movement, and always look ahead. Every time is always the first time, and it may be the last. Don't forget! You may have put your foot down well to take a proper step but you never know if suddenly there might be a loose gravel stone in your path and you would end up stumbling over it. And who would believe you if you said you'd put your foot down properly? You can't defend the truth. It's not the step you take that counts. It's only the step that is seen that counts," he used to think. And then he would think exactly the opposite, "No, no, that's not true, that's not true..."

"There he is! There he is, look folks!" the villagers continued shouting. It was something quite out of the ordinary for them to go down to the quay watching the ships come in to berth, to welcome some relative or someone they knew. They were the sort of people who rarely left their village, if at all. They only came there to witness the bustle around the port, to wish that someday a ship would arrive that would invite them aboard for a joy ride, a brief sail beyond those shores, without going too far away, on the condition that they would be brought back soon, without them getting lost somewhere along the way, or left adrift in the middle of the sea. They used to hear people telling tales about huge fish living in the sea that were constantly hungry, however much they ate, and they would also eat humans. Men and women and children of all ages. Even when there was fair weather, the calm seas lapping the harbour was another world, and it was not theirs.

"Which step counts? The one your foot takes or the one that's seen from afar in people's eyes?" Fr. Grejbel was still worrying, turning this thought over and over in his mind. "But why are you having such thoughts today of all days, Fr. Grejbel? You never learn, do you? But you're getting on in years!" he admonished himself. "Now is not the time to indulge in such thoughts. This is a joyful moment. Come on, Fr. Grejbel, smile, move your lips, let your smile dent your cheeks so that everyone can see your happiness. You've won out in the end! Smile, lift up your eyes and walk straight!" he kept repeating to himself. Holding up the edge of his soutane with the fingertips of one hand, he began waving with his other hand because he noticed that there were people welcoming him. They could not be his relatives because he had none. Those had found their resting place in the little cemetery a long time before, being crowded in a small family grave, lying next to each other in that village cemetery. "But now, leave off from these sad thoughts, Fr. Grejbel!" he urged himself once more. But these thoughts kept buzzing around in his head however much he wished to get rid of them. He had a mental picture of them as he looked down at the deep sea, imagining them like small waves coming and going and after a pause coming once more. He continued waving, waving to everybody. "How kind these people are!" he congratulated himself.

The people arrayed on the quay continued to wave at him.

"But no, Fr. Grejbel, not everybody is kind. You should know better than anyone...No, no," he went on pondering, "all of them, yes all of them are kind, and in the coming days I want to show them how much I feel they deserve a place in Heaven. If I don't manage to carry all of them off with me up there, it'll be my fault! Dear Lord, let not a single one of them get lost! That's what my job is all about, to get them to that door. And then, it's up to them what they do once they're inside! They'd be able to find their relatives, their friends, just as if they were back in the village, at home or in the square. They'd know what to do without getting confused or getting into trouble. Ah, there wouldn't be any more knotty problems to unravel. But in the meantime, I'd better get down this gangplank. This soutane is certainly out of place, here."

As soon as he disembarked, treading solid ground, he approached the waiting villagers and they ran to him and took turns to hug him. He recognised some of them but soon realized he had forgotten some faces. And some of them he had never seen before.

"Let's push off for the village, my friends! Let's go from here, back to the village now!" one of them shouted. "Leave Fr. Grejbel in my hands. He's coming to the village with me."

Fr. Grejbel, his eyes bright with tears, looking lost and embarrassed more than ever, could not utter a single word.

"Look here, Fr. Grejbel, you can sit here, on the handsomest horse the village can boast of!" that man declared with delight. "If you ever come across a more handsome horse, come and tell me, and I'll give you what he's worth. That horse, ahh, he's a proud one, and so is his owner! I chose him especially for you because he's proud, and has reason to stand tall. Look at him! That's what today's occasion demands!"

"Me, on that horse? Dear Lord! When have I ever ridden a horse? How will I hold on up there, all along the way? He is beautiful, simply beautiful but..." Fr. Grejbel replied, overcome with shyness.

"You may never have ridden a horse up to now, but I have, Fr. Grejbel, and there's nothing to it, don't worry. I will lead you, right up to the village. I'll be holding the reins and it'll be as if I'll be on the saddle myself. Your place is up there, high above everyone, your face to the light, looking up, and everyone can greet you respectfully, because in the village no one can stand higher than on the back of a horse, and such a horse! You should see him go up the ramp, sweet and easy!" the man went on earnestly. "And that's a great honour. Now you'll see for yourself how beautifully he steps out, holds up his head and obeys. No sooner do I give a command then he's prompt to put it into action. I hardly have time to open my mouth. I know how to deal with him and he understands everything, as if he was human, or slightly more than that! Whether I tut-tut or cough, or grouse or flatter him, he totally understands. He's ever so pleased whenever I have words of praise for him! He's got used to me when I ride him, my handling of the reins and my every movement. Lately I've mentioned you to him and you should have seen how glad he was! These last few days I've been telling him, 'Now, make sure that you'll show your paces to everybody. Stay calm, there's no other horse to touch you! That's why you're going to ride him, Fr. Grejbel. You don't know him yet, but you will. 'Don't let me down, neither with him nor with anybody. He is worthy of you and you are worthy of him.' That's what I told him, Fr. Grejbel. He shook his head, began to neigh and that was it. We'd come to an agreement. It wasn't the first time but I told him this time it was very special. He won't forget and after a good feed of clover he'll continue dreaming about it."

Fr. Grejbel climbed as best he could onto the horse's back, careful not to get tangled up in his soutane. "Now I have to be very careful not to get entangled in it, even up here! Just imagine were I to get tangled up in it and fall! What would happen to me? This is something new!" he smilingly said to himself.

The man went up onto the other horse and with the reins in one of his hands, his other hand held the reins of Fr. Grejbel's horse, just a few paces away. "Everything alright, Fr. Grejbel? See here now, we're off!" he said.

"Very well, my friend. I never imagined after sailing on a ship I'd be riding a horse. This is really all new to me! Lately I've been doing nothing but having journeys, by sea and on land," Fr. Grejbel replied. "I didn't know the ship's captain but this time round the captain..."

"Is me. Leave it all in my hands and sit tight. You've always held fast, solid and stable as the carob tree. And what's more solid and stable than a carob tree? A tree that lives for entire centuries and can withstand anything, summer and winter. It's a deluded man who thinks he can overwhelm it! Well then, you know how to hold on fast, today as well," the man replied. Next, he lowered his head to talk to the horse, as if to whisper in his ears; he uttered some endearments to encourage the beast and then, in a loud voice purposefully made to carry to everyone present, he cried, "Giddy-up my beauty, on to the village! Look at the lovely ribbon I've decked you with today! All the village horses will envy you. You know the way, and make sure that today you'll show Fr. Grejbel how well you know it by heart! This is a race too!" The man raised his head and turning to the priest he said, "Can you see, Fr. Grejbel, how obedient and well-mannered he is? He's absorbed every single word I've taught him. There's no other friend like him!"

People began moving about on their carts to follow them. Every draught animal was decorated with ribbons and bows, with tassels and tiny bells, with anything and everything the villagers used to adorn their donkeys and horses on special occasions.

"And now we're on our way to the village, I suppose, aren't we?" Fr. Grejbel asked. "From up here the street looks very different from the way I remember it, but we're making for the village I think."

"Of course we are. Of course, straight to the village. To the village square," the man astride the horse answered.

"The village square?"

"Now don't you worry your head about anything. I let you up on my horse and presently I'll let you down from it. An obedient horse will bring you to your destination safe and sound. The honour is for the three of us to share: you, me and him. We all need one another."

"Truth to say, I did expect someone would come to greet me, but such an enormous welcome as this is completely unexpected. How could I have possibly ever imagined such a thing where I was at the time?"

"You didn't expect it? Well then, prepare yourself Fr. Grejbel! The best is yet to come!"

"Is yet to come! Oh Dear Lord!" the priest exclaimed.

"Whatever villagers do, they do it out of conviction, believing in it entirely. And they take it to heart. You know what I'm trying to say. You're a priest, true enough, but you're also a villager. This occasion is a feast, and it must be celebrated from beginning to end."

Fr. Grejbel remained silent, and spoke to himself. "I trust, Oh Lord, You're still in control of this situation, and that You can spare the time to watch over the village from up there. In the meantime, during these last few years I've come to realize that You need to look after a vast world, but please, don't forget Your old friends. I would like to tell you that Your ways are truly mysterious, winding in unimaginable twists and turns. I bless them, all of them, with all my heart, before I even come to know them, and more so when I do. That's what we'd agreed upon in the beginning, and You've never let me down. You once told me that in Heaven You have a map for everyone, and our village, a very tiny dot, barely visible even in full daylight, is there, and You can see it. One needs a magnifying lens to see it. But Lord, You see everything close up, with love, whether one stands in the centre or on the margins. As for me, from atop this horse, however well-mannered it is, I can see the world whirling me around much more than before. I can't keep from You that I'm feeling dizzy. Whether up here or down there, it's a giddy world for me. Sometimes I think it would have been better if the world didn't go round. Wouldn't it be better if one day You could stop it for a while? I don't want to poke my nose into Your affairs. My ideas stop right here. It's in Your hands! That's what we'd agreed upon once, and now I want to renew our contract," Fr. Grejbel went on praying. "The conditions remain the same. As it was in the beginning, now and forever shall be, amen...Blessed are You forever."

"We're making good time, Fr. Grejbel! Everything is going as it should!" The man on the horse drew his attention. The two horses were keeping pace with one another, as if they were siblings in total accord with one another.

Amongst all the noises, the clip-clop of the horses' hooves was the loudest. Their simplicity, their steady unchanging rhythm and the pace they set, all gave a solemn proud air, a natural mien to the whole proceedings. The admiring and inquisitive glances, especially from children, were all directed at the four legs, thin but sturdy, of each beast, stepping smartly forward with an unfailing measured beat, even when they stepped on some stone lying across their path. They gave an impression of total loyalty and order.

"The whole village awaits you, eagerly, as happens throughout the days of the village feast, exactly like when we're celebrating the feast when everything is different, special. No more, no less. As soon as we learnt of your return we decided to celebrate it as if it was a feast day. If we don't do it well, it would be better not to do it at all, that's what we've learnt. And we've brought out all the feast decorations and we've decked the church and streets in all their finery. All of it!" the rider let on.

"Like the village feast? Like the feast dedicated to the patron saint of our village, you mean to say? But how can that be? A feast for me?" Fr. Grejbel was astounded.

"Yes, a feast for you! Up to now we've had one saint in the village. From today onwards we'll have two!"

"Two?"

"One of them in Heaven and the other one down here with us, Fr. Grejbel. One who's known to all and another one who's known only to us. Don't we have the right to have our own saint? A village saint, planted in our own fields, in our own backyard! We made you one; today we pronounce you one. It's all up to us. We found one saint already made, and the other we've fashioned ourselves, using our own skills, good or bad. Otherwise, how can we redeem our mistake? This feast is for our benefit too. Leave it all to us. God knows what's in our heart and mind. It's right and fitting for you, it is. Soon you'll see just how much the villagers love you."

"I never doubted it."

"There was a time when you could have had doubts, and I don't blame you if you had, but today you'll know for certain."

They entered the village and rode their horses up to the church square. The rider had spoken the truth. Every street and alleyway had been decorated, and most of all, the village square, at the moment crammed with villagers. Faces known of old, new ones, all looking at him, halfway between smiling and astonishment, full of curiosity. And they greeted him. Babies were held in their mothers' arms, staring and sucking on their big soother tied with a ribbon and attached to a buttonhole in their dress. Slightly older children clung to their mother's skirts, pleading to be held up in her arms like their siblings, to see all that was happening. Tired feet were brought forward as an excuse, and that down there in the crowd they were going to get lost. Nearly all the boys were wearing a cap like the men and sometimes it was clear that the cap was too big for their small head.

"Take off your cap! Take it off, he's here," the mothers and fathers began to tell their sons as soon as they saw the priest's horse approaching.

The bells were ringing out in celebration, not stopping for a single moment. On each bell, around the clapper's round shape, a small bunch of flowers had been tied and a long ribbon fluttered down, easily seen down in the square, swaying with each stroke of the bell.

"Dear God, greatness is truly Yours! I can think of no other word to describe You. My eloquence stops here. Your ways are truly mysterious, Lord!" Fr. Grejbel kept repeating to himself under his breath, greeting people all the time. "I never for a moment feared You'd abandon me. You taught me to walk down the long road and then, when You saw me stumble, You lifted me up just in time. You also taught me to wait. Patience. Patience, that's what my mother used to say when she talked to me about You, once, a long time ago, somewhere in this warren of streets. What can I tell You, now? Thank you? What kind of thanks could possibly be enough? Oh Lord, my words are too stark. Rustic words. And my Latin is rusty too. How often I studied Latin by candlelight! I don't know how many times I woke up earlier than usual in the hope that a fresh mind would make me remember! That blessed ablative absolute case, and participles, and the gerund, and declensions, *dominus, domine, dominum*...and then the conjugations... Nowadays I can hardly understand the words in my missal. Still, at least I can remember the most important verb: *sum, es, est, sumus, estis, sunt.* Oh good, I haven't forgotten everything! *Ego sum!* Here I am! I am, I exist! And the *oratio obliqua*, indirect speech oh Lord! Let me see: the sentence 'He is a good man' in Latin is: *Ille vir bonus est*. But in indirect speech, wonder of wonders, it translates differently: 'We think that he is a good man' – *Putamus illum virum esse bonum*. But as for You, Lord, what language can't You understand? And I think You consider all languages equal and the same. They are all beautiful and whole, and that goes for all of them. Up to now, You've always understood me when I speak in dialect. And these villagers have only spoken to You in dialect, like I have, though they think I read thick books in Latin. Aren't I just like them? Didn't You tell me from the very first that I was to remain like that right to the end? You'd said, 'Make sure you don't change your ways, because I too don't change mine. And if you change, I won't recognize you any longer.' Do You remember?"

The rider made the horses go right up to the church and with both hands signalled to the bell-ringers to silence the bells straightaway. The last notes rang out more strongly, and the crowd's noise dwindled and died down.

For a few moments, Fr. Grejbel remained with bowed head, silent. Then he raised his head and gazed in the empty space before his eyes, towards the fields spread out next to each other, beyond the square. He could not utter a thing and the first words came out hoarsely, haltingly. He coughed twice to clear his throat and fell silent once more, overwhelmed with emotion. The villagers stood silent, still. He made a tremendous effort, drew in his breath and began to speak, "There, do you see? We had thought, all of us, that we had lost our way on this journey, and that we'd forgotten how to retrace our steps to this square. We are all gathered here together once more, as if nothing had happened, and, just like before, I want to tell you all that I love you..."

The square remained enveloped in silence. An array of rapt faces was spread before him, gazing at him like placid vegetables covering the face of the earth in the fields.

"I love you because you've remained in my thoughts, and I've continued to pray for you, and because I knew that you too were praying for me. Don't ask me how I knew!" Fr. Grejbel addressed them with a smile. "I don't know how to prove to you all what I feel, and anyway, I don't need to prove anything. If we are sure of something we're certain, and that's that. Whatever our feelings are, they're there, growing inside as we ourselves grow older. Our hearts can speak and understand, even from afar, without any need of words. Tell me if that isn't so. Now, here and now, can we say that what we used to believe before isn't what we've come to know now? Before we used to believe, in blind faith, but now we know it for certain. That's the miracle that's happened in the meantime. Today's celebration means that what we've always believed in wasn't empty belief, and that sometimes, the Lord chooses to break His everlasting silence to show us that He's here with us. Our wisdom grows and comes entirely from our surrounding fields. I remained firm in my beliefs, and you remained steadfast too, and today we have the proof that we didn't believe and hope in vain...in the meantime we didn't stray and get lost."

"Forgive us, Fr. Grejbel!" someone in the crowd shouted.

The crowd kept its silence and some people turned their faces in the direction from where the voice had come.

"The distance between us, though very great, wasn't enough to keep us apart and now, after all these years, we're reunited once more. This means that our hearts, though far away from each other, kept good faith and waited. And since they waited, they remained open. We've waited, you and I, and we haven't waited in vain. There was something bigger than us that kept us together. You felt it right here, and I felt it, far away where I was."

"Forgive us, Fr. Grejbel!" another voice called out, stronger than the one before.

Fr. Grejbel pretended not to have heard and he continued, "Today, we should remember those who are no longer with us, who, in the meantime, have departed to the other side of the village from where there's no return. They lie distant from us but nearby, all the same. Let us remember also those who are still with us, burdened by years, and pray to God that they may walk in His path to the end. They are the ones who built and shaped our village for us and they are the ones who taught us our beliefs and feelings. Though they could not read or write, they knew how to fashion something even more important than that. They knew how to feel, and they wanted us to follow in their footsteps and know how to feel as well. They had a good memory and wanted to pass everything on to us. They succeeded!"

The multitude remained quiet, straining to hear his every word.

Amongst the faces turned to him, immobile, he suddenly caught sight of Susanna, and then he noticed that she was holding hands with a little boy. He was startled, and with joy welling up in his heart was about to lose the thread of his thoughts and speech. He paused, as if choosing his words carefully and went on, "And let us remember those who are just starting out on their path and are still only a few years old, so that God may show them the way clearly from now...and so that they may always walk on the straight and narrow. All good paths lead to Him."

"Forgive us, Fr. Grejbel," someone else shouted.

"God forgives us all, my dear brothers and sisters. Only He knows how to read our heart, and hearts cannot be seen. Each one of us carried out his duty as he saw it; each of us felt we did the right thing. Set your minds at rest about it, each of us heard our conscience as best we could. This is what I've learnt most of all during the time I've spent away from you. Don't call for my forgiveness. I mean it, don't ask me that. And if you will permit me, I would like to be the one to ask something from you, today. Just one thing."

Silence reigned among that sea of faces.

"I ask you all to be as we used to, happy with each other, whoever we are. No one amongst us is a stranger. This is the only signal that God has forgiven us all. And that's why we can have this feast to celebrate. All that we've gone through hasn't been for nothing," he cried out and fell silent.

As soon as he saw Fr. Grejbel finish his speech, the horse rider raised his hands in signal once more to the people in the bell-tower. At once, the bells pealed out again and the villagers broke out in applause. Torn between tears and joy, the villagers crowded around the priest, hugging him, and he smiled at everybody and had a kind word for each and every one. The extreme embarrassment he had felt at the beginning had begun to wane and he finally began to feel more himself. Children, sent by their mother and father, came to him, hands clasped together and crossed on their chest, eyes straight, a hurried word on their lips asking for his blessing. He spread out his right hand over their heads and made the Sign of the Cross with a slight movement of his hand in the four directions. The children smiled, lifted up their heads and uncrossed their arms, and flew back to their parents, happy and proud.

In a short while, people drifted back to their homes, the bells were stilled and the church was closed, and the square had nearly emptied.

Just at that moment, an elderly man approached the priest, as if he did not want to startle him. He gave a slight bob in front of the priest, as far down as his knees allowed, and he took the priest's right hand in his respectfully, to kiss it. "Fr. Grejbel, here I am, I'm still here and I don't know what to say! All I know is that I never expected such a wonderful moment as this," he managed to say in a broken voice.

"Our sacristan! How are you? How are you?" Fr. Grejbel hugged him for a long moment.

"From tomorrow onwards, count on me to be with you to see to all your needs," the sacristan declared.

"From tomorrow?"

"Yes, right from tomorrow. Set your mind at rest, Fr. Grejbel!"

"And why not from this very evening?" Fr. Grejbel asked him with a smile.

"From this very evening? And why not? From this very moment! More than ever before!"

"I would like you to accompany me to the cemetery. I would like to pay my respects to my mother."

"Let us go, Fr. Grejbel, right this minute. But the keys are at home. Wait for me till I go and get them. You know I don't live far from here."

"No, no, there's no need for that. Today I will visit her at a distance. Tomorrow I can go in and stand right next to her."

"Let's go then," the sacristan replied in agreement.

When they got there, they stopped in front of the closed iron gates, and Fr. Grejbel pressed his face against the iron rods and brought up both his hands to grasp them, clenching his fists as if to break through the bars and enter the place. The candles and little oil containers, all coloured red, threw a dim, obscure light onto the graves. The flames they threw off looked like tiny lanterns silhouetted against the evening's dusk, declaring that even at night, the dead were not forgotten by the living. Only the wind had the power to douse them all, and to blow away every flower from where it had been placed. The silence was only broken by the sound of the cicadas. Their screeching drone, mournful, endlessly repeated over and over again, filled up the solitude of that place.

"And now, Fr. Grejbel, I must tell you that together with your mother, only a few paces away from her, lies someone who was very dear to you," the sacristan ventured to inform the priest and then held his tongue.

The priest turned to face him, lost for words.

"Someone you used to respect immensely, and who respected you just as much. Fr. Anselmu."

"Fr. Anselmu?" Fr. Grejbel recollected the many times he had gone to that elderly cleric, laid bare his heart and mind to ask for advice, the only one available to him. For a very long time he had considered Fr. Anselmu as a man full of wisdom and prudence, a humble but decisive man...the person who could point him on his way through the obstacles and surprises strewn across his path, out of the experience he had garnered in a lifetime and which made him eschew the day-to-day contact with people and spend his last years in the tranquillity of reading and praying. He had shared both sorrow and joy with him, and it was to him that Fr. Grejbel had turned whenever he felt confused or alone. Nobody knew Fr. Grejbel as well as Fr. Anselmu. To Fr. Grejbel, Fr. Anselmu was what remained of a whole family.

Fr. Anselmu spoke of you right till the very end," the sacristan said, to try and console him. "He remained steadfast in holding you dear and believing in you. He never changed his mind. I assure you."

"His grave, which is his grave?" Fr. Grejbel stammered.

"That one, look, that one there," the sacristan answered, pointing to a grave. He thought for a while and then went on, "But you can't see it in the dark. It's quite some way off from here and the graves all look the same."

Fr. Grejbel felt his tears fall and he moaned, "I came as soon as I could, this same evening, as soon as I got back, Fr. Anselmu, even though so many years have passed." He clenched the gate harder still and bowed his head, almost pressing it into the iron bars till it hurt. He then raised it again and gazed upwards, as if he was speaking to himself but not knowing which way to look. "I'd have given anything to have been at his side when his end came. It was my duty to have been there, after he had accompanied me for so long, throughout my life. Alone...alone...he too was all alone..."

The sacristan felt his own heart wrung with emotion. "It's not your fault you weren't with him. You couldn't do otherwise," he sympathized in a low voice, as if he was speaking to himself. "You were with him still." Then he changed his tone, "He asked after you many times, and even on his last day he hoped against hope to behold you once more. Nothing could make him lose heart. He died waiting for the day you would come knocking at his door and go up to him. He waited for you as if there was some arrangement between you, as if...as if you were simply late."

Fr. Grejbel wrenched himself away from the iron gate and looked eagerly at the sacristan, saying, "Thank you for everything. But now we'd better be going. We'll come again tomorrow and you can tell me all that you recall about Fr. Anselmu's last days, please. It'll make me feel better about it, perhaps, and maybe I could set my mind at rest that he didn't suffer too much on my behalf. In spite of everything that's happened, that's what I'd like to believe. I need to make myself think that way."

They began to walk away from the clump of darkness shrouding the cemetery. The streets were deserted. Their footsteps, though regular and without haste, seemed to change from one moment to the next in rhythm with the words they spoke, sometimes quickly and sometimes slowly. Even the merest breath made itself heard, and accordingly, they spoke in low tones, nearly beneath their breath.

"There was only one thing however, that grieved Fr. Anselmu, more than anything else, Fr. Grejbel. And I'd like get it off my chest now, since you've just returned," the sacristan confided. He lifted his gaze to the priest to try and read the reaction etched on his face, in the dim light lingering in the street, and to pluck up his courage to continue.

"Something that grieved his heart more than anything? I know that all I went through saddened him. I feel guilty about that, whether it was my fault or not, all the same. But I don't understand what you're getting at."

"One day, when he knew his time was up, well, at that point...It was evening, and he only used to go out to come to church, and he was shaky on his legs. He'd begun to go out less and less in the evenings and finally he stopped coming to church to recite the Rosary and receive the Blessing altogether...One day, I was about to tell you, he came up to me and whispered in my ear, as if he was feeling embarrassed and because he didn't want anyone to overhear, 'Listen, when you can spare a moment, please come to my house because I'd like to have a word with you.' And I told him, 'Of course, Fr. Anselmu, if you want, I'll come by this very evening, this very evening.' And I went along and found him waiting for me by the door. 'I'd like to send a letter but I can't write any longer,' he confessed. 'I don't know what to do. I'd like to write it and I've memorised all that I'd like to say, here in my mind...word for word...one after the other, I know them...I know them all but I can't put pen to paper, you know, the state of my health...' he told me, distracted with worry".

"He wanted to write a letter? To whom?" Fr. Grejbel asked half astonished and half amused.

"To whom?" the sacristan promptly took him up on his word. "To you! Who do you think? He invited me into his dining room and to sit down at the table and he brought a sheet of paper and a pencil, and then he asked me, 'Please, I want you to write a letter for me addressed to Fr. Grejbel.' And then I told him that I too could not write, because I don't know how. I've never written anything. He took it hard but then I was inspired to suggest something. I told him, 'Don't worry. I know a clerk. He writes very well because he's got a good ink pen and he's got black ink and also red, whichever you want. He has a ruler and a blotting paper to dry the ink immediately so none of the words get smeared and blurred. He writes in a fine hand, neatly, both cursive script and in block letters.' Fr. Anselmu enquired whether I knew him well. I answered, 'I'm only acquainted with him but the little I know of him is all to the good. Many people go to him to have letters written for them. He is a trustworthy person, a man of few words and he doesn't charge much.' He answered, "I don't care how much he charges me. As long as he writes down every single word I dictate, that's all that matters.' 'He's a very successful clerk.' I put his mind at rest. 'Will you take me to him, please?' he asked me. And I replied, 'Willingly, out of respect for you and for Fr. Grejbel.' We went to the clerk's house and he invited us in, to the room where he served his clients."

Fr. Grejbel remained thunderstruck, listening to all this.

"The clerk opened his small wooden case, took out his ink pen, smoothed down a sheet of paper and everything. He looked to be a wise man from the way he spoke," the sacristan went on with his tale, keen to impart all the details. "From time to time he dipped his nib in the ink. Fr. Anselmu began reciting the words from memory, word by word, as if he'd learnt everything by heart, and the clerk wrote it all down, slowly and carefully. Sometimes he interrupted Fr. Anselmu's flow to check whether he'd heard him correctly, and sometimes he'd repeat the passage he'd just written to set his mind at rest that he'd taken it all down, exactly. And finally he put his pen aside, took up the blotting paper and gently covered the letter, pressing down to have it absorb the excess ink, and then he paused and looked at it to see if Fr. Anselmu wanted to add something. A truly good clerk."

"A letter for me...? A letter from Fr. Anselmu?" Fr. Grejbel stammered, more amazed than before.

"And then he gave his last instruction, 'And now, Sir, please write this, 'Bless you for the last time. And remain a good priest as you have always been. Fr. Anselmu.' And while he was dictating these words, he lifted up his hands with what strength he had left, made the Sign of the Cross and blessed you for real. That's what he dictated and that was the end of the letter. Even the clerk appeared impressed with the words he'd taken in dictation," the sacristan informed Fr. Grejbel, with bowed head.

"What else did he say in this letter? Is there something you can clearly remember?" Fr. Grejbel asked him, hoping to hear something else about the letter.

"Something I can clearly remember? Why, everything! But," the sacristan paused to think, "Hmm, yes, there's one thing that stands out more than anything else in my mind...and I can tell you word for word."

Fr. Grejbel stared back at him, eyes wide open, indicating a good guess on his part as to what that something was.

"Yes, Fr. Grejbel, I remember it well. Fr. Anselmu also wanted the clerk to write what I think you are expecting me to say. He told him, 'Write and tell him that I am certain he is not guilty. Reassure him that I still consider him, all the same, all the...all the same, how he's ever been, a good man.' The clerk lifted the ink pen off the paper and stared at me, paused to think and then lowered his head and wrote the words down."

Fr. Grejbel raised both his hands to his face, in the manner of one at prayer, closed his eyes, and drew in a long breath pulling down his head sharply, without vouchsafing a single word.

"That's what I wanted to tell you. He kept waiting for a reply from you."

"A reply? From me? To this letter?"

"Even one word would have done. He kept coming to me and asking right till the very end. He used to say, 'Has Fr. Grejbel sent word? One word would suffice. He can write, not like me, my eyes are worn out and my hands shake. Why hasn't he written to me? Maybe he doesn't have paper and ink where he is? Whatever, he doesn't need a clerk, that's for sure.' That's what he used to tell me. And I would reply, 'Fr. Grejbel is in a distant land. They do say the world is a very large place. Letters take a long time to arrive and goodness knows what paths they cross to arrive here! Our village is completely cut off from others. Goodness knows how many people handle the letters from one ship to another, from one hand to another!' I wanted to set his mind at rest. And I used to console him like that." The sacristan looked at Fr. Grejbel, expectation written large on his face; a clear answer was called for.

Fr. Grejbel, overwhelmed, with a sorrowful look on his face, heavy gaze pointing to the ground, remained silent.

"I don't know if it was wrong of me to tell you all this, and this very evening, too. Perhaps I should have held my tongue for a while, but...I had to tell you sometime, whether today or tomorrow. For me, keeping silent is as good as lying."

"I never received that letter. I know nothing about it!"

"You never received it? Didn't they send you the letter?" The sacristan shook his head and exhaled loudly in angry disbelief. "I can hardly believe it, but I know you've never told a lie. You don't even know how."

Fr. Grejbel shook his head in denial but did not speak.

"You never got it!" the sacristan kept repeating in disgust.

The village seemed cradled in tranquillity. Some parts of it lay in complete darkness and in others a dim light shone in clumps here and there. All the windows were closed. Only their footsteps could be heard, and they seemed to intrude at that time of evening, seemingly too loud. In a short while the sacristan bid him goodnight and they went their separate way.

Everything in the rooms of that house remained the same, the way Fr. Grejbel had left it before he departed. He made his way from room to room, touching things lightly, as if discovering a new place, one he had never laid eyes on before. Nothing had lost its colour. Nothing had been moved. He looked at everything and began to smile, and then he sat down at the dining room table, pleased to find himself surrounded by the plates and cups and the cutlery and all the things he had grown up with. Most of the things, simple, cheap and cheerful, had been given to him by his mother. The thought leapt forward in his mind as if for a little while he had forgotten something which was never far away from his thoughts.

Fr. Grejbel got up from his chair with a lurch, lit the candle in front of the crucifix and flung himself to his knees. During the hour's silence that followed, he made an enormous effort to stifle his weeping. He did not want to wake his neighbours who would have heard the least sound. He began to sob and contained the echoing sound of his lamentation within his cupped hands, raised to his face. "Oh God! Oh God! How much the taste of Your chalice plumbs deep!" he moaned, seeking solace in prayer. "How long those three hours on the cross pass by! But how unshaken is Your promise to stay close by! You keep Your word. I've never complained about You and I'm not about to start now. You have never forgotten me. You left me neither to emptiness nor to wastefulness. I realize now that You wanted me to suffer all those trials to strengthen my resolve, to be convinced more than ever before, and after the courage You engendered in me, I'd be able to help others climb the long hard road. You wanted me to get closer to You, to feel as You, to understand a little the pain of the crown of thorns and of the nails driven through flesh and bones. You wanted me to grow a bit more so I wouldn't let the emptiness of the day carry me away. The hill is there and it will stay there till the very end. It's the pathway that leads to You. I've known all this for quite some time. The uphill climb is hard and full of grief. It's not lovely at all. There's nothing about it to appeal to my mind or body. I don't like it, but somewhere in its aura there's a hint of You, a taste, and it's sweet and tranquil. It reminds me of the sweetness of these fields, forgotten by all but remembered by You. I know You too are a rustic countryman, Lord Jesus! Who could understand all that I feel? You know because You too climbed up that hill alone. And Your mother was some way away from You, alone, unable to give You aid and succour. And that grieved her all the more. Sympathize if I cry and smile at the same time. Sympathize if I lean from one side to another. My heart is my own, yet it's not mine. I am a poor man as You were, but I am a poor man of good will. I am simply a man...a man like any other...a country priest...here...at the edge of the world, Lord. Wring me out and You'll see what emerges! Heap sorrow and grief on me and see me bear it! Beat me and see me stand without complaint! Send me trials and see my faith in You hold fast! I am little but my will is far greater than me. Lord, You won me over once, and now You've won me over forever with my miserable existence and all. With every step I take, the way I know how, I want to approach You ever closer. Lately, You've taken me away from this village to teach me about great distances. You wanted me to learn to be astonished, looking at grandness and thereby appreciating the small and humble things. Perhaps they're the same, the grandness out there and the smallness in here? The two pans of the scales lie in Your hands. Everywhere can be considered a village, wherever a human resides. And now You've returned me to this village to make me understand that for You there's no distance or nearby. Even on this patch of ground at the edge of the world, You recognize who belongs to You, whether they are on the edge or in the centre, because Your sight reaches everywhere."

Chapter 7

It was a lovely day. The first sounds of a working day, after a night of perfect silence, began to eddy around the neighbourhood, rising in volume with each passing moment. Soon the entire street would be full of life, a normal working day. Life could not go on as usual without its accompanying noise and bustle. The cockerels and hens, locked up in their coops on the roof of most houses, or ranging around freely on the farms, had started waking up everybody a long time before. This was the villagers' oldest clock; their every morning wake-up call, precise, courteous. The sacristan too, relied on their call, even though he often had to be up betimes, before them. Summer or winter, he knew what it meant to walk the streets when no one was about, and to open up the church when people were still languishing in bed.

Susanna opened the window and peered out, holding the two slatted shutters in her hands and feeling happiness well up inside her on seeing the sun shining brightly everywhere. Just like people's moods, the weather was changeable and the different kind of days they had often ran into a whole week. Some way off, beyond the area full of fields, she could see that the bright day promised fine weather more than could be discerned in the fastness of her humble dwelling. The glowing brightness of such a day could change her mood instantly, making her feel proud to be village born, a girl that had emerged from somewhere amongst the farms, the alleyways, and the winding paths hemmed in between vines, olive trees and carob trees resting their branches on the rubble walls. All of them led to some other place beyond, in wide open spaces, where land and sky met and lived together in harmony. In the depths of her heart, Susanna admitted to herself that she loved the village, and every grief she suffered and whimpered through because of it, was, after all, part of the price she had to pay for everything that was beautiful and good.

Wistin, above all.

He too was the land's offspring, like all her people going back generation after generation, and like his father's. Part of his make-up included all that had been fashioned during entire centuries, those same centuries she hardly knew anything about because they had only merited a brief mention in books. But the ancient stones stood there, around her, and every house and every hut stood witness there before her that the story had begun a very long time before she had come on the scene. Wistin, she reassured herself, should find this cradle ready for him. His cradle was this old village with all that kept it steadfast – a solid rock in which entire centuries had barely made a dent. Though she was not too sure about that.

"Ever since my mother brought Wistin back to me, many things have changed in the village," Susanna mused. Not everybody looked askance at her, indeed the smiles and greetings from people, especially from women, had increased. People change very slowly...in time, she thought. This notion pleased her.

"Mummy, Mummy, is it time?" Wistin called out to her from his bed.

"It's a very beautiful day today," she answered him. "Come and see for yourself. But before you hang out of the window make sure to go and wash your face. You have fresh water, it's ready in the basin and there's a clean towel next to it. Don't forget. You must wash your face thoroughly, bring up water to your face cupped in both your hands, once, twice, three times and that's enough, and then wipe it dry. Don't forget your ears, wash them properly too! And this is something you should do every day, now and forever. Such things don't change. You must learn to do it from now so that you'll always do it."

"Even when I grow up and become a man?"

"Of course, even more so. When you become a man you'll need to wash your face more often. The more you grow up..."

"Why more so?"

Susanna did not answer.

"Tell me, Mummy."

After a short while, Wistin appeared in front of her. He was still drowsy and swayed as he walked. He slowly approached the dining table, pulled a chair and climbed up to sit on it.

"You haven't washed your face, I see! Did you think I wouldn't notice?"

"I don't feel like it today."

"You don't feel like it? As if feeling like it comes into it! You have to wash your face. Duty is not a question of feeling like it, son. Come, get up. Come and from today onwards you mustn't fail to do what must be done as soon as you wake up and get out of bed. That's what everybody does. And if everybody does it, well then, so must Wistin..."

"How do you know what everybody does, Mummy?"

"Ahh, I'm your mother, and I know. A mother always knows many things."

"But they, other people I mean, do they always feel like washing their face as soon as they get up?"

"Always. Every day, every day. They wake up early on purpose to wash their face."

"They never, but absolutely never, wake up and don't feel like washing their face?"

"Never, absolutely never."

"But I do feel like it."

"Well then, why didn't you wash your face on your own?"

"I tricked you! That's not what I feel like doing. I'm not going to tell you, you must guess. One, two, three, guess Mummy..."

"You feel like giving your mother a big kiss."

"Yes, but after I tell you what I feel like doing."

"Well hurry up and tell me!"

"I feel like going to fly my kite."

Susanna looked at him happily; she smiled at him and told him, "Yes, if that's what you want, let's go and fly the kite. Now don't forget what you've promised me!"

Wistin hugged his mother and kissed her many times on her cheek.

"And now let me tell you something. Today there's hardly any wind so the kite won't rise easily and maybe it won't rise at all. What do you think, should we go tomorrow or some other day when it's a bit windier?"

"No, Mummy, no, no, no! Today! I want to go now! The wind will come." His puling voice held a note betraying a spoilt child who knows his wishes are always granted.

"Well then, you know what? I'll prepare a picnic to take with us, some ħobż biż-żejt, bread with tomatoes and olive oil, some lettuce and capers and basil leaves and olives. This is the kind of food I grew up eating ever since I was your age, thought up by my forebears and you'll get to like it too," she promised him. She crammed everything in her ġewlaq, shoved a couple of napkins inside and everything else that would keep their hunger at bay. "You'll work up an appetite in the fresh air, Wistin, just you wait. And you'll gobble everything up," she assured him gleefully.

"But I won't have time to eat. I'll be flying my kite," he replied with pride.

Susanna looked him full in the face, shook her head and put her hands on her waist as if to tell him, "Since you say so, well that's what we'll do! But the wind doesn't blow as your fancy takes you! Now if the wind ever came into my hands, well, then that would be a different story!" She did not regret giving in to his every whim; she knew no better than to spoil him.

They left the house and began walking away, she laden with her straw basket in one hand and holding on to her son's hand with the other, while her son held on fast to his kite, the reel gripped tightly between his fingers. Wistin was nearly hidden by the kite, and its size was making him feel important. From time to time he lifted it up to see whether it would move and to show his mother that he knew what he had to do on his own. Sometimes he pursed his lips and blew, imitating the wind. He could see with his own eyes that not even a leaf in the trees stirred in the still air. And trees there were in great number. A settled calm lay over everything. He began to suspect as much himself. His mother was always right, or nearly so. She knew the answer to his every question, about all the different things he asked her about, and he never would rest till she had given him the exact answer he wished to hear. Sometimes she said that she did not know the answer because, after all, she did not know all that there was to know. But she always did her best not to leave him without some sort of reply.

"I don't know, son, I don't know everything; actually I know only so much. When you're older, ask someone who knows more than I do. Wait. But don't forget the question," she would tell him. "If you don't ask questions, you cannot grow up."

They continued walking holding hands, looking delighted with each other's company. Though they often went for walks together, they had never gone on such a long walk and at such an early hour. And all because of that kite that had him spellbound at first sight, more fascinated by it than anything else he had ever laid eyes on, Susanna observed. The minute he had discovered it, Wistin had laid aside all other toys.

"Mummy, where are we going, now? Are we going to keep on walking straight ahead?"

"Are you tired? No, you aren't, surely? You're still young. Walking is a new pastime for children your age. However much you walk, you feel light on your feet and want to walk on. You're still brand new, son!"

"Of course I'm not tired! I still want to fly my kite, Mummy, and to do that I must stay on my feet and walk, sometimes forward and sometimes backward. Then I must let the string spool out of the reel, play it out till the kite starts to rise slowly, slowly and then it will catch the wind and will rise faster and start racing, and rise so high up it will look like a pigeon, and this pigeon will fly here and there without hitting anything, and there will be no one to stop it or knock against it, and it will go up and up, without fear or looking back..."

"And then?" Susanna interrupted him gently.

"And then...Let me think, Mummy, 'cause I don't know. And then, and then, I'll want to bring it back down. I wouldn't want it to blow away 'cause then I'll be left alone."

"Alone? What do you mean alone? Aren't I here with you? Am I not enough for you?"

"Yes, Mummy, but I was talking about the kite. The kite isn't a woman. You don't fly. Do you wish you could fly, Mummy, just like that, as if you were a kite or a pigeon with wings that can take you anywhere and when you wanted to you could go down to the ground or fly up and hide yourself up there, near Baby Jesus?"

Susanna looked at him, wordless. She pressed his hand as if to reassure herself that he was indeed there by her side, keeping pace with her, up the path she herself had opened up for him. "I don't fly, son," she said in her heart. "And it hasn't been all that long since I learnt to walk. There was a time when I simply crawled. I couldn't move forward in any other way."

"Will the kite fly up very high in the sky, today, Mummy?" he asked her.

They continued walking and she remained silent for quite a while. She could recall it all so well. There it was, the edge of the village where the Valley began...down there...well hidden among the ancient carob trees, densely decked with foliage. Every tree had a thick trunk and branches, all of them intertwined so closely that they resembled a series of walls offering shelter from rain and shade from the hot sun. Once upon a time, Susanna had been here, amongst the densely leaved trees, in the hidey-hole down here, when her beloved wanted proof of her love for him. And she had felt a strong shiver run down her spine and envelop her whole body, and she had wanted to...and at the same time had been reluctant. She could not recall whether she had told him no. Now she was afraid to remember what answer she had once given that young man, as if that answer meant wanting Wistin or not. "Yes, yes," she told herself. Wistin had been conceived here, somewhere in that hidden place; she knew the exact spot. Precisely where it all began. Nothing had changed, and the trees appeared exactly the same; they did not appear to have aged even by one day. Withered leaves in yellow and red hues rustled beneath their feet, just like they had done once, as if they were the very same leaves.

"Mummy, Mummy, can't you hear me? Will the kite rise high up in the air, today?"

"I don't know, son. We'll see, it depends on what wind we'll find. Everything depends on the wind. There can be a light breeze or a strong one, a gust or a gale. The wind is its own master."

"But there's no wind at all, Mummy."

"Let's call it up, Wistin! Shall we call it up?"

"How do we call up the wind, Mummy?"

"We call it up," she prevaricated, thinking furiously, "we call it up, look, by calling to it! North Wind! Come, come North Wind! And we can call it by other names too. Leading Wind! Or Head Wind! Or Wind of Fortune! How shall we call it, Wistin? Which name do you choose? Make sure to call it courteously, because it holds all the power in its hands. It's in command."

Wistin did not heed her words. "Mummy, where are we going? Tell me where? I've never been in these parts and I don't know where we are. Where are we?"

"Don't you want to explore this place? Don't you like the Valley? This is a beautiful place full of greenery. I'd like you to see it. Walk with me, here, hold my hand and you won't fall. There's some more walking left. The Valley is a vast place and when you enter it you forget the rest of the world, because all the world can be found here. Everything is gathered in this place, son, in the Valley."

"You know this place, Mummy?"

"Now just pay attention where you're stepping. If you're not careful you can take a wrong step and stumble and fall. And if you fall you can hurt yourself badly. I know what I'm saying. But don't be afraid, I'll hold your hand all the time. Don't let go of my hand," she quickly added when she thought he was about to let go of her hand. "Hold on tightly and look at the ground. There are rocks scattered around...and they've taken on shapes sculpted by time, the wind, the rain, and the waters. Rainwater collects here, see, and when it rains puddles form and you can sail paper boats on them. That's what children like to do. This is the Valley, son. This is it."

"What is the Valley, Mummy?"

"The Valley, son, is a place where life is born. The Valley means life. It's surrounded by high ground as if walls enclose it in, protecting it."

"The Valley?" Wistin repeated listlessly, devoid of any interest. "But I can't fly my kite down here! If I try to make it fly it'll get stuck in the branches and get entangled. Let's go away from here, Mummy. I don't like this place."

Susanna paused, her hand in his. "Look around you, Wistin, so you'll know. Life begins down here...Every tree was a sapling once and every sapling was once a seed. That's the way life goes on in this world of ours."

"Let's go, Mummy, let's go!" Wistin whimpered. "I don't like it here!"

Susanna stood still, seemingly deaf to his cries. "You don't like it here? You'll like it in the future, I reckon. This is where it all starts. And then, to fly the kite we must go elsewhere. Wait a little, it won't take us long to get there. Nothing happens in a flash, son. We have to pass from this place as part of our way. We have to walk along it together, the two of us. We came down together down here and together we'll climb out of it again. Leave it to me, Wistin."

"Alright. You're like the wind, Mummy, you're in command. This is the path you walk," he told her against his will. "But it's not mine. I don't like it here."

She made him walk further on for a while and then she told him, "Let's climb back up to the fields, now, to the wide open spaces and we'll be able to fly the kite there."

As soon as they reached the high ground and found themselves facing a large green area, thickly overgrown with grass, Wistin let go of his mother's hand and ran off, holding up the kite as far up over his head as he could manage. He ran faster and faster, frequently looking back over his shoulder to see it. "Fly, fly, go up, go up, go on, go up there, come on now!" he shouted. "Let's fly away together, far away from that Valley, up up!"

"Don't go far away, and when you run don't keep looking back," Susanna called out to him when he had gone quite a distance. "If you look back you can fall."

"Mummy, Mummy, can you hear me from there?" he shouted back at her, stopping in his tracks. "Look at me coming back there, me and the kite! When I run, it will start to rise because the wind will come! Call to it! Call to it! You're in command and the wind will surely listen to you!"

"Run, let me see who's the fastest of the two of you!"

"Let's go. Run, run!" Wistin told the kite. "Fly up, fly up!" With his mouth, he made noises like the wind gusting away, his mouth forming a half circle, and he enjoyed listening to the sounds he produced.

Susanna stood waiting for him, holding the straw basket by her side, and as soon as he reached her she caught him up in her skirts and then knelt on the grass to embrace him. Gently she disengaged his hand from the kite and put it down on the ground next to them. He left her embrace and picked up the reel. She took it from his hand in one smooth movement and helped him unravel it slowly.

"Like this, Mummy, isn't it? Look, look!" he exclaimed straightening up with the kite in front of his face.

The kite made no movement. There was not even a slight puff of wind that could make it stir, however slightly, off the patch of grass. Not one leaf moved, however sluggishly.

"You see, Wistin! Your mother was right!"

"How did you know, Mummy, that the kite wouldn't fly?"

"How? I learnt it one day as I was reading a story."

"Tell me the story then, Mummy, tell it to me," he importuned her, seeming to have forgotten all about his kite lying beside him. "Did you read it a long time ago, long, long ago when kites could still talk?"

"No, Wistin, a long time before that. It was a time when we still played with paper boats, when we used to sail them in the puddles that formed after some downpour. Or else we used to sail them in the puddles down in the Valley. We had to wait for the rains, Wistin, to find puddles. We needed them. Wherever some rain collected, a boat could be floated. Boats cannot stay on dry land. And ships carry people on board, children and adults. We used to imagine ourselves at the harbour, where real ships come and berth. And sometimes these ships brought babies. At other times they brought people who disembarked for a rest and to forget shipboard life. In the harbour everyone feels small because the ships are very large, very high, and the sea is very deep, and it hardly ever moves, except when it's angry."

"Does the sea get angry too, Mummy?"

"Yes, Wistin, the sea gets angry too. The sea is male. But not around here because our village is far away from the sea."

"Everybody used to come by ship, Mummy?"

"If they were coming over the sea, yes, everyone came by ship."

"And everyone comes by ship, Mummy?"

Susanna lost command of herself. "Yes, everyone," she stammered. "People are always coming and going. The harbour is open. It bids farewell to those who leave and welcomes those who arrive."

"Do ships come in everyday, Mummy?"

"Of course they do, every day."

"At what time?"

"At any time. Whenever people arrive from abroad and want to disembark."

"And when will my father arrive, Mummy?"

"There are many people queuing up to arrive, son. Each person has to wait a long time, behind the people who came before him, till his turn comes. In the world, out there beyond our village, there are many people wanting to set sail, but there are only a handful of ships. That's why they take a long time to get to their destination."

"You've been telling me for ages that he should be arriving."

"There are many people waiting to board. Each one behind the other, and nobody can jump the queue. Just like when we're at the market doing our shopping. We wait in line. Don't you remember? Can we jump ahead of someone?"

"No, we can't. Everybody has to wait for his turn. And who gets down from the ship first, children or grown-ups?"

"Who do you think, Wistin?"

"Whoever had been waiting the longest, I suppose."

"Is that what you think? Well then, that's how it is."

"But then why did I arrive here before my father? Maybe there are ships only for children, Mummy, and others only for grown-ups. The children's ships are small and those for grown-ups are big, so that there'll be enough space for all of them. That's what I think, 'cause otherwise...But my father's been waiting ever so long! Do you know how long he's been waiting, Mummy? Let me tell you, Mummy."

Susanna looked gravely at him.

"As long as I have years," and he started counting on his fingers, one after another. "I know the numbers well, all of them. One, two, three, four..."

Susanna reached out and gently closed his fingers one by one and clasped his hands so that their four hands together looked like one whole thing. She raised his hands to her lips and gave them a gentle kiss. Her head was bowed.

"Four..." Wistin was about to go on.

Susanna's right hand covered his mouth. "And what about the story? Hadn't we better continue it?"

"Isn't this another story, Mummy? One day I'll be the one to tell you a story, Mummy. Would you like that? And you'll sit and listen to me."

"And how does that story begin, Wistin?"

"I'll start off like this, listen. Once upon a time, there was a little boy who was always waiting to see the ships come into harbour, because there were some ships that brought children over and others that brought grown-ups...The harbour remained open, day and night."

"That's a nice story," she told him somewhat curtly, as if she had taken offence all of a sudden. "Would you like to eat a piece of bread, now?" she asked him as she spread out a large napkin on the ground and started getting the food out of her straw basket. "I brought the food for us to eat it; I don't want to carry it back home. If you eat some bread the basket will get lighter. What do you say?"

But Wistin continued with his story. "And this boy was always gazing hard, across the sea, and waiting, and asking all the people there, "Have you seen anyone? Have you seen a man?" He would go up to every man he saw and ask him if he was his father."

"Wistin, here, take this piece of bread. After all this time in the fresh air you must be very hungry, and don't forget what we said before we left home. In all this fresh air we work up an appetite. We're far away from the Valley."

"But I felt like flying my kite, Mummy."

In the distance, on the edge of the field, Katarina came striding purposefully towards them, and Wistin saw her at once.

"Wistin! Wistin!" Katarina called out to her grandson, and waved energetically at him as if she had not set eyes on him for a long time.

"Granny! Granny!" Wistin shouted happily running towards her.

Katarina knelt down on the grass and lifted him up, stood up with him in her arms and brought him to Susanna. "My goodness, how heavy you're getting to be, you little scamp! I'm no longer as strong as I was! Do you know I can hardly lift you up? Goodness knows how many times I lifted up your mother in my arms! She felt as light as a feather!" She let him down and patted his hair into place.

"Would you like to join us and have some bread, Mother? I thought you might turn up. I suppose you went looking for us at home," Susanna greeted her mother.

"Where would you have me search and find you, daughter? At home, of course, I looked for you at home," Katarina replied.

"We came here early because Wistin wanted to fly his kite."

"Today of all days, my dear? In this weather? Not even a leaf stirs," Katarina replied. Then she encouraged the boy to play some way off. He took up his kite and went off at a run with it raised over his head.

Susanna raised her eyes, intent on watching him. "Wistin, make sure you don't run far, out of my sight."

"Listen, daughter, now I can speak freely to you," Katarina began as soon as she saw the boy put some distance between them. "Look here, the worst is over!

Finally we're going to have fair weather. God answered my prayers, and all that Fr. Grejbel did was not in vain. Everyone is overjoyed to have him back. Nowadays, the villagers love him more than ever before. Your son is with you. You lack for nothing, daughter. There's only one thing you lack, and it's not a small insignificant matter. I pray you, go back to your husband. Arturu will always be your husband. Go and speak to Fr. Grejbel. He will help you for sure."

"Mother, you've stood by me through thick and thin. You're the only person I have left. But these matters aren't as easy as you're making them out. Lately you seem to think that everything will fall out the way you'd like them to, just like that."

"No, daughter, I haven't changed all that much. I was a woman of my word and I still am. I know that things have to take their time, slowly."

"Maybe not all that much, but nearly so."

"Nearly so, indeed, nearly so." After a short pause Katarina went on. "What do you say, huh? If you dash all my hopes, you'll cut off all the life that's left to me."

"Do you think it gives me any pleasure to deny you? How can I not say yes to you?" Susanna replied handing her a cup of tea.

Her mother's face lit up with happiness. "I'm going, let me go straightaway to find him and tell him that you'd like to speak to him. Dear daughter, bless you! I bless you with both my hands and with all the strength that's left to me, now and till the last breath I draw."

"Wait a moment, Mother, just wait. Here, drink some tea first. Where shall I go to speak to him, and when?"

"Leave it to me. I'll fix it. I'm going now and I bless you again with both hands, the way Fr. Grejbel will when he sees you once more. My blessing counts for something, but his may count for much more."

"Fr. Grejbel saw me at some distance, and he saw my son with me, the same way he saw you, in the crowd."

"I know he saw us, and I'm sure he was very glad to see us all! I'll explain everything to him, myself," Katarina said bubbling with joy. She gathered her long skirts spread all around her on the ground, got up and brushed her clothes quickly and looked in the direction where the boy was playing. "Wistin, Granny has to go! She's too busy for words these days! Bless you, you too! Even blessings need work! Bless you both," she shouted.

"All these loud blessings are going to make people think you're blessing the whole world, dear Mother!"

"The world? How would I know the whole world? My hands reach only as far as the edges of our village. That's my whole world, Susanna. That's how it always was and that's how it should always be. And what should people think, after all? When I'm happy, I'm happy! My happiness is loud and clear! That's me! Don't I deserve some happiness in my last years? Don't you know what sort of oppression I had to live under? But there, let me keep silent about that. I don't want to fall into error and let my tongue run away with me and endanger my soul's salvation. Marriage is for life and it's a closed box. After all, your father will always remain your father."

"God rest his soul!" Susanna said the time-worn phrase under her breath.

"God rest his soul!" her mother echoed her and went off in haste.

The thoroughfare between the field and the village square ran in a direct line and Katarina soon entered the church, went down on her knees as if she was about to start praying, made the Sign of the Cross and glanced around. Fr. Grejbel was not there so she went to look for him inside the vestry, which was quite small. Not finding him there she went on to his house and after rapping on the door twice, she found herself face-to-face with him.

His face lit up as soon as he saw her and he smiled, and feeling as if he had something stuck in his throat he gestured for her to enter. She bowed her head, keeping her hands together as if still at prayer in church and waited for him to speak and invite her to sit down. After a few moments of silence, she lifted her gaze to his and burst out weeping.

He went to her side and clasped her hands in sympathy. His eyes were brimming with tears as well but he made an enormous effort to appear steadfast and calm.

"I wanted to speak with you again. I'm not going to keep on thanking you because there aren't enough words to describe...Since you came back, I took heart and I've been trying to urge Susanna, a word here or there, to come and talk to you about her marriage to Arturu. I've always mentioned you and that's the only reason she's listened to me. Your name, not that I want to flatter you, but your name opens doors. I cannot reach up to where you can."

"They've remained separated, meanwhile? They've never approached each other?"

"Since you left, Fr. Grejbel, nothing's changed between them. He's on one side and she's on the other. And now there's the boy stuck in the middle, and he's not Arturu's son."

"You've managed no mean feat there, bringing her son back to her. God bless him, I saw him in the crowd, at a distance. You cannot have done a finer thing than that, Katarina."

Katarina recounted the whole sorry story to him. "You remember my husband, Saverju, and you know how nothing would ever make him change his mind. If he thought something should be one way, that's how it had to remain whatever happened. He had taken it to heart that Susanna was with child out of wedlock and he spent a long time refusing even to see her. And then you know what he did, so that when Susanna gave birth, her baby was immediately taken away from her and left in an orphanage. He did his best to hide things from me as well. But as you can imagine, I did my utmost to find out where the baby was and I didn't rest till I was certain of his whereabouts. Sometimes I saw that Saverju closed an eye to my activities. I knew who was taking care of the baby. I sometimes paid the little mite a visit, behind Saverju's back. I set my mind at rest that at least the baby was in good hands and well-taken care of. But Saverju was always dogging my footsteps; he didn't trust me in this matter. He was afraid I would somehow betray him. And I felt that way too, that I shouldn't let him down...He remained stoutly in denial right up to the end...And on his deathbed he never said a single word to Susanna about her baby."

"I know, I know,"

"You were there. You've always been there for us, Fr. Grejbel, throughout our sorrows."

"And even in your joys..."

"Yes, even in our joys, truly. When Susanna married Arturu, you mean. My husband and I weren't there that day. He didn't want to attend her wedding. He didn't even want to speak to Arturu. And if my husband didn't want to go, then I couldn't, either. Poor girl, she didn't deserve all that she's had to face!"

"Don't fret, don't fret, in the meantime you still loved her, and she felt your love, surely, even at a distance."

"How could I let her down? I could only do so much, with my husband around. And then he passed away. But then your troubles came. They were all our fault, all our fault."

"No, no, don't say that, don't think that. It wasn't your fault. Every good gesture causes some movement and that can hurt. Whenever we do some good, we have to cause some pain, somehow or other. But it's not wasted suffering. That's all. If we realize this, we understand the why. It doesn't become any easier to bear but at least we don't remain in the dark. Tranquillity...we call this tranquillity."

Katarina was still puzzling over the idea. "Well then, whose fault was it? You did nothing but good, not just to my family but to all the villagers. It was our fault."

"That's life for you, that's how it is. That's how it's always been, now and forever and everywhere. That's how it was in the beginning and that's how it will remain till the end. The important thing is to do our best, even if we come to the brink."

"And you did get to the brink, Fr. Grejbel..."

"But see, life brings its own consolations, too. Now we find ourselves here, at this point, so that we may look ahead. And then...I would like you to continue with your story..."

"Well, then, when your troubles came about, I didn't have the courage to do something to bring the boy back. I feel I let you down, at least in my thoughts, Fr. Grejbel. It's as if during all that time, I too accused you of wrongdoing. My silence confirmed your guilt, even though all I was doing was staying loyal to my husband. I had to remain loyal to him, whatever happened. Marriage is for life, and continues in the afterlife. I pray you understand, I too am village born..."

"Of course I understand, but this idea shouldn't even cross your mind."

"Our village had never gone through such an experience before. I felt withdrawn into myself, almost forgetting my daughter and her son, everything. I thought, everything is in ruins and there's nothing left to pick up. In my eyes, my husband appeared to be the only one who had been right all along. I started telling myself, 'So much time had to pass, and now that he's dead, he's been proved right, and by the entire village.' But I was wrong, and he too was wrong..."

"Don't say that. Say that he did all that he thought was the right thing to do. Each person did his duty as he saw it and felt he must do. And when our different duties meet each other head on, what happens? They clash. There's conflict. A bolt of lightning comes out of the blue. And somebody is caught in the middle, in a vice. It may be that everybody is caught in such a way. But then time passes and it's all water under the bridge and the water runs clear. That's all that's happened," Fr. Grejbel soothed her gently with infinite kindness.

"Where did you come by such tranquillity, Fr. Grejbel? Where did you find such peace?" she asked him wonderingly. "You never did lose it, did you, throughout your troubles?" She fell silent and gazed at him. In a different tone she briskly took up the tale, speaking decisively. "But then, when I learnt that you had been sent far away from here, I started feeling guilty. I said to myself, 'This is as far as I go, obeying my husband blindly, even after his death. Now I must do something to redeem all the victims.' The victims were you, Susanna and Wistin. And I didn't rest till Susanna and the boy were re-united. Well, re-united in a manner of speaking because they had never been together except during her pregnancy. And they weren't a happy nine months, either."

"But look at what's come about from those difficult nine months! Aren't you happy with such a victorious outcome? Be glad and proud of all that you've achieved."

"Proud, of myself? After I've collected all these years? If it weren't for the sacrifice you made, then..."

"Everyone had a part to play. And now?" he asked her with a rising inflection in his voice, showing her plainly that he could make a good guess about the matter she wanted to discuss.

"And now, Fr. Grejbel, I would like you to do your utmost to bring Susanna and Arturu back together. I had never imagined that my daughter would one day enter that house to serve Arturu and his mother and she would remain there and end up becoming his wife. Not only did I never imagine such a thing but I almost wished it had never happened. But it did, and today they are man and wife. What a shame, they've spent more years apart than together! From the little I know about their marriage, I know he was ready to welcome her back with her son. Susanna says he often told her so and I believe her."

"Truly, I can reassure you on this point myself. Arturu made this promise in front of me. More than once."

"There you are then, you see! If only they can come together again! Marriage is for life! For life!" she repeated over and over again, sadly but with a hint of hope.

"Do you want me to speak to her? I don't want to make a false move, either do too much or too little. And after all, it's important to see how she feels about it, at this stage."

"What do you think, Fr. Grejbel? Can you please talk to her? Open her eyes. She'll listen to you, as she's always done."

"I'll do my best. You've done all you could as her mother and you deserve some help in this."

"With your help, Fr. Grejbel. I needn't repeat it all. That's what I say to whoever asks after my daughter and her son," she confessed, turning round to leave. She stopped and raised her open palms to her face, as if thinking twice about saying more. "I don't think I'd be doing the right thing if I didn't add something else," she hesitated. "My husband Saverju seemed to believe that after his death I would go and fetch the baby. But he wanted to have nothing to do with it. Absolutely nothing. He remained hard and unforgiving till the end but he didn't want me to be stubborn about it like him, forever. I felt that he expected me to do my part, in time. If this wasn't so, he wouldn't have let me know where the baby was being brought up. He just wanted me to keep silent and wait."

"We all waited, do you see? We do well to wait. Hope is our ability to wait. There's no limit to how long we must wait. Sometimes only a short while and sometimes for a very long time. The important thing is not to lose our way in the meantime. Have hope, now as well."

"Are you telling me, in all this time, you've never felt the least bit aggrieved with my husband? You waited without feeling anything?"

Fr. Grejbel merely smiled at her and lowered his head. She went out and he closed the door behind her. As she walked, she went over in her mind how she was going to tell Susanna about it. Her lips moved soundlessly and various expressions chased each other across her face. She had forgotten she was walking in the street.

Chapter 8

As soon as he arrived at the main door of the Curia, left ajar as if on purpose to greet him, Fr. Grejbel found the doorkeeper waiting for him. He removed his hat and held it in his left hand whilst he shook hands. They went inside and a priest appeared at once.

"Please follow me," the Priest of the Corridor informed Fr. Grejbel.

Fr. Grejbel glanced at him briefly but said nothing.

The doorkeeper stayed where he was, as if unwilling to take a step too far, and he returned to stand at the main door, his hands crossed at his back. He had spent most of his life there, close to the world outside but detached from it. It was there that he had asked himself innumerable questions, relating to Heaven and Earth but they had only served to confuse him. And it was there that he persisted in nurturing an innocent child's attitude and he did not want to worry his head too much about things. He often concluded that were he to lose the simplicity of his life, he would lose everything at the last minute. His hair had gone white and his teeth had seen better days. He was wise enough to continue believing that he could save his soul out of the goodness of his heart, more than through the knowledge in his head.

"Too much knowledge can bring confusing thoughts," he used to like repeating to himself as he stood looking upon the world on the threshold of that massive door. "It's better to have one less thought than one more. Better to know a bit less than a bit more. That's where the error of our ways begins...from thinking." He used to talk to himself as if he was a little boy engrossed in playing with his toys, and he did not mind arguing with himself, on his own, even making hand gestures as if some doctor of law was hearing him out. He used to enjoy fancying himself with an admirer listening to him, lost in admiration. But as soon as he saw someone approach, he would quickly change his hand gestures and pretend to go through the motions of wiping his face or rearranging his hair, and he would look in a different direction and keep silent. And then, as soon as the coast was clear, he would embark once more on his fantasy. He had no one with whom he could pass the time of day, but he was blessed with a fertile imagination and he could fill the empty hours he daily spent on his own, keeping watch at the door and greeting visitors, accompanying them inside for a few paces.

He had heard of Fr. Grejbel but had never seen him from up close before. When he found himself face-to-face with him, the doorkeeper stared at him, elated, wishing he had the opportunity to chat for a while. His impression of the priest was of a good and decent man, a country person through and through from the looks of him, and loyal to his cloth. The doorkeeper could not help looking back at him, once, twice, as he walked back to the doorway.

The enormous antique clock dominated the corridor, almost to the exclusion of everything else. The long pendulum moved in an unchanging rhythm, and no other sound interrupted its repetitive strokes. One of the doorkeeper's daily tasks was to open the glass door of its cabinet and wind it up. Another of his duties was to patiently endure its loud, regular strokes.

"I wish you'd become hoarse! And mute! I've patiently borne your presence all these long years! What an annoying clock you are! And those words written in large letters above your face, as if anyone can miss seeing them – *Tem-po-ra mut-an-tur et nos mut-am-ur in il-lis*. Someone had once explained what each word meant, that over time we change. The world is a wheel! That's all there is to it! How can I not have learnt those words by heart after all these years staring at you? You go on ticking away every second and every quarter of an hour sets you off on a long panegyric, as if you still haven't got used to life after all these years! And when the time for striking the hour arrives, oh dearie me, no-one and nothing can stop you, what a to-do you make! And for all the noise you make, you're older than me by far! Those lumbering minute hands you've got have passed over you too, lurching on their way as usual, and that dratted pendulum doesn't know what it wants...tick-tock, tick-tock, always one then the other, tick-tock," the doorkeeper used to address it. "If it was up to me, I'd not wind you up for the day, and wait to see what happens. Ah, but you're no fool, you know the doorkeeper was here and will remain here, willy-nilly, tick-tock just like you, like your pendulum."

Fr. Grejbel immediately realized that today's summons was of a different sort. As he made his way down the long wide corridor he noticed the Bishop waiting for him at the door to his room. He had a slight smile spread all across his face, as if he had been waiting for him for quite some time. But Fr. Grejbel still felt very shy as he walked up to him with his shoes tapping loudly on the floor tiles. He needed those heels to walk properly but they annoyed him. It was not the first time that he asked the village cobbler to try and reduce the sound those heels made...now every tap sounded three times as loud, as if it wanted to pierce the ground and embarrass him.

"I sound like a soldier on my way to the general after a battle!" he said to himself. He tried to walk on tip-toe, as if about to start dancing involuntarily, but he nearly slipped and that embarrassed him even more. He quickly held on to the wall, put his feet down firmly on the ground and resumed walking. The corridor seemed like a street getting ever longer in front of him as he walked along, as if it was teasing him, and making him laugh, too.

That silence was too oppressive for his liking, too solemn, and gave him a level of importance which he felt he did not deserve and which he, in any case, had no wish to assume. He did not like it; it was like a bright hot flame lit in front of his face, to make him feel too hot and turn his face fiery red. He was used to content himself with the dim light in his humble house, and with candles in his small village church. And there were also burning rays of the sun penetrating the large windows. The blazing light threw a white glare in every corner, almost reaching shadowy crannies. And this, more than ever, made Fr. Grejbel feel that light was beautiful when it did not hurt one's eyes.

The Priest of the Corridor accompanied him for some way but as soon as they had nearly reached the Bishop standing at the door to his room, he bid Fr. Grejbel goodbye and stopped on the spot, letting him walk the few steps left on his own.

The Bishop gave Fr. Grejbel a brief smile and shook his hand, gently gesturing him inside without a word.

Fr. Grejbel made a slight bob, an act of reverence, and tried to kiss the Bishop's right hand but the Bishop drew back quickly not giving him time. Fr. Grejbel was startled and nearly tripped over his soutane. The Bishop smiled once more and invited him to sit down. He had prepared a special armchair for the priest, all curves and full of baroque designs. It was one of those magnificent looking armchairs which made it difficult to sit comfortably. The stuffing of its red damask seat was too full and raised in the centre. He began to feel as if he was about to fall or slide down from it. He preferred the flat stool, listing to one side, that his mother had left him, or the village rush-bottomed chairs, flat as well and soft and comfortable like every other simple thing. He sat down, got up again and gazed from beneath his brow, but felt self-conscious once more and sat down again.

The two of them looked at each other for a few moments, and the long time that had elapsed and separated them from each other seemed to be starting again. Remembrance lit up every corner of the room and brought up everything on a small raised stage in front of them. Both of them were at a loss how to begin, but Fr. Grejbel felt certain that it was not up to him to make the first move. He did not wish to give the impression of being arrogant, or hard-hearted, or even offended. And he was adult enough to know the value of keeping silent; it carried less chance of committing mistakes than talking.

"I was told you were treated to a warm welcome by the village folk. A marvellous welcome! I soon got the news that they celebrated a great feast in your honour, just like the one they put on to honour the patron saint of the village," the Bishop spoke to him heartily.

Fr. Grejbel lifted his gaze to the Bishop and smiled blissfully. He nodded his head twice in assent.

"Just like the village feast in honour of the patron saint, I was told. How pleased you must have felt!"

"I don't know how the saint feels during the feast in his honour, your Excellency," Fr. Grejbel told him in jest. "And I don't know how he would feel in my place, either."

"But you can imagine! Are you content now that you're back in our midst once more?" the Bishop inquired in a tone calculated to sound determined but kind.

"Content, yes. I'm content," Fr. Grejbel answered, still waging an inner war with his shyness.

The Bishop made a gesture with his hand, inviting Fr. Grejbel to elaborate and waited in silence.

"You know I've always done my best," Fr. Grejbel managed to say after making a huge effort. "If I failed in something it was because I could only go so far. And I always bowed my head and obeyed, whatever was asked of me. I've been through a very hard time as you know, but I always believed it would pass and happier times would come. That's the way I was brought up and that's the way I still feel. I waited and here I am today. Everything happened as if by itself, one thing after another."

"And happier times have come!"

Fr. Grejbel bowed his head and tried hard not to be heard weeping. He could not help feeling a constriction in his chest and he was mortified, but at the same time he did not want to disown his feelings.

"Come now, Fr. Grejbel, remain steadfast," the Bishop told him encouragingly, going to him and patting his shoulder several times. "The villagers' welcome means that you're still their shepherd; these people still trust you and believe in you, believe that you remained loyal, to God and to everyone else. In the beginning something held them back from coming to that conclusion," he continued and walked a few paces away and then stopped. "Tradition, as you very well know, stands four-square and nobody flies in its face without betraying himself. Flout it? That goes against all reason, both that with which we're born and that which we've learnt and succeeded in shaping over time. We've toiled hard to build it, stone by stone, in fair weather and foul, one storey on top of another, till we saw it rise. Tradition is much bigger than us all. From down here we can't see what's up there, and if we climb right up to the top and look back down, we might feel dizzy...and still not see anything. It's a huge, tall edifice and there are those who live in it and those who stay in front of it, around it. It's a tower with deep foundations that are rooted in centuries upon centuries. Like a carob tree, or an olive tree, centuries and centuries of life. And that's what the village is, this is the notion that takes centuries to shape and become a conviction which no one can contradict. You need an earthquake to change this notion. And if the ground shakes and cleaves apart..."

"Somebody must be buried beneath the rubble," Fr. Grejbel continued in a very small voice, and with his head bowed.

"Somebody must die for the sake of the crowd. It is written. That's how it was from the very beginning, and that's how it must remain. That person is pitiful indeed in that fateful hour, and everything judders and tumbles down on him. But then, afterwards, he is blessed indeed."

"You know I bowed to all this because I saw it as God's will. His will, for me. Set your mind at rest, your Excellency."

"Thank you for telling me this. This stands witness to your kind heart. But as for me, now, here and now, I still need to set my mind completely at rest that even I did well in all that I did. I too have the right to fully understand God's will in my regard."

"You did your duty, your Excellency."

"I did my duty, Fr. Grejbel. But you have no idea how difficult it is to perform your duty well when the supreme law that directs everything is love, and not the law itself! Love is a law unto itself, far above the law itself, but at the same time it must be the law that directs love. This is the paradox we have to live with, that all in all we're nothing but human beings, but human beings with a duty that is far larger than us. Heavier than us! This is a heavy burden on our shoulders and there's nothing natural about it. It's a privilege, and perhaps it's a cross we must bear, as well."

"Duty, your Excellency," Fr. Grejbel spoke in a very low voice, trying to say something. "I'd better keep my mouth shut," he mumbled beneath his breath taking himself to task.

"I'm not happy that in this entire saga there was so much heartache and pain. One sorrow after another, and every woe greater than the one before. Answer me this, help me here, Fr. Grejbel," the Bishop continued speaking earnestly, going back to his seat. "Help me, please..."

"Me help you, your Excellency? Me? Today? I'm only a village priest, nothing more. That's what I was and am still."

"Today you must help me out, Fr. Grejbel. And it must be you, a village priest. Today, now that we can both observe the past clearly in front of our eyes. Help me. It's your duty to help me! I wish, if that were possible, to order you to help me, and if I could, punish you if you were to deny me. Understand what I'm trying to tell you, because this is the great struggle with myself, now, before my God, and before you. And even in front of that woman, Susanna and her baby, who's grown into childhood." The Bishop fell silent and bowed his head, as if he was listening to something only he could hear.

Fr. Grejbel was dumbstruck, bewildered. He did not know what to do with his hands or where to look. With one hand he began playing with his soutane, pleating the cloth covering his knee and letting it go again, smoothing it out with his fingers splayed out. He did this once, twice and then stopped. With his other hand he gripped his hat.

"Could I have washed my hands of the whole affair?" the Bishop burst out in a voice half-way between a wail and a command. It was not clear what frame of mind he was in. "Imagine this story I'm going to tell myself, here, as if I was alone...and I'll say it in front of you not to remind you but so that I myself can understand it better, and so that you'll see it from my side of things...From here, from this armchair, the world is not the same planet. Just go to the main door or peer out into the street from the window or go up on the roof and look around you. You'll see houses on houses, and people, all with a different story to tell, a personal history, and everyone under the same sky. Imagine yourself in my place and I in yours...Look upon the neighbourhood and see how difficult it is to distinguish what you're seeing."

Fr. Grejbel looked at him, plainly ready to listen to all that the Bishop had to say.

"Imagine this. Once upon a time...A little village, in the distance, far away from noise and bustle. A young woman falls pregnant and a priest uses all his resources to help her. Such resources as his limitations could provide. No one knows the baby's father. Time passes. She marries someone else but then they separate and the priest does his best to help, and he does the right thing. He does the right thing...up to the point of making people wrongly suspect him! But he sticks to his chosen path and looks ahead. This is all very well but all is not right, still. And I, a bishop, from within this room, that naturally overlooks onto the street, I, from in here, have a duty to see to it that all is done well and in a proper manner. The voice of the people, is it the voice of God or not? *Vox populi, vox Dei*? Did I have to let time pass and allow all this to happen, for me to learn whether I should follow this precept, or not? Is a law, law or not? *Vox populi est aut non est vox Dei*? Tell me, I pray you, Fr. Grejbel!"

"Me, your Excellency? I tell you? It is you who direct me, not I you. You've studied much more than I have, a simple village priest. I...umm...how far can I possibly drive my thoughts? I barely understood the Latin words you've quoted at me. I've lived with country folk and I'm one of them, a villager from a village at the world's edge. I've christened, married and buried many people, always wearing the same soutane and surplice. I've never stopped concerning myself with these things. Always the same routine, from the cradle to the grave." Fr. Grejbel fell silent as if he felt he had said too much, and he lowered his head once more.

The Bishop waited for him to continue. "Go on, go on, I'd like to hear what you have to say, Fr. Grejbel. Your every word gives me something to think."

"I've seen people come and go, from performing baptism to administering the last rites, and the road has always been one with two doors. White and black clothes, smiles and tears. I've lived between the two. Without pause. But I never thought about the things you're telling me. Or maybe I did without knowing. I'm not one for thinking too deeply about things even though I feel questions welling up inside me. But without wanting to. I've tried to be everything for everybody and to be there for them, your Excellency! Always! I tried to laugh and make others laugh along with me even though in my heart I felt burdened with a sack of sorrows. And I had to cry when I felt happy inside. I can only talk about these things, your Excellency, about a small village of unimportant folk, and not about abstract principles. My mind cannot go beyond my concerns and reach out to there. All I have is a life lived to the full. Like the decades in the Rosary: the Glorious ones and the Sorrowful ones. Of experience, if you'll permit me to say, yes, I had, but of abstract wisdom, no, your Excellency. I can distinguish reality, but I can't pass judgement on it. I see it, try to understand it and straighten it out, if I manage to do that, and if I don't end up just as mixed-up myself..." Fr. Grejbel told the Bishop while gesticulating with his hands as if he was endeavouring to bend something hard. "But to pass judgement about reality, ahh, no, no, I'm not up to that..."

"Yes you are! You are indeed, though you might not think so yourself, Fr. Grejbel! So much so that while you were going about your work you didn't consider the perils involved, you only considered what you needed to do at any cost, even at the cost of being ruined. And your life was in ruins and you became a broken man. But do you know where you were broken, Fr. Grejbel?"

"Where I was broken? Tell me, your Excellency!"

"You were broken on the mount of Golgotha! Up there, alone, and you trudged up under a hail of blows, and with solitude on all sides, and with pain, and the greatest was – the lack of faith in you. A man is made of flesh and blood, and...what else?" he asked the priest. "Tell me, go on. Tell me that word. I want to hear you say it."

Fr. Grejbel was completely dumbstruck and did not answer.

"And faith. Flesh and blood and faith. You had lost people's faith in you, starting with mine, but you remained loyal. And you toiled up, all alone, till you lay down on the cross and only spoke a few words. And none of them was a word too much or full of revenge. None, Fr. Grejbel! I know!" The Bishop came to a halt and then went on. "You remained absolutely silent! Where did you learn such perfect silence?"

Fr. Grejbel stared back at him in amazement, like a boy hearing an incomprehensible story far removed from him. His face betrayed all the signs of one ignorant of the fact that he was the subject of the story.

"From where did you draw all this strength that lies in you?" the Bishop asked wonderingly in a voice that trembled. "What did you do to nurture it so, inside you? Give me some of it, just a bit of it. Don't I have the right to share in the power that lies in you, dear Fr. Grejbel? You don't need to keep it all for yourself...You have too much of it, almost more than need be. It's not there only for you."

"Don't speak to me like that, your Excellency! You're confusing me! All I did was do my duty. It was the most natural thing in the world for me, and very simple. Duty is natural and simple. Even though it may not be easy."

"Is our duty a privilege or a cross to bear?"

"The cross is...a privilege, your Excellency," Fr. Grejbel replied with a quaver in his voice.

The Bishop stared back at him when he gave this reply, and then ventured on, "Was it your duty to go as far as being put on the cross? Couldn't you have stopped mid-way, and then turned back? You'd have done what you could, till the limit was reached. But you didn't do that. You kept toiling up, not taking any notice of how grievous it was. Beyond the limits it becomes heroism. That's what being a Christian means. You are blessed indeed."

Fr. Grejbel could no longer stifle the sobs that rose to his throat, and his weeping became audible.

"What could I do, Fr. Grejbel? What should I have done? How could I have remained silent? But, really and truly, what was expected of me so that I would neither fall into error nor cause anyone pain? Could I have washed my hands of the whole affair, just like that, in front of everybody? Could I have ignored the law? Do law and mercy go together? And what is left of love in the meantime? Up to which point can mercy hold sway, and where does love come into it, when the sword of law is ready to slash through, leaving no doubts behind?" entreated the Bishop, visibly moved. He stopped there for a few moments, overcome with emotion, spreading his right hand wide across the armchair's side with his forefinger pointing to empty space, all the while staring beseechingly at the priest, and then he asked, "Do you know what I needed? The one thing I wished I had? Can you tell me that?"

Fr. Grejbel made a mighty effort to control his sobbing and raised his head slowly to give the Bishop his full attention, each slight movement alive to the expressions fleeing across the Bishop's face.

"Do you know what I needed? A very common thing, Fr. Grejbel, and it's also very rare. A doubt! Even the hint of a doubt! The merest whiff of a doubt!" The Bishop's words exploded in the room as he raised his right hand and pressed the first three fingertips together. His gesture recalled the laying of ashes on people's head during the ceremony celebrated on Ash Wednesday. "That would have saved me and given me all the excuse I needed. I would have stopped all the proceedings right there. But I didn't have any doubts. And time had to pass before I could find the benefit of the doubt, mercy at the core of doubt. And then I needed to find mercy at the core of certainty..."

"Doubts, and certainty," echoed Fr. Grejbel beneath his breath.

"Certainty, Fr. Grejbel, of which you were an example to us all. When I finally became convinced of it, I took immediate steps to have you return. Every moment of delay meant an extra burden on my shoulders. And the feast that was celebrated in your honour was at my instigation. I wanted the villagers themselves to welcome you back in the manner you deserved. And it did happen, they took me upon my word straightaway. The news of your return was disclosed here and it quickly spread. Everyone was of the same mind."

"*Vox populi*, your Excellency..."

"*Vox populi*, indeed, Fr. Grejbel, but when? In which mood? Today it's one sort and the next day it's the complete opposite. Which season falls down from the sky? There are too many seasons. There always is *vox populi* echoing in our ears. Ahh, you have no idea how difficult it is to be in this seat and to have to decide whether it's truly *vox Dei*! Many errors of the past were committed in this way. That's what has happened and that's how it will remain." The Bishop stopped and changed to a gentler tone, "It wasn't just me who wanted your return celebrated as a feast, but, but...now I have a wonderful surprise for you."

"A surprise for me? What could come as a surprise, nowadays for me, your Excellency?" Fr. Grejbel snatched at the edges of his hat with both hands in agitation, and gripped it so hard that he nearly bent it. Unconsciously, he tried to straighten it to its former shape.

"A surprise! I've also decided that you should serve in a much bigger village, a more important one, where there are many more people. In these circumstances I feel it's a promotion that's not only richly deserved but long-awaited. It is a reward, to make amends. Justice obliges me to make it known to all and sundry that you've been rewarded."

Fr. Grejbel was taken aback, raising his head in alarm and wanting to say something. However, he did not succeed in expressing himself.

"Happy now?" the Bishop went on, drawing near. "This way everybody will know how valued and respected you are. It's my duty to make it known. What do you say, Fr. Grejbel?"

"What can I say?" Fr. Grejbel answered, beginning to crumple the hat all anyhow, once again. He stood up and lifted the squashed hat to his chest.

The Bishop looked at the hat with amusement.

"Your Excellency, thank you very much. I want to thank you from the bottom of my heart. This is certainly proof of how much you hold me in respect..."

"Nowadays I hold you in far greater terms than respect. I admire you. And, as I've just told you, I'm deeply sorry for what's past. Regretfully, it all arose out of my duty which I faithfully carried out, but I'll carry the remorse to my grave. But that's beside the point now. Today I want to celebrate with you."

"Thank you, thank you, your Excellency. I'd like to ask you a favour, if I may, please."

"If I can, I'll grant you whatever you wish for, at this moment. If it's something within my power, you can be certain of getting it. I'm in your debt and I wish to start redeeming myself straightaway."

"It is something within your power, your Excellency. If you want to, you can grant me this favour."

"Are you sure?"

Fr. Grejbel nodded assent.

"Well then, go on, tell me. It's no problem."

"Your Excellency, I would like to remain in my village."

"In your village? Where you've always been? On the edge of the world, is that where you want to stay? Even now, now that you've been out in the world? You deserve far more than that."

"Nowhere is better than that village, for me, your Excellency. A simple priest like me is best left there, forever, till the very end. I'll go wherever you want to send me, but if it's at all possible, please..."

"There's nowhere else that suits you better?"

"Now that I'm back, your Excellency, I don't have the least doubt that there can be anywhere better than that village, for me."

"I can't deny anything any longer, Fr. Grejbel. Very well, alright. I grant your wish. You may stay there. Besides, the villagers certainly want you to remain with them. *Vox populi – vox populi!*"

Fr. Grejbel shook his head in modesty, respectfully motioning the Bishop to leave off uttering more words of praise.

The Bishop stopped talking and changed his tone. "There's something else I want to speak to you about. Fr. Anselmu, you knew Fr. Anselmu well...I mean to say, you were very close to Fr. Anselmu."

"Yes, your Excellency, he was my confessor."

"He had sent you a letter. I felt I shouldn't send it on to you. It would have taken a long time to reach you and then you'd have been feeling lonely and far away from your loved ones and it would have made you feel worse. More than that, I wished to keep it by me, to use it, and partly base my decision to ask for your return. I don't want you to run away with the idea that I kept it back out of disrespect. Quite the opposite, in fact."

"I understand, I understand, your Excellency."

"Here's the letter," the Bishop replied, taking it from under a pile of papers on his desk and handing it to him. "Read it, and please do so aloud because I want to hear it too. It's been a long time since I read it."

Fr. Grejbel took the letter from the Bishop's outstretched hand and held it firmly, beginning to read. But after a while something seemed to catch at his throat and he stopped.

"Go on, go on, never fear," the Bishop encouraged him.

Fr. Grejbel went on reading. "I want you to know that there are many people who know you are not guilty and that you did everything with the best of intentions and to honour God above all else. Let me give you my blessing for the last time. And I urge you to remain a good priest, the way you've always been. Fr. Anselmu."

The Bishop remained staring at the priest, waiting for Fr. Grejbel to hand him back the letter. "This will remain in the archives, a document in your favour to serve as witness, both today and in the future. A keepsake of another priest. But it wasn't this letter, Fr. Grejbel, that prompted my doubts and which then made me take the decision to have you return. As you can imagine, there were many people who still respected you, many people, but not enough of them. Numbers count for something, and not every number carries an equal weight. Not even Susanna's entreaties or her mother's. All these moved me somewhat but not enough to set my mind fully at rest and ease my conscience. Doubts, Fr. Grejbel...I needed to have some doubt."

"Then who, your Excellency?"

"Can't you guess?"

Fr. Grejbel stared back at him wide-eyed, shaking his head as if trying to remember all the faces of people he knew, bringing them to mind. "I don't know, I don't know. I can't think of anybody."

"Can't you deduce who was truly convinced of your innocence and more?"

"Your Excellency, I hope that everyone thought so, always, even though circumstances forced them to choose otherwise. Everyone, and always. For me, the truth has always been simple and crystal clear. Maybe I wasn't aware that the world was not as I pictured it in my mind. But even now, I don't want to change my opinion about people, your Excellency. I would like to keep giving them the benefit of..."

"The doubt. The benefit of the doubt. You don't know who it was. Well then, let me tell you because he himself would like me to reveal this. He spoke very highly of you and it wasn't easy for me to continue the discussion with him. I think he left here convinced I was going to recall you after my conversation with him, even though I hadn't specifically said that. Who was it?"

"Who? A very kind soul, for sure! And a special person, for you to have attached such importance to him or her, your Excellency."

"Stiefnu."

Fr. Grejbel stared back at him, nonplussed. "Stiefnu, who?"

"You've never met him? Is that what you're saying?"

"I don't know who he is."

"Susanna never introduced you to him?"

"Susanna only introduced me to her husband, your Excellency."

"Stiefnu is the baby's father."

"Wistin's father? Then the village has truly undergone some changes."

"Yes, Fr. Grejbel, it has changed, and changed for the better. And do you know how? With God's help, as always, but this time with yours as well!"

"Then what I did wasn't in vain. And all that I went through didn't go to waste."

"We don't do anything for nothing, and nothing goes to waste, least of all that which happens on the hill of Golgotha. But you know all this, Fr. Grejbel, very well indeed, and you've lived it and taught us the lesson. This time your sermons weren't addressed only to the village folk. This time a strong wind blew them here, too."

"No, no, your Excellency, don't say that again. Your words bring me gladness but they also alarm me."

"Alarm you? You should be full of renewed courage. What's there to alarm you?"

"Because you make me feel as if I'll be carrying a much bigger responsibility than I can bear."

"You've already borne much, and I should think that from now onwards your burdens will become lighter. After the Crucifixion comes..."

"The Resurrection, your Excellency."

"You can't have one without the other, and in that order, one after the other."

Fr. Grejbel drew closer to the Bishop and slowly made as if to kiss his hand. The Bishop quickly drew back his hand, once more, and accompanied him to the main door which was open on one side. The doorkeeper was at his post and he immediately went to lift the latch and open the other side of the door.

"Wide open, today we'll open the door wide open," the Bishop said to the doorkeeper with a smile.

The doorkeeper was astonished to see that only Fr. Grejbel was leaving. He hadn't opened the door wide open for him. He remained on the side and politely bobbed his head.

The Bishop remained standing on the top step, outside the door.

Fr. Grejbel felt overcome with confusion and embarrassment, and while he slowly put on his hat he nearly tripped over his soutane.

The doorkeeper stole a glance at the Bishop to check whether he could openly show his amusement. The Bishop too had a smiling countenance. The doorkeeper shook his head in admiration and kept silent.

"Dear Lord! There's no getting used to this soutane! It so often threatens to trip me up...of all the places where it had to happen, did it have to do it here and now?" Fr. Grejbel muttered to himself as he went on his way. "It's always the same, even when I'm about to get up on a *karozzin*!"

The doorkeeper waited for the Bishop to walk back inside, gave him a respectful bob as he passed and began to push the door to close it once more.

The Bishop walked straight back to his room, went in and went to stand directly in front of the Crucifix hanging on the wall, and addressed it. "Master, my job isn't easy at all. And it's not always clear. Even when I'm certain about something, I keep getting doubts. I know the rule of law through and through and besides, there isn't just what I feel I have to do but I also must take into account the people out there, the crowd. Where do You stand in all this, Lord, where are You? In which part of the square can I find You? I heard all that there was to be said, weighed it all up and prayed for guidance. Then I had to make a decision. I faced the crowd and asked, 'Is this what you believe? Is this what you want? Choose! Either this man or the other!' But where was Barabbas this time? And who was he? If the accused was actually innocent, and if I accused him and sent him away as a punishment without entertaining the least doubt, adhering to the letter of the law, who was there by my side to point out my error? Didn't I too have the right to be enlightened? Even at that very moment, was I truly alone? Lord, someone has to die for people's sake. I know this only too well. And for someone to die for an entire nation, there must be someone who metes out the punishment. For every victim there must be an aggressor. I didn't know this before. So many years had to pass before I could see all this unfolding in front of my eyes, now, when I thought my life was completely fulfilled, and that I no longer needed anything except confirmation, affirmation of all I'd gone through. Did it have to be me?"

Perfect silence held the room in thrall.

"Lord, have mercy on me," he continued, voicing his thoughts and turmoil. "Don't imagine me more of a man than I can ever be. Don't expect bigger things than I can cope with. My abilities don't extend beyond the law, and the law is the written word, and when it's unwritten, it's the voice of the people. Isn't it? What other way open to me must I enter? I have to admit I don't know. I had to come to this point before realizing that I don't know. Were You always by my side? I believe so. And did You want me to take each step on my own? I think the answer is yes, again. Where were You? You were silent. I haven't always understood Your silence. For what am I to blame?" the Bishop burst out saying with a loud moan. He had fallen to his knees.

A light knock on his door made him break off abruptly.

"Come in, come in," he called out startled, turning towards the door.

"Do you need something, your Excellency?" the Priest of the Corridor asked him, standing in the doorway.

The Bishop did not answer immediately but stared back at him. He got to his feet and went to the door, saying, "Do I need something?"

"Yes, your Excellency. We heard you talking and felt concerned. You were alone in here. We were worried about you, if you must know. That's all," the Priest of the Corridor explained.

A little way off, in the middle of the corridor, stood the doorkeeper with his hands clasped together across his chest, as if he was praying. He was reluctant to draw any nearer.

The Bishop went out into the corridor and told them, "Is there something I need? To understand, my friends. Something we all need. Since we believe, it only remains for us to understand. You heard me talking, did you? Perhaps you thought I was whimpering in pain?"

Both the Priest of the Corridor and the doorkeeper nodded assent.

"Today, I have once again asked the Almighty what His silence signifies. Just look, look! Here we are in the Praetorium," he spoke to them in a kindly voice, holding up his hands palm upwards and wide apart as if delivering a sermon. He walked a few paces away and then stopped and turned to face them, speaking out once more. "A large building signifying power – the Praetorium. A large building, just like this Curia. A Governor, the accused and the crowd. They didn't go in so the Governor had to go outside to address them and he asked them what accusation were they levelling against that man they'd brought before him. They were certain of his blame, had all the facts. 'If this man was innocent, we wouldn't have brought him here before you,' they cried. The Governor was perplexed. Could he entertain any doubts? When more than one idea is bandied about...the mind searches for an answer here and there, until it takes up a position. 'There's no need to question anything!' the mob told him and then reminded him, 'You hold all the power in your hands.' They were of the same mind, all of them. The accused was a man of few words. Sometimes, when he was with people, he wouldn't utter a single word. He remained silent and silence was his only defence. 'Are you guilty of all that they're accusing you?' the

Governor questioned the accused. 'Who has accused me of all this?' the accused man wanted to know. 'Them,' answered the Governor. 'They know you well and they're the ones who brought you here.' The Governor could have no more doubts then. Not even the slightest hint of one. The accused then mentioned the word truth. 'The truth? What is this truth?' the Governor asked him. But the man held his peace. And this is where Barabbas comes in..."

"Barabbas?" exclaimed the Priest of the Corridor and the doorkeeper in unison, looking at the Bishop in amazement, hardly believing what they had just heard.

"Where was Barabbas? If he had also been present it would have been an easy choice, a clear one. Between an innocent man and a ruffian...the Governor's choice would have been easy to make. Or would it? The crowd was there, and it had not the least doubt," the Bishop explained firmly.

"The crowd never has any doubts, your Excellency. The crowd always sticks to one word," the Priest of the Corridor opined.

"And what word is that?"

"A single word, whichever it happens to be on that particular occasion, your Excellency," the Priest of the Corridor elaborated.

"The word can be changed to suit the occasion, you mean to say?" the Bishop asked him as he paced the corridor, stopping in the middle.

"Yes, your Excellency."

"The crowd can shout any word. You mean, whichever word. That's what you're trying to say, isn't it?"

"Yes, your Excellency."

"The crowd doesn't think, then..."

"I'm afraid so, your Excellency."

The Bishop turned to the doorkeeper, who had kept quiet so far, and took a few steps towards him. "And you, speak up, you too, go on, speak up. What do you think? You're right here too, in the square, just imagine yourself in a crowded square, amongst the milling crowds, and you're one of them, just like them, nothing more, nothing less. What do you think, what does your brain tell you?" he asked him, coming closer still and lightly tapping his forehead.

"Me? What do I think? What can I think, your Excellency? I'm part of the crowd, and nothing more," the doorkeeper replied.

"And as part of the crowd, then, what do you think?"

"I don't think anything, your Excellency, I don't think, there's no need for me to think anything, I don't know," the doorkeeper gabbled on in agitation, trembling from head to foot but speaking firmly. "There's someone else with the right and obligation to think for me. My role is different."

"That's a very wise answer," the Bishop complimented the doorkeeper.

The Priest of the Corridor and the doorkeeper stood together, still astonished, looking at the Bishop.

"But doesn't any word come to mind, or a phrase, not even one? Spoken by the crowd?" the Bishop queried the doorkeeper.

"A word, a word or phrase that comes to mind..." he replied thinking hard. "*Hos-an-na*! *Hos-an-na*! *Hos-an-na*! Your Excellency!" he exclaimed.

"*Hosanna*! *Hosanna*!" the Bishop stopped to reflect. "The same word. For how many times?"

"Once, twice...Thrice...I think for as many times as need be, your Excellency." The doorkeeper still spoke decisively.

"And what does this word mean?"

"It means that the crowd is happy and content."

"Are you sure that's what it means?"

"That's what people make of it. Therefore that's what it means, your Excellency."

"If that's the situation, then it's a very lovely word. It would be a good thing if things were always so."

The doorkeeper plucked up his courage and continued, "And then there's another phrase, your Excellency..."

"Another phrase? Do you really think there's another?" the Bishop asked him eagerly, full of admiration. "Isn't the word *hosanna* enough? Isn't the crowd happy and content enough?"

The doorkeeper shrugged, reluctant to speak, almost frightened. "There is another phrase, your Excellency, and I know it – *Crucify him*! *Crucify him*!"

"So the crowd says two things...amongst others," the Bishop agreed.

"*Hosanna*! *Crucify him*! *Hosanna*! *Crucify him*!" the Priest of the Corridor and the doorkeeper repeated in unison, as if they formed a small choir.

"But which one of the two? Which one? It's got to be either one or the other!" the Bishop beseeched them.

"The two of them together! The two of them!" they countered.

"And how do you know all this?"

"We're part of the crowd, your Excellency," they gave him their answer.

After a few moments' silence, the Bishop took up his tale again. "The story continues. As I was saying...The accused man stood silent. 'Don't you know that I have the power to free you or punish you?' the Governor attempted to get him to speak. That silence, how could the Governor interpret his silence? How do you think this tale will end?"

"*Crucify him*! *Crucify him*!" the two of them cried together.

"That's right. You've said it. And that was a mistake, the biggest mistake," the Bishop told them, drawing near, coming between them to rest a hand on their arm and gently lead them along the long high-ceilinged corridor. "It was the biggest mistake in our entire history, when the law was but a dim-lit oil-lamp and illumination was far, far away. But only the dim light of that oil-lamp was available. A feeble oil-lamp," he pondered aloud and then he changed his tone of voice. "And you, what do both of you think about that man? Just imagine if you will. The Governor had him stand on a raised dais in full view of everyone, and as soon as they saw him the crowd shouted as one..."

"*Crucify him*! *Crucify him*!" promptly cried as one the Priest of the Corridor and the doorkeeper.

"You've given me the right answer. Straightaway! Both of you. Could there be any doubt? This is what I'm asking you," the Bishop explained. "I only want to know this from you. The question asked by someone who is alone. He always has to remain alone, otherwise he couldn't be what he was supposed to be. His privilege, his punishment – to be alone, up there."

"Is that all you'd like us to tell you, your Excellency?" the Priest of the Corridor ventured to ask.

"That's all I'd like to know. That's all I need, for the moment. Could there be any doubt?"

"No, there couldn't be," the two of them chorused together.

"And why is that?"

"Because the law was the crowd and the crowd was the law," the Priest of the Corridor stated.

The Bishop looked at the doorkeeper, expecting an answer from him as well. "And you, what do you say? Why?"

"Why? Because there had to be somebody to die for the sake of all," the doorkeeper declared with simplicity and certitude.

"And why did it have to be him?" the Bishop asked him.

"I don't know, your Excellency. Don't ask me any more than that. Maybe I can answer you, to the best of my knowledge, but I can't tell you the reason why. I know the answer but not its explanation." The doorkeeper bowed his head, amazed that he had shown such presence of mind when speaking to the Bishop for the first time. He had never dared open his mouth in front of people before, and he was unable to speak his thoughts without trembling uncontrollably.

"Is that what you think?" the Bishop asked him.

The doorkeeper stared back at him open-mouthed, and then replied, "Yes, that's what I think; I've thought so for a long time but I've never asked myself why, without knowing the reason. Whatever I think I just think from the top of my head, without any internal discussion."

"You don't know why?"

"And I don't even need to know why. I just don't feel the need."

"If you truly feel that, you've touched on the mystery then, my son," the Bishop told him admiringly. "Where did you learn all this? It's exceptional wisdom."

"Me? Where did I get it? From that doorstep, your Excellency. I've spent many years looking and thinking, and speaking to myself. A doorkeeper is one who has to spend his life alone, always waiting."

"Well then, even a doorkeeper can have deep thoughts," the Bishop observed.

"Of course, your Excellency."

"If he's not part of the crowd, then..."

"Yes, your Excellency, only if he's not part of the crowd."

"But your Bishop wasn't part of the crowd..."

"But he was still having to face the crowd, all the same, your Excellency," the doorkeeper soothed him.

The Bishop took his hands off both their shoulders. Then he walked a few paces away, on his own. He turned back to them and told them, "Our day ends here, today. I think we've learnt a lot. We'll meet again tomorrow, God willing."

144

Chapter 9

It was not yet dark but the street was deserted, all the same. The slatted windows latched ajar were the only signs of life, and behind them lived people engrossed in their own little world that was their home. Maybe a face would partially peer out and then withdraw, and a pair of hands would take hold of the two shutters and pull them shut with a loud bang. The lights indoors, though dim, spilled outside through the slats and could still be seen, and indeed seemed quite conspicuous. When, however, the windows and solid shutters were closed, unrelieved gloom took over. Most probably, all the members of the family would be safe and sound at home. Even the cats and dogs would know the day was at an end, and all the running around and chores would gradually wind down and be laid to rest.

Nothing else remained to be done except to partake of a light evening meal followed by the reciting of five decades of the Rosary. More often than not, the Rosary would be led by the mother, word after word, in the sing-song chant of one who knows it by heart, and is proud of being able to remember it entirely, without minding, endlessly saying it over and over again, and without getting confused along the way or in its repetition. Its very repetition was not common to everybody. Even prayers were inherited from one generation to the next, each family endowing it with its own nuances. With each decade, especially in the Sorrowful Mysteries, the recitation became more devout, the tonality would change and a sound would emerge as a laboured breath from some hidden space of the soul. Down there, far away from the neighbours' inquisitive eyes, lay the secret store of the family's joys and tribulations. The sound of the village folk at prayer could be heard in the street too, along with the rattling of the rosary beads. Some mothers had the habit of bunching up the rosary beads when they came to the end of a decade and then opening their palm to let the string of rosary beads fall as soon as they embarked on the next decade. The dear departed were always mentioned by name during the recitation, one after another, especially the grandparents, to have them share in the credit and in this way the living helped them go up to Heaven as quickly as possible. It was them, the dear departed, who had formed the family and protected it over the years. It was the duty of their descendants to think of them and pay their dues towards them. The word of one's ancestors still held sway from the cemetery, a few paces away from the house and streets of the living, even now.

That is the way each generation grew and was brought up, one after the other, for a long time. The street, just like every other part of the village, had never changed the rules and regulations of each day, not even during feast days, eagerly anticipated from a long time before, when the programme is slightly changed. The Rosary brought together the father and mother and their children at the same time, for the same purpose, in the same room. A large holy picture, illuminated by a candle lit before it, was enough to change the room into a church. Sometimes there would be a painting and sometimes a statue in plaster.

A small glass full of lamp-oil would be kept burning in front of the sacred image, like a strong desire rising to the ceiling, splitting the beams apart and piercing the silent sky, high above. Floating on the oil's surface, a tiny piece of cork carried a tin prong, fastened to it on three sides. The wick emerged out of a tiny hole in this prong. This humble light was the heart of each house. Some people placed this light on the windowsill whenever it was known that a priest would be passing by to go and give Holy Communion to a dying person.

At this time of day the large iron keys left in the door locks on the outside would be removed. Housewives would open their door to take the key in and lock the door behind them. Little by little all the windows would be in total darkness and the street would have fallen asleep as usual. The dusk would gradually deepen into night and black would be the sovereign ruler, as if this was a rule not to be broken by anything or anybody. The dim light thrown by the lamp at the street corner was like a ray of comfort, a sentry spending the entire night waiting for dawn, and for the sun to change everything. Darkness and light, black and white, those were the village colours, and they ran around each other nose to tail as if they were a cat and a dog chasing each other round in circles. The village seasons were characterized and recognized in fine detail. Every cloud, every gust of wind, every sprouting, everything had its precise moment. Every exception was a disgrace. Every unbroken rule was a miracle. Life was one entire miracle, and nobody could have reason to doubt this.

Total darkness had not yet fallen, and the windows were still ajar, on the latch, and each window could contribute some light to the length of the street.

Stiefnu scrutinized each and every door and came to the conclusion that the one he was looking for was right before him. It was a small door, commonplace, well-kept and clean, no more no less, the same as the window at the side of the door. It looked to be a tiny house but in spite of its small size, it was large enough to house several people. Many children could have been born there and brought up, safely, in a nest watched over zealously by a pair of eyes, night and day. Windows acted as ears for the nest and mothers remained mothers, even when fathers were the heads of the households. If both of them happened to embark on a struggle to gain the upper hand, they knew quite well that there was a contract between them built on common sense. And such common sense as this was a centuries old heritage, inherited from their ancestors who had been laid to rest forever at the edge of the village, in a patch of ground assigned to them from the very beginning, with a lit candle burning on top of them, with a few flowers and with many prayers recited before them. Every villager's thoughts frequently zigzagged between the cradle and the grave, both of them present in the village, maybe several years distant from each other, with some people counting only on a few while others groaned under their weight. There was no escape, and the church stood four-square there, at the centre of everything, making sure that the newly-arrived would be welcomed in the family and that the newly-departed would be sent off in a befitting manner and laid to rest forever in their appointed place. A greeting on their arrival, a greeting on their departure. The bell tolling the dead reminded all the villagers that one of them had passed away.

In that silence, Stiefnu's footsteps rang out loudly. The least movement at this time of day was untimely and the least noise was an exception to the rule. For Stiefnu, however, this was a time like any other. The day had yet to come to an end. As soon as his footsteps approached the door, the faint light of a candle wavering behind the slatted window beside the door, could be discerned. He noticed it but pretended to be unaware of it.

"She's not here, she isn't here," he spoke softly beneath his breath. The silence discouraged him from knocking on the door. He was afraid of waking everybody up with the least noise. Little by little, other windows seemed to come alive all of a sudden. Faint glimmers of light could be seen behind every window, making no noise, and a dark shadow moved slightly behind all of them...Maybe a lamp or a tiny oil-lamp, maybe a candle, some sort of light moving about...he raised his head and observed that he was surrounded by windows each of which looked like a flickering flame, prudently but with a determination that hung palpably in the air. He bowed his head once more and the lights grew fainter and retreated, quite as if they had agreed on it.

"Where is she if she's not at home?" he said to himself, and he began to walk away.

"She's not at home!" a woman's voice came to him from behind a slatted window still left ajar.

Stiefnu raised his head and looked in the direction from which the voice had come, but saw nothing. He realized that the woman who had spoken was giving him the answer without his having to knock at doors.

"There's no one about, everyone's at home," he thought, "And I'm the only one running around, the last person out abroad at this time, even though it's still early, not yet time to go to bed. But a family's bed time isn't the same as mine. I'm a single man, a free agent, and my mind is the only thing that keeps me back. I can go wherever I want at whatever time I feel like it...But perhaps this isn't the best choice I could have made. Otherwise why would I have come back here, searching for..." he pondered as he retraced his steps. He looked back once, twice, but saw no change in the street. The house was locked up and there was no one at home, he decided. He had come to this street on a few occasions, waiting to see her come out, and he had knocked on her door to see her look out from behind the slatted window, and sometimes she had smiled at him before withdrawing, without closing the shutters. This was enough for him to think she still loved him, or at least, that she still had some warm feelings for him, even if just a very little.

Many years had passed since Stiefnu had met Susanna and together they had gone down to the Valley and made love...and he had been very attracted to her...and had desired her...and she had not refused his advances...and both of them had given in to the passion that united them...and then she had fallen pregnant...and he wanted to have nothing to do with any of it. Her kin had shown her the door but she had found all the help she needed from Fr. Grejbel. But Fr. Grejbel had soon found the whole world had set its face against him till at length he was exiled far away. Her marriage to Arturu and the subsequent separation did not deter Susanna and she remained hopeful of finding her son, and so it came to pass.

A sense of guilt still troubled Stiefnu, as if it was a wind pushing him down and contradicting his decisive character. Ever since he had gone to see the Bishop however, things were becoming clearer. Time had to pass before he could pluck up the courage, but when he set his mind to it no more doubts gnawed at him.

"Did you go to the Bishop to speak to him about Fr. Grejbel?" Susanna had asked him once.

"Of course! How could I not insist with him that Fr. Grejbel was blameless, nay, the opposite of guilty? The Bishop was pleased to grant me an audience and he welcomed me as if he'd known me for a long time, and he didn't reproach me as I expected him to. Indeed he discussed everything at length with me, and he understood what had not been clear to him or the village folk for many a long year," he told her, looking at her with admiration glowing in his eyes.

She was lying on the grass in the middle of a field with her long skirt spread out like a carpet complementing her beauty. With one hand she was doodling imaginary circles and squares over the grass, the short grasses running riot across the entire field, grasses which people called weeds but which she loved. Large stretches of cape sorrel in flower, yellow with tall stalks, abounded. Yellow carpets, innocent ones. Children enjoyed nibbling the grass and sucking the stalks, relishing the bitter sap. Adults, Susanna amongst them, liked to wave this tall-stemmed flower in the air, as if it was a little wand. The cape sorrel was a humble flower and Susanna loved it.

"That's nothing but a weed!" Stiefnu told her to tease her.

"I like it and it's not a weed. If you come and lie down next to it you'll see how sweet and lovely it is, like all the other grasses. When you see something from up close, you can appreciate it properly but you can't do that from a distance. Why are you saying it's a weed?"

"Because people don't think much of it, I suppose."

"That still doesn't make it a weed. Is that what you really think? I never knew you to think in that way. But even our thoughts change with time."

"How well you can speak, Susanna! And I think you've learnt to read meanwhile, haven't you?" Stiefnu marvelled noticing a small book lying near her, cradled in the flowers next to her straw basket full of food at her side.

"Time alone teaches you. Yes, I know how to read."

"What are you reading?" he inquired with some curiosity making to pick it up and riffle through it but losing interest as soon as he picked it up, and letting it fall back.

"A story book!"

"A story book? You mean...one of those that people invent? Made up just like that, out of nothing? Like smoke? Why?"

"I have to tell one every day, every night, and sometimes more than one."

"For the boy?"

"Yes, for my son. Your son, Stiefnu likes stories. You have a son who likes to dream. I don't know if he was born like that or whether it's something he inherited. But, ever since I've known him, that's how he's been. Maybe I encouraged him to begin with but that's how he's remained."

"So, he likes stories, does he?"

"Very much, and he believes them wholeheartedly. And I too have come to love them. Both those I know by heart and the others I invent myself."

"You invent stories yourself?"

"Yes, Stiefnu, I invent stories."

"Just like that, from the top of your head?" Stiefnu asked her in amazement.

Susanna paused to collect her thoughts. "Yes, from the top of my head, perhaps. But, no, no, more likely I think they come from my heart."

"Will you tell me one?" Stiefnu demanded in a teasing drawl, imitating the voice and gestures of a child. "I too, like to hear stories, Susanna."

"Stories are only for children, Stiefnu. They can be a bad influence on adults. And I don't wish that on you, not even now, in spite of everything. That's what I've learnt."

"And I'm not a child then? Wasn't I one, once? Perhaps you think I'm still a child up to this day, huh? Am I one or what?"

Susanna smiled at him from beneath her brow and with bent head continued caressing the grass and drawing imaginary circles over the delicate flower heads, spread out in a wide expanse all around her. She felt happy amidst the vast green space surrounding her.

"Do you think I'm still a boy, even now? Well then, you must tell me a story, there can't be any problem."

"There's just one little problem..."

"A problem?"

"I don't know where to begin. A story isn't just a tale. It's also a journey, and the journey must have a destination. And I don't know what direction a story for you should take, simply for you."

"What direction? Look around you," he replied with an air of self-confidence. "I suppose you can choose the direction the flock of sheep takes, where there's a shepherd in charge and all the sheep walk according to where he wills, wherever he takes them because he loves them. When night draws near he leads them to a place of shelter and leaves them on their own, guarded by dogs who stake their lives for them. The least word that falls from the shepherd's lips is clearly understood by them because it is the usual word he says. They wait for a little while, ready and willing whole-heartedly. Isn't that the right direction, Susanna? Or perhaps that of a flock of birds, flying towards a place they all know how to find and how to return to, the nest. Or the direction clouds take..."

"Do you know in which direction the clouds move then, Stiefnu?" she interrupted him brusquely.

"You're right. I don't know...But even clouds move in some direction."

"I don't know much about clouds, except that I see them up there. They're too high up for me to reach, and they move too fast for me to remember what shapes they form."

"My heart tells me you actually know a lot about clouds, Susanna," he told her with a wry smile.

"Yes, yes I do know a bit. There are humid clouds that sort of smear things and make everything sweat, and then there are wispy soft clouds that form dew on the grass. And then there are rain clouds..."

"That bring rain, I suppose, isn't that right, Susanna? What a lot you know about clouds! Go on, go on," he invited her to continue but with a taunt in his voice. "I like learning!"

"And there are also streaks of clouds on the horizon...beyond, if you look closely at the horizon you'll see them, streaks of clouds," she responded in all seriousness.

"On the horizon. From here you can't see the horizon."

"But it's there, Stiefnu, somewhere behind the hills surrounding the village. You know this well enough."

Stiefnu remained silent.

"And then there are also the clouds of...the clouds of stormy weather."

"Stormy weather?" Stiefnu repeated her words. "You mean..."

"Storm clouds that herald a tempest. That's what, Stiefnu!"

"How brilliantly you've learnt to speak! It really shows you've taken up reading!" he exclaimed, trying to change the charged atmosphere that had built up between them. "Goodness knows how many thick books you've handled and how many pages you've read closely word by word, under the dim light of a room filled right up to the ceiling with volumes, huh? See, I too can think with my mind. Volumes upon volumes, paper upon paper, all shedding wisdom and all ready to enter that open mind waiting for those words of wisdom. Susanna's mind. Susanna ended up searching for wisdom."

"Susanna lived out her life amongst the fields, under the clouds, under all types of clouds, that's all, Stiefnu!" she spoke up with a somewhat scornful tone, keeping her gaze on the grass. "Could I have spent all these years here without getting used to the clouds? Could I have gone by without learning their names? These fields here are open books, too."

"What a long time it's been since we went down to the Valley, huh? Anyway, are you going to tell me a story? There are many I don't know."

"And if I tell you a story you already know, will it matter, Stiefnu?"

"Not at all. Whatever you say; I enjoy hearing you speak..."

"Once upon a time, a long, long time ago," Susanna began, changing her expression to look like a child once more, a child who greets everything with joy, full of enthusiasm for each new idea or some new movement around her. She paused and gazed round all around her, as if wanting to make sure that there was no one nearby.

Stiefnu continued to stare intently at her. He too was sitting down on the grass, sometimes pulling out a handful of grass and flinging it away from him. Without any words, by her look alone, Susanna gave him to understand that she could not see the reason why he had to exert such unnecessary force in this least of actions. She wanted to tell him that even the grass was blameless, and that it was tender. His eyes though, did not change their expression. They looked like two large candles, burning before her, with passion and determination, and she had long realized this.

"Well, there was once a ship..." she went on.

"Oh very well, very well...there was a ship," Stiefnu roughly interjected. And then he went on to unfold a story with an ending that had been envisaged, in a mocking tone, but his voice betrayed he had also been slightly offended.

"And there was a ship that brought children, because as you know...you know, children come by ship..."

Susanna raised her head while her hand still scrabbled among the grass, and she smiled back at him and took up the tale, "and they come by ship, and storms lashed the ship on its journey, and sometimes the ship was about to lose its way and change direction..."

"Because of the clouds," Stiefnu brought her to a halt.

"It's the clouds that count, because clouds bring on the rain," Susanna went on, raising her head to the sky and glancing all around. "Dark black clouds threaten storms, but not all storms bring rain in their wake. The gales sometimes dry everything up and blow everything away, far, far away, no one knows where, and you have to wait years before you can see some vessel entering the harbour again."

"And this vessel, small and tiny, was a rowing boat, and the boatman rowed hard," Stiefnu took up the tale, "and risked everything to bring his boat safely to the quay, because on his boat he held a great treasure. And that precious cargo was a forgotten treasure, kept far away for years without count from where it should have stayed, right from the beginning." Stiefnu kept his gaze fixed on Susanna as he talked, eager for her approval. "And the boatman was ready to drown and be eaten by the huge fish in the harbour, but he kept a steady heart and rowed and rowed, on and on, without fear of the waves, his thoughts turned only to the shore where a beautiful girl waited for him, and he could see her in the distance and he waved to her to reassure her that all would end well in the way she hoped for. And that young woman was called..." Stiefnu stopped talking, a very solemn tone in his voice.

Susanna stared back at him her eyes swimming in tears, her face expressing all she felt as if it was a thick book revealing everything. Her hand still played with the grass stems teeming around her.

"She was called Susanna!" Stiefnu exclaimed, admiration written in large capitals across his face.

She wanted to draw closer to him but she was afraid and held back.

"And that treasure was called..."

"It was called Wistin!" she burst out.

"And the boatman?" he asked her.

"Who could the boatman be? Somebody who risked going under for all our sakes, Stiefnu."

"I know, I know, Susanna. That's why the time had to come for a great feast to be celebrated in his honour. Well then, this story first had a sad ending and then a happy one, Susanna. I don't know what sort of ending you give to the stories you tell our son. With a happy ending or a sad one? Or maybe with no ending at all? But this one finishes like this – with all the characters reunited together, Susanna. Don't you like this ending?"

Susanna lifted her hands to her face, crying her heart out. She scrabbled about in her deep pockets on either side of her skirt and brought up a handkerchief. She wiped her eyes which had gone red but which still held sparks of joy. Her weeping seemed to underscore how happy and proud she felt.

"Don't you like such stories, Susanna? The mother, the son and..."

Susanna continued to sob avoiding his eyes.

"The mother, the son...and the father! Susanna, why not? Isn't that how it should be? After all this time being separated, after all the troubles it brought about, now the time for rejoicing has arrived. Isn't that what we were taught? After the Sorrowful period comes the Glorious one. After the storm, fair weather arrives. You know all the lore about clouds. I was a fool, I didn't know how to shoulder my responsibilities, and many things got in the way, preventing me from doing so. I was in my youth, a time when all my thoughts were frittered away in the Valley with the butterflies and birds. My mind was like a cloud, truly, and everything came too early, began much too early. It was a time for fairytales..."

"Was it really like a fairytale for you?"

"Yes, like a fairytale, Susanna. You know full well. I've never read books like you have..."

"Don't mention books! Both of us were brought up outside in the countryside...Our books were the seasons."

"Oh very well I won't mention books, and anyway they came afterwards, when I'd gone far away."

"It was a time for fairytales, I agree, both for you and for me. But true stories, nonetheless," she responded, as her sobbing lessened. She kept her handkerchief crushed into a ball in one hand and rested her weight on the other, palm downwards on the grassy surface. "True stories because my father didn't move an inch and my mother was helpless before him. She only managed to gather some scraps of strength and courage after he died. And Fr. Grejbel had to face ruin in the process and many years had to pass by. I waited nine months to give birth to Wistin but then had to wait for years on end to see him before my eyes. But there, it's all water under the bridge, now!"

"Well done, Susanna, well done! I'm so very sorry I didn't realize all this before."

"Never mind, at least you can appreciate it now. Better late than never. Forgiveness, Stiefnu, is a great thing and I've learnt it. Fr. Grejbel taught it to me and I saw him forgive others as if he was simply drawing breath and nothing more, without any great effort, even though he had a very heavy cross to bear. The strength in that man's soul is greater by far than himself."

"You're making me so happy with these words Susanna! This means a new time has arrived."

"The time when stories are over and done with. Forgiveness means a new beginning. It's love, that's what Fr. Grejbel taught me and that's what he taught all the others. He always said the same few words, and there was nothing in his heart but love. He couldn't make anything else out of it because that's all he had," Susanna shared her conclusions with Stiefnu, all the time twirling a cape sorrel stem round and round her fingers.

Stiefnu was all attention and openly admiring her.

"How can I not forgive? If I don't, every hurt I've suffered would have been wasted, useless. I haven't been brought up to let things go to waste. We had nothing extra. My father didn't want a single thing thrown away capriciously.

Not a single morsel of bread, the least word or the least thought. Not even on his deathbed did he waste any words on me...he did not open his mouth."

"Susanna, did you forgive your father, too?"

"I forgave him, Stiefnu, him too, a long time ago. And I pray for his soul too. I often visit his grave and light the little lamps. Sometimes I even think there was nothing to forgive because he held to his beliefs. That's what I was taught."

"Have you forgiven everyone then, Susanna?"

"If forgiveness isn't total and complete it won't be forgiveness. It's either complete or nothing."

"Have you forgiven everyone?"

"Is it so amazing?" she turned to him, incredulous. "I've seen all this happen, learnt it from another and did the same."

Stiefnu reiterated his question. "Have you forgiven everyone?"

"Everyone, Stiefnu, set your mind at rest. New times have come round and they must be good times, at least for the sake of that boy."

"Have you forgiven me too?" he asked her very humbly.

"Yes, Stiefnu, I've forgiven you too, a long time ago. Ever since I found my son again and since Fr. Grejbel's return. From that day onwards nothing was left to keep hurting me."

Stiefnu gazed back at her with feeling. He bent his head and his eyes were brimming with tears. He wiped them away by lifting a hand from the grass and passing it to and fro across his face. He lowered his hand to the grass once more and made a tentative gesture towards her with the other, but stopped short of actually touching her. His face plainly showed a desire to kiss her.

Susanna remained where she was, looking back at him with kindness. "I've forgiven you, rest assured. I'd be at odds with everything I have, with Wistin and even with myself if I didn't forgive you. Without forgiveness, my whole world will fall apart, tumble down around my ears. I don't want that."

Stiefnu made to kiss her.

Susanna drew back violently, immediately making her refusal plain.

"And can you understand it was all just youthful folly on my part?"

"I try to understand that, Stiefnu. We were all brought up in this same little world of ours. We're not all that different from each other. We can't be."

His heart was full of courage as never before with these words. He drew closer to her and embraced her, but she was startled. She gave him a slight hug but quickly sought to disengage herself from his arms.

"Susanna! I love you!" he cried passionately.

"Life teaches you how to live life at the very moment of living it!" she replied straightaway, in the tone of voice of someone revealing a great truth, in the sing-song manner of one reciting a hymn by heart. Her mother knew many such hymns and she frequently recited them, even at home, to show off her prodigious memory.

"If you've forgiven me it means you love me. Forgiveness means love. That's what you said to me and it's true."

"Forgiveness also means duty, and the wheel of life can't turn without it. Without it life gets stuck in a rut!"

"Susanna! Wistin is my son. And you are my son's mother! For the first time we can be united together. After all, I'm your son's father."

Susanna threw away the grass stem and smoothed her skirts with both hands. She made as if to get up but remained where she was. She did not want him to get up and follow her.

Stiefnu declared his love for her one more time.

"You're the father of my son. But you're not my husband. You can never be my husband."

Stiefnu remained silent and ducked his head in an effort to control his tears. The naughty young man he had been before now seemed like a very young boy in front of her, disarmed and looking lost. "I love you, Susanna! I promise you, I love you! I made a mistake but I've paid for it now, and I'm ready to make it up to you even more, and to the boy, our son..."

"I love you Stiefnu, the way I did in the Valley, and the way I love you today as the father of my son. But nothing more than that! Today, it's me who must ask for your forgiveness, Stiefnu, even though I'm not letting you down. If you truly love me, don't ever imagine me as your wife! Forget that idea!"

"Never?"

"Marriage can only be entered into once, Stiefnu. Marriage is for life. That's what my mother always said and I say the same thing, now, before God and everybody."

"But if you and Arturu separated, what love could there be between you?"

"Arturu and I are married to each other, before God and the rest of the world. That's how we were and will always remain to the very end. Separated but still married. This time, you must forgive me please, Stiefnu, even though none of it's my fault. I have never let you down but you're asking me something I can never grant you."

"Do you wish you could though, Susanna?"

Susanna paused to collect her thoughts and then replied, "I don't know. I don't think so. I'm not sure what to tell you. If I have that desire in me, it's only one of the many dreams and desires I've learnt to store and hide away in the dark recesses of my heart. I have many wishes stored there so I won't search them out."

"Are you quite decided?"

She avoided his gaze but nodded her head in assent.

At that very moment, at the corner of the field, in the distance, a woman and a boy could be seen approaching. They kept coming nearer and their voices became audible.

Susanna became aware of them immediately. "Stiefnu, go, go away! My mother's coming with Wistin! Please go away at once! Go, go, go! I beg you to go. Don't let my mother see you here."

Stiefnu was startled. "I'm going, Susanna," he replied. "This time round I can't not give way to you. If that's what you want...But, I'd like to meet Wistin, see him from up close and embrace him."

"Yes, yes, of course, but some other time. The day will come. Take my word for it."

"When, when? You don't live where you used to any longer. You've gone back to your mother's house, I suppose?"

"Yes, yes. I'll tell you all about it then. But now please go. If my mother sees you, she'll bombard me with questions...I don't want to lie to her but I don't want to tell her what's what. Even if I keep my mouth shut I won't ever change her mind."

"And I also want to tell you all that's happened to me in all these years. I'm no longer that country bumpkin you knew. My life, now, revolves around the sea," he managed to snatch some words out. "I don't care for village life anymore."

"The sea? You've become a seafarer?" she asked him in amazement. "But, you've got to go now, quickly, quickly..." The sea was beyond the village limits, far away, though not at a great distance, Susanna thought, waiting for him to vanish from there.

Stiefnu rose from his grassy seat, brushed off bits of grass stuck to his clothes and set off. Suddenly, as if he felt the need to hurry all at once, he sprinted and ran away.

"Susanna, I love you!" she seemed to hear him shout in a loud voice that echoed all around the fields. "I love you; I've always loved you, even in my folly. It was a fairytale time, when dreams and reality, wishes and desires were one. It was a wonderful time, wasn't it, Susanna? Down there, at the edge of the village, on the edge of the world, as they used to tell us, down there we had all the happiness we wanted. All the trees gave us shelter, from the cold that nature has in store and from the heat that people produce. Don't you wish we could become young again like that day we first exchanged a kiss? Don't you want me to show you how well I can love you? Why do you want us to grow up and leave behind our youth, with carefree soul flitting here and there like butterflies, as free as clouds journeying across the sky, not tied to one place? Wasn't our village a closed place, tiny and forgotten? Or was it heaven on earth without us realizing it? We lacked nothing, didn't we? Didn't we love each other? Didn't we run after each other and imagine that was the entire world for us, and it was a big enough place? What have we discovered now? The city? Adulthood? Susanna, come back, I'm waiting for you! I'm no longer the Stiefnu of long ago! Susanna, I loved you when I was foolish. I loved you when I was carefree. Imagine how much more I love you now that I've grown up and learnt some wisdom!"

As she saw him growing ever distant and vanishing on the horizon of that wide open space, Susanna kept imagining she could still hear that powerful, decisive voice. She wanted to silence him at once, or at least convince him to lower his voice. But she imagined that the more she tried to silence him, the more he shouted, repeating, "Susanna, Susanna, I want to publicly declare my feelings to everyone everywhere! I am Wistin's father, and I'm Susanna's husband! Wistin is the most charming boy in the whole village and Susanna is the most beautiful woman in all the world! They are mine, only mine, that's how they've always been and forever will remain! End of story!"

Katarina and Wistin were nearly upon her. Both of them started waving to her. The elderly woman held up her skirt slightly off the ground so as not to trip over it or soil it. Wistin was walking quickly, his hand in hers. Both of them were swinging their joined hands, each movement like a swing going backwards and forwards, keeping time to the rhythm of a traditional song. Katarina was singing such a song and it filled the air all around.

Tomorrow I'll come and with me bring
A bowl of water for you to drink.
Tomorrow I'll visit my garden and pick
Some roses for you, the best, I think.

Tomorrow my vine I'll circle and ring
And every bunch away I will pry.
Tomorrow I'll tear my heart from my chest
To give to you. Tomorrow I'll die.

She had learnt those verses from her family as they worked in the fields, and she still remembered them by heart, without ever making a mistake. Her family used to tell her, "We don't know how to write, or think deeply, but we know how to feel, and since we feel our emotions we have to express them somehow. And we have nothing but a few songs for that, songs handed down to us by word of mouth because otherwise they'll be snatched away by the wind. That's all we have in our minds where we store everything. These songs shouldn't be lost and forgotten; otherwise nothing will be left of what we've felt. Our heart is in those songs. The farmhouses, stone huts and rubble walls are a legacy of our hands, and the songs are the sounds our heart made when we wanted something to be heard".

Suddenly, Wistin let go of his grandmother's hand and went towards his mother at a run.

"Look out, he's coming to you!" Katarina shouted.

Wistin was holding the kite above his head, taking pleasure in moving it to and fro to catch the slight breeze wafting by. He felt satisfied with the least movement it made. There was no strong wind to lift it off the ground, as had happened time and time again, and it did not skim the air and soar up high. Wistin kept hoping to see it fly. It was one of those wishes that could not be fulfilled immediately merely by wishing it so, but it was too soon for him to realize these things.

Susanna had realized it because he had frequently asked her to bring him out here in the wide open air to fly his kite, and see the string unwind and reel out, spooling out from the large reel held between his two small hands, for all the world looking like the hands of a ship's captain at the helm. Wistin's kite was still labouring to get off the ground, Susanna thought, yet he went on wishing and that was the reason he still used to ask her to bring him to this wide open place, where the breeze would one day become a strong wind and getting ever stronger it would make the string spool out entirely, all of it, and Wistin would be able to feel the kite pulling from a great height. Everyone needed to wait. The right kind of wind had not yet arrived.

"What are you thinking about, Susanna?" her mother asked, looking at her with some curiosity as soon as she came right up to her. She too flung herself down onto the grass, spreading her skirts carefully about her and then re-iterating her question, "What are you thinking about?"

"Nothing...nothing, Mother."

"We left you waiting for a long time, didn't we? But the market was packed with people and Wistin was determined to stop and look at everything. You know his way. He wants constant affection and attention even out in the streets. I can't buy him everything he fancies, my dear, but I can let him have a look at least. You know, he walked by my side quite like a little gentleman, holding on to that blessed kite and bumping into I don't know how many people with it. But no one minded and they smiled affectionately at him saying, 'Ah, Susanna's boy! How sweet he is! She's got a likely-looking lad there! God bless him and watch over him!' And I took great pleasure from hearing all this. I need to get used to behaving like a grandma, with my daughter's son at my side, what do you say?"

Susanna kept silent.

"What are you thinking? Tell me! Now don't say you're miffed because we took ages to get here! I couldn't help it. And anyway, you yourself wanted to come here early, first thing," Katarina reasoned. "And I don't think you minded waiting in the fresh air. There's no more beautiful place than this wide open space here. Far better than those tiny four rooms we call home. But we fit snugly inside that house, don't worry. You were brought up there as my daughter and now you can bring up your son in the same place. It's better like this, and time will tell and you'll see for yourself that it's best this way."

Susanna remained staring upwards into vacant space, beyond where she lay, at the point where green earth and blue sky met and merged. She seemed to be still hearing Stiefnu telling her..."Susanna, I love you! I love you! Believe it, I truly love you! Everything has changed for the better, even I. I'm no longer that carefree youth with the rogue lock on my forehead. Whenever you want to, and feel ready for it, I'll come for you and take you away with me, and I'll do my best to see that you and Wistin will want for nothing. I'll find work and earn money, and when we've saved up a good sum we'll go abroad. We'll board a ship that'll take us far, far away. We'll take the same ship that brought Wistin here, and we'll ask to be taken back to where he came from, where Wistin used to live before he set foot in the village. Do you like the idea? Tell me and I'll make all the arrangements with the captain. I know how to deal with those in authority. I've already convinced the Bishop to have Fr. Grejbel brought back. And I've already convinced you I'm no longer that wayward youth I used to be. What else is left to be done? What else must I do? Doesn't everybody make mistakes? Don't we all stray occasionally from the path when we're young? Doesn't everyone go down to the Valley someday and then try to climb back up? Susanna, I'm older and wiser now, and I gave you a son."

Susanna kept hearing all this echoing round in her head. She imagined it being said loudly, and that the whole village could hear him, starting with her mother right beside her. She lifted her gaze to her mother and found her staring back at her.

"May I know what it is you're thinking of?" her mother asked her. "Don't forget, a mother's heart portends."

"Wistin, don't go far," Susanna spoke up to fill the gap.

"He's in my sights, don't worry. I'm watching him all the time," her mother reassured her. "But tell me, what's up?"

"Shall we have a bite, Mother? I've brought *ħobż biż-żejt* sandwiches. Everything's in my straw basket," Susanna replied.

"Oh very well, let me get them."

Susanna remained staring into vacant space. She still could hear Stiefnu's voice, this time softly, telling her, "Look here, Susanna, you've always put your trust in Fr. Grejbel, because he's a saintly man, a man of God. Tell him you've got a man who loves you, the father of your son, and the only thing he needs to do is to be with you both from now onwards. He will hear you out as he's always done...Whatever he tells you to do will be the right thing. Go and tell him and do what he says. He'll surely say that Stiefnu is right." Susanna tried to change her thoughts but they remained the same, stuck in her mind.

Wistin was approaching them but Susanna urged him to move away to play some more. "I'll be calling you soon, darling," she told him, her thoughts on her mother.

"Hmm, I suppose you know who came round looking for you?" her mother guessed.

Susanna did not reply.

"What did he tell you? May I know what he had to say for himself? Do I have a right to know, or not?"

Susanna stared back open-mouthed, involuntarily betraying the fact that she knew her mother had seen him beside her.

"Who was that man standing here with you? I saw him when Wistin and I were coming...My eyesight is still pretty good, even to see things far away. Where is your heart leading you, daughter dear?"

"Very well, you saw him. It was him. What else do you want to know, Mother?"

"What did he say, daughter? I'm neither your father, nor anything like him. You know all this very well, and you know to what lengths I went for your sake and for your son. I humbled myself with everyone, forgot all my pride when need be, so that your son would be returned to you. That was the right thing to do! Time heals everything. But whatever was good remains good and whatever was bad remains bad. That's what your father believed, and so do I. And we're right! You'll never grow too old to be my daughter, forever youthful however old you become. And however old I grow, I will always be that same mother I was in the very beginning...the same one. And even when you became a mother yourself, you remained my own daughter, the very same one who had just learnt to walk. I came into this world before you did and will leave it before you, but all that I say to you doesn't hold true only for that particular moment. If it was right then, it still is right now. It holds true for all time."

"Mother, there's no need to be telling me all this. I know it all already, and I believe and feel it with all my heart."

"Bless you, daughter! I give you my blessing till the end!" Katarina exclaimed, her voice full of emotion which suffused her face. "I pray that your faith remains whole, body and soul. You only marry once."

"You only marry once, Mother. That's what you've always taught me and that's what I still believe, never fear. Don't you think that now I've reached this stage, now that I'm all grown up, I can't think straight?"

"You don't just need to think straight, you need to think right, too. I will always remain your mother. Your mother, mind, not your father! I'm not the one to start issuing orders. The one who did so now lies there...there, look...not far away from here...Don't expect any commands from me. All you can expect from me is to feel with you, everything in the same way you yourself feel, because I carried you inside me for nine whole months, daughter, none other than me. Do you think I no longer feel the void you left inside me?"

"Don't children come by ship anymore, Mother?"

"The truth is there for you, daughter, but for your son there's a story. For him, children should still arrive in the village in the way you say..."

"And in the way you liked to tell me," Susanna joined in with an attempt to pass it off lightly.

"Yes, in the way I used to tell you, true enough, because that's what was necessary at the time. Everything in its time and place. When he grows up, well then...then he'll find out life is more than just a lovely story. When you grew up, you found out what I truly felt in reality."

"Of course, of course I know what you felt, Mother. I too felt this way."

"Of course you felt this way, and more! You went through more than other mothers do, and that's why I'm so proud of you, because I wish you to win through completely. It's what you deserve," Katarina declared, looking lovingly at her daughter. "What did that man say to you, daughter?"

"What do you think? That he loves me."

"He loves you?" Katarina protested, her voice betraying her anger.

"What do you wish he'd said? That he hates me?"

"This isn't a laughing matter, daughter. I don't want him to hate you but neither do I wish him to love you in the sense... in the sense two people love each other, umm... you know what I mean, when they come to love each other. To respect you, yes, and esteem you. You're the mother of his son after all, but nothing more than that. Are we agreed on this?"

"Agreed."

"You need to ask yourself, 'Do I love him?' And your answer must be, 'No!'"

"I've already asked myself that question, Mother, and I'm not sure where I stand in all this. My mind tells me one thing but my heart leads me in a different direction. I turn this way and that. If I was a bird I'd flap my wings and take off, but I can only be what I am."

"What are you telling me?"

"I'm telling you exactly what I feel. I can't lie to you."

"I don't want you to lie to me. I've never known you lie to me. But, at the same time I wish you didn't feel this way. Your husband remains your husband, wherever he is," Katarina went on. "See what a good thing it was that you left that house and came to live safely with me? Now Mister Stiefnu may understand that his dearest wish is yesterday's wish. Even wishes grow old and the time comes for them to pass away. He should have loved you before..."

"He should have loved me before, I know. But could he have done that, Mother?"

"No, daughter, you're right. Even if he wanted to, he couldn't have, out in the open or in secret. Even a father's heart has premonitions. I don't really know but I think so. That's what your father once said."

"Everything happened all at once and he just didn't want to know, Mother. It was only in time that he changed his mind completely. Today he is a man."

"If he thinks he's changed, it's only time that can take the credit! You did the right thing in coming to live with me. Now he can realize the story has come to an end. There's no need for him to keep trying to see you."

"He knows that, Mother. But he's still that little boy's father," Susanna replied with a look at Wistin, absorbed in playing with his kite and imagining it was flying. Everything was still calm and at peace. "He'd like to meet Wistin. At least see him from up close."

"Meet Wistin? Where and when?"

Susanna called out to Wistin and got to her feet at the same time, running to him and kissing him, taking the kite out of his hand and telling him, "Shall we try to fly it together, you and I? Who knows? Maybe a breeze will come suddenly and the kite will rise and we'll let out more string, and the higher it rises, the higher we'll go too. What do you say, Wistin?"

"Yes, Mummy, I'd like that. Shall we go then, Mummy? Look, tell you what! I'll hold the kite in my hand and you lift me up, and as soon as the breeze comes we'll jump up and go..."

"And where would you like us to go, Wistin?"

"Let's go to that land where the ship bringing my father home is about to leave. Since he doesn't want to come, we'll go there ourselves, me and you, and we'll meet him and tell him, 'Here we are! We've been waiting a long time for you and now we've finally got here. You didn't know where we lived but we had this kite and we got here, far easier and lighter than coming by ship...' That's what we'll tell him, Mummy," Wistin went on, imagining himself high up in the air, above the clouds, with the village nestling beneath him. "Look there, Mummy, there's Granny's house, and a bit further off the house we used to live in before, me and you. But now we're going far, far away..."

"And now Wistin, hold on tight, 'cause a strong wind is going to blow and we'll go higher up."

"Better and better, Mummy. That way we'll get there sooner."

"But a strong wind can blow us to a different country altogether, by mistake, and we won't arrive at the Port where the ship would be weighing its anchor to leave."

"Then let's send a message to my father. A message for Wistin's father. 'Please tell him to remain at the Port because we're on our way to meet him. And we're coming with goodwill and a sackful of kisses for him. We don't have a lot of money but we lack for nothing, and with the help of our kite we're still able to come to him. Tell him to keep waiting for us!' That's the message we'll send him, Mummy."

"But for how long will he wait for us, Wistin?"

"But Mummy, just think how long we've been waiting for him! I've been waiting for him all this time..."

Susanna and Wistin kept on flying through the air...in their imagination...and strong winds blew them hither and thither.

"It seems as if the wind's changed, Wistin," Susanna said. "We don't seem to be going in the same direction as before. We're going somewhere else. Look, look, it seems we're going back...We've passed this place already. What's happening? How can this be?"

"Did the weather change, Mummy?"

"The weather's changed, son," she affirmed holding him tighter to her.

"Are we near the Port yet, Mummy? We've been flying for so long!"

The strong winds were slowly blowing more gently until at last there was only a light breeze, and then even that was gone and Susanna and Wistin found themselves back in the field. They imagined themselves landing hard on the ground but since they landed on soft grass they were unhurt. They were locked in each other's arms, facing the border of the field where sky met earth. Right in front of their eyes, aligned with their face and wide expanse of ground, there was a tiny flower, and on it lay a ladybird.

Susanna picked a cape sorrel flower and twirled it round her finger.

"Granny! Granny!" Wistin shouted.

Some distance away, Grandmother Katarina was contentedly looking at the two of them. She felt like crying, out of sheer contentment, but she drew in her breath sharply and managed to hold back the tears that threatened to engulf her with an overwhelming emotion. She inclined her head sideways, still smiling at them and said to herself, "Those two are my children, Susanna and Wistin. And as for her father, ohh, her father! My husband, dear Lord, my husband...With you here it's one thing and without you it's something else. In spite of everything, I wish you could be here by my side to bask in such happiness. You deserve to have your share of it, too. What dreams we shared together and what pains we went through to make our humble house more comfortable when she started walking, and when she spoke her first words, and how many stories I invented for her and how many lullabies I sang over her cradle! Where did all those sweet words come from to trip over my tongue? How many dresses I sewed for her and what pleasure it gave me to see her as well turned out as anyone! And how many dolls I made up for her out of rags! You too, Saverju, were immensely proud of her, even though you didn't like to show it openly. If you were here today, you'd feel so proud! If I close my eyes, just a little, I'll see everything clearly, in colour, like a beautiful dream that I wish would last. How passing strange!" she was quite astonished, "if I open my eyes I can see everything right in front of my eyes, but if I close them I can see all that I left behind, in the past!"

Wistin went to his grandmother at a run, and Susanna walked leisurely behind him.

"He'd like to meet his son...I was asking you...And where? And when, Susanna?" her mother asked her once more. "You know what we were talking about," she spoke in such a way that Wistin would not understand.

"Where? Here, of course! This is the best place..."

"And when, daughter?"

"When you're doing your shopping and won't be around. And then when you arrive, the meeting would come to an end."

Katarina looked relieved at these words. She gave a small nod of satisfaction and smiled, as if about to burst into laughter. "It seems like a bit of a farce, all this, as if it's one they put up on the village stage and we're there to see it."

"Isn't that life for you, dear Mother?"

"But this part is serious theatre, my dear daughter."

"Comic theatre is serious too, Mother, even though it makes us laugh. We can laugh because we see it at the theatre, not if we're on the stage ourselves."

"How well you've learnt to talk, my dear daughter! And since you speak so finely, you must have wonderful thoughts running through your head!"

"Don't you know that I still like to read? Now I've got used to enjoying reading books."

"I can just imagine when you began to read books. Dear oh dear, you'd do well to keep on reading, till you join your husband!"

"I still need to read a bit more, Mother. I haven't read enough, yet. Everything in its own good time. Isn't that what you're always telling me?"

"Yes, daughter, everything in its own good time...But there's late fruit and early fruit as well. Time doesn't always seem to move at the same pace. Maybe I don't always see properly. I spent my entire life waiting on things, with my eyes closed. Waiting, without realizing that I'd be waiting for something. Well then, let me wait for this, too. And then all my work would have been completed, and I can pass on to join your father – and I'd go all happy and content!"

"Because up to now you're nearly content."

"Nearly, my dear daughter..." Katarina said to Susanna with a smile on her lips.

Chapter 10

It was time to go shopping as usual. Katarina hurried as much as she could to make her purchases from the market stalls, and with her *ġewlaq* full to the brim, she made off in the direction of the church. That *ġewlaq*, made of straw, old and patched up in parts with rags, somewhat cumbersome as it was, had long become dear to her heart. It was a keepsake from her youth, and it gave the impression of loyalty because time had not set it aside. Her veil often slipped down to her forehead, and she had spent all her life tipping it back up on her head. It did not bother her, but neither did it please her, in the same way many things around her felt to her. In the village women's eyes, hair was considered a vanity rather than a sin, a beautiful thing that attracted attention without causing trouble. She took hold of both ends of the veil and holding them together pinched between two fingers at her throat, she continued on her way with a firm and decisive step.

Suddenly, she jerked to a halt in front of the side door of the church. As soon as she saw Fr. Grejbel coming out, she stepped forward slowly letting him notice her. He greeted her warmly, the way he greeted everyone, and came to a stop with his head inclined, waiting for her to speak up. She lowered her head and was silent, nodding a greeting, so he continued on his way home. She walked down the whole length of the street wondering how to overcome the shyness that overwhelmed her.

There was hardly a soul in the vicinity and her words could not be overheard.

"How am I going to broach this?" she asked herself. "I should greet him first, saying 'Sir, Fr. Grejbel...' and then the Good Lord will help me out and the words I need to say will come. There's no one to order me about and hold me back, now, and I always used to know what to say, and even what to sing, come to that! Am I less than anyone else? And after all, Fr. Grejbel is a saintly man and when I come to a halt I think he'll know how to help me continue..." She did not slacken her pace as she was speaking.

Fr. Grejbel opened his front door and was about to enter when he noticed from the corner of his eye that the woman had nearly arrived at his side; she was only a few paces away. She held the same posture as before, with the fingertips of her right hand holding onto her veil at her throat and with her other hand gripping her *ġewlaq*. Its heavy load was beginning to tell on her now.

That was how Fr. Grejbel pictured all the village women in his mind, and how he always saw them - both near and far. "If I was a painter," he liked to tell himself, "that's how I'd paint the village women. Retiring, their veil slipping across their hair, a shy look on their face, not knowing where to look, and words tripping over their tongue. Ahh, these women, these women...As a priest, they are there for me to admire from afar, as if in a colourful painting, just like those painted all over the ceiling in the village church. But nothing more than that. God created them so that as a priest I can only look upon them from a distance, and sometimes a bit more close to, and I can tell Him, 'Well done, Lord, well done, all the same, even though it's none of my business. They look truly beautiful in the paintings on the church ceiling and in other paintings, but down here they are even more beautiful. Lord, whatever is beautiful remains so. And I want to come closer to You by admiring them without going too close.' That's what I'd say." Fr. Grejbel was always keeping up a conversation with himself, and that is what kept him hale and hearty like the farms and stone huts surrounding the village. The very stones of the village were there to put heart into him because whatever the villagers made, the rocks and stones were part of it. He turned round to look at Katarina in some astonishment, as if he wanted to ask her why she had not spoken to him before.

In that profound world, dark but shot with colours, of the *għonnella* and the *ċulqana*, or the *geżwira* wraparound gown, or any other ordinary dress, a woman carried a whiff of mystery around with her, down the entire length of the street...and this was only made possible because she concealed her charms and one was left to unveil her mysteries all by oneself, in one's imagination. Holding her *qoffa* or *bomblu* on her head, her rush basket or pottery jug, or a sack, a woman could show everybody that she could carry the whole village all by herself if she had a mind to, walking all the while with elegant steps, a natural stride, nothing studied about it.

"Just one word with you, if you please, Fr. Grejbel! I'd like to have a word...may I?"

"Of course you may, of course."

Katarina waited for him to invite her in. "Stiefnu and Susanna have met," she said quietly.

"Sit down, and put down your basket," he calmly invited her, looking unsurprised by her news.

"I seem to be too agitated to speak, maybe I'm feeling too embarrassed...no, not maybe! I really am embarrassed." Her basket was still clutched in her hand, held with its two handles bunched together, both sewn with a covering rag for a more comfortable grip. She put it down on the ground glancing at it. Her money was safe under her skirt, in a fabric pouch tied to her waist. She put her hand inside her slit side pocket to reassure herself that the little money she had and her house key were still there. She scrabbled around for a while because she was wearing two skirts on top of each other.

"There's no need to feel agitated, and you shouldn't feel shy. It's my duty, plain and simple. Go on, and in the meantime I'm going to prepare some coffee," he told her.

"You're just the same as ever...you've remained the same," she answered with admiration. "Going abroad has not changed you; it's even improved you. The entire village is of this opinion. Everyone sings your praises, that you've remained the same as if you've gone through a storm without letting it affect you in the least."

Fr. Grejbel smiled. "The coffee will be ready soon, Katarina," he told her as if to stop her fulsome praise and change the subject.

"Yes, yes I know that the coffee's ready. It doesn't take long to prepare."

164

"Katarina" he began, turning round to face her, "storms come to bring fair weather in their wake, but fine days won't come if we don't withstand the storm. Sorrows remain sorrows, no more no less. They're there to bring some goodness out of them. They're not there for our pleasure. But...but I'm going on doing the little I know, making a good cup of coffee..."

"I was telling you that Stiefnu and Susanna have met. What do you think of that?"

"They met because he's the father of your daughter's son. Why not? How can he not feel a bond with his son?" Fr. Grejbel reasoned, trying to ease her doubts. "That's a far greater bond than us, bestowed on us by nature without our asking. It's a bond that holds through every situation. Nature's laws are fixed and cannot be overruled easily, even if we might like to think the contrary, or think along lines that we ourselves have made up," Fr. Grejbel spoke gently but firmly to her, placing a cup of coffee on the table next to her. "You know all this better than I do."

"Me? Know more than you, Fr. Grejbel? Me?"

"These are things you've been through already, in the nature of things, and God created nature. And nature obliges us to understand it in the light of who created it. Don't get confused over nothing of importance, Katarina, even during stormy times. You know the way because you've walked along a great distance on this path," he reassured her.

"I don't want them to love each other, Fr. Grejbel. He's her son's father but he's not her husband..."

"That's the problem Susanna has to solve, now..."

"Dear Lord, a chain of problems. One link bringing up the other. First Susanna fell pregnant, then the baby disappeared, then Susanna married Arturu, then she bore a child that died, then Susanna and Arturu began quarrelling with each other and ended up separating, and then...then, no, I don't even want to continue. Dear God! How long can this chain be? Can you tell me how many links it has, Fr. Grejbel? Tell me, how many more are left to come...It's too much, too much!"

"There are as many links in it as we have life, and the last link will be the last. And then a new chain will come, one without any links..."

"No more links? All our troubles will disappear? And every happiness will truly bring contentment?" she asked him eagerly.

"Only contentment..." he affirmed.

"I wonder how that place looks, with only contentment there!"

"How would you like it to be? How do you imagine it?" Fr. Grejbel queried.

"How do I imagine it? I imagine it as..." she mused aloud, closing her eyes, "a place full of fragrant flowers, all with different colours and leaves of every shape, that never wither and die like those we cultivate around us. And the sun will never set in that place and there will be neither strong winds nor too much heat. And everybody will be there. And we will never get fed up, or wish for more. It would be like a village that needs nothing more...Flowers on flowers. A village of flowers, a village of friends. And during the feast everyone would be holding a special bunch of flowers; you would have carnations, I would have roses, and I imagine Saverju holding a bunch of narcissus, God forgive him..."

Katarina was eloquent, with tears in her eyes. "He used to love narcissus, because it grows wild and alone in the fields. Saverju was the sort of man who liked to be alone..."

"A village that lacks nothing, where everywhere is tranquil, in repose, beautiful, and good..."

"A perfect village...then," Katarina broke in.

"A perfect village," assented Fr. Grejbel, to agree with her. "And on the doorway the word 'Heaven' will be written."

"But I don't know how to read, Fr. Grejbel!"

"You won't need to know how to read over there, Katarina. And on the doorway there will also be written 'Only Children May Enter'!"

"Only children?" she asked in astonishment, looking alarmed.

"No Adults!" he replied seriously but with a smile splitting his face in two. "Adults will only enter if they manage to become like children once more. 'If you don't become like children...you won't enter here!' Do you remember these words?"

"I remember, I remember. Well then, Heaven is a village holding only children," Katarina exclaimed, pleased with herself for having found the right words to say. "And those children are us, our forebears, and our friends, of yesterday and of today and of tomorrow, relatives and friends. Am I right, Fr. Grejbel?"

"You're right. Isn't that what we've always known and believed, Katarina? Otherwise we'd be a bunch of fools, starting with me. We need to wait. Always wait because we're always convinced of this. We're not waiting around in vain."

"You really haven't changed one bit, Fr. Grejbel. And the village has realized you're still the same, but I've told you this already and I don't want to keep buzzing around you telling you things I've said before. But at the same time, how can I not say it?"

"You were starting to tell me..." Fr. Grejbel headed her off, in a gentle tone of voice.

"I was telling you Stiefnu isn't her husband."

"But he's a father, all the same. And what else?"

"What else? I don't know. I only know her husband is somewhere else. What do you think about all this? That's what I came to find out."

"Today, does Wistin have the right to know who his father is, now that he's growing up? Is it in his best interests to know that? Will he feel hurt when he learns of it?"

"But what do you think, Fr. Grejbel?"

"What use is it to see what I think and what everybody thinks? Only that person who gets hurt can say what he thinks. The only suffering is that borne by the one who goes through it. And the same with happiness, to be fair, since only that person who's happy can feel it. You're happy. And Wistin must certainly be to find himself with his mother, at last."

"And Stiefnu too, is surely content to be seeing his son and the boy's mother. But...but what is the best thing to do, now?"

Fr. Grejbel brought to mind all that had occurred. Even after all these years, every corner of the room, every nuance in a word, everything had remained fresh in his mind's eye, as if it was a pristine painting with its colours crystal clear. He could picture himself in the house where Lady and Arturu lived. Lady was dying and she sent for him to be with her in her final moments to advise her on her conduct. Arturu was in the room and she asked him to leave to be able to confide in Fr. Grejbel privately. She revealed that Arturu was her late husband's son but not her own. She also told the priest that Arturu was unaware of this and she had never said a word about it. She had brought him up out of love for her husband. She wanted Fr. Grejbel to keep her secret and bound him to it, together with the responsibility of looking after Arturu, conceding that time might bring better counsel and Fr. Grejbel might tell Arturu everything. It was up to Fr. Grejbel to decide what would be best.

"Did I lie to myself and to others? Yes, I did," Lady had declared on her dying bed. "But most of all I lied to my husband's son...I'm in two minds whether to be afraid or not. Did I lie to God? No one can lie to Him. But, I'd like to explain it all," she said to Fr. Grejbel, asking for direction.

Fr. Grejbel was in a reverie; it was plain to see even though he was behaving courteously. Katarina felt him to be miles away in his own thoughts. Did he have far more important things than her on his mind that day? Was she wasting his time? She stared at him, waiting for him to speak. He came to all of a sudden, gave a jerk and looked intently at her. Just as when someone would have been talking to himself for a long time and would suddenly realize that someone was in front of him, looking at him and hearing him, and waiting for him to speak, Fr. Grejbel raised his voice a little and told her, "Katarina, everyone resorts to a lie occasionally, to sustain his own truth. Like a walking stick that changes nothing but helps us prop ourselves and prevent us from falling. We may stumble but not fall. It's not a bad lie, just a necessary one, and it may be a virtue and save the situation which otherwise might be utterly ruined by pronouncing the truth."

"Truth itself, Fr. Grejbel? The truth could bring about ruin?" Katarina asked in disbelief, having long known the priest to weigh carefully his every word.

"In this world of ours, in people's hands, everything can be brought to ruin and prove wrong. Our hands don't always fashion clay properly. Truth is important but love is necessary. Truth without love can lead to war, and love, by itself, is already a good thing. On its own, love can be foolish but it's the sort of foolishness that brings none ill. That's why silence is something that keeps truth and love from quarrelling and bringing wholesale destruction. We are here in this life to make do. Pure, absolute clarity lies elsewhere. We must wait. Wait patiently because it's not in vain. Don't you believe this, Katarina? You've brought up a daughter with a strong character! You've done something truly momentous..."

"Me, Fr. Grejbel?" she asked, as if she was praying in front of a statue inside the church, before one of the many niches set aside for private devotions.

"You're Susanna's mother," the priest declared, pointing his forefinger delicately at her. "You were the one to take pains growing a most beautiful flower, with fresh dewdrops always on her petals. You brought up Susanna, a flower in a flowerpot which you fashioned yourself. You and your husband together. Even your husband, in his own way, watered this flower. And the flower is beautiful not because it is real but because it has love in it."

In a flash, the past entered that room.

"Truth or love? Tell me, which one do you choose?" he asked her.

"Love. If it was up to me I'd choose love," she responded firmly, a woman not beset by doubts any longer.

"You told me Susanna and Stiefnu have met. Stiefnu is a good soul; he's grown up and realized that time changes us..."

"I know, I know, time shapes us and nothing gets done unless in its own good time. Just like fruit and trees, I know, I know, and Stiefnu too...They've met because he wanted to see Wistin. They met in the fields, where Susanna takes the boy to fly his kite. That's where we take him, but sometimes there's not enough wind to make the kite rise above the grass that covers the whole place. But they enjoy themselves there, and spend many happy hours. She tells him stories occasionally and plays with him at other times. I go in search of them there, after doing my shopping. On the day Susanna and Stiefnu were going to meet, I didn't go. I didn't go on purpose, so that they could be alone together, a united family – she and him and the boy. Then I was supposed to go later so that Susanna could set her mind at rest that Stiefnu would leave. Because he always leaves as soon as he sees me coming, in the distance...I went to that field, but nobody was there. I was startled and continued on across the grass till I came to the spot where Susanna liked to spread a tablecloth and place food from her basket on it. And then, as I was walking, I came across a broken kite, torn and discarded. I recognized it at once and said to myself, 'This is Wistin's kite. What can have happened?' I walked on but found nothing else except that kite...I picked it up and took it away with me, as if I was still a child."

Fr. Grejbel was all attention.

"I was confused and left the fields. I kept asking myself where could they have got to. They weren't at home...no one was at home...and they weren't at church, either. The village isn't that big a place. Where could Susanna have gone, after all, with her son at her side? I stopped to think and the Good Lord enlightened me. I suddenly thought of looking in the cemetery and that's where I found them, the three of them. And do you know where they were, actually? In front of my husband's grave! And so I thought to myself, 'Susanna took both of them to see where my husband lay. He's the boy's grandfather, after all.' Whether he wants to or no, my husband, my poor husband, God forgive him, will always remain the grandfather of his daughter's son. Even down there where he lies, he's a grandfather, all the same. What a world we live in, to be sure! A grandfather even after his death, forever and ever."

"Everything is forever."

"Everything, even me, a grandmother, forever. We should have understood this clearly at the beginning, after all, Fr. Grejbel. But, but it wasn't my fault... Let me go on. I saw them from some distance away. I was near the iron gates of the cemetery. As soon as they realized I was there they looked at me and I plucked up courage to go to them. I was feeling a bit scared, though not too much. I don't know. It's as if God was with me at that moment, too. I walked forward and said to myself, 'Finally, I'm seeing my daughter's family united together.' There they were, the three of them. Never, but never had I seen all three of them together. I looked upon them, mother, father, and son, there, and wished to embrace them and show them how happy I was, finally. And down below, silent, without a word, without a single command, lying straight in his place, was my husband, who did not change his mind till the very end. But I still went ahead and did what I had to do, as you know. And I found Susanna's son, because my husband knew that somehow or other I would manage to unravel that tangled ball of wool. At the end of the day, it was he himself who left the dangling end of it in my hands. He let me know who was the child and where he could be found. 'As long as,' he told me once, 'as long as time passes. Not just yet! For now it must be kept secret!' He had terrified me with those words, but you have no idea how happy I felt and how much I cried with joy! I went into the other room and prayed to Our Lady. 'Blessed indeed are you, Mary our Mother; you've touched his heart.' And I looked for the boy. And I found him...Saverju had left the door ajar, for me to find, and I could go through when the time came." She looked at Fr. Grejbel as if seeking his approval.

"Go on, go on," he encouraged her.

Katarina remained silent, as if she was seeing it all happen right before her eyes. It was as if she was painting the scene in skilful villager fashion that remembers all the little details and can read hearts, and with a woman's skill, one who has always felt things keenly and expressed herself, though never finding the need to learn how to write. Fr. Grejbel did not interrupt or distract her, supposing she did not feel like recounting any details. And he waited for her to finish the narrative taking place inside her...

~ 0~

Katarina's head was bowed down as she was thinking...

"Granny! Granny!" Wistin shouted as soon as he noticed her at the cemetery gates. "The kite! The kite! That's my kite! We left it behind 'cause it tore, Granny!"

She remained where she was and made a sign with her finger in front of her mouth, warning him not to make a noise in the cemetery. They were used to keeping silent there, just as they did in church. Susanna helped him make the Sign of the Cross, moving his hand with her own, covering his, first moving it to his forehead, then down to his chest, and then to his left shoulder...and then he removed her hand and wanted to continue on his own.

Wistin held a bunch of flowers in his other hand.

"Now then, Wistin, put the flowers on the grave, and greet your grandfather, and tell him, 'I love you,' go on, say that," Susanna coaxed him.

"I-love-you," the boy repeated dutifully.

The three of them started walking back to the iron gates, Wistin between the adults, with one hand holding his mother's hand and with the other holding his father's.

Katarina smiled at them from where she stood. Stiefnu gave her a small nod in greeting, bid goodbye to Susanna and Wistin and left.

"How did it turn out?" the old woman asked Susanna.

"He was very happy, Mother. Content that we met, the three of us together. He told me he's no longer that country lad, the way we used to be and how I remembered him when I came to know him at first. His livelihood nowadays depends on the sea. He's become a seafarer, he told me. Instead of knowing every inch of our fields, he now knows the Port and its surroundings. That's all, Mother."

"A seafarer? Earning his livelihood at the quayside?" her mother frowned worriedly. "We don't know the sea, dear daughter. We're people of the earth, earning our livelihood from the soil. Our water comes down from the sky, when the skies open their doors up above and the water falls down to the very depths. They call water the sea and we call it rain. Do you understand me?"

"There's no land without the sea, Mother, and no sea without the land," Susanna spoke up, her voice betraying a hint of annoyance. "I told you the whole story and now enough of it. End of story!"

"And did he mention Fr. Grejbel? What did he have to say about him? Has he spoken to him since his return?" Katarina wanted to know.

"Yes, of course he's spoken to him, and he's told him everything there is to know. I should think it was up to Fr. Grejbel, once more, to say words of comfort for the good of all, and to say them in such a way to move you. Stiefnu understands how the situation stands. They spoke together for a long time and I never imagined in the least that everything would simply fall into place, so very easily."

"Simple? Easy? What do you mean?" Katarina asked Susanna, perplexed, at the same time checking to see that Wistin was far away enough not to overhear them, absorbed in his play with the kite, trying to mend it and not giving up. "Blessed is the world of children!" she exclaimed. "That's the really simple world! In an adult world, what is simple...if adults don't become children again?"

"Yes, simple, Mother, very simple!" Susanna insisted. "Stiefnu understands that I'm a married woman now, and that wherever I end up because of all that's happened, I still remain so. Stiefnu is still free of such ties, as I've always known him, and I don't think he'll enter into such a commitment in a hurry. He's learnt a lot from life now, but he was always a free bird and that's how he's stayed and how he wants to stay. His wings don't need to rest because they don't get tired. I know that he loves me..."

"He loves you?" Katarina gasped.

"He loves me, yes, Mother, and I love him too, but set your mind at rest..."

"Set my mind at rest?"

"We've all grown a lot, Mother, and most of all in the sentiments we hold dear."

"Don't speak to me that way, with difficult words, my dear! I know you like to read books..."

"It's very simple, Mother. See how you've already understood me without knowing it. We're no longer children, running after butterflies and clambering about tall trees and branches. That's all! He's going on his way and I'm going to keep on walking down my own path. See, isn't it simple, Mother?"

"Simple indeed, daughter. If that's so, it's all very simple and if I've understood it, everyone can. My mind isn't what it was but the things I need to remember, I remember well. Fr. Grejbel will be so pleased when he hears! At least, all that he went through because of us won't have happened in vain. I can hardly believe matters have panned out so well, my dear!"

"Are you happy and content now, Mother?"

"Yes, happy dear daughter, and nearly content!" beamed her mother, snatching another look at Wistin to reassure herself that he could not possibly overhear their conversation from where he was.

~ 0~

Fr. Grejbel was still listening to her with full attention.

Katarina told him, "That's the whole story, Fr. Grejbel..." She paused and drew breath, and slumped back against the back of the chair. Her eyes turned to her shopping basket.

In the meantime, Fr. Grejbel had been pacing the floor, back and forth across the room, all the while looking at her beneath his brow to show her he was still very interested in what she was telling him and he was not in any hurry for her to finish. She could take as long as she wanted to recount the whole story.

"I told her I was content...nearly content!" she told him, crossing her arms and raising her face to look at him. "She understood what I was telling her. She knows what I wish for, and she's known it from the start. But at the same time I don't want to burden her with my own hopes and dreams. She's borne enough already...if not too much."

"That's very true, Katarina."

"Well then, what do you think, Fr. Grejbel?" she asked again, longing to hear him say she was in the right of it. "I'll abide by whatever you say."

"You can imagine what I think. I agree with what you're saying. If you impose your wishes it will not count, and it will neither last nor make it binding. Nothing is of value unless it comes from the heart."

Katarina would have liked to ask him what had been said between him and Stiefnu. She had already formed the question in her mind, but she bit her lower lip and stayed the words. She knew he could not betray a confidence and that he would be imprudent if he even opened his mouth. The question 'Truth or love?' kept going round and round in her mind. She remembered he had already answered her by asking another question and she thought she should not tempt him to be imprudent.

The brief silence that followed was enough for him to realize that she was waiting for one last word of encouragement from him.

"Time itself shows us what we should do. Every season has its own features and they're all different. We live in the midst of fields and we can observe nature from up close and learn from it all the time. Nature's lessons are the best. The best thing to do is to wait," the priest said to her.

Katarina took her leave and went out. She remembered his every word clearly. A few days later it was her turn to tell Wistin a story.

It was evening and the three of them had finished their supper and were ready for bed. Katarina closed the slatted shutters and windows and checked that the front door was locked.

"Granny, you tell me a story tonight. Tell me a story about Grandpa..."

"A story about Grandpa, dearest? What story about him could I tell you, Wistin?"

Susanna could hear everything from the next room. "I told you, Mother! One fine day it's going to be your turn to say stories! Go on, Mother, imagine it's me you're telling the story to, back in time, somewhere in this same house, and that I'm listening to you all agog! Once upon a time..." Susanna teased her mother. "Go on, Mother, go back in time, use your head, and you'll see..."

"About Grandpa, about Grandpa!" Wistin kept insisting.

Katarina was lost in thought.

"Once upon a time...look, Mother, you can begin like that...Once upon a time there was an old man, and this old man..." Susanna began inventing a tale.

"Oh very well, very well, let me start, look...umm..." Katarina broke in, closing her eyes in an effort to concentrate. She opened her eyes, looked for a long moment into space and began, "And this old man..."

"Lived in the middle of the fields, Granny..." Wistin interjected.

"Well done, Wistin, well done! He lived surrounded by fields, and he had a beautiful horse," Katarina went on.

"And one day the horse told him...told this old man," Susanna interrupted this time.

"Hey, as if horses can talk!" Wistin exclaimed with a teasing tone in his voice but one full of doubts, too.

"A long time ago, of course they did. Don't forget Wistin, this story happened at the very beginning, when everything was very different from what it is today. Birds nested on the bottom of the sea, and fish could fly through the air, and people were always dreaming, thinking of nothing, always dreaming and imagining things. They didn't even sleep so that they could stay dreaming."

"How can that be, Granny?"

"At that time, yes, it was possible. They never felt sleepy."

"What a wonderful time that was, then, Granny!"

"Yes it was wonderful, dearest, because everything could be done simply by dreaming it. For example, this old man once dreamt that his horse could take him somewhere far away, far from the village. And he told his horse, 'Look, tonight we'll have an early night and then we'll wake up early and go somewhere.' And the horse understood and went to sleep and very early in the morning he got up and called his master...and he told him, 'Master, don't forget it's time! You need to get up too so we can leave...' That's what the horse said to his master."

"Is this all true, Granny? I don't think it could be true, but what a lovely story it is! I wish it was real. It's more beautiful than real ones. In the stables next door there are two horses that always look at us when we're passing by and maybe they'll talk if you talk to them. 'You need to get up too' he told him. Go on, Granny, go on..."

"And the old man climbed onto his horse and they set off and left the village. The horse told him, 'Look Master, I'm going to show you the world and you'll see what a very big place it is. And you'll see that the rest of the world is different from the village, even though the village is a lovely place. You're going to see that there are many people living on this earth...' That's what the horse told him," Katarina said. She was in full swing, remembering what Fr. Grejbel had recently described to her when he had come back from his travels and had recounted all that had happened to him.

"The world outside is like a dream world to us, Katarina," the priest had said to her. "It's like a village and at the same time, it isn't."

Katarina paused, uncertain how to go on.

Susanna realized and tried to help. She took up the tale, "And the horse told the old man it was time to return to the village..."

Katarina took it from there. "Let's go back to the village..."

"And they came back to the village? Did they find their way back?" Wistin wanted to know.

"Of course, dear heart," Katarina smiled at him.

"And they didn't bring anyone back with them?"

"No, no one, dearest," Susanna answered him.

Katarina hurriedly continued the story, "And the two of them went through the pathways and past the trees, sometimes stopping to rest or to talk between themselves until at last they arrived..."

There was complete silence in the room.

"I think he's fallen asleep," Susanna whispered softly to her mother, approaching him very slowly.

"May Jesus keep him safe and give him sweet dreams!" Katarina prayed.

The two of them left the room silently, walking on the tips of their toes. They sat down at the table and looked contentedly at each other.

"Mother, you have no idea how happy and content I am to be together again. Something inside me tells me that even my father, from where he lies, shares in our happiness. Maybe he's changed his mind, now; maybe he's given up his position and doesn't hold it against me anymore. Once I was told that people change their minds when they go to Heaven. They don't think in the same way as they did when they lived in this world," Susanna said hopefully.

"Change their mind for the better, that's what you're saying, isn't it?"

"If they're in Heaven, Mother, doesn't it have to be for the better?"

"Your father hadn't taken against you, daughter. Your father loved you very much."

"I know, I know that he loved me."

"He loved you in the way he knew how... sternly... curtly... not giving way by an inch."

"I know, I know. I've heard all this before, even though I couldn't believe it, let alone understand it, at first."

"You were lucky, daughter. In your life you had a lamp shining brightly on you, illuminating your steps, and you didn't lose your way. You know to whom I'm referring. God lights our way during the day and when it gets dark He lights His lamps. There's never complete darkness that way and our paths are not closed off. Just like the lamplighter who comes to light the lamps in the street and leaves the light shining behind him. The wind can blow them out, but the seasons aren't the same."

"I know, I know, and that's why I'm happy and content."

"And I'm happy too, and nearly content."

"Tomorrow, Mother, I'd like you to show Wistin all that my father left him when he died."

"Yes, the time has come for that as well, Susanna."

The next day they did not go to the fields and the two of them woke up with the happy thought of opening all the drawers, and looking for all the things Saverju had left on purpose, for his grandson, Wistin. Katarina, in the manner of her folk, had wanted time to pass and more than that, she had felt no desire to be rummaging about in drawers before Susanna and Wistin had met and were living together.

"Where shall I start?" Katarina spoke with a hint of pride in her voice, not expecting an answer from Susanna. She wanted to arouse her daughter's curiosity now that this experience would be taking her back in time. "I have to start remembering everything again. Anyway, recall all that I cannot begin to forget. How can I possibly forget my husband's death and all that we lived through and succeeded in, together? Ahh, time...But there, it's not fair to make you sad. We've agreed that from now onwards we won't cry anymore. What foolishness!" she stopped there and continuing to search the drawers she exclaimed, "It's not foolishness really, just a fond wish. A lovely wish but foolish too! There, do you see, daughter, I'm learning to reason things out, too! It's never too late but I could have begun earlier. Don't you sympathize? They used to tell us that a woman is just a woman, and nothing more. A woman can cope without numbers and letters. She shouldn't bother her head with complicated things. There's always someone else who can tot up numbers and read papers for her. She has other work to do, and it's all work she has to do by hand. And in the meantime she must love, weave and wait."

"I don't just sympathize but I'm truly impressed with the way you think and talk!" Susanna spoke jestingly to her mother. "Go on, Mother, go on." And she applauded her lightly.

"It's as if I've become another woman ever since...no, no, I'd better not say any more, God forgive him. It's as if I've grown a pair of wings...a very small pair mind you...they don't belong to some eagle...but then, when have I ever seen an eagle in the village?"

"On the painted ceiling of the church there is an eagle, Mother, actually there are two, one on one side and the other on the other side. On a par with each other. One lone eagle wouldn't have anyone to talk to, or to quarrel with."

"Do you look up at the ceiling when you're in church, then, daughter? And out of so many figures, were the eagles the ones to catch your eye? There are so many angels! I've never seen these eagles you speak of. I've always gazed straight ahead."

"That's why you've never seen anything else but people, but they're there, and they've been there for a long time, looking at you from a great height. One day, Mother, you must look at them, too..."

"As if! I'll end up having nightmares because of them!"

"They're not real, Mother!"

"But I know real eagles exist...far away from here, they say, but they must be somewhere," Katarina went on, all the while searching through the drawers and seeing what to bring out and place on the table. "Eagles, dear heart! What do eagles have anything to do with us?" She scolded herself. "They used to tell us that women's tears were like fair weather in winter. Which means they weren't real."

"Then they weren't like the eagles, Mother," Susanna teased her.

"And they used to say that a woman's stomach was large enough to hold a loaf of bread but she couldn't keep a single word. Or listen to this, they used to say that one deranged man could win over seven sane women together! One saying capping another, daughter!"

"And where did you hear all this, Mother?"

"From my own mother, where else? That's for sure! I heard them! How I heard them...I heard them with my ears and I cried them with my heart in this house. You never even knew. You used to be absorbed doing other things, and I would look at you, from a distance, silently, and say to myself, 'If Susanna only knew what grief is festering inside me...' And I never wanted you to know, and today I know for sure, more than ever before, that I did the right thing."

"Yes, you did the right thing, Mother."

"My goodness me, how much I'm boasting today! When did I ever boast? I've never boasted and neither has anyone ever praised me."

Susanna was saddened and thought to change the subject. "Do you know what I hear them saying, Mother? However old a beautiful woman becomes, she's always good enough to adorn a window. Do you like that? And do you know who this beautiful woman is? Guess!"

Katarina dropped all the things she was holding and hugged Susanna. "Me, a beautiful woman? Maybe I was beautiful, once upon a time, and when I was, I wasn't happy. Now that I'm no longer beautiful, I'm discovering what contentment means, perhaps. With your help...But even with your father's help, God forgive him. What's happened is all water under the bridge, now."

They began uncovering the *pasturi*, clay figurines that peopled the traditional Christmas cribs, hand-made, colourfully painted. They were poking out of layers of straw, faces, heads and finally the entire figurines. Susanna was full of glee even hearing the rustling of the straw and she could smell its special smell as well. There was the shepherd and one of his sheep, and then another and another, a whole flock of sheep; the baker with his wooden paddle holding a loaf; the farmer; the cow; the donkey; the camel; the three kings, one holding incense, the other gold and the third one myrrh; and there was the man who was greeting the scene; the water seller; the servant; the sleeper; the climber. All the figurines were dressed in country fashion. There were some men wearing a waistcoat and sash around their waist. Other rustic figures were wearing berets or caps on their head, while other personages held a knapsack or were wrapped up in a hooded cloak. The female figurines had their form hidden under long skirts or a long loose gown and their hair covered up under a *għonnella*, whilst younger women wore long headscarves. All of them had their head covered, as if they were in church. St. Joseph looked like an old kind man, with his head inclined to one side, kneeling in worship, and holding a long staff in his hand, almost too big for him. Our Lady was fashioned as a young woman, with a serious and serene gaze. She too was kneeling, her hands clasped in prayer. Baby Jesus was smiling and his arms were open wide, with his legs slightly upraised to rest comfortably on the straw. The manger was made out of sticks tied together with dry grass twine.

"These were your father's pride and joy. Look what beautiful colours they have! They're all made out of clay. He used to enjoy telling me how they were made. As winter approached and the first rains came, the craftsmen who made them would go into the fields to gather clods of clay. They would dampen the wet clumps and leave them for as long as was necessary. Then they would knead them well with their bare hands. The moulds would be crammed with clay and then the figurine would emerge to be given colour. And every *pastur* would be finished the way you see here. It wasn't just you that your father didn't allow to touch them. He didn't even like anyone to look at them, daughter...Not even me. Everything was ours, but at a distance. They were his. But, perhaps not because of that. He took great care of them and was worried that they might break. Whatever is made out of clay, daughter...just like us...we're made of clay as well...can break."

"I used to see them only briefly, when they were set up in the crib."

"And there's one of them there which was his favourite. Can you guess which one it was? Have a guess!"

Susanna looked them over one by one, picked some of them up and observed them closely, smiled but held her tongue. "The climber?"

"No, it wasn't the climber."

"One of the three kings, then?"

"Neither," Katarina answered with a note of pride in her voice. "The one that stares and gapes; that one fascinated him. It's the figurine of a man holding out his arms out wide, his mouth open wide too, in wonder, his gaze turned upwards, with staring eyes. Your father liked to move it about from place to place in the crib, sometimes making it stare at one place and sometimes at another. And so this awestruck man ended up being amazed at the entire crib. Sometimes, Saverju turned it around to make it look at him. The two of them gaping at each other. I never interfered. Your father could stare and gape at anything he liked, I didn't care. After all, it was only at a figurine. That figurine was someone special in your father's eyes. Your father was awestruck with the figurine and I was awestruck with your father, without letting him notice it."

"Why, Mother?" Susanna asked worriedly.

Katarina drew breath sharply. "Are you asking me? Your father remained awestruck till the very end, daughter, because every different thing he came across was a surprise to him. He could never get used to anything, not even the breath he took. The least deviation that changed the day slightly was like a bolt from the blue for him. He wanted life to be always one thing, the same thing. That's why he raised his voice over trifles."

Susanna picked up the figurine and removed it from the rest. "I'll wrap it up on its own," she informed her mother.

"When he no longer felt astonished, I knew that he'd realized his days had come to an end. He lost all interest in things, not giving up but to reassure himself that his work was done. And with his final breath he reminded me that these figurines were to be given to your son. His exact words were, 'Give them to the boy, not just yet but when the time comes, and tell him that they belonged to my father who had them from his father, I think, an inheritance passed on from father to son. And tell the boy that now they belong to him. Tell him to look after them well, as I did. They can break easily, they're nothing but clay. Everything made out of clay. They're not dear but they're old, and since they're old they're worth a bob or two,' that's what he told me."

"Really, Mother? Is that what he said?"

"Yes, Susanna, really."

"And you've never breathed a word to me about it! And then they say a woman can't keep a secret."

"The time hadn't yet come. I didn't always know when I had to speak up or when to keep silent. Old sins cast long shadows and I seem to do the same, being a woman."

"I'm a woman too, Mother."

Katarina levelled a brooding glance at her daughter from beneath her brows, shook her head and did not answer. "The day had to come when I needed to show you that your father loved you till the end, but in the way he knew. Each one of us loves others in our own way."

"Can you imagine Wistin's delight as soon as he wakes up and finds these spread out in front of his eyes?" Susanna cried in excited anticipation. "Let's not wake him up just yet so we'll give him a surprise, just like the figurine who stares and gapes..."

"Let's open the other drawers too. All that they hold are for you and Wistin. They're not some precious treasure but they're for both of you, from us with all our heart."

Susanna waited to be given permission to open the drawers. She felt convinced that whatever was left of the bond between her mother and father lay inside them, and she did not want to come between them in any way. The special drawers, large and heavy, reeking of mothballs and soap, were not there to be opened capriciously. They were beautiful drawers precisely because they were always closed, arousing curiosity. She too had lived in the shadow of the man who had ruled the household keeping a tight rein on everything and she had grown up wary of making any move, even in the same rooms where she was born and bred.

"These are all his clothes," Katarina began. "Look, this is a large shirt made of carded cotton. And this is the cloak made of lambswool. He always wore it in winter, and when an acquaintance or friend of his died, he used to wear it inside-out as a sign of mourning. And this is a waistcoat with silver buttons. He only wore it during the village feast, and maybe on the occasional Sunday for mass, letting people glimpse it. I hadn't the heart to bury him in it. And here it is now, goodness knows what would have become of it below ground...Do you see these buttons? They're elongated like a pear. That's what we used to call them – pear buttons. Many men have these sort of buttons, they're nothing special. But these are the ones we have and they're for Wistin."

Meanwhile, Susanna kept on looking at her mother with a smile on her face but did not interrupt.

Katarina kept opening drawers. "Look, here's the sash, see! It's a sash of carded cotton, woven on the loom. And this is a pair of leather sandals. He never liked going outside barefoot. We never did so, neither one of us. Nor you, did we ever take you outside barefoot? Try and remember. Many people used to carry their sandals in their hands and then decide later whether to wear them or not. But never us. He did not want us to do that...This is his knapsack. It opens in the middle but is sewn closed at the ends. He used to throw it over his shoulder with half across his chest and the other half resting against his back. He carried small objects in it and it served as two pockets. But he didn't like to weigh it down with heavy things. 'It doesn't look good if it looks like two pockets overflowing with rubbish!' he liked to say."

"And this is his pipe. A reed pipe. He always carried it around with him," Susanna recalled.

"And he had another one, a white clay-pipe, like the ones sailors have. I scrubbed it thoroughly to remove its smell. It just wouldn't go. That goaded me into a fit of pique and I didn't rest till I'd got rid of it. He never used it much. We'll find it presently. It must be here, somewhere. And this is his cap with a brim. And this is his hat, look what a wide brim it has! And this is his straw hat. There are two pairs of cotton trousers, one which he wore on weekdays and the other on Sundays. He wore this Sunday one for early mass and then spent some time with it but then changed out of it as soon as he came home. He also wore it during feast days. It was always kept clean in the drawer and that's why it's still as good as new."

Susanna stared at all the things without uttering a single word.

"What are you thinking, Susanna?" Katarina asked, shielding some object with her hand so as to reveal it to her daughter with a flourish. "Close your eyes and then open them when I tell you to!"

"What a beautiful fan, Mother!"

"This is for you, too. It was part of my dowry, from my mother. I hardly ever used it."

"I don't recall you ever using it. That's why it's still in such a good condition."

"And this is the *għonnella* I used to wear during feast days, a silk *għonnella*," Katarina said proudly.

Susanna went to her mother and hugged her. Unbidden, a thought came to her of the *polka*, the curb link chain of a pocket watch – a long silver chain with a silver watch hung at one end. Her mother did not show it to her. It hadn't emerged from the drawers opened before her eyes. She could distinctly remember her father wearing it; though they were not rich, he liked to keep up a good appearance and never went anywhere without it. That *polka* was a link with his side of the family. He used to feel a whole man wearing it, and he was in control of every minute of the day with it, as if the entire world revolved around those two diminutive hands which never lost time and went wrong, according to him. Just like him! He too was never in error, Susanna thought. She could not remember a single instance when he had admitted to being in the wrong or that the world was not exactly how he saw and understood it. His certainty dangled on the end of that chain, too. She asked herself where that chain and pocket watch could have got to, and why had her mother not even mentioned them.

Susanna did not bring it up.

What was her father without that *polka*? Though he had never told her, she knew it was the custom for young men to wear it when they became betrothed. He would pass the chain through one of the buttonholes of his waistcoat and the chain would hang down to one of the side pockets. The watch would be kept in the pocket hung at the end of the chain and wound up with a tiny key. She remembered her father winding it up every night, always at the same time, just before going to bed. He never forgot and during the night, he would put the watch on the chest of drawers next to his side of the bed. Reassured that the watch was beside him, he would sleep soundly. No-one ever laid a finger on it, no-one dared. Sometimes, in the silence of the night there were times when the faint ticking of that watch could be heard. On the other end of the chain there was a tiny box, made of silver too, and in it he used to keep some gold coins.

Susanna glided silently out of the room. She tried to drive the thoughts away because she felt she was letting her mother down. But those thoughts kept flitting through her mind.

"That's all, my dear daughter, that's all that was left to me to pass on to you," Katarina declared. "I have nothing more. More than that I've either dreamt of or stolen away! I've discharged my entire duty now."

Wistin was still fast asleep but they did not wake him up. The day had dawned a long time before and the windows had long been thrown wide open. It looked to be a fine day, but in that house the day waited on the little boy to truly begin.

Chapter 11

"Susanna, if you come you can see with your own eyes how different the life I chose is. Today I don't intend to look back. Everything's changed for me, meanwhile. Come, let me show you," Stiefnu told her, in the voice of one trying his hardest to impress her. "It's like nothing you can possibly imagine from here. It's like another world, full of people and movement. It's a far more realistic and colourful story than the ones they used to tell us when we were children. If you don't see for yourself, you won't believe me."

"Is it different from the way we were brought up in the streets and alleyways of the village and the Valley?" she asked him.

"It's as different as a boy's life is different from a man's. I'm a man, now. Just as now you're a woman. We've grown up but the paths we've chosen have forked and they'll never meet up at any point. But don't be afraid, let me show you," he had continued insisting. "This time you won't think of me as a thoughtless and carefree boy any longer, one who doesn't know how to do anything."

"Are you telling me that village life was a good thing when we were children? Only good till childhood? And then no good for anyone after that?"

"Yes, that's what I mean, Susanna."

"And when we grow up..."

"When we grow up we want something else. A different place. Beyond the village. And do you know why? Because the village does not grow along with us. It's like clothes we've outgrown."

In her heart of hearts Susanna knew she was in total disagreement with him. She remembered Stiefnu saying something of the sort to her many years back, down in the Valley. That day too, he had wanted to give her the impression that he was a man, all grown up, decisive, and he wanted to prove it to her. He wanted her to see him as a man who knew his way about the world. Though he had never yet set foot outside the village, he had been certain that there could be nothing to fluster or hold him back as he was growing up. He was already certain that he was man enough for anything. He had kissed her many times, embraced her...and the rest. And she had discovered a different life existed to that quiet one spent at her mother's side and in the shadow of her father's stern gaze. She thought that her mother and father were people from an older time which yet was still valid and would never become obsolete. These were thoughts that she felt right inside her, at the core of her being, but had never expressed in words. Now along had come this young man, smart, full of self-confidence, from just a couple of streets away from her own, and he opened up a vista without limits for her. It all seemed like yesterday when the two of them were still happily playing about among the trees and clouds, with grass and each other. For a little while, both of them had believed that they needed nothing else but these. Everything was still new, tender, and life was still simple. Even her father's grim gaze was nothing more than part of the large sheltering wall that surrounded her.

"Are you coming? I'll be waiting for you," he said to her.

"And what am I going to say to my mother? Mother will understand straightaway without me saying anything."

"That's her job. Otherwise what sort of mother would she be?"

"I don't know how I can duck out of her sight, even for a short while."

"You're of age now. Go out, walk on and keep up a steady pace. You're not a child any longer. Tell your mother, 'Look here, I'm going out. A bird has come calling to me. I can hear his song, whether I like it or not.' That's what you should tell her. Open your wings and fly, like I've done," he urged her, full of himself.

"I could never bring myself to speak to my mother that way."

"That's the village mentality inside you talking...You can keep it, Susanna! I want to have nothing to do with it," he replied in a tone full of pique.

Susanna ignored his outburst and continued where she had left off. "My mother understands everything quickly. She can interpret even a glance, or half a word, or a gesture. She can read my thoughts, as if I was a book," she had told him.

"Since when did your mother learn to read books?" he taunted her but then stopped. "Forgive me, that was uncalled for. I meant you. Do you still read books? I know you began to read and found somebody to teach you. See how lucky you've been! Go on reading books, because they've got many pages, they're never-ending. The more you read, the more you want to keep on reading, isn't that so?"

"How do you know?"

"Hadn't you better tell me that? Where is that person who taught you to read?"

Susanna remained silent. She tried hard not to feel offended. She knew all too well what he meant when he mentioned books. She wanted to appear not to have taken any notice. Books could only mean one person in both their experience.

"Are you coming? Come here! Go on, run away just for a short while and then tell me what you think of this life I've chosen to lead. I want to have led you into this, too, far away from the trees and flowers, from the fields and alleys. Far away from all that we were brought up in. Without the least choice on our part. At least, I speak for myself, away from all that I grew up in. I left all that behind me. Maybe I broke the rules too soon..."

"And I broke them with you," she replied half-heartedly. "I too broke them, and I'd be lying if I didn't admit it."

"Every epoch has its own rules. And every person is different!" he declared. "There, see, I too can think and use my head, even though I've never read any books! You'll be amazed when you see how I've learnt to think ahead and decide what steps to take, one thing after another, and succeeding without anyone's words of wisdom," he continued. "Are you coming?"

"And what shall I tell my mother?"

"Tell her, 'Mother, I'm going for a walk, far, far away, to the other side.' That's all! Can you manage that?"

"And don't you tell your parents anything? Don't they have any interest in your life?"

"My mother and father have their own pair of wings. And they are the only ones who can use them," he answered her with a provocative lilt to his voice.

"Do you have wings?"

"Come, and you'll see for yourself. I use them to fly above the seawater and they're so good I've never got wet. And what if I do get wet?"

Susanna felt as if Stiefnu was challenging her in all that she held dear and was important to her. Did she really lack all initiative to decide to go out briefly wherever she wanted without having to answer to her mother's long, detailed questions? And now that her father had long been silenced by death's rules, could she not feel free like this man? This man is truly a free agent, she said to herself. "Very well, I'll come!" she decided on the spur of the moment.

"At last! Finally you're moving out of your rut! And even this time round, it had to be me to make you move!" Stiefnu preened himself.

"Very well" she answered somewhat listlessly. "And at what time will you be there?"

"At what time? I begin at the crack of dawn and stay on till the night draws in. It depends. If I can earn a penny, as little as a penny, I don't turn it down. You can never tell what time some trade might be had. Each moment means money and it can mean starvation too. My job is to grab whatever I can. I grab any opportunity, that's all. What do you say to that, huh?"

Susanna realized, deep in her heart, that she could never love this man, even had she wanted to.

There was a yawning gulf between the village and the Port.

~ 0~

"I'm going out," Susanna called out to her mother a few days later.

"I don't want to ask you where you're going," Katarina replied. "There's no need to interfere. I wish I neither saw nor heard anything, nor thought anything either. But that's wishing for something that cannot be. As long as I muddle through here, I can't do otherwise."

"Better not ask, Mother. But set your mind at rest. I know my way back very well. I can go far away but I can never get lost. This time no," her daughter declared.

"It really shows you read books, my dear daughter!" her mother teased her, giving her a quick glance from between her lashes. "But be careful what you read. I've never read any books, and I can't read and neither could your father. And we still lived our life to the full. But..."

"Do you hold it against anybody who can read books, Mother?" Susanna responded with a taunt.

"No, no, as if! On the contrary!" her mother was quick to take her up on her words. "I love books and I also love who reads them. Books bring about good things, they open minds, enlighten people, and I hope that..."

"Oh very well, Mother. I know what you're going to say. I'm going out now."

Susanna arrived at the quayside and stopped to gaze all around her. A completely different scene from the neighbourhood she had grown up in met her eyes.

The Port was teeming with shipping, merchant ships and war vessels. Hardly any space was left between them. Some ships were tied to huge buoys of which only the upper part could be seen moving on the water's surface. Other ships were berthed along the Quay. A long, thick rope seemed to be the only link between land and those murky depths, where violence lurked just below its present calm exterior. On the decks of tall ships the men looked like tiny dots, like the figurines in a mechanical nativity crib that move slightly, constantly, in a glide rather than with a jerk. But they were always there...though this was not significant in any way. There were many of them, all dressed in the same uniform. This had its own particular colours which distinguished the men from the rest of the ship and from the fixed dun colour of the water. The movement that the sailors made seemed to change their very appearance. They had to follow strict orders in the pace they took and they observed the rules even during their leisure time away from the eagle eye of their superior officers, though they occasionally broke them. The uniform did not simply cover them from head to toe; it was a force that changed them from inside.

The Port signified, first and foremost, vessels that were constantly entering or leaving – everything taking place in some unseen order. Every frigate had its own characteristics, even though they seemed indistinguishable from each other as they lay berthed together. The sailors created constant movement as if to signify that on the sea there could be no dozing off, by day or by night. A battalion meant hundreds of men and the arrival of a ship in port meant a large amount of trade and commerce on land. Aboard ship the crew had plenty of food and drink. They were well looked after and not kept on half-rations. But making landfall meant an invitation, or something even stronger than that, urging them to quickly disembark. The land held a strong fascination for all those who lived at sea. The neighbourhood around the Port was seething with sailors and soldiers, and officers. Their uniforms looked like small flames on the move. When they walked as a group, their gait had a single rhythm. It was the regular military step, second-nature to them, something they could not leave behind them even when they sought to break all their ties and indulge themselves for a little while in the liberty found in the streets. Some would take up a song or ditty; others would drink beer and make passes at young women. The people living in those localities not only waited for them to arrive but took new life from their presence. Life would seem to jerk forward once more, for tradesmen and beggars both.

The passenger boats plied their trade to and fro, filling the harbour with their unceasing movement. Each boat held two ferrymen and some held passengers. They zigzagged across the harbour, letting passengers disembark and waiting for others to come on board. A large fleet in the Port, holding several regiments, lit up many people's fantasy, making them wish to see such vessels from up close.

The passenger boat would take them after they had negotiated the fare with the ferrymen.

Some boats held no passengers and the men at the oars would look around them trying to pick up a fare. They would row up to the Quay and urge people to take a trip. All the boats were gaily coloured, painted with care and attention and looked to be greatly cherished by their owners. All the boats had two oars. When one approached the Quay to stop, the boatman would hold it steady from the prow to allow passengers to embark or disembark. As he was approaching the side of the quay, the boatman would let go of one of the oars and paddle the outer one till he was in position. Every movement was precise, the result of years working at sea, always the same and yet always new, unpredictable. The sea was a friend who could not be trusted more than it was wise to do so.

The boatmen were men whose livelihood depended entirely on their boat. They could not afford to be too courteous or weak, because the waves on the sea had long taught them that life was one entire storm, even when fair weather was about since there was no telling how long that would last. The weather could change suddenly without the least warning, and the boatman would need to change all his movements if he wanted to return safe and sound to his wife. Sometimes he risked his life because the large vessels were tall and clumsy and a constant threat to the little boats, swaying with each capricious movement of the waves and sometimes swinging wildly with a terrific jolt that could capsize them.

Some ferrymen were haggling over fares with some people. Every journey could ignite a quarrel since a few of the boatmen would squabble over a few pence, and the row would flare up in a trice. If the passengers were foreigners, there was no fixed price and a courteous request would be enough to ensure payment with quiet satisfaction on both sides.

"Give us whatever you think fair, Sir! You look kind! We'll leave it in your hands how much to give us, you know best, Sir!"

The sailors and soldiers and officers were not mean with money and were thus eagerly sought after.

Life spent on the surface of the deep sea was not something they could put their trust in. Every day was a new day, every wave spelt a new challenge, but each man was sure of one responsibility – he had to return home safe and sound with a small pouch full of pennies. Those were his badges of honour, for that day he would have proved himself a man and need not bother with any other proofs.

"A man is worth as much as he can earn," the boatmen would nod wisely at each other. "Our boat is our fortune and our manhood depends entirely on it. Let anyone who makes a pass at our wives beware but hard luck on us if our wives aren't happy with our day's earnings! We're men whose value depends on what each day is worth."

Susanna walked slowly along the Quay marvelling at all she looked upon. "How deep the sea is! And how many foreigners there are! They came through that wide gap, on a ship," she thought, and smiled.

Calm or storm-tossed, the sea was one and it was always this sea that showed how man was stronger than the waves. It was the sort of life that could not be entirely subdued, even though every man jack of them was a past master in rowing and swimming. Every boatman spoke to himself on each voyage he made. He prayed on his own, fell silent on his own, dreamt and worried on his own, and expressed his anger on his own. Who could hear him except the large fish at the bottom of the sea and God? Two boatmen on each boat represented good fortune and bad, and they made a story of their life, recounting and singing it during their journeys from one side of the harbour to the other, or next to the Quay when they were inviting people to step aboard. A good part of their trade relied on the beauty of their boat. That is why all the boats had names and one outdid the other in the beauty stakes. No boat could afford to be left scratched or with fading colours. Each part of the boat held a certain fascination – the helm, the gunwale, the rowlock, the forefoot, the bar keel, the bench, the coaming, the stern, the oar pegs on the left and on the right, the futtocks, the floor timbers...every part had to be shown off to its best advantage, as if it was part of a woman's figure.

The boat was female. It had to meet every challenge. On fine days it had to show a man there was no trouble about and during a storm it had to show him it would pull him through, keep him skimming above the waves and save him from drowning. In any case, it had to be the boat to make him believe himself a man, a whole man, standing tall even when he returned home with less money than usual. He never had to feel embarrassed or lose any of his self-confidence. He was a seafarer precisely because he did not know how to be afraid, whether on the outer or inner part of the Quay.

"Where is Stiefnu? I can't see him from here," Susanna began asking herself.

A harbour launch passed by, going to and fro between the two harbour sides. On each journey it carried many passengers, some seated and some standing up. The helmsman stared straight ahead, carefully turning the helm and steering the launch forward. There was another crewman on board taking care of the engine. Another man was in charge of the coal which powered the launch. The Port was an important coal bunkering station. And the last crewman was a sailor whose job was to untie the ropes and tie them up again as soon as the steam launch left the quayside or returned to it. The sides of the steam launch had benches, and the passengers were engrossed in looking back towards the sea, enjoying the spectacle that their voyage afforded. There was another bench in the prow and others in the little glassed-in cabin.

The Port was bustling with activity. Merchandise was constantly being transported from one ship to another. Some boats were waiting till the tanks of leftover swill were lowered from the ships and transported to land, and from there they would be taken to a place where portions were sold to people who were waiting, hungry and full of curiosity to see what sort of supper they would be having. The mixture of meat, potatoes, bread and other food, which were leftovers from the sailors' dinner, provided meals for people. There would be a long queue with people of all ages waiting to eat, and no one dared jump the queue. Some soup in a tin, a portion of food wrapped in newspaper or some other scrap of paper, and supper would have come down from the ocean to people's houses in the neighbourhood for people who needed to eat without spending much.

Susanna remembered the time she had spent relying on a plate of hot food offered to her by the Friars. Beggars used to congregate on the doorstep of a convent waiting to smell the aroma coming from a large cooking pot. The men would enter into the hallway but the women would remain on the doorstep. The Friar would make the Sign of the Cross and they would all begin to eat without saying a word.

"I've always given you good food to eat! I've never fed you swill! I spoilt you...and spoiling leads to spoilt children," her father had thundered once at her in a fury. "What can you complain of here? Go outside and you'll see what hunger there is in the outside world! I've fed you wholesome produce from the land, crops that we've grown ourselves! From the evergreen fields around. The village is self-sufficient. It needs no outsiders! The village can feed itself! If I was in command, I would surround the village with high bastions, or walls...we need no one from the edges of the village inwards! Whoever is outside these limits can stay outside and whoever is in can remain safe inside!"

Susanna had gaped back at him in astonishment, and her father had realized that she did not understand all his words.

"Of course you don't know what swill is! You eat wholesome food here, freshly pulled out by its roots from the soil. The village is not a city. Don't spit in the wind, daughter, because if you do...If you're not understanding me let me explain what swill is!" her father had ranted at her in a rage.

"Swill...it's a huge amount of leftover food, taken down from the big ships..." she remembered, her thoughts running on. "But where is Stiefnu? I cannot see him anywhere! The Port is here, so he must be here somewhere."

Other boats were circling the big ships, and their owners were trying to sell all the goods they had stored aboard. There was not an inch of free space in these bumboats, loaded up with all manner of goods for sale. The traders' boats quickly homed in on ships seen entering harbour. Some of them approached very close and the traders tied their bumboat to the ship and called to the crew on board urging them to buy their goods. Sometimes they even ventured up the ship with an armful of their goods to sell. Proud, happy and anxious, the trader would array the goods on the deck and call to the sailors and passengers to approach and handle the goods, offering special prices and assuring them of bargains they would not readily find ashore.

"Going cheap! Everything's going cheap here! And it's all genuine stuff! It's a one-time opportunity! Special prices today! Welcome Sirs! Welcome! Come, come! I came aboard especially for you, bringing you bargains!" one of the tradesmen cried, having obtained permission to go on board.

The other bumboats kept circling the ship, trying as best they could to sell their wares from their boat. The sailors and passengers would often take advantage of the opportunity and after inspecting the goods would finally make up their mind and buy something. The eager voices of the traders could be heard even on the Quay, though the big ship would be at quite a distance from the quayside. The sold goods would be raised onto the deck in baskets fashioned from plaited ropes. For those men who did not have permission to go on board, a piece of wood with a string tied to it was enough to display their wares, have them inspected and finally sold. The people on board inspected everything, desired some objects and negotiated a fair price.

"Inspect it properly! Take your time! Have a good think and appreciate what you're buying here! It's genuine! Everything's genuine! At a good price!" the seller would cry, waiting for the piece of wood to be lowered back.

There was not a single moment of respite in this kind of job. They were men who needed to sell everything they had before dusk fell, and before their wife would ask them how their day had gone when they returned home. Their children would gather round them and would ask the same question. These men could not afford to do less than their best. After all, they needed to save face, not simply line their pockets. If they did not manage to sell everything there was always bartering as a last resort.

Suddenly, one of the boats began approaching the Quay. A man was rowing with all his might, coming in Susanna's direction, and she saw him at once. She saw a powerful pair of arms rowing to a single rhythm, a measured stroke back to front. And the boat drew nearer leaving a small ripple in its wake. The sea frothed at its sides next to the oars and the boat approached the Quay. The sound it made grew louder, water slapping against wood. No unnecessary movement, no break in the rhythm, and a fixed gaze, decisive, the gaze of a man who knew his destination. Stroke after stroke, with no hint of fatigue on his face, he drew near.

"That's Stiefnu! How can it be?" Susanna was startled.

The boat was loaded up with objects, all piled on top of each other filling every nook and cranny of that bumboat, from its cleat to its stool and even right up to its prow. There were many bars of soap, and packets of postcards and notepaper, and packets of tea and coffee, bags of sugar, and perfume and sweets, and lengths of lace, and shirts and caps in different sizes, and quality silk and pencils and ink. Stiefnu had pieces of chocolate and bottles of alcoholic drinks. He also carried small framed pictures of Our Lady and of St. Joseph.

"Susanna! Susanna! Here I am, I've arrived!" he called out when he was still some distance away. "Can you see now what I told you? I have samples of everything! Choose whatever you want and take it! I have a special price for you! And what you can't see I can find for you in the boxes or bundles or sacks that I have. You can find anything in my boat! Ask away and you'll find out it's true!"

Susanna smiled at him tremulously, gazing back at him with awe. Without saying anything she wanted to express her admiration because she felt truly impressed with the spectacle he presented. She had imagined a lot of things as she was making her way to the Port on her own, but she had never imagined she would be seeing so much.

"Did you ever imagine all this, Susanna?" he asked her. "This is the Port! It's all mine!" he told her in jest but with a serious underlying note to his voice.

"Stiefnu, well done! I'm marvelling at you rowing without pause, one stroke after another. That was a long voyage from that ship out there to the Quay," she said, feeling she had to say something.

"Is that what you think? That's nothing!"

"That voyage is nothing, Stiefnu? I've never gone on such a voyage and it astounds me. I could never begin to imagine myself rowing from there to here."

"This is men's work, Susanna. And not all men are up to it. The long voyage I really made isn't that one. My longest journey was from the fields in the village to this Port. That was a far harder journey and...Anyway, that's it, I won't say anymore. How are you?"

Susanna did not answer him but smiled back, astonished and at the same time startled by that environment. Life in the Port, crowded, fast and full of movement had made her dizzy already.

The bumboat drew closer to the quayside and Stiefnu quickly controlled it to prevent it hitting the wall. He was wary of causing the slightest extra movement through carelessness. The least glance sideways could suddenly cause the boat to hit the wall and get scratched. Every moment counted and it could make him poorer in a flash. This time the sea was not churned up in motion and his oars could make the precise movements the rower wanted and the boat was in his full control.

"Would you like a ride, Susanna?" Stiefnu asked her.

Susanna became flustered. "Where do you want me to wriggle in?" she answered cheekily. "Among all those things! Your boat is crammed to the hilt! There's no place for me."

"There is one place," he replied. "Haven't you noticed? There is one place I've left free, on purpose. Look carefully."

Susanna stared. Soap bars, lengths of lace, sweets, bags of sugar, filigree, handkerchiefs, perfume... "I don't know, I can't see anything," she answered feeling rather shy, more than before. She was also a little apprehensive.

"Seafarers are used to looking carefully, in every direction, because danger can come from any quarter. Perils can lurk high above near the clouds or down all around them near the waves. And do you know where else? At the bottom, where there are huge and hungry fish..."

"How well you speak, Stiefnu!"

"At the bottom of the sea, down here, Susanna, there are fish that eat and fish that are eaten. You either eat or get eaten. That's how the sea below us is. This water means wealth and health but it can also mean hardship and death. It all depends from which direction the wind is blowing. Life doesn't give you anything for nothing."

Susanna was spellbound listening to him speak. "How well you speak!"

"And I don't even read books. Imagine how much better I'd talk then!"

"Very well," she said, slightly offended. She was about to turn her gaze towards the vessels berthed in the distance.

"Look carefully. Look again and you'll certainly see it. Here, in the boat, near the sea-cock..." he invited her speaking with a note of pride. "Read what's written there."

"Wistin! Wistin!" Susanna exclaimed, reading the word 'Wistin' painted in a bright colour that stood out against the background. Without wanting to, she was amazed at herself for not having seen that word before. "Wistin!" she exclaimed once more.

"Now look at the stern," he told her.

Susanna looked towards the back of the boat and there she saw the image of St. Joseph.

"What do you see?"

"St. Joseph!" she answered happily.

"Look more closely!" he urged her.

"St. Joseph, the patron of our village. His face is the same as that of the statue in our village. It's exactly the same. What made you do that?"

"You don't know why? Try and guess."

Susanna kept silent.

"The saint to whom I made a vow! That's his face!" he told her in a voice that was half command and half challenge.

"Which vow? What are you talking about?"

"Don't you know?" he queried, with a smile that was half serious and half banter.

Susanna remained silent.

Stiefnu came alongside and alighted. The boat swung gently as if he hardly rocked it when he moved, and came to a complete stop. He approached Susanna and looked her full in the face. "This is my job. I trade on my bumboat!"

"A trader on a bumboat?"

"Yes, a trader on a bumboat!" he said to her, "And I'm very happy and proud of it."

"What's a bumboat?"

"You don't know what a bumboat is? Just as you didn't know what a sea-cock and a stern were, isn't that so? You know nothing about all the things in connection with the sea...You're right; you've remained a child of the soil. A bumboat is a boat full of supplies of all sorts for people on board ships and the trader is the man who steers his boat towards a vessel, moors alongside it, and sells all his goods to the people on board. I earn good money, Susanna, in spite of everything! The ship captains are my friends, and I know how to be friendly with one and all, even with other men who are my sort, boatmen and ship chandlers." He stopped there and raised his head sideways to avoid her direct gaze and to look straight at the other side of the Port. "Everyone offers things from what he owns, that's the way of the world. There, do you see, Susanna? With all your book learning you had no idea what a trader on a bumboat was. I'm one. A little distance away, along this wharf, I have a room where I store all my supplies. Look, look there," he entreated her, pointing to his bumboat overflowing with objects. "My luck is all tied up in that and my wife is that boat. She's never let me down, so far. And I've never let her down, up to now, too. I can only say up to now because times change. It's like a contract, nothing more. Maybe in the future...if the wind changes," he went on in a changed voice.

"In the future? What do you want for the future?"

"In the future, maybe when I've run out of things to sell, the bumboat will be empty...completely empty, and I would end up on my own...and I'll become a ship chandler."

"A ship chandler!" she repeated after him, astonished. "What's that?"

"A ship chandler is a man who can supply provisions for an entire ship. Life on board ship depends on him. The ship chandler is an important merchant, employing several men. He directs everything. The ship chandler is close to the ship captain and to the officers, too. Officers are men, and if you go around this neighbourhood for a while, you'll see foreign nursemaids dressed in a smart white uniform, looking after their babies. The nursemaids wear a starched cap. You can recognize them straightaway. The officers have a handsome uniform. Servants look after their children. That's how a ship chandler is. There are foreigners and then there are villagers. Rich folk and beggars, like the fish at the bottom of the sea! The Port has many different colours."

"So that's what a ship chandler is!" Susanna said with a noticeable lack of interest.

"Yes, that's what a ship chandler is! He only waits for his ship to enter harbour. He would be expecting it, and when he wouldn't know beforehand, he'd ask. Then he would go aboard with no trouble at all and speak to the captain. 'Here I am!' he'd tell him. 'Tell me what you need and I'll soon send it along. All the food supplies that you want, just tell me, and you'll see it arrive. I'll bring you some from my stores straightaway and the rest I'll be buying as soon as I disembark. Whatever isn't in my stores will be in someone else's! Absolutely no problem at all.' That's what the ship chandler tells the captain."

"That's what the ship chandler tells the captain, huh?" Susanna exclaimed in amazement. "Why, then the ship chandler..."

"I'm a ship chandler...just imagine!"

"Then you're an important man..."

"And the ship chandler speaks to the officers, too. The ship chandler does his best so that the people on board will lack nothing. And when he doesn't find all that he needs from here, do you know what he does? He goes aboard one of those ships and leaves from that open door to the world. And from out there he'll bring what he didn't find in here. Look there, Susanna of the Valley, there is the great door of the Port," he told her pointing with his finger towards the place. "All the ships enter harbour from there, and that's from where they leave as well. When children come by ship, Susanna, it's from there that they come, and the adults leave on board from there, too. Doesn't it all remind you of the Valley, huh? With one difference, and it's a big difference – in the Valley there are farmers, and in this Port here there are the foreigners. And they mean money, a fortune!"

Susanna clasped her hands together and bowed her head, all the while gazing at the name of the boat. "Wistin, my Wistin, don't worry, I'll soon be back home with you," she said in her heart.

"What vow? You asked me that question. You don't know? Have you forgotten? How could you possibly forget? Isn't that what you told me once?" Stiefnu suddenly put his hand under her shoulder and led her forward slowly, as if he was driving her towards something.

"I don't know, truly...I didn't make any vows. I prayed, yes, but..." she stammered.

"But...you may not have made a vow, but your mother made one instead. And she made it to St. Joseph, the patron saint of the village."

"How do you know that?"

"Can you see now how someone looking to be a ship chandler in the future can use his brains? The sea taught me much, in the same way someone else taught you to read books!"

"Yes, I know, even a ship chandler can use his brains."

"And your mother made a vow asking for the boy to be found..."

"True, she made it for the sake of our son. What's wrong with that?"

"She also made a vow so that you and I would never see each other again."

"How do you know that?" she asked defensively, almost as if she wanted to defend her mother.

"How...St. Joseph came and told me." He paused and took on a new tone. "She told me herself. Do you believe me?"

"I believe you," she whispered.

Stiefnu took hold of her again by her shoulders and stepped forward once more, "and do you know why you believe me? Because your mother and father aren't any different from each other. Your father was in command all the time and your mother obeyed all the time. It's one and the same thing. At the time your father didn't want me. Now it's your mother who doesn't. And today, I don't want you. I don't want any of you."

"That's not the real reason. It's because in the meantime I..."

"In the meantime you got married. I know you're married. That is your problem, only yours. You could have waited...Time goes by slowly. You know very well how the seasons of the village move on."

Susanna was silent.

In front of her eyes she could see the bustling Port...and the fields and farmhouses and the country paths and the flocks and the villagers were so very far away from there. She glanced around her wondering which path she had taken to arrive there, in that place where Stiefnu had asked her to come and see him.

"You're very different from the last time I saw you," she declared.

"No, no, I haven't changed so quickly. I'd already changed, but I was waiting for this moment. I didn't want to say the final word before I could show you that I've found my place in life. This way, the whole vow can be fulfilled. Your mother will be completely contented, not just nearly content. Here's my place in life, far away from those closed-in streets and the Valley where you've remained locked up."

"Your place is here, in this wide open space of deep sea, where big ships take up all the space..."

"And where my oars can take me close up to them to show them my boat full of wares for sale. Sometimes I buy things and sometimes I barter them. Can you see now that I'm no longer that carefree boy you once knew? Tell your mother that I've grown up as well, and that I've learnt to swim strongly. I know how to float on the surface and whenever I feel like it I can explore what's below the surface, too. In this sea there aren't any lizards or butterflies but large fish, and I can go down to the bottom as well, otherwise the smallest wave could overturn me. Tell her Stiefnu knows how to forge ahead on his own."

"I'll tell her, and I think she'll be pleased to know."

"When everything falls into place, everybody should be happy."

"I'm glad you've changed your tune, now..."

"Is that what you think?" he asked her. "Susanna, you've remained a country girl but I became a town person a long time ago. Our paths don't cross. I am Stiefnu the trader on a bumboat. Maybe Wistin, too, will come out of that village and discover all that I've discovered myself, in these localities. And maybe he'll become a ship chandler as well. He'll earn good money, as long as he has something of everything to sell. He'll need to trust himself and his boat. The boat is a woman. The future is still some time away and maybe he'll come here on his own when he grows up."

"Every season teaches us to make a good choice."

"Wistin...Look after him well, and bring him up as you know very well how to. Remind him that his father loves him, in the way he knows how. Not everybody is made the same way. Tell him that one day ships will be taking his father away with them, but not just yet. If you get used to living in wide open spaces you cannot get used to living in enclosed ones. I cannot think or be any different if I want to be at peace with myself. Don't I have the right to be at peace? Even grown-ups come by ship. If this wasn't so, I wouldn't be able to live, I, Stiefnu the trader on a bumboat who'll become a ship chandler one fine day."

Susanna kept her head down and did not utter a word.

Stiefnu went up to her and squeezed her hand lightly, moved away from her again and walked to the edge of the Quay. He went down to his boat which rocked alarmingly with his weight. He was not perturbed.

Susanna feared he was going to fall in the sea and gasped aloud.

Her startled cry moved him and he wanted to reassure her that he was not precariously balanced, but he said nothing. He untied the rope, pushed off and took up the oars rowing himself further and further away. With sudden vigour he sped across the water and did not look back till he had arrived next to the ships. Then he stopped and waved to her with one hand. His other hand held on to the oar, as if he did not dare leave the boat on its own for even a moment.

Susanna was still gazing back at him, seeing him get more and more distant till he stopped where he wanted. She waved back to him perfunctorily and turned round to leave, making her way back slowly and not giving him a second glance. She shook her head as if she was arguing with someone, plunged her hands deep into her large skirt pockets and walked along the quay for the last time.

Karozzini plying their trade to and fro were a signal that a fleet had entered harbour. The thin ringing sound of their bell, the heavy rhythmic tread of their wheels and the snatches of conversation coming from the coachmen of these horse-drawn cabs, seemed to come from every direction. Couples walking hand-in-hand, arms around each other holding the other like a venerated statue, formed one long procession. Small groups of happy sailors, singing and swaying with their arms locked over each other's shoulders, filled the air all around with a gaily festive mood. Children in rags ran after them importuning them with open palms for a penny or two. Some sailors waved them away but others delved inside their pocket and flung them a coin. When it was thrown up in the air the children jumped up knocking their heads together and falling in a heap on the ground all over each other. Some other coins would roll away on the ground and all the children would get down on their hands and knees and scrabble after them. The children would happily report what they had earned. The unlucky ones without a coin would keep zigzagging in front of the sailors till they too received some money. As they walked away, the children would boast about the money they had, gloating at the coins spread out on one of their hands while with the other they shielded their hoard from the other children, not trusting anyone not to snatch it away.

Beggars were seen in those parts, too, and some of them slept in sheltered corners in the vicinity of the Port. For them, the arrival of people disembarking from the ships meant hope, as it did for all sorts of trade, by day and by night.

"That's better," Susanna sighed in relief. As she put some distance between her and the sea, she observed that all around her on land there was a small world, full of colour, sleeping by day to stir and come vigorously alive by night. The Port never slept, and the sea remained a dark colour, even on fine days. Beyond the enormous smoke-stacks and narrow masts of the ships, the sky was a lovely clear blue. "Somewhere there lies the village, and my mother and Wistin are waiting for me," she thought happily and continued on her way.

As soon as she arrived in the village street, she noticed her mother waiting for her on the doorstep, one arm resting on the doorjamb. Susanna smiled and waved at her.

Katarina looked relieved to see her. "Wistin is waiting for you; he hasn't stopped asking for you. And I too, as you can imagine," she said to Susanna.

"There's no need to make a mountain out of a molehill, Mother, imagining we're on the edge of a precipice."

"Don't you know that this place is on the edge of the world? Isn't that what they say? I'm not going to be the one to move the place of the village," Katarina attempted to joke, trying to see what was on her daughter's mind.

"This place is at one end, and the other place is also at one end, the other one. The Port, Mother, and the bustling life around it..." Susanna started saying, in the eager tone of voice of one having a lot to say, "the ends aren't the same."

"I'm not with you. What news are you going to give me? Don't worry me. My heart has been beating enough, sometimes quickly and sometimes slowly. I hope you're not going to tell me that you want to leave the village and another wind is going to start blowing and carrying you off with it..."

"Not every wind that blows carries you away, Mother. I'm going to tell you something that will keep you as happy and content as you are now."

"As happy and content as I am now? Yes, I'm happy true enough, and to be perfectly honest, nearly content," Katarina answered giving her daughter a quick smile.

"This time, Mother, you'll be perfectly content."

"Really? Are you going to tell me that the prayer for my vow will be granted, all of it?"

"You know what sort of vow you made, Mother."

"St. Joseph and I know it. That's between us. He keeps all confidences and I do too. But you can imagine what it is. You read books."

Susanna went to her mother and embraced her fondly. Two large tears rolled down her cheeks and her mother saw them.

"You're crying. With joy or in sadness?"

"The two together, Mother."

"Choose joy then, dear daughter! I'm sure St. Joseph has stood with us once more. He always does, bless him!"

Wistin emerged from the room next door and rushed into his mother's arms. "Granny told me you went far away from here. And you saw the sea and many ships. She told me that's a very different place from here. The people there are different. And I asked her many more questions but she wouldn't answer. Is it true, Mummy?"

"Yes, it's true. Granny doesn't lie, Wistin. Granny waits."

The next morning, Katarina rose very early without telling anyone what she meant to do. She went straight to church and asked the sacristan for the key to open the niche where the statue of St. Joseph stood.

"Another vow, Katarina?" he asked her full of curiosity. "That's a good sign if it's so."

Katarina nodded but kept silent.

"Wait here for me a bit. You won't have long to wait, neither you nor St. Joseph," he told her. "The key is always there, ready and waiting for kind-hearted people like you."

Katarina raised her shopping basket from the ground and rested it on a chair. She delved deep into it with both her hands, looking all the while at the sacristan and the statue of the saint. "This was to fulfil my vow. My husband's cap. If you look closely you'll see it matches his walking stick."

"The cap matches the walking stick?"

"That's what Saverju always believed. Now don't you start contradicting me! He used to look after them as if they were made of gold. And he always went out with the two of them together. Do you understand now? And if not, it doesn't matter. After all, the vow I made hasn't got to please you."

"It's St. Joseph's turn to understand! But St. Joseph looks to one's heart, not to presents. With all the patience he has, I imagine he's pleased with everything."

"St Joseph didn't just understand me a long time ago but he was ready to hear me. I just need one more vow to be fulfilled."

"It won't be long before I see you in front of this niche, then!"

"I don't know when that will be. Everything must take its time. He knows when. I just have to pray and wait."

"You can come by anytime you want. The key will be waiting for you in its usual place."

Chapter 12

Suddenly, a considerable number of men began arriving from every corner and they gathered around as if they had agreed on it. They started forming a queue, though it seemed as if it was a difficult thing for them. They raised their hands and began to shout angrily, and the queue somehow took shape. One could not quite make out what they were saying in a nervous, hasty flow of words, even from a few paces away; it was as if they were speaking a different language of their own. They were expressing a natural anger, quite usual for that particular time and at other times when hunger and fatigue overcame them, and everything looked blacker than ever before. Another day was ending, a day spent in carrying loads, at a run, and a never-ending repetition of work, all for a few miserable daily pence that were not enough to live on. The life of the Port.

"They're coming, at last! Finally, they're coming!" the men said amongst themselves, while some of them pointed with outflung arms and straight fingers.

These were men who had finished work for the day. Some of their colleagues were still hard at it though, as if their work had no end in sight. These were stevedores, strong, powerfully built men, with swarthy faces darkened by the sun, barefoot, and many of them wore long wide trousers, patched up and coming below their stomach which was rather larger than it should have been. Some were carrying a sack over their head and some others carried it over their back. It served as a hat to protect them from the sun and from rain and they made do with it. Those two elements, the sun and the rain, were their enemy all year long and when they were not suffering the hot sun beating down they had to put up with the sticky, cold slaps of rain. No season, even when it was calm, could treat them kindly. They had spent their entire working life carrying huge baskets of coal. In spite of its grandeur and majesty, the Port was nothing without them. Some ships entered harbour to take on coal for their next voyage. Others used to bring coal for the other ships. Some workers took the coal to the coal bunkers or to lighters which served ships directly they weighed anchor. They used to wait till the ship's prow touched the Quay. As soon as the ship berthed, they put up planks between the quayside and the prow and started carrying the coal baskets aboard. Other workmen took care to stow the coal. Coal was not only the means to move ships but also to provide the means to live for many men and their families.

From the Quay, each stevedore, strong and powerful though he was, looked like an ant scurrying across the plank, overarching the deep dark sea, solid-looking with an oily surface, unmoving. Even during a storm, the water in the Port seemed loath to stir. The stevedores' shoulders were used to the weight of the loaded coal baskets, and the bruise produced in their flesh became part of them, a natural consequence, just like sweat in summer and shivers in winter. Fat or thin, short or tall, these men were light on their feet, taking no rest in their dash between the ship's deck and the stores where they unloaded the consignment. They were used to the jog across the long plank which bounced with their weight and frequently made horrendous noises as if it were on the point of breaking.

The stevedores knew only too well that there was nothing to break their fall except the unscrupulous deep sea. They did not feel afraid, but they had no choice, either. Their faces were blackened with soot except for two small white circles around their eyes, mute witnesses to the fact that their job had almost penetrated their very skin. On land, on deck, at the bunker, on the tug boat, in the stores along the wharf, these men had nothing to declare except the precise day's wages. They had no time to waste or slouch about. None of them could afford to do that. They only had time for sipping some tea or coffee, sold by people armed for the purpose on small boats arrayed like a little bar, swaying gently on the sea's surface and moving along where they were needed. Necessity was the mother of invention and people thought up of all sorts of things to do to earn some money. The Port was a place that did not lack anything. Men formed a scene of unceasing work, but only the men. The women were someplace else.

"They're coming, at last! Finally, they're coming!" the men spoke amongst themselves, consoling each other for their long wait.

The large carts that held the boxes of swill had just arrived. The large boxes contained the leftovers that the sailors and soldiers had not eaten that day. Each worker hoped to find a piece of meat and some potatoes and peas, and a tomato, and some gobbets of bread, perhaps already spread with a bit of salted or unsalted butter in his portion that was his lot. Those who longed for some soup, made from meaty bones, brought a can with them which the swill seller would dunk in the large pot and bring up full to the brim. If it overflowed, the seller would tilt the can and empty some of it, a precise amount. Every drop of soup was worth money and all eyes would be on each other, closely observing that none took more than their money's worth. All the food came from the kitchens that served the sailors and troops aboard ship or from their barracks on land. Food was prepared in far greater quantities than were consumed by the sailors and soldiers, and the extra was put in large boxes and sold off, plate by plate. The workmen would be waiting for this moment otherwise their backbreaking day's work would also end in hunger.

The neighbourhoods around the Port were full of brightly lit bars, during the day but more so when evening drew in. They were not the sort of bars that felt tired and went to sleep, and the music played there went on continuously. They readily welcomed foreigners but also workmen who went there to eat and drink some more or to eat a better meal. Each workman had a deep pocket from which he brought up the few coins he had earned. The jingling of coins in a pocket meant that that man had worked and earned money that day. It was quite common to see a workman walking along with his hands in his pocket and jingling the coins there, to show how happy he was and that he did not have empty pockets. By no means would he be a rich man, but every jingling coin belonged to him.

Barefoot children wearing caps on their head ran about those localities, pestering every sailor and foreigner they came across.

"Give me a penny, give me a penny!" they chanted, all the while dogging their footsteps.

Arturu entered one of the bars, approached the counter behind which was the landlord and sat down on one of the vacant high stools. A dense fug of cigarette smoke rose circling in the air all around and its smell was so strong that it could be smelt over the aroma of food and the smell of the crowd of people. Dim lighting gave illumination and the place itself was rather dark. All in all, the whole ambience was steeped in a dark red hue.

The landlord went up to Arturu from behind the bar counter, smiling and saying, "Welcome, Sir! What may I get you, Sir?"

"A beer!" Arturu began tapping the counter with both hands. The counter was a wide and thin slab of white marble, with black veins stippling it all over and with a bevelled edge.

Soon a brimming glass was placed in front of him. The landlord flashed him another smile and waited to be paid.

Arturu put his hand inside his pocket to take out a coin.

"Here! See if this covers it!" somebody said to the landlord over Arturu's shoulder. A long hand snaked past him held rigidly straight, hesitated for a moment and then promptly handed over the money to the landlord.

Arturu was taken aback and he raised his head and looked at the large mirror in front of him that was hanging on the wall behind the landlord. He was conscious of the five fingers of a hand splayed out behind his head. The mirror reflected the entire room with all its corners and it had advertisements for beers and spirits painted on it. Some people were playing cards, others were looking around and waiting, and nearly all of them were smoking. The strongly-smelling smoke, looking like soft columns swirling in the air, did not appear to bother anyone. Each person's head in there lanced through the smoke rings as if they were not there. People were inured to everything.

The face could not be clearly made out in the dim light in there.

"This evening I'll pay for you! Put your money back inside, maybe you'll need it some other time, Mr. Arturu!"

Hardly aware of what he was doing, Arturu put his hand back in his pocket, slowly took it out again and turned to face the person who had paid for his beer.

"Drink up, Mr. Arturu, and I'll join you!"

Arturu did not touch his drink.

"Drink, Mr. Arturu, drink it!" the voice said again but this time with a steely note of command. "Don't you know that when someone pays you a compliment and buys you a drink, you're supposed to join in? You should know these things because you can read and write, and you own books and read them. And if you still haven't learnt them by now, remember – you're no longer in the village. You are in town. Foreigners stay here, too."

Arturu remained staring back at him, unable to hide his amazement.

"How's the village, Mr. Arturu? Here in town, the country air doesn't penetrate. The air is different here, as you can see for yourself."

"And you, how are you?"

"Do you recognize me?"

Arturu stared back at him, at a loss for words.

"Stiefnu, the trader on a bumboat. That's who I am. Look at me!" Stiefnu proclaimed proudly, stretching out his right hand as if he was an actor receiving applause. "I am more than that to you. But if you don't know me well enough, then this is a good way to get to know me. You've found me here, after I've just had a meal of swill, Mr. Arturu. If you had come by earlier, you'd have seen me sitting on the Quay eating and drinking. I'd have offered you some. A piece of meat, two potatoes and some peas! And two slices of buttered bread! Where there is a meal for one, two persons can eat, isn't that so? I'm a nocturnal bird, but I have to fly all day long if I don't want my wings to harden up. Otherwise, what sort of bird would I be?"

"I came here because of you. There are some things we need to discuss, you and I," Arturu spoke up.

"Drink up, and when you've done so I'll offer you some more, until you've drunk enough to admit the truth, Mr. Arturu. Look there, see, some lovely ladies will soon come out from there to sing and dance. Look at them to see what the world has to offer, away from those high walls where you've stayed locked up, and then tell me what you think," Stiefnu spoke in a harsh voice. "Bring him another beer! The same!" he called to the landlord in a loud voice. "Mr. Arturu is also a man and he can drink some more."

There was a sudden stir among the patrons as soon as the band, made up of a few men advanced in age, struck up some long, strong notes and then fell silent just as suddenly, with a jolt. A trombone, a trumpet, a tuba, a horn, a saxophone, a euphonium ...a few notes issued from them and an expectant atmosphere immediately made itself felt. At the same time, the curtain stirred and out of a little side door came four tall women with a curvaceous figure. Swaying their hips in unison and glancing at the bar patrons from between their eyelashes, they waited for the signal to begin dancing and singing. A short burst of applause greeted them without any noticeable enthusiasm and it soon petered out. Conversations became muted in the dance hall but everyone kept smoking and drinking, and went on with their conversation in whispers. All attention was riveted in one direction. Smiling faces and provocative glances. Slightly chubby legs encased in long transparent stockings, were raised and lowered in one single synchronized movement onto the small wooden stage. Long, tapering hands twirled sinuously around each body's curve. Their high heels clattered in a single rhythm. The lyrics were simple and centred on love and the melodies were sweet and tuneful with an air that was halfway between happiness and sadness, and which could easily be remembered though only heard for a short while.

Stiefnu rested his elbow on the counter, hardened his face and tone of voice and turned to Arturu, "What do you have to say to me?"

Arturu was silent, holding the glass in his hand and watching the spectacle.

"Mr. Arturu, you've made a long journey from the village to here, and it seems you're not yet acclimatized to these parts. I made this journey a long time ago, and I'm used to the distance, and I know how to measure it as well. Don't you worry; you too can see the difference. But as far as I can see, you don't like to admit it. Isn't the music to your liking? Don't you find those women fascinating? Don't you know how to find a woman somewhere beyond those walls in which you've locked yourself up?"

"You're a country person too, Mr. Stiefnu, and it's the Valley that you know most of all. The Valley is the bottom of the village."

"I used to know the Valley, and that's where I started from, but nowadays I know the sea too. The sea is far away from the Valley. Don't count me in as another one of you. I don't want to be one of you and sometimes I wish I'd never been."

"If you left the village, it means that the village rejected you. Or it means that you weren't good enough for it."

"Since when have you learnt so much about love, Mr. Arturu? Teach us then, go on, teach us! You needed to bring home a servant girl before you finally began to learn something about life."

"I brought home a servant girl who's worth as much as any other woman, and it wasn't me who threw her over when she was most in need of someone to stand by her."

"Oh no? It wasn't you? Don't you know that she too made her acquaintance with the Port a long time ago? She ended up here from the palace you made her mad about. It did her some good after all, because she learnt that the Valley was only the beginning. The Valley is a closed place."

"It wasn't the best of beginnings for her. You simply made use of her and turned out a coward."

"A coward, I? Afraid of the villagers? Afraid of the parish priest? I was afraid of who? And after all, what do we have to do with each other nowadays? Haven't you made your decision?"

"And she's made hers as well," Arturu answered him decisively.

Stiefnu lowered his glass to the counter with a bang, and made his hand into a fist and shoved it between his lips. Anger was writ large across his face.

People noticed their quarrel and looked in their direction. A hubbub arose suddenly and Arturu was startled. The band slowly came to a halt, one instrument after another and the women stopped dancing.

"It's nothing! It's nothing! Just the usual..." said the landlord, coming out from behind the counter and approaching Stiefnu.

"Mr. Arturu is a wealthy man, as you can see. Look how smartly dressed he is. Not like us seafarers. Nor like sailors and soldiers," Stiefnu sneered, addressing one and all. "Now since you're a wealthy man, Mr. Arturu, and since you're kind-hearted, put your hands in your pocket and pay for another bottle of beer..." he went on with a command in his voice. "We're near the sea, here, and the sea makes us work up an appetite. There's no fixed time for drinking, here. The bar is always open. We feel thirsty all day long. It's thirst that keeps us alive and encourages us to live fully."

"Gladly," Arturu replied in his customary courteous voice. "Bring him another bottle, if you please," he turned to the landlord.

"Another bottle? Only one? No. I'm not used to drinking alone. A bottle for everyone. Either everybody drinks or none. Stand a round for all, if you're a man," Stiefnu demanded.

A titter ran round the dance hall.

"If that's your wish, of course! No problem!" Arturu said calmly. He dipped his hand in his pocket once more and brought up money while he made a sign to the landlord to count heads.

"And this is just the beginning, Mr. Arturu," Stiefnu went on. "The price is far higher than this."

The band began to play again and the women continued their dance.

"Nobody gives something for nothing in return...If you want to take something you must pay for it," Stiefnu went on. "If you succeed in taking something, it means you've won. I give in. Very well, very well, I give in. But you must pay."

Arturu left in a hurry. Stiefnu stayed put, nonchalant, as if nothing had occurred and continued drinking his beer. Then he glanced around, put down his glass on the counter and left as well. Two barefoot boys, beggars, met him in the doorway and begged him for a penny with their hand stretched out, but he shoved them away roughly and kept on walking. The boys ran after him for a short distance but soon gave it up as a bad job.

The Port was already lit up for the night. The sea was a solid block of darkness, dark and light at the same time, reflecting the long winding outlines of the large ships and other sea craft. Apart from the singing, almost tired but cheerful, being drawled out by some sailors and soldiers, nothing could be heard. The sailors and soldiers were street choirs, filling the air with their plaintive voice. The long drawn out laugh of a young woman could break the silence and show that the world did not consist only of men, even though there were far more men than women in these places.

Arturu kept walking along the Quay. He put his hands in his pockets and tried hard to appear tranquil, without a care in the world, as the people who crossed his path that evening appeared to be. He heard firm footsteps following him and at last he stopped and turned round, saying, "There's no need to beg as you did in the dance hall, asking me to put my hands in my pocket for you. I never dreamt you'd end up begging."

"Did it seem to you that I was begging in there, Mr. Arturu?" Stiefnu demanded, arriving at his side.

"It's not a question of whether it seemed like that or not. Everyone heard you ask me to pay for you. And I paid for you. That's what being a man means."

"I didn't ask you, I ordered you. And this evening I have another order for you, and it will be the last."

"What do you mean? And when you explain please understand that there's no call to take this attitude. Whatever we have to say to each other, will finally be said today. And today it will be the last time."

"That's the way it'll be. Here I am at home. But not you, you're far away from home. The village lies at quite a distance from here. Look around you, see if you manage to see something that reminds you of that fastness of yours."

"The village...that's from where you left, you too, after all. A few years have gone by and they made you forget everything. Is your memory really so short? How can that be?"

"The years that have passed haven't made me forget. But they've taught me a lot. They taught me, first of all, that whatever I want I need to work for, I, myself. I didn't find anything ready and waiting for me, and nobody left me things as an inheritance. I think you're well able to understand that, Mr. Arturu."

"Is it my fault there were things I could inherit?"

"It's not your fault, no, but it doesn't do you any credit, either. Everything fell into your lap. You lay down on a bed that had already been made."

"If that's what you want to say, go ahead and say it. I agree with you. That's where I have the edge over you. I don't find it difficult to boast about it all."

Without them noticing, they had continued to walk along the Quay without deciding in which direction they wished to go.

"I'm the opposite, whatever I possess I got through my efforts," Stiefnu spoke to Arturu with pride. "For each penny I have, I sweated and risked my life. That sea there, look, that's drowning and risk, but it's wealth, too. We earn pennies here on land but sometimes we have to dive down to the bottom for them. Life hasn't given me anything for nothing, and it's often taken more from me. What have I done not to have life spoil me the way it's spoilt you, Mr. Arturu? Aren't you spoilt?"

"I, too, have paid for what I own."

"Did you pay for it yourself? You found all that you were born with ready and waiting for you. And all that you own today, Mr. Arturu, I gave to you – all of it!"

"Don't you worry, I too am going to see that whatever I have I'll earn, so that I can buy it and it will be mine – not yours!"

"Do you want it all? Take it! I want nothing that you desire. I am a seafarer, I row and fly over the waves, recognize the waves and see ships entering and leaving harbour day and night. Over here there's never a single lifeless moment. The ships are our lifeblood."

"The ships that bring children, you mean to say, Stiefnu!"

"The ships that enter and leave. That's what ships mean to me. The ships that bring wealth. The ships that bring children? Are you joking? Do you think I was so foolish to believe that, at the time?"

"You had a long journey to arrive here at the Port from the Valley."

"If it wasn't for that Valley you'd have nothing. Everything began in the Valley for you. Who could ever imagine things turning out this way?"

Arturu looked intently at Stiefnu, went slowly up to him and stretched out his hand to grip the other man's shoulder.

"What do you say to that, Mr. Arturu? Can you see now, that even a trader on a bumboat knows how to use his head? And he doesn't forget!"

Arturu kept his hand on Stiefnu's shoulder. "I didn't come here to quarrel with you. I came here..."

"To tell me how much you need to pay."

"Another bottle of beer?" Arturu responded with a joke. "Here, take it," he continued, taking out a coin and holding it up between two fingers to taunt Stiefnu.

"Only one coin? No, no, a bit more than that, Mr. Arturu," Stiefnu answered him with a sour smile. "My life was only a game. I played it as best I could and always hoped for good luck. It has always been like that from the beginning. When I went down into the Valley I had nothing to lose and nothing to gain. It was an adventure. Everything was new to me. From my parents' small house I could see the wide open space of the Valley down there. I needed some air. And I searched for it. Perhaps you did not feel the need. You had the wide open space of a garden. And you had books, they told me. Books, which means you could wander around and fly and even go back in time for many centuries. Do you see now that I too have learnt something? Who can lord it over you in those pages, one on top of the other? I've never read anything. That's a world without end for me. But I could not live out my life in the closed-up space of four tiny rooms. I know how my mother and father slept together. I knew when they kissed and when they quarrelled. I knew each and every hug and fight. I remember all that they whispered underneath the bed covers. I saw them loving each other and I saw them fighting together. I saw their every season with my own eyes. And every time after a fight, I saw them lie down on the same bed, him on one side and her on the other, as if nothing had happened. That's the way it had to be. Whether with a hug or with an insult, they spent their entire life like that. What sort of life is that, Mr. Arturu? Can you tell me? The harshest word wasn't strong enough to make them separate and the sweetest word wasn't enough to make them truly love each other. Somewhere in between...One minute they'd be insulting each other and the next minute they'd be praying together, and then they would snore together, all night long in one unbroken sleep till dawn. There was only one thing I didn't know – what their dreams were. But I think they dreamt of each other. And I, in the middle of all that closeness, needed wide open spaces...Those rooms were too small. They choked me. Do you still want to condemn me now?" Stiefnu shouted.

"You needed the Valley."

"I needed the Valley, and the Valley saved me, in spite of everything. That's where I became a man, and started to believe in myself, and I believed I was worth it... I was man enough and showed it. Mr. Arturu, the Valley wasn't far, even for you if you had wanted it. The village streets criss-cross each other and they meet down there. The rain water stops there. Why didn't you go down there, too? We weren't far from each other. Just a couple of streets away. The villages lie next to each other, as if they're one village."

"I didn't come here to answer all these questions."

"Mr. Arturu, tonight you must understand that I too went far away from down there. Just like you did, who's never even been there. The only difference is that I had to escape from the village and find out what to do with myself. I played the game and I'm still playing it. I'm still taking on dares whenever I put my hand in my pocket and don't hear any jingling. I cannot have any ties, at sea or on the Quay. I feel both of them moving beneath my feet and moving me along. Sometimes a day comes when there's enough work and I earn a pretty penny and can go and have a square meal somewhere under a roof. But on other days when I don't earn much, or not at all, I have to swallow swill and do it outside wherever I can find a place to sit," Stiefnu said in a voice full of emotion, and then he paused. "Please, don't let me eat heartily all on my own. May I offer you some swill?" he went on in an ironic tone. "This time, it's my turn to offer you something, a piece of meat, two potatoes and some peas...for free!"

"Swill," Arturu murmured.

"What's swill? Aren't you going to ask me that, Mr. Arturu? Go on ask me, and I'll tell you what sort of taste everyday soup has. What food and bread taste like. I'll tell you everything, as long as you ask me. I already know the taste of tomorrow and what the day after tomorrow will have. I suck on it and chew it and it's always the same. That gap in the Port is my only hope. You want to lock yourself away and I'm waiting for the day when I can spread my wings and fly far away from here."

"The two of us are content, then, in a different way."

"The two of us will be content if we agree on the rules of the game. And it's the one who's winning that makes the rules."

"I wasn't aware that I was playing a game, Stiefnu."

"Of course you knew. If I was playing a game, then you too had to be taking part, willy-nilly. A game needs at least two players to be played. Walk a bit further and I'll show you. The Quay makes for a nice stroll."

The two of them walked on till they came to a boat full of objects. It was tied to the Quay, swaying gently.

"Is this your boat?" Arturu asked.

"Yes, this is my boat. The evening has drawn in but as you can see, my boat is still full of things. So, everything is still for sale, even now. Perfumes, sweets, lace, shirts, pencils, ink, soap...That's how it was this morning when I rowed out to the ships. At the dance hall I try to forget for a while and spend what I'd have earned on other days. In there, life is soft and sweet but out here it's hard."

"I'm sorry for that."

Stiefnu hesitated and then he stuck out a hand as if expecting money and said in a decisive voice, "Pay me, Mr. Arturu!"

"Pay you? What do you mean? Pay you for what?" Arturu replied in surprise.

"Pay me! Buy all this day's worth of goods. Take everything in there, all of it, and give me whatever sum you will. But don't be mean or I'll know. And don't be too extravagant either, because I know my limits. The sea teaches us to measure all things. There, do you see? Even I can feel and sympathize."

"Give you whatever sum of money I think of? I have no idea what sort of price you expect. And besides, I don't need those things."

"You don't need them? Is it possible you don't need anything from that lot? There's nothing I can offer you?"

"Well, if that's what you want...How much do you want?" Arturu replied completely flustered. "I don't know what all those things you have filling up the boat are worth. I'm not acquainted with these parts."

"Give me what I paid for them, at least. I don't want to make a profit from you but at least..."

"I don't know how much they're worth, Stiefnu."

"Give me a few pennies, Sir. Charity! Charity! A few pennies, at least so that I may say I've earned something today," Stiefnu answered with a taunt in his voice.

"But how much? I don't know..."

"You don't know how much? How much is a young woman from the Valley worth? A lovely young woman...and have you managed to win her? And how much is that boy worth? You've won him too. Where did you get all this power so that both of them have become yours? Are you able to buy everything?"

"I've done nothing more than live the life according to the times we lived in."

"And don't you think that I too lived my life according to the times I found myself in? Is there some other way?"

"That's true, we both obeyed the rules according to our circumstances..."

"With the difference that you won and I lost because the entire village favours you."

""Not only that...and anyway, I think it wasn't like that at all," Arturu answered him, taking out coins from his pocket. He raised his eyes to Stiefnu and wordlessly asked how much he had to give him.

Stiefnu shrugged, giving him to understand that he was free to pay him as much as he wanted. "Give me whatever you want, as much as you think will help me eat and drink something. I'll be grateful for every farthing you fling. It's up to you. I leave everything in your kind hands. You know how beggars are and what they want. And if you've forgotten, just take a look around you. The Port is full of beggars. They own nothing but themselves. Some of them sleep here, in the corners, with a sack next to their head containing all they possess. And there are beggars of every age, even children. Some of the children try to climb aboard the ships with a large can to beg for swill. Their mother and father would have sent them."

Arturu remained listening, giving Stiefnu his full attention.

Suddenly, Stiefnu changed his voice and said, "Imagine me one of them. Me, Stiefnu the beggar. Don't be mean with me, remember I eat whatever I earn. Charity, Sir, charity," he begged in an ironic voice, cupping his hands to receive money.

Arturu threw a pile of coins in his hands.

"Charity, Sir, charity, give me some more," Stiefnu pleaded putting on a broken voice.

Arturu threw him some more coins.

"More!" Stiefnu ordered in a voice of steel.

Arturu plunged his hand in his pocket again and brought up more coins.

"More! Much more!" Stiefnu continued, his commanding voice getting sharper. Then he got down on his knees, bowed his head and continued to accept the coins. He then raised his head and gave Arturu a long, hard stare. In a split second he hardened his features and opened his cupped hands letting the coins stream down slowly to the ground, as if he was pouring water.

Arturu was taken aback.

"You can pick them up, now, Mr. Arturu. Now you can pick them up and make sure you don't leave any on the ground. Over here it's only the sailors who drop money, and children or beggars pick them up instantly. The sailors come by ship from abroad and they bring riches with them. When the fancy takes them, they drop some coins overboard to see starving people dive for them. In this Port, people dive to the bottom even for chunks of coal. Even coal falls into the sea, down to the very bottom, Mr. Arturu, and it sinks straight down, clump after clump, like money. You showed me that you can pay, that you wanted to pay, and I showed you that I don't need your money. You can keep it all. And do you know why, Mr. Arturu? Because all that you've won from me I cannot buy with money."

"What did I ever win from you? What are you talking about?"

"Don't you know what you've won from me?"

"That's not what I mean. I mean to say that circumstances fell that way."

"Susanna's heart belongs to you. I've known this for a long time. But never mind. My ropes were never tightly knotted and they untie very quickly. I know how to untie and how to tie. A seafarer must know these things. You can't imagine how well I can row that boat. Someday I'll row it out of the Port and never come back. I'm not tied to anybody or anything."

"The oar instead of the plough. Is this the choice you made?"

"The oar leads you outside and takes you on many journeys. The plough hardens in the soil. There's nothing here to bind me to the soil. Even the Valley was some way off from the heart of the village, but it was no different. The sea is something else altogether." Again he paused and bowing his head continued, "Pick up those coins, from now onwards all that money is yours, all of it. I'm giving them back to you."

Arturu gave him a savage look, but controlled the rage that threatened to overcome him.

"I don't need your money, Mr. Arturu. Today, I too have grown enough to be independent. Look at the Port. It's alive and it doesn't know how to rest because it never gets tired. It gives us hope, by day and by night. Your village is dead on its feet, by day and by night," Stiefnu spoke scornfully, putting his hands in his pocket and jingling the coins he had. "I earn good money."

"I don't know why you should take up this aggressive attitude with me. I'm not to blame for anything that's happened. I've always been far away from you, even though circumstances brought us together somehow. Nobody can predict circumstances. You should have learnt this lesson too from the sea."

"You're not to blame, that's true. But the fact remains that you and I found ourselves on the same path and we ended up having to fight each other. You didn't want to and neither did I. And you won, maybe without even knowing me, and I lost. Do you think I shouldn't feel anything, being the loser?"

"I didn't know you, certainly."

The sea before them was a large spread of reflections, like straight and swaying lines going down to the bottom. It buried inside itself the continuous babble of words coming from aboard the ships, uttered without being understood. Even from the quayside, life aboard ship could be seen from the movement people made, looking tiny.

"Today or tomorrow, this rage inside me had to erupt," Stiefnu went on in a calmer tone. "And I wanted to show you that I too have some pride. I've never let myself weep in all these years. I thought and asked questions, yes, but wept, no. I don't want to cry. I desired something, and what I desired cannot be, and I understand that. Our desires aren't there to come true, all of them. From the time I lived with the Valley till now I've learnt many things."

"I too have learnt a lot."

"I tried to make you angry this evening, Mr. Arturu, but I didn't succeed. You won against me in this, too. At first I thought it was because you're a calm person, but now I can see that this isn't so. It's more than that. I can imagine where you got all this. From the village. But all the same, the village is no longer for me."

"But the village is within you, all the same, if I may tell you so. And it will remain in you. It blends with the city in you and the mixture will be good. Don't you think so?"

"Aren't you the least bit angry with me, Mr. Arturu? I wanted to humiliate you as much as possible this evening. I didn't just see you as yourself but as a whole village. And you still did not say an extra word and you didn't lose your patience. We're not like each other, the two of us."

"Then it's not the town and village that are different from each other."

"Are you saying that I was born with wings from the very beginning, and you were born without them? The open space of the Valley wasn't enough for me but the fastness of the walls was enough for you? Two different streets that never meet." Stiefnu paused and approached Arturu. "Excuse me, Mr. Arturu! All that I've done, I've done to show you that I too did not waste all these years that have passed."

"Truly, all that you've succeeded in doing is a credit to you."

"My boat needs to grow more. That's what I hope for. And I understand the choice Susanna made. I cannot be grateful for all that Fr. Grejbel did and not respect Susanna's decision. You can whisper in your heart, 'This man has no ties, neither with the sea nor with the soil.' That's true, that's how I am. But that isn't the real reason, the most true one. I cannot go against Fr. Grejbel, today more than ever. My anger against you was simply an effort. And I'll get over it. That's what the sea does to you, Mr. Arturu. It changes ever so quickly, one minute it's rough and the next minute it's calm, suddenly there are large waves and just as suddenly there's a gentle swell. You can never tell. And I'm just like that. Excuse me, please."

"Don't worry about it. I can understand. And we can shake hands over it..."

"For today and whatever the future may hold," Stiefnu assented, going up to Arturu and embracing him. "Our paths are very different but they briefly crossed each other somewhere where it all began...and Fr. Grejbel intervened and risked his all. He suffered a great deal but I did my part, all that I had to do..."

"You?"

"Yes, me. Late, very late, but I did it. And Fr. Grejbel came back..."

They continued walking while Arturu looked at him in amazement.

"Let me tell you the whole story. But first, I'd like you to come with me on the boat. Don't be afraid, I row very well," Stiefnu assured him. "And the sea is very calm. It's like oil, hardly moving at all. There's no need to be afraid. And you'll see how different the world looks from out there, everything seems to be moving, everything at a distance, and nothing stays still. Mr. Arturu, the sea is a village without walls, and the Port is a door leading to some other place. Will you come with me?"

Arturu went in the boat against his will. Gradually, the fear that he felt in the beginning abated. "Truly, even though the sea is calm, the whole world seems to be on the move, and nothing stays still. Imagine then how it will be during a storm!" he said to himself. His mind was bent on going back soon to the village.

Chapter 13

In Baskal's wine tavern, everything was prepared for that evening's special occasion. Since early morning Baskal had taken pains to have everything in order: he dusted every inch of the place, arranged the bottles on the shelves, placed the glasses symmetrically, and looked at the tavern from all angles, arranging and then re-arranging everything to his satisfaction, as if he was preparing some large place, much bigger than his tavern was in reality. He never hoped to have a bigger place. Custom never flagged, though it came from a handful of regular clients, and his wine had never failed to satisfy and even gladden people's heart and make them open their mouth. What with one word or another, between one story and another tale, his tavern was a long yarn representing the simple life, a kind of refuge for whoever entered and spent an hour there, drinking, discussing, and hoping to win some argument or other. That's where dreams and wishes, complaints, jokes, angry incidents, suspicions, and most of all memories, were aired and expressed.

Remembrance was the strongest magnet that tavern possessed. Each person who sat down at a table had to recount some memory, otherwise he would not feel thirsty, or if he did feel thirsty, the wine would not be enough to slake his thirst. That was where people's reputations were built up or destroyed, with words and impressions that the village could not do without if it wanted to remain the same – the place untouched by time because it did not allow any movement that could bring about a change.

"This was such a good idea for this evening's entertainment, you know, a really good idea," Ġwakkin began to say. "The best idea that ever entered your tavern, Baskal. It must mean there's an open door somewhere, letting in fresh air!"

"My doors are always open, Ġwakkin, and everybody is welcome. The village heartbeat is here. Not in the village square, but here...A good idea, yes, a good idea, of course it was a good idea. This is where the story began and this is where it must end. It's one of the most important rules of the village, that, Ġwakkin. And I'm telling this to you and to everybody!" he declared in a tone where seriousness blended with irony, straightening up as he spoke, as if he was addressing a large crowd.

The men raised their heads, looking at him with great attention.

"It had to come about. One day or another we had to meet him and welcome him. After all, we've always respected him, and we never thought or spoke a word except as country folk. A thought, after all, can fly away and disappear, out of the village. But we still remain here, the same people. We're not too different from each other, all of us born and bred in this place," Baskal continued saying.

"We're not different, no, how could we be? Maybe sometimes the wine goes to our head and sometimes it makes tempers flare. It's too capricious for words.

It's unpredictable. You can't even trust it with an empty glass, the rascal," Ġwakkin piped up.

"A rascal? Wait...wait a minute. Who are you calling a rascal?" Baskal quickly cut him short.

"The wine! Wasn't it about the wine that I was talking? It's a friend to us all..." Ġwakkin reassured him. "Everything depends on our friend. Go on," he ordered.

"I am going on. Anyway, I was saying...And so? We do say more than we should, sometimes, there's no denying, because one word leads to another and the tavern doesn't keep going strong only with alcohol. It also needs thoughts," Baskal began holding forth once more. In the meantime he had not stopped for a single moment from cleaning the clean glasses, and polishing them and rearranging them like someone arranging a display hoping to win a prize. "The tavern is spotless, isn't it? What do you think? The occasion merits that! And I brought some flowers too, to change the everyday appearance and to perfume the place with their fragrance. Look, look there at that vase in the middle, full of flowers, nicely arranged by someone whose hands are never still and there we are, everything takes on a new life. Baskal's wine tavern. What other place in the village can compete with Baskal's wine tavern? Tell me, what does it lack in comparison with the large bars, all colours and decorations of all sorts that they say they have in the towns? What don't you have that others do, my little palace?" he exclaimed, opening his arms wide. He went to the door and stepped out, glancing here and there, straightened up and came back inside, gazing all around his tavern. "It needs nothing more! And that's my final say!"

"He needs to come," Ġamri interjected, glancing at all his mates.

"True. You're right, Ġamri. He needs to come," Kieli agreed.

"He promised he would come as soon as he closed up the church. You know what people are like...Some old people never stop praying. They ramble on and on and on, and never stop. They know many prayers, and they know them by heart, and they can repeat them without mixing them up and without getting tired. Not even the sacristan with his candle-snuffer can make them stop. What other signal do they have to see to realize that the day has come to an end and that the church has got to be closed?" Baskal grumbled. "The sacristan is also a man, after all, and even he deserves to rest after a whole day spent on his feet. I say so even though he's never shown his face in here and made me earn a penny."

"They're better people than we are, though, because they pray a lot. We, well...we don't follow their lead, much," Ġwakkin muttered. "We do pray, of course we do, but then we put our lips to other work."

"Speak for yourself, Ġwakkin!" Ġamri snapped at him. "I can't say I can drone on like those old women in church, but don't you think I pray too? What sort of villager would that make me? But now, apart from all this..."

"He's coming as soon as he closes the church," Baskal reiterated. "That's what he promised me and that's what he'll do."

"I hope he won't be long in coming. I'm feeling very thirsty. A thirsty man cannot stand around for long. He's like a dry plant. Then, as soon as you water it, it perks up! Give it some water and you'll see! And if you water it a lot there's no holding it back! And a man is just the same! Otherwise, what sort of man would he be? Aren't you all thirsty?"

"Of course we're thirsty. But this evening we must wait for him; that's the right thing to do. We'll drink when he comes, and we'll drink with him. And then there'll be nothing to stop us. We must wait a bit more," Ġamri affirmed.

"No, no, not a drop for now," Baskal confirmed. "It's not really to my advantage to say this, you know, because it's through you and your drinking that I earn some money. Drink up then, my friends! Drink, drink...and always drink up, my friends! But this time – no. This evening, that's what's required and so I have to say, 'No, for now, no drinks!' And that's an order! Even this is my final say!" he declared with a smile.

"Now, my friends, as soon as he comes we must get up and greet him!" Kieli suggested. "We must behave like well-educated people."

"That's rich! As if we need you to tell us what we should do! We know how these things are done. We're not complete rustics from the back of beyond, behind high, large mountains as they say," Ġwakkin interjected, "though we've none of us ever seen these mountains they talk about. Funny isn't it? We don't live behind these mountains but in the meantime we don't have a clue where these blessed mountains can be found! And we don't even know what they look like!"

"No, no! We're not from the back of beyond, behind high mountains, as if! Not behind them nor in front of them, but somewhere around, a bit here and there, most of all when a drop of wine reveals the truth. The grape isn't like other fruit. It's the queen of fruit. The vine's woody stems produce twigs that have no fixed shape and you can't see where they begin or end. It's a fruit for the brain, it goes to your head and the head reasons with it, and it reasons better. The grape is an intelligent fruit. So what can be better than wine? The truth lies in wine! Which means, what can be better than the truth?" Ġamri rambled on.

"But not only that, Ġamri, not only," Baskal butted in with the tone of a learned man who wants to pass on a lesson. "We now know that truth isn't to be found only in wine. We've drunk enough and thought enough to realize this."

"Of course it's not only to be found in wine," the others mumbled together with a serious air.

"Not only in wine," Baskal repeated. "And let me tell you something else, my friends. It seems that truth can't be found in my wine tavern...I say this against my will, after all these years I've opened up shop in here, but that's how it is. The truth is the truth." Baskal spoke these words humbly but with a hint of pride in them, rising and walking to the door to peer out. As soon as he looked, he sharply pulled his head back and with his hands at his back stood to attention.

The others nodded their head in a single motion as if it had been agreed amongst them and gazed at him in astonishment. They were about to get up and move away all at once but they remained where they sat.

"He's coming, he's coming, my friends!" Baskal announced with a dramatic whisper, and he went to the doorway again and waited, standing as straight as straight can be in the doorway, this time with his hands clasped in front of him as if he was in church.

The others all stood up, standing straight as well.

Fr. Grejbel arrived, shook hands with Baskal and then embraced him. He then went up to the others and also shook hands with them and embraced them. There were a few moments of silence which could be cut with a knife. They all remained standing up as if they did not know what came next. In that moment, the confident air they always had in that tavern evaporated in an instant. They looked like men who had never set foot inside that place, and who did not know each other or were regular drinkers and as if they had never seen the priest with their eyes before. They gave him a long, fixed stare...from head to toe and from toe to head. And there were a few moments when they looked as if they were about to smile nervously. And for a few moments they were about to put on a serious air. They looked here and there...at nothing in particular and at each other...and at the empty table, empty as it had never been all these long years. It was as if they were seeing a special scene, one they could not believe was truly happening.

The bottles of wine were in their place, and the brightly polished glasses were gleaming on the shelves.

"May we sit down, my friends?" Fr. Grejbel said to break the silence, and to lighten the atmosphere. "Baskal, it's your say, this is your tavern. What do you say, landlord?"

Baskal remained with his hands grasping the edges of his apron, nervous and shy. Then he lifted up his hands clasped together in front of his chest, bowed his head and replied, "Of course, of course, Sir, sit down, sit down please, all of you. We were waiting for you. Usually I direct things in this place...but today it's up to you. That's the proper thing to do."

Everybody sat down.

"I made you wait, but I couldn't come any earlier," Fr. Grejbel began.

"It doesn't matter. It doesn't matter," they chorused.

Baskal brought out some glasses and came to their table, putting a glass in front of each person. He went back to the bar counter and picked up a bottle of wine, bringing it to the table. He raised it proudly for everyone to see, uncorked it, smelt it, gave it a smile and began to pour.

"I rarely drink. Only during the feast, as the occasion demands. But today I will gladly drink with you, not a lot but still, I'll drink some wine with you," Fr. Grejbel told them. "It's as if it's a feast day, today!"

They all stood up and raised their full glass.

"To your good health!" he toasted them with great joy.

"To your good health, Sir! To your good health!" they spoke as one.

"I'm not Sir! You know my name, what it was and still is," he replied with a smile. "We're all country folk, and we stick together. The same way we were, are, and will be."

"To your good health, then Fr. Grejbel!" Baskal shouted.

"To Fr. Grejbel's good health!" the others took up the toast.

"We're going to wake up the entire village this evening...all this noise..." Fr. Grejbel said guiltily, feeling embarrassed.

"It doesn't matter, it doesn't matter," Ġwakkin said. "If it's in your honour, it doesn't matter."

"If need be, we'll hold another feast in your honour," Ġamri stated. "We'll hold another feast for you. We don't need telling twice to hold a feast."

"No, no, one was enough, and it was extra, really. I never expected all this. The saint is that one in the niche, and as for us, as long as we remain down here, we're only men and women. Between ourselves," Fr. Grejbel bent his head and lowered his voice as far as it would go, "I won't shout so he won't hear me. I don't want the saint in his niche to be touchy because of me. He might begin to say, in his heart of hearts, 'Just see Fr. Grejbel these days, how puffed up with himself he is! Since when has he been trying to take my place?' As if! He can't imagine how much I...But enough of that. This evening is not the time to deliver a sermon."

"Oh well, instead of one saint we'll have two," Ġamri spoke up.

"Oh no! God forbid!" Fr. Grejbel laughed heartily.

"We'll make you a niche, Fr. Grejbel, the same way we made all those niches in the church. And we'll make it even lovelier! And do you know why we'll make it for you? Because we were the ones to make you go through all that martyrdom. That's the truth of it." Baskal declared.

"That's true! That's all very true!" one of the men said fervently, and then all the others joined in. "That's true! That's all very true!..."

"You know how I feel on this subject. What's past is past. All that there's left is to see what good came out of it all, and not just for me personally, but for you too," Fr. Grejbel was insistent. "Tell me, how have you passed the time since I've been away?"

"Without you here, Fr. Grejbel?" Ġamri burst in.

"No, not without me here, not because I wasn't here...how has the time passed here?" the priest asked once more.

"Without you here the village seemed to be flustered. We still spent our days as usual, from our fields to home, from home to church. It all stayed the same because life goes on. But no, without you we weren't the same as before," Ġamri went on. "Ask anybody, and you'll see. Everyone will say the same thing. That's what we villagers have in our favour. We agree on things!"

"What can we tell you? Who was born and who died? How much it rained and how hot it was? How much fruit we had? As to that, the same as usual, the village was and will stay what it's always been," Kieli said.

"That doesn't mean we didn't learn a lot from all that has happened. We did learn, and we've changed too," Ġamri said.

With a huge smile on his face, Fr. Grejbel wanted to show them how pleased he was to be hearing all that they were saying. "Bless you! Bless you all! That's why time moves on, and if we change along with it, why then it won't have come and gone for nothing."

"We're blessed, Fr. Grejbel? We're blessed? And are we blessed now, now that we're old?" Baskal asked the priest in surprise.

"We're blessed?" murmured the rest in unison.

"You are blessed now, though you think you weren't before. It's never too late. But tell me, how have you spent all this time?" he asked them once more.

The five men remained silent, looking straight at their glasses and waiting for him to go on speaking.

"Nothing? There's nothing you can tell me?"

"Nothing!" they answered him, almost amazed.

Ġamri stood up and told him, "Fr. Grejbel, you can tell us many things, that's certain. We've stayed right here. Our minds have stayed the same. We give it wine to drink so it may think, but when we do that what does it do? It roams where it will, nothing more. When the wine's influence passes, it comes back and brings us back right here with it, where we were before. Playing *Ring-a-ring-a-rosies*, that's how we were and that's how we still are. But you left this place and went far away from here, and crossed the sea. We've hardly ridden over the ground but you've ridden over the waves. That's what they said. Tell us something yourself," he asked him and then paused. "Imagine how many things you have in your mind that are completely new to us!"

"He's right. What he's saying is very true." The rest spoke together.

"Is that what you think?" Fr. Grejbel asked them. "Well then, what would you like me to tell you? Go on. Ask me and I'll do my best to answer you. You can start, Ġamri. Someone has to go first, and then the rest take heart."

"Me? Start off? Well then, let me see," Ġamri nodded and thought for a while. "Very well! Is it true that the world is a very large place? People often say that. Is it true or not?"

"That's a good question," the others approved, looking at each other with a satisfied look and taking it all very seriously. "Good, that's good."

"Yes, it's true that the world is a very large place, and it's far too big for us, who live in this village, to understand what that means. There are enormous distances, that never seem to have limits," Fr. Grejbel answered.

"Enormous?" they chorused. "And how big is that?"

"Enormous! Words cannot begin to describe them!" he told them, awe apparent in his voice though he spoke half-seriously and half in jest. "Truly enormous," he went on opening his hands wide like children do, as if he wanted to embrace all that was in front of him.

They were thunderstruck and opened their arms in likewise fashion.

"Larger than our fields?" Ġwakkin wanted to know.

"Much larger than our fields, Ġwakkin."

"But how much larger? Let's say as large as the entire village?" Kieli took up the thread.

"No, Kieli, far larger than that!"

All of them showed themselves full of interest, and astonished with each thought that flitted through their mind, they bombarded him with questions, in all seriousness, like very young children who want to know things.

"And is it true that there are mountains?"

"Certainly there are mountains."

"And are they big?" someone else asked.

"Very big."

"And is it true that there are rivers?"

"True, as well."

"And is it true that there are savage, ferocious animals?"

"That's true as well."

"Animals with large pointed teeth?"

"Yes, it's true."

"Tigers? Lions? Crocodiles? Snakes?"

"Of course, and many other kinds, too."

"And is it true that there are ferocious animals that kill each other?"

"That's true as well."

"And do they really eat people, too?"

"Yes, they do."

"Is it true that there are oceans and seas?"

"True, yes."

"And there is the Pacific Ocean, the Atlantic Ocean, the Arctic Ocean..."

"Yes."

"And is it true that there are many volcanoes on Earth?"

"Yes, it's true."

"And there are dormant volcanoes and active ones?"

"Yes."

"And is it true that there are hurricanes, cyclones, snow and ice?"

"Yes, it's true."

Fr. Grejbel went on answering their eager questions, fascinated by their amazement, that grew with each question they posed.

"But now, if you please, stop for a while, my friends!" Baskal interrupted their babble all of a sudden. "I never imagined my tavern would end up a great house of learning like this. You're making me feel extremely ignorant." He turned to the priest and told him, "Sir, the good fruit of the vine I've given them is already doing its work. They've started using their imagination. Usually it's about our streets and paths and alleys, but tonight they've gone abroad and are going far away. Don't be offended with them, or rather with us, because I'm one of them."

"Oh leave off, Baskal!" Ġamri bit his head off.

"We're only asking him sensible questions, Baskal! Questions that require some hard thinking," Ġwakkin shouted.

"You've asked him some questions too, yourself, Baskal!" Kieli put his oar in.

"I began to ask him questions but then I stopped. A few questions are enough. But not all these. I know these things exist. These aren't fables and fairy tales, my friends. These are real. But we can't learn everything in one evening. Where's the hurry? And the gentleman is tired tonight! All these questions! How much can a man remember and know?" Baskal asserted, a landlord's authority behind his respectful tone towards the priest. "And I have something to say, to all of you. It's not something to my advantage, on the contrary, but I must say it. From now onwards I'm not going to sell any more wine. I'm going to close! I, Baskal, declare here and now, that Baskal's wine tavern is closed! And, most of all, out of respect for you, Sir, so that our friends can learn some proper conduct! I'm closed!"

"Closed? You're closing?" they asked in astonishment and dismay.

"From now onwards, that is, I mean tonight, till I close up," Baskal quickly corrected himself.

"Ahh, now! That's something else!" they responded together in relief. "You've set our mind at rest!"

"Don't give us such a fright," Kieli objected. "Don't joke this way!"

"Sir, you asked us what's happened here since that time," Ġwakkin turned to Fr. Grejbel. "What's happened is that we realized we don't know what lies beyond the village. You left, and we thought of you, always asking 'Where did that man go? Far away? But what does far away mean? What does it really mean? There are some who say that the world is round, but we've always seen it flat. Ever since we were children we've seen it this way."

"And there are some who say that the world is always turning round with us on it. But see, we're here around a table but we don't move. We don't feel any movement, not a stir, not even a small jerk – nothing! What's all this, then, Sir?" Kieli said puzzled, putting down his glass and touching the table to show how fast it stood.

"These people want to have their little joke, Sir," Baskal interposed. "Am I right or not to take control of the wine?"

"No, no, Baskal, we're not joking about these matters. You too want to ask the gentleman many things, especially since we've finally found this opportunity," Kieli went on determinedly.

"Well, you're right there...that's true," Baskal conceded. "There are many things that come to my mind, unbidden, without me knowing how they get there, and without wanting to. But I've never asked anyone about them. And I've always said to myself, 'If I've made do, so far, the way I am, I can make do tomorrow, too.' And the same goes for the day after tomorrow and the day after that, always the same. If you make do once, you can always make do."

"We don't know anything, Sir. Absolutely nothing!" Ġamri declared in the tone of a man who has completely given up.

"And more than that, we know..." Ġwakkin continued to say.

"What do we know?" the others were quick to snap at him.

"We know that we know nothing," Ġwakkin replied.

"We've only just realized lately," the others assented together.

"All of us know only so much, Ġamri," Fr. Grejbel spoke reassuringly. "We know as much as we can to make do. If there's as much as we've mentioned, there's something we know for sure. Wherever we go there are people just like us."

"That means that we, villagers, could be living on top of mountains," Ġwakkin concluded

"Or next to a river," Kieli said.

"Or..." the others were going to continue.

"We could have been born anywhere; we're no different from each other, my friends," Fr. Grejbel said to them. "You can be sure that everywhere there are people who have a mind that wants to understand, and they have a heart to feel, all the time. In lands where you cannot see any limits, where seasons bring many great changes with them, there are people just like us who live in this village, at the edge of the world, right on the edge..."

"Right on the edge, huh? That's where...we are," Ġwakkin reflected.

"And for all that, we still don't fall over, huh! It would be unbelievable if it wasn't true!" Kieli mused in amazement.

"Well then the world must be round..." Baskal went on. "Where would you find a better proof than this?"

"And it's turning round!" Ġamri concluded.

"That's it, my friends! The world is round, or nearly so...and it's turning round with us on it..." Fr. Grejbel informed them.

"Right at this minute?" they all asked him.

"Right at this very minute, my friends! Hold on tight because we're moving! Let us stand fast!" he smiled back at them.

They stared back at him in amazement, as if they were struggling hard to believe him. Their face displayed a rather disappointed and sour look. They did not want to show less than complete faith in him, but it was no mean feat for them to reason like him. "How can that be?" they all thought.

"That's it! Wherever we are, if we look up we'll all see the same sky," Fr. Grejbel asserted, pausing to see their reaction.

There was perfect silence. The men looked at each other, their faces showing surprise, more than ever before.

"Let me be the one to tell you what happened, then, Sir," Baskal made an attempt to explain after a few moments of silence. "A little while ago, right here under this very roof, we ended up discussing whether the world went round the sun or whether it was the sun that went round the Earth. We couldn't conclude if that was how some people thought or if that was the way we saw and felt ourselves. From here, in our fields, we've always seen the sun rise from behind the hills early in the morning, and then we always saw it set behind those same hills in the evening. Our hills surround our village. They've been there since before our time. We said to ourselves, 'There's no other way to resolve this mystery except to go somewhere near the sea and see what happens with our own eyes.' We needed positive proof from the sea itself! The sea is far away from here but we had to go."

"The sea is far away, too far away," they chorused.

"And one evening we agreed to go to bed early and then we rose very early, earlier than usual," Baskal went on. "We took food and drink with us. We took water, only water! And fresh water at that, to keep our mind fresh and alert. No wine! And at last we arrived at another village from where we could see the sea in front of us. There it was. And we chose a good spot and stayed there. The ground was sure and solid. Not a soul could be seen and not a sound could be heard. We could concentrate. Not even the sea was making the least movement, let alone the Earth. Usually the sea stirs a bit, with a gentle swell if anything, but that day no. We were all staring, without saying a single word. Our thoughts were all concentrated on one thing. We waited and waited. And there it was!" Baskal continued, spreading his hands open. "There it was! Suddenly we saw the sun slowly, slowly appear from behind the horizon, or anyway, it was touching it. The point is that the sun was moving. We couldn't contradict what our own eyes were telling us. 'There it is. There it is. That's it, my friends...it's rising. Rising!' we shouted in certainty. We stayed there seeing it rise, up and up, on its own, up to the clouds above. What a moment that was! We'll never forget it!"

"True, that's all very true what he's saying," the three other men nodded wisely.

Fr. Grejbel listened to it all with a very serious air of attention.

"But this wasn't enough for us, Sir," Baskal spoke again. "We also had to see if at the end of the day the sun would go down or not. We thought that if it could go up, it could also stay up there. Who could gainsay it? We stayed there for the entire day, concentrating on it. And we stayed there till evening, without moving about. And there it was, then! 'There it is. There it is. The very same!' we shouted once more. We also saw it go down, always going further and further down till it disappeared behind the horizon. The sun had risen and had then set, in front of our eyes. We had spent the entire day in the same place, without moving, without even a little shuffle. Not even a little jerk as when you're on a cart...nothing!"

"Not even one little jerk!" they all said together to Fr. Grejbel.

"What a shame! If we'd had a boat, we could have gone after it, towards the horizon, and we'd have been able to see where it slept during the night," Ġwakkin declared. "We were dying of curiosity. But we didn't have a boat. None of us were familiar with the sea. The horizon wasn't that far away."

"No, it wasn't far away. The horizon wasn't far away," the others affirmed.

"Leave me be to go on telling him..." Baskal broke in brusquely, now that he had got the bit between his teeth. "We said to ourselves, 'Well then, we must see the world turn every time we drink wine. If we don't let it go to our head, we won't turn. So it must be the sun that turns and our world doesn't.' That day I had to close shop, unwillingly, but it was necessary. But these friends of mine here took care of me all the same, and they promised to come to my tavern on the morrow to drink wine, and not only the usual amount but double that, to make it up to me...and they kept their word." Baskal smiled with satisfaction at the memory.

"We had two days' thirst to slake. In all those hours we spent facing the sea, we only drank water, only water, to make sure that we saw properly," Kieli remembered. "And we only had one thing on our minds. But not the next day, the next day we went to drink as usual."

"And we started seeing the world turn once more, but we were sure that it wasn't true. So, there's no truth in wine, then..." Ġamri said with a worried frown.

"But tonight, Sir, you've changed our mind. From what you say, the world is round and it turns round," Baskal concluded.

"That's it, my friends!" Fr. Grejbel smiled back at them.

"And has it been turning round like that for long?" they wanted to know.

"It's been going on like that from the very beginning," he answered.

"Both the world and the village?" they asked him together with one voice.

"Of course, it's the same everywhere," Fr. Grejbel smiled again.

"Even now? At this very moment?" Baskal asked in amazement, looking at the ceiling and at every corner of his tavern, and he moved his legs and stamped on the floor, like a soldier, to stand fast.

"Of course, even now," Fr. Grejbel reassured him.

"What a huge mistake we made!" they all exclaimed together.

"We needn't have got up so early, that time!" Ġwakkin grumbled.

"And we had such a long trek, for nothing!" Ġamri groused.

"And we lost out on a day's drinking!" Kieli joined in the general complaint.

"We'll never bring back all that wine we missed out on!" Baskal mourned.

"And so, from where you were Sir, when you looked up at the sky you were seeing the same sky that we were seeing from here, meanwhile! That's it, isn't it?" Ġwakkin crowed.

"That's it," Fr. Grejbel confirmed.

"You're a good man, and a good man always looks up at the sky...Well then, in all that time, you were looking at the sky over our village, too," Ġwakkin continued. "The same sky..."

"All the time, yes," the priest replied.

"And we never realized," Kieli observed.

"Even if it was stormy?" Ġamri asked.

"And if it was a fine day?" Ġwakkin wanted to know.

"Of course, because stormy weather and fine weather are very close to each other, even though they're not good friends," Fr. Grejbel remarked. "The two go together. We see a year passing by when the seasons come by, and there is a season for storms and a season for fair weather." He rose and adjusted his soutane, and clasped his hands together as a signal that it was time for him to leave.

"No, Sir. Tonight we can't keep on drinking when you leave. This is your evening," Baskal told him. "Tonight I'll close up as soon as you leave. Tonight we'll all leave together."

The others agreed with him.

"You still haven't told me what you've all been doing in all this time," Fr. Grejbel reminded them with a smile.

"Nothing, we did nothing, Sir," they all said.

Ġamri shook his head. "The gentleman is right to ask us what we did," he said, turning to his mates. "Well, let's tell him then. We only did one thing, Sir! We set up a village theatrical company! We set it up as a joke, talking amongst ourselves, on the same day news came that you were coming back!" he said, pointing his forefinger at the priest.

"Really? What a good idea! You set up a theatrical company? And what have you done, since?" he asked them.

"Nothing! What do we know about it, Sir?" Kieli asked.

"We're not actors," Ġwakkin went on.

"We've been play-acting every single day between ourselves, all this time, Gentlemen!" Ġamri told them with satisfaction.

"We don't even know how to write! We have to remember everything by heart, or invent. We play-act as we know how," Kieli interposed.

"In Baskal's tavern, Sir!" Ġamri declared full of faith in that little band of men.

"Ġamri's in the right of it, Sir," Baskal stated. "This tavern is a little theatre. And many short plays have been performed, with unexpected beginnings and endings. Everyone recounting stories by digging into his memory. That's a deep well, cut into the rock, and everyone dredging something up, and its waters never run dry. It's not always sweet tasting fresh water that comes up...But the bucket never comes up empty. You have no idea how many stories came up...That's the beauty of it all. But that's the pity of it, too. Just like life. Where there's wine..."

"There's truth!" the others answered him with one voice.

"And there's also imagination!" Baskal declared. "The world appears flat but it's actually round. And it seems not to move, but in fact it does. It's been doing it all this time but we've only just realized it, and really and truly, we still find it hard to believe. Things aren't always what they appear, then, that's all." Abruptly he fell silent, satisfied with what he had said, and he cleared his throat to change his tone. "Fr. Grejbel, when will you come here again? This evening you've brought much happiness with you..."

"Because of you we've felt ourselves like young children again, in spite of our age," Ġwakkin told him.

"I've never asked so many questions in all my life, Sir," Kieli said to him. "I never had the courage."

"And I'd never realized how many questions there were that I'd never felt bothered to ask," Ġamri put in his bit.

"And as for me, what should I say, Fr. Grejbel?" Baskal groused. "Should I say that I stopped these friends from asking you more questions? One question right after another! And do you know why I stopped them? Because as they were asking you, they took me back to when I was a youngster clinging to my mother's skirts. I used to bombard her with questions about everything I saw. It wasn't right. Poor Mother! She used to try to give me an answer and rack her brain, and make up things to tell me and go on and on. And I would pretend along...I thought that since she was my mother, she should know everything, God forgive her," he said while he made the Sign of the Cross and kissed the tips of his fingers of his right hand. "And I used to ask her in the same way we've done today with you, whether children came by ship...and she used to give me an answer full of fantasy. Ships were always something far away from us. Tall. Huge, heavy and mysterious... How do they float with all that load while a stone sinks right down to the bottom? That time of asking questions had gone by for us, once and for all. But today, because of you, we lived it once more."

Perfect silence reigned in that tavern.

"Come again, Fr. Grejbel," they pleaded all together.

"I shall come, and on that day we will play-act together. And do you know what that little play will be called?" Fr. Grejbel posed them the question with a contented laugh, smiling from ear to ear. "It will be called 'Even Adults Come By Ship'."

They felt too shy to laugh with him and remained silent. They went up to him, one by one, and embraced him. There were tears in their eyes.

Fr. Grejbel took note. "Man cries with sadness, and also with joy," he observed. "Joy and sorrow are mixed together. And tonight we're crying with happiness! You and I together!"

"You've brought us all this joy from afar, Fr. Grejbel!" Baskal rejoiced. "From across the sea..."

Chapter 14

Fr. Grejbel was due to arrive any minute at Arturu's house. Arturu had been pacing the floor in the hallway for a long time, with his hands clasped behind his back, sometimes raising and waving them about as if he was speaking alone but imagining someone facing him.

"He shouldn't be long," Arturu said to himself, going out on the doorstep to check and coming back inside.

He was still the same, a person who liked to be wearing a smart suit whatever the time of day, as if he was on the point of attending a feast. Above all, he liked to wear a waistcoat and it seemed he never took it off. His hair was always combed back in the same fashion – presenting an example of a man who took pains to keep up his groomed appearance since a man is often judged a gentleman according to his mode of dress and general appearance. It was the custom in his family and he was not about to break with tradition, now that he had ended up on his own. His mother had spent her entire life urging him to keep up a good appearance, because a good suit bestows worth both in the eyes of the villagers and of outsiders. The person with a slovenly appearance gets trampled upon; she used to like repeating with the conviction of a woman without the least doubt in her old and fixed principles.

One of these well-known principles was that *clothes maketh the man,* judged a gentleman according to his appearance, and other values would follow suit. He had learnt this lesson very well and followed it to the letter with no bother at all. In actual fact he had no choice. An entire vision of life had opened up before his eyes when he was still a little boy, without a hint of rebelliousness on his part, and all he had to do was to see that it made sense, was for his own good, and without it there was nothing – except dishonour.

He could never forget his mother. She had been the sort of woman who brings up children with great discipline; everything was done in good measure and at the right time. For her, the large house, richly furnished, was a palace from which she could observe the large, bustling world outside, quietly and at a distance, without too much time spent at a window looking out. For her, an entire house was like a ventilator in a humble villager's home. She did not like to go out and about much, and when she ventured outside she always kept herself to herself.

"Good morning and Good evening, and the rest is all superfluous. Better one hundred words less than one extra word," Lady used to impress upon Arturu. She was a reserved person according to her own nature but also because she cultivated such detachment. She was of the opinion that in this way she had earned the villagers' respect and also her own. She could never forgive herself for the least mistake. She would present herself in front of the large hall mirror as the accused party needing her own defence. She would go up to the mirror and look balefully at her reflection, then change her expression once or twice and move around to strike up the right pose...Lady used to realize when she had committed an error and when she had behaved well according to her lights. "You alone don't lie to me," she would tell the mirror. "First of all, if you lie I'll catch you out. And secondly, if you lie it gains you nothing. You'll remain what you've always been – simply a reflection of what's real. Console yourself with that!"

The streets of the village were a mystery to her. Alleyways criss-crossing each other. Narrow streets eventually leading to the square. Living in that large villa bequeathed to her by her late husband, it was easy for her to conclude that all the world to her was that small space in which she lived, without wandering beyond its limits. She had no need to.

Beyond were the villagers, people who were different.

All these teachings had reached every corner of Arturu's mind. And his respect for Lady remained, seeing her as a monument to measured order, loyalty, and everything that was good and serious. Every corner in the house reminded him of her, and the last words she said to him remained etched in his mind, as if they were the only words he had ever heard. These were no different from the words she had said before. The fact that she always insisted on the same things impressed him. She too, he used to think, never changed.

"I too have reason to pity you. At least I know who my mother is," Susanna had taunted him once, in a moment of anger.

"What do you mean by that?" he had asked her. "Who told you that?"

He could remember every little detail of that quarrel. Susanna had held her tongue after that outburst, and he had immediately realized that she was penitent about letting her tongue run away with her.

Arturu's temper had flared. He felt anger take hold of him and icily had told her, "I'm ordering you to tell me! What do you mean by that?"

Susanna had found the opportunity to speak. It was the moment she had been waiting for, and now, at least for once in his life, Arturu seemed to be on his knees before her, a loser, humiliated by his own identity. That same identity of which he was so proud. A long, exalted family tradition that saw her as Lady's maid, which meant his too, in that enormous house that was a living memory of his father. His father was a large framed portrait which Susanna often liked to look at, trying to see Arturu's resemblance to him.

After that, all he could remember was his own strong outburst. "The father of your child never once showed his face to you again, and he didn't want you and he left you to fend on your own," he had said to her, throwing it into her face several times. He had exaggerated and he too had let his tongue run away with him. "I shouldn't have gone on, saying those words," he reproached himself in disgust. And then he remembered his cruel taunt which had wounded her to the quick. "You soon sent off the child I fathered below ground. What sort of mother are you?"

One thought led to another and the memories were woven together.

"No, no, no!" he moaned alone, cupping his hands together and pressing them against his forehead. "Susanna, I too am a man who makes mistakes. I'm a man too, after all, only a man," he kept on telling himself.

~ 0~

It all seemed as if it had happened the day before. It began when he had been struck by Susanna's beauty, her simplicity, her love for life, and at the same time by the fact that she had already passed through pathways of life that he hardly knew existed. She knew how to tease a person without trying, and to bewitch a man effortlessly. She did not even realize this herself, or at least, that is what Arturu still thought. There was something beautiful about her that was innate.

If she had taught him something this was that there was natural intelligence. He had been brought up with books, and she had learned everything quietly from the trees, birds, winds and the Valley, where she had come to understand that a man was a different world. But she had also learnt things he had taught her, because he encouraged her to read. He used to set aside a book for her and tell her, "I've chosen a book for you from all those in the library. Take it home with you, read it, and you'll see how you'll start seeing the world in a way you've never seen before."

"If I read it, will I start seeing the world as more beautiful or less?" she had asked him.

"You'll see it better. It depends on the way you look at it. You have to find a place, and then, from that point you'll start seeing..."

"Is that the book? Are you telling me, then, that I don't see properly as I am, now?"

"Compare and then you can come to your own conclusions."

Susanna used to admire him, knowing that from that moment onwards he would not just be the son of her mistress, but a youth who had promised to accept her as herself, and who would remain with her to the very end. There was nothing he wished for more, the lad who hardly knew the streets in the village and who rarely approached the towns, far, far away. He too, after all, was the offspring of the village, and the big house and wealth in it did not make him a different person. A short while after meeting each other, he and Susanna could understand each other and could come to love one another in the way they knew.

"How did it all happen?" Arturu asked himself countless times. "What would my mother have said if she'd remained alive? And what would my father have said? My father, ahh, my father was canny. And he left early from this village, from the place he loved, on that armchair in the room he loved best, the library. My mother continued to relive that moment, and it was at that moment when life stopped for her. There was nothing anymore. Nothing else happened from that moment onwards for her, and nothing ever would. She was a faithful woman and therefore a good woman. She was a woman of few words but showed that she was always thinking about something. Maybe she gave the impression of being proud, but that was how a lady was supposed to behave, a rich lady living in a big house in the middle of a village...When my mother died, changes started taking place. Susanna bore a child but it was taken away from her and they told her nothing more about it. I would never have imagined that her father would be so hard on her, and he remained like that till the day he died, not saying one word to her on his deathbed...She told me she had pleaded with him, but in vain. Susanna was left on her own but I loved her still and we soon got married. What did I do wrong in all this? I did not go against my mother's wishes but then, I could not seek her advice either. I was sorry when my mother died, but after all, that way I could start walking on my own path. My time had to come one day. She herself frequently used to tell me that she would like to see me safely married and with my own household."

He paused for a moment as if he was trying to find the right answer.

"Safely married? But not to Susanna!" Arturu seemed to hear a distant voice repeating and echoing these words inside him. "Go, go out and look for a young woman. That's how parents have always wished their sons to do. You'll see there are many well-behaved young women..." he felt his mother telling him.

"A young woman has only to be well-behaved to please you, Mother?" he felt himself answering.

"She has to be well-behaved above everything else, but not only," he heard his mother tell him. "Good behaviour on its own has no strength."

"And be rich?"

"Her father will be rich. Not she, but him. Money and wealth belong to the father. Depending on whose daughter she is. If she's rich, that would be better. That would mean that her father was circumspect and respectable. And more than anything else, make sure that you would have seen her in church," she had spoken to him decisively.

"And she must be lovely too, what do you think? A lovely young woman is always a lovely young woman," he had said a little shyly.

"Of course, of course, if she's lovely all the better," he seemed to hear her say, feeling she wanted to cut short the conversation.

Beauty was not mentioned in that house, or only very rarely and then it occasioned much blushing and downcast eyes.

"Like Susanna then, Mother, because Susanna is a very beautiful young woman, well-behaved and she goes regularly to church," he imagined himself whispering to his mother, hardly moving his lips to make certain his mother did not hear. "You have no idea how beautiful Susanna is, Mother! She's lovelier than those portraits of women in the drawing room, all curls, looking sideways with their hair down to their shoulders, standing next to a vase of flowers. She's a child of the soil, and she is still beautiful, suntanned by the sun shining down on the fields, and full of life because she has to fend on her own. She's not lettered and hasn't read any books, but I'm teaching her to read, little by little, and she learns fast, with no difficulty. All that she never learnt in years she's soaking up like a sponge now, all at once. She reads every book that I lend her to read. Well, maybe not from cover to cover but she gets the gist of it. If you only knew, Mother, how intelligent she is!" Arturu continued pondering.

Susanna appeared in front of his eyes like a brand new framed portrait, the most beautiful one amongst the old ones filling the entire house. There she was, with long hair, looking into the distance, a little smile on her face, with curls peeping out from underneath her veil and with the air of one waiting for the future to begin. He used to spend a long time looking at her and he used to congratulate himself that now, finally, something beautiful had fallen into his lap, unexpectedly. And he had been wise enough to snatch it. These rural areas had their own treasures to boast of, as well.

But then, the two of them had started to squabble and fight, time and time again, and the two of them thought that they were incompatible, not right for each other. They agreed on that, at least. A large house was not small enough to keep the two of them together in one room. This was something that Arturu felt keenly. "If we had lived in a small house, with only a few rooms...Maybe we'd have learnt to get on better with each other, and maybe not. Our differences continued to keep us apart," he thought. "No, no, that wasn't it," he came to a different conclusion soon after. Many a long hour he spent, stopping to reflect on the same thought, repeating it in different words to try and understand it better, and to finally accept it or reject it. He wanted to explain many things to himself after all this time.

He did not throw her out of the house; she was the one who left of her own accord. She had spent a long time weighing things up before arriving at her decision. When she had made up her mind nothing could change it. She could not afford to hurry and take another false step, needlessly. He understood all this in her words and in her silence. He used to pity her at a distance, seemingly against his will, even at the very moment when he felt his heart harden towards her. He could not explain what was happening to him and she too was confused about her whole situation. The silence between them stretched longer and longer, and it was a crueller blow than the hard words they had exchanged, and it echoed more loudly than any other sound in all those rooms. She had arrived at the conclusion that Arturu had never truly loved her, and that maybe, she too had not truly loved him, either.

All in all, he was certain that he was not the one who had slammed the door in her face. This thought consoled him a little but he knew that Susanna had her own pride. He thought her pride was the same sort that her father used to hold fiercely on to. Her father, curt and decisive as he had been, had passed on to her something that she herself never realized was her father's. Was she then like her father without wanting to and without knowing it? Arturu knew that he himself resembled his own father.

"You won't see me anymore!" she had exclaimed once with unusual determination, as he had soon realized.

This was too great a humiliation for him. Alone in that house, king of his own castle, he felt like a helpless prisoner. He possessed money and property, and they brought him respect from many, but he could not move a woman's heart. He could well imagine that if she left his house she would live in poverty. She had no roof over her head under which she could shelter.

Remembrance could take him as far back as he wished, and everything was still crystal clear in front of his eyes. The sense of all this was, in one way or another, part of the inheritance Lady had left somewhere inside him. Now more than ever, he realized that her words had not been uttered in vain. She had left a far greater impression on him than he had realized at the time.

"Make sure that your conduct remains irreproachable and always seek advice from Fr. Grejbel," Lady had warned him on her deathbed.

~ 0 ~

"But where was Fr. Grejbel, meanwhile? He was close for such a long time! Where is he now?" Arturu often asked himself.

The years went by and Arturu's house remained the same, silent and full of past memories. Every object that he inherited or was there for his use, took him back to his father when he had been in his prime. Whatever Arturu did not know from experience, he could imagine with a little effort. Everything around him built up a different world for him.

The days were always long and Arturu did his utmost to spend them pleasantly. He convinced himself that a whole world was there for him inside that house and he needed nothing else. But Susanna filled up his rooms more than all his objects did.

"I shouldn't have treated her that way. Perhaps we were not to blame that she was brought up in one way and I was brought up in another. It wasn't wealth that separated us or our family. Her father had died, leaving her in such a condition that she didn't know what to do with herself. Her mother remained estranged from her out of loyalty to her husband, almost more so after his death than when he was alive. And she had nowhere to live," he kept on thinking. "Was she obstinate? Yes? Should I have given in to her? I don't know! I only know that..."

At that very moment, Fr. Grejbel appeared on the doorstep.

Arturu invited him in and the two of them sat down on an armchair in the drawing room.

"This house always reminds me that in our village there are far more interesting things inside houses than there are in the streets and alleys and the square. If you knock on every door, you'll find a village in miniature. And if you enter a house like yours here, well, you'll find an unbelievable universe. It's a museum of objects dating back to centuries ago. The same with the village...its present lies in the past," Fr. Grejbel observed.

"You haven't forgotten this village," Arturu remarked.

"Forget it? How can I? The villages, separated by a few low walls, resemble each other greatly. The same winds blow over them and the same sun warms them up. Between one village and another there are just a few fields, and the same seasons pass over the fields."

"No, no, I meant that you still love the village. You saw another world, far bigger and very different, but you still kept loving the village."

"I came to love it more. Its solitude, I have to say, is not a disadvantage but a privilege. Out there everything happens in an adult world, and here we still seem to live in a children's world. We're spoilt. Not because we're children. We were children once, and we can never go back to childhood. We're adults, like everybody else, but our very smallness and closeness have their own beauty. They're an exception in an adult world. It seems as if they lessen problems. They grow all out of proportion the way children tend to make them, but then they deflate and go away on their own because they would be children's problems."

"Is that what you think, Fr. Grejbel? In a small village like this one...closed in on itself...are problems necessarily small and insignificant?"

"No, they're not small and insignificant...I wish to believe they are. But when they're really not insurmountable, they're less than those you find in larger lands. That's what I mean. As for the rest, well, we're people like everybody everywhere."

"You certainly know from your own experience," Arturu cut him short.

"They're not small, no, no, they're not," Fr. Grejbel went on musing, "because people are always people, everywhere. But at the end of the day, the confined space we jostle each other in serves to make us realize that it's too small a space to really make war."

"And your war, Fr. Grejbel, wasn't it real?"

"At its apex it was, but today I think that it was a war that came from outside. It was an idea engendered in town that made it happen. Authority is not invested in the village, or the church and sacristy a few paces away from this spot..."

"You mean to say if..."

"I mean, Arturu, that if everyone truly forgets the village, the village would be heaven on earth. The seasons are able to guide us well, all by themselves."

"But, don't people remain people, the way they are everywhere?"

"They remain, true, as long as the rules are not broken."

"There we are, Fr. Grejbel! And so?"

"Maybe this is just a dream of mine. Perhaps today I need to start thinking in a different way. I know what grief and hurts are now, more than ever before..."

"That's what I wanted to tell you," Arturu cut him short again.

"Don't worry, don't worry Arturu, and don't get confused. I don't want it to be me to confuse you with vain hopes and dreams. Happiness shouldn't be cut off from its roots, leaving the roots to wither. All that we ever thought in long years past, in moments of truth, still hold, and will do so till the very end. That's the crux of it all. That's what strikes us as people everywhere. But for those of us who live here, in these little streets and alleyways, where everything belongs to us, that's a different story...I would like to keep on thinking that the village is the courtyard of Heaven...A courtyard with a thin curtain in the doorway, and behind that curtain lies Heaven. If you go and move that curtain...just a little bit...you'll find yourself there...wearing the same clothes you had. I would like to keep on thinking so."

"Even if you find out it's not like that..."

"Yes, even if I learn that, Arturu."

"And I think you do know. You found out a long time ago."

"Let's just say that I knew from the very beginning. Every village, this one or another, is one large spread-out space. The stone walls, put up with one stone on top of another, separate them but they themselves are the same...Just think for a bit, Arturu, how many years it took to build up those walls. They were built so that within them, everyone could imagine that his whole world lay there."

"But that's not real, Fr. Grejbel!"

"It's not real! No, it's not real, and it never was, but as long as people thought so, that little space they had was all the world to them. And all that they dreamed about was linked only to that small patch of ground belonging to them.

And do you know what they did if they could not find something? They simply never dreamed of it!"

"And were they content?"

"Yes, I think they were content, Arturu."

"A contentment that was not real?"

"If they were content, well then, it was real enough......well anyway...why are we letting our thoughts stray? How are you?"

"Me? I'm fine thank you, Fr. Grejbel. Fine." He then paused deliberately and stared for a long time at Fr. Grejbel. "I find your ideas very interesting. I've always found your conversations interesting, and not just me. People have always listened to you, Fr. Grejbel. And do you know when they paid you most attention?"

The priest looked back at Arturu with a smile but looked somewhat embarrassed.

"When you were silent! Ever since the silence you left behind you started making its presence felt, people began remembering all that you used to tell them. They needed a lie to start appreciating the truth."

"Arturu, what are you saying?" Fr. Grejbel exclaimed, joy spreading across his face and amazement too.

"Precisely what you've just been telling me when I tried to contradict you. Do you know what I'm feeling at this very moment?" Arturu asked him, settling himself down more comfortably in his armchair. "I feel as if the two of us have just picked up the conversation from where we left it off years ago..."

"You're right, Arturu, and if you want we can end it as well."

"With all my heart and grateful thanks. That's why I asked you for a meeting. It almost seems that without knowing, you've already provided me with the answer to the question I want to ask. And I have just one question for you. What am I going to do?"

"What do you wish for most of all, Arturu? Try and gather all your thoughts in a few words and tell me, and tell yourself, more than anything else! What do you want?"

Arturu rose from the armchair and went to peer out of the large window. "I only want one thing, Fr. Grejbel. Whether it's cheap or expensive; whatever its price, I want to buy it. I want to be content, that's all I want."

"Like the closed-in world of the village then."

"If the closed-in world of the village is content – even if I cannot see it properly from here because it's in the distance, well, that's the world I want."

"If I understand you correctly..."

"I'm sure you do understand me, very well indeed, Fr. Grejbel," Arturu broke in, turning to face the priest. After a pause he went on, "You know that when Susanna and I quarrelled seriously, and ended up separating for ever, she hurt me, hurt me grievously. She told me that at least she knew who her mother was. She meant, you know...you know, or don't you? That hurt me but I had been hurting her too, for a long time. It almost seems to me that when I hurt her I was trying to forgive her and in that way she could forgive me, too. I hurt her and she hurt me. A tie. I needed to feel that. That's what I'm trying to say. That way, I'm not a loser."

"No, you're not a loser, Arturu."

"What do I gain if I stand my ground and remain hard and unfeeling? Meanwhile, I feel as if I'm letting the years left to me to slip through my fingers. Why do I need to ask about the truth when all I really am searching for is contentment?"

"You're right about that. The truth or contentment? The two together, but which one is greater?"

"Today, here, sitting on this armchair, I must admit that I don't have more time to lose, or sentiments to waste. Contentment. The past is past, and all I need is time, and I wish it to be different, this time. And I have to admit that I've already wasted too much time, because my future began when I met Susanna, here in this house, and she, with her sweet and natural simplicity, managed to show me that I had not yet started to really live...in spite of all I possessed, I still had nothing. This is my great loss, Fr. Grejbel!"

"I see that you still love her, Arturu!"

"Yes, I still love her, and these years since we've been apart made me understand that I loved her much more deeply than I had thought. I had too much pride to admit it to myself. But now I've had enough time to understand myself."

Fr. Grejbel rose from the armchair, went up to Arturu and embraced him. "You are blessed, as well, Arturu. Out of all the joys I've experienced since I came back, this is the greatest. This is truly a day for celebration! Time itself taught us the path we must follow, and we all had to fall and get hurt. You got hurt, and so did I, and so did Susanna..."

"Susanna was hurt, and I too hurt her."

"We all got hurt, and do you know when? At the moment it was ordained that we were to get hurt. It's part of the rule of life. Now the moment has come for us to get up, brush off the dust and walk on."

"There's another thing that's constantly on my mind, Fr. Grejbel. And it's not leaving me any peace, urging me to take this step."

Fr. Grejbel smiled. He did not utter a word but kept smiling at Arturu to show him he understood the whole situation.

"Are you smiling, Fr. Grejbel? Do you know, then, what I'm going to say?"

"Shall I guess? Should I try?"

"Yes, try to guess. I would like to confirm that the same thing you have in mind to do is what is buzzing around in my head."

"You're thinking, you're asking yourself..." Fr. Grejbel began and then paused to find the right words. "You're saying, 'If those two who loved me so much were here, what would they wish me to do?'"

Arturu felt too overcome by emotion to speak. Holding back his tears, he nodded affirmation.

"Why should we waste what's left and is still good in our life, Arturu?"

"That's what I feel, too." Arturu closed his eyes, took a deep breath and said, "Do you think Susanna will accept?"

"What do you think?" Fr. Grejbel asked with evident joy in his voice that seemed like an answer in itself.

"I think she'll accept. And what will her mother say?"

"What do you think?"

"I think her mother will be very happy."

"And the boy's father, what will he say? I would like to have your word on this, too."

"He's already accepted the fact that Susanna is married already," Arturu told him and then he fell silent for a few moments. "All in all, when I look back I realize how lucky I've been. Today I can understand my father's and mother's silence. I understand your silence, too, before and now...And it was necessary that this silence and understanding took years in the making."

Fr. Grejbel lowered his head to avoid Arturu's gaze. He rose to pace the room and went straight to the window, stopping there, with both hands stretched straight behind his back, still gazing outside.

Arturu went up to him and putting his hands under the priest's forearms, invited him to stroll around with him. "You still haven't told me what my mother told you just before she died, Fr. Grejbel. Circumstances arose and somehow or other I came to realize on my own that my father sired me from a woman whose identity I've never managed to find out. All these years that you've been far away from here served to get me out of the closed-in rooms of this house. In my mother's silence, because that woman remains the mother that raised me, I understood that she wanted only what was best for me. Your silence too meant you only wish the same thing for me. Don't speak, say nothing!" he told the priest in a tone of gentle command, all the while making him keep pace with himself while holding him from below his forearms. "You need to keep to your silence...I know, Fr. Grejbel, we all need some lie to live. And it's a good lie, watered with tears and rooted in the soil of truth. And I've also learnt when it should be planted. It must be planted whenever the need arises."

Fr. Grejbel kept walking beside Arturu, step by step.

"I pray you, Fr. Grejbel, don't worry about not keeping your word. I'm not going to ask you to say too much. Necessity showed me what I had to do to go outside for a while, out of these walls that surround me. And I managed to go out, with the help of, amongst other things, your strict silence. You taught me to be honest and I think that the woman who brought me up was silent because she too was honest. Keep to your silence, Fr. Grejbel, and I can keep respecting you as a whole person, a priest that stands straight. Thank you once again."

Fr. Grejbel remained with bowed head, silent.

Arturu took him to the door of the room where his mother had died. He opened the door slowly and allowed Fr. Grejbel to precede him.

Fr. Grejbel glanced around and saw that everything was exactly the same as when he had been in here last.

Arturu saw his reaction and was glad. "You're right in your thinking, Fr. Grejbel. Time has stood still in here, and when it stopped we three of us were in this room: she...you...and I...Do you remember?"

Fr. Grejbel gave a small nod of assent but remained silent.

"And today I also understand the harsh words Susanna said to me when we were fighting," he went on. "They were unexpected words, but words that I needed too. All that's happened served to make me put the pieces of the puzzle together. I've gone through all the books in this house. I searched the pages and found holy picture on holy picture. I found some scribbles, a copybook full of memories, but nothing else. And I told myself, 'But why am I searching for the truth in written pages? How many people amongst us know how to read and write, after all? This time, truth is a person. But tell me...where is this person to be found?' That's what I asked myself."

Fr. Grejbel kept his hands locked behind his back. He half-turned, with a fixed look in his eyes, and lowered his head again. "You have a whole future ahead of you, Arturu, and you yourself declared that it's a wonderful future..."

"True, but for me this is the beginning of the future. I began pondering about this when we buried our baby. Do you remember? Susanna was brought to bed with a baby boy, but after a while he began to weaken. And I came searching for you to baptise him quickly. He had been born only to die. You remember all this, too. Fr. Grejbel, this isn't a secret, there's no confessional silence involved..."

"I remember it all, there was just you and I..." the priest spoke, visibly relieved that this time there was no need to hold back from expressing his thoughts.

"And the baby, in a white coffin. Do you remember?"

"That's right, Arturu, and the baby's name was Arturu. Susanna had bestowed that name on it, for you. Can you see how much she loved you? And she still does...The future lies before you, and it will begin from this house, no, from this room, and from today, now, yes, now, if you want! Let the past go, Arturu!"

"Set your mind at rest, Fr. Grejbel. I understand, and this time too I will do as you say. But there's this story that I feel I have to tell you at last, or otherwise I would be failing you..."

"If that's your wish, I'll hear it. But don't forget, Arturu, from now onwards, this house will be full, it will be yours more than ever before. It will come alive for you."

Arturu seemed lost in a world of his own, not seeming to hear the priest address him. "Listen to this story, Fr. Grejbel...look the other way and let me be the only one to speak, so that I won't even know what you're thinking, what expression you have on your face...I appreciate both your words and your silence."

Fr. Grejbel moved away from him and stood straight, alone, looking out of the window, with his hands held rigidly behind his back.

"Once upon a time there was a good, kind woman, Lady, who was on her deathbed, and before she passed away she sent for a kind priest. He lived far away, he wasn't from that same village, but she wanted only him. She sent her son to look for him, and her son didn't rest till he found the priest. It was a stormy night. On the point of death she wanted to open her heart to the priest. She trusted only him. She told him that she had loved her husband very much but it had pleased God to take him early. Her husband had a son from a woman with whom he had lived for a long time but had never married. When the boy was born he had sent him to an orphanage. He had not wanted him to grow up in a household where the man and woman were not married. The woman had been separated from her own husband, which is why they could not get married. In time, the baby's father had left her and she had gone back to her husband. But this happened only after one condition had been met - every marriage, Fr. Grejbel, imposes some form of condition, and it seems to be different every time. This one condition was that her husband would never get to know that she had borne a son to another man. The baby's father kept the secret. A short while later, he met another woman, Lady. You know who Lady was. The two of them fell deeply in love with each other. They met in a dancehall, far away from the village. She was a young woman on the lookout for a personable young man who was well off. He was in a hurry to meet a woman who would accept his son. He wanted a new beginning. She could not bear children and had no choice. They soon got married and brought the child home from the orphanage. They brought him up in a large house, full of opulent furnishings and books. She always treated the boy as if he were her son. She was happy and content to have found a man who treated her as a married woman. She wanted to be a married woman and a mother to that boy." Arturu paused briefly and then continued. "She always believed that it was this secret that saved her."

Fr. Grejbel stayed where he was, standing straight and looking at the window.

"This woman, Lady, as the people of the neighbourhood knew her, asked the priest if she had lied," Arturu went on with his tale. "And she herself admitted that in fact that was what she had done, she had lied. Above all, she had lied to her husband's son. Sometimes she had felt it was wrong of her, but she had quickly realized that the lie was necessary to keep harmony in the household. She was feeling afraid because it was time to meet her Maker, and she wanted the priest to reassure her. She was afraid that she had lied to God as well. 'Did I lie to God?' she had asked the priest. She knew nobody could lie to God. God knows everything from the beginning. She wanted to explain the situation to him, she said. Her greatest worry was her doubt whether she had somehow harmed the boy by not telling him that she wasn't his real mother. That's why she wanted the priest at her side at that moment. Otherwise, she had no sins to confess."

Fr. Grejbel remained where he was, silent, standing straight, alone. He endeavoured to appear impassive, detached from what he was hearing...as if he was not in that room...almost as if he did not wish to hear.

"And then Lady asked the priest, 'Aren't you going to tell me something?' She wanted to know what she had to say to God in a short while, when she died. The priest had to answer her, at last. He told her that God's ways are mysterious and that we don't always understand them. He told her that she had behaved in the best way she could. And then he told her something extremely important. 'I don't feel you've done anything wrong, in God's eyes and with regards to the boy.' And by that she understood that he thought she had to keep silent. And the priest agreed with her. Finally, she begged him to tell the boy himself if the day came when he thought the boy should learn the truth."

Arturu stopped, moved towards Fr. Grejbel and spoke to him behind his back in a decisive voice, "After telling you the story, Lady sent for the boy to come to her and with one hand she held the boy's hand and with the other she took hold of the priest's hand. She begged them to remain close to each other.

She asked the priest to consider the boy as his own son, and she asked the boy to heed the priest's words of wisdom whenever he needed to take a decision. And she wanted the boy to swear to it. And he had to vow to do so."

There was total silence in the room. In that hushed moment the grandeur of that house seemed more palpable.

"From here onwards, Fr. Grejbel, we must respect that silence. My whole story ends here. I know nothing more because then Lady wanted to confess her sins," Arturu said to him, and then continued, "I know this well - a confession is a confession."

Fr. Grejbel turned round slowly, astounded, like a statue fixed to the ground, which only moves when the ground beneath it moves.

"That's the entire tale, Fr. Grejbel. The boy was called Arturu, and the priest was called..." Arturu spoke with a note of satisfaction in his voice and with a serious smile on his face.

Fr. Grejbel kept silent, all the same. He tried his best to hide any emotion, even the least hint of expression on his face that could reveal his thoughts. Deep within he could feel nothing but amazement.

"I imagine you'd like to know how I came to know all this. Who told me? What happened since that day for me to learn the whole story? You didn't tell me..."

Fr. Grejbel shook his head vehemently to confirm that he had never spoken a word since Lady had called him to her as she lay breathing her last. Arturu was witness to that.

"There comes a time when everyone commits a sin, Fr. Grejbel. And a man sins even if it's a case of clinging on to an anchor to save himself from drowning. I sinned on that day. When she asked me to leave the room I left. But when I heard her immediately insisting that you close the door, do you know what I felt? I felt that that was the last chance I had to understand that woman's silence...the great discipline in which she'd raised me and conducted her household, in all prudence and reserve, keeping to the daily rules that never changed, and above all, with the order that nothing should be touched in my father's library...She frequently used to tell me, 'One day I'll tell you a story,' because in these parts, in the villages, since time immemorial, mothers keep to the custom of telling stories to their children. This is a village where mothers use their imagination. In my case, this didn't happen, and in my early childhood, in the orphanage, we used to go to sleep early. We would say a prayer and that was it. When they took me out of there I was too old to begin hearing stories. But she still kept telling me, 'One day I'll tell you a story,' and the day came when she did begin to tell me this story. She began, but I got fed up and she realized it. I was no longer a little child, happy to stay put hearing stories...That's what I thought at the time. That evening, all this suddenly came before my eyes. As soon as you closed the door, I was filled with curiosity, and I listened at the door, overhearing every single word she uttered. I said to myself, 'Now that she's about to die, she's going to reveal the story she had to tell me.' That's what I thought, and that's what happened."

Fr. Grejbel kept mute, standing in the same position.

"I remember every word she said, word for word, as if I'd learnt a part I had to perform by heart. You know if what I'm saying is true or not. You can't deny it."

"Arturu, please don't put me in an awkward position. You understand only too well what my situation is."

"I know, I know, you can't show any reaction. Neither yes nor no. But Lady told you that the decision must be yours. In the meantime you've remained silent. And I did the same. After all, I could only defend myself through silence. Without knowing it, I was on the point of getting married, and I needed to show Susanna that I too, had my own dignity to uphold, here within these walls. One way or another, I had to keep up family tradition, my superiority. Today, after all this time, I can understand and appreciate better the position you took. I want to thank you once more."

Fr. Grejbel remained silent.

"Fr. Grejbel, I implore you, speak. You won't be compromising your prudence in any way. Now you know the whole situation entirely."

"If from what all that you've told me, some good will come out of it for your future with Susanna..."

"And for my future with her son...you mean."

"And with her son, certainly...If from all this some good will come out, well then, Arturu, even your actions will have been worthwhile."

"You're referring to my sin, the fact that I overheard the words she said which weren't meant for my ears...Yes, I do understand that Susanna's boy's situation is no different from mine."

As he was hearing Arturu out, Fr. Grejbel was picturing in his mind the agony Susanna's father had gone through. Time had passed...Susanna had not seen her father for a long time, but she was there at his bedside, now. He himself was on his way to their house to administer the Last Rites. Without undue haste, but without pause, he was leading the procession of the *Viaticum*, the Holy Eucharist that was to be given to a dying person, with altar boys at his side, praying and holding a lighted lamp in their hands, accompanied by the ringing of a small thin bell. He had entered the room in silence.

Susanna had approached, going closer to the bed and taking up her father's hand. He looked happy to be seeing her again after so long. Susanna had gone down on her knees next to the bed, putting her mouth close to his ear and in a trembling voice had pleaded to know where her baby was. He still had not vouchsafed a single word, had turned his head away and had slowly closed his eyes. She had continued imploring him to speak for his laboured breathing terrified her.

Suddenly, her father had opened his eyes and said...he told her these exact words which Fr. Grejbel could remember without any difficulty, 'Susanna, I've always done my duty, and I shall do so now, right at the end. I bless you, for the last time, my daughter, but don't ask me for anything more. I've done nothing but my duty, and I'm not going to fail in my duty now that I'm about to leave this world. I only have one soul.' That's how Susanna's father died, and Fr. Grejbel went on remembering it all.

For a few moments, perfect silence reigned in the room. A silence that seemed to stretch too long. Both Fr. Grejbel and Arturu could not find the right word to break it.

It had never occurred to Fr. Grejbel that the two deaths had so much in common. "The deathbed. A woman kept her silence in her own way, and a man did the same in his own way..." he thought to himself.

When Arturu saw that Fr. Grejbel was not going to speak, he continued saying, "All this time has passed and it served to show me things in a different light, and to prevent me from turning the past against myself – both my past and that of Susanna's. The two resemble each other, don't you think so? We were born to families that were very different in many ways, but we were born in the same sort of neighbourhood, meaning we're much more alike than we had thought. Tradition, huh, Fr. Grejbel? But today I can admit that without it we're nothing, perhaps. Not even dreams can exist without tradition. And this is the house *par excellence* of tradition! Just look around you and you'll see, everything speaks to you of yesterday. But what would I have been able to achieve here today, now in this place, without yesterday?"

"Arturu's situation really resembles that of Susanna's son," Fr. Grejbel was thinking in silence. He could not hide his gladness any longer and so he broke his self-enforced silence. "All those who did everything with the best of intentions, Arturu, always deserve our appreciation. Everyone is judged according to their goodwill. God judges the rest. Whatever place we reach, the important thing is to walk on."

"This time, too, I won't put more responsibilities on your shoulders, Fr. Grejbel. All I ask is that you listen to me. Susanna herself had told me how her father had kept his silence as he lay dying. I know that she continued pleading with him till the very end."

Fr. Grejbel would have liked to keep silent but he realized that there was no longer any need. "Every person carries out his duty as he sees fit, Arturu."

"There are some questions I had asked you a long time ago. Sometimes you answered me with words, and you did the right thing. At other times you answered me with silence, and again that was the right thing to do. Silence and words, you taught me that they are two sides of the same coin and they're not whole without each other."

"And now, Arturu?" Fr. Grejbel asked him with a big smile lighting up his face. He walked towards Arturu as if he was about to shake hands. "And now, what's left?"

"Don't you know what's left to be done?"

"I know very well what's to be done but if the silence has to be broken, you have to be the one to do it, Arturu."

"A silence that's lasted years. I too have let her down."

"It's never too late."

"What else is left? Susanna needs to come back."

"Bless you, Arturu. And when?"

"Whenever you want, Fr. Grejbel! It was always you who put back the broken pieces together. You have the wisdom and you have the patience. And this time too, it's in your hands."

"Another responsibility for me."

"There are only responsibilities for you, Fr. Grejbel. Sometimes to stay mute and sometimes to break the silence...but always to make good things happen."

Fr. Grejbel rose to leave the room.

"I want to show you something, Fr. Grejbel. Come with me," Arturu invited the priest and put his hands under his forearms, like a friend in a special moment. "This house has remained the same all this time. That's how my father wanted it and also my mother, Lady, as Susanna used to call her. I kept everything the way they wanted, with no changes to mar the rule of time. And the rule decreed that a married couple sleeps in the main bedroom. My mother did not want the room where my father had died to be touched, and I too wanted untouched the room where my love had died..."

"Your love didn't die, Arturu."

"It didn't die, no, but time has long stood still in this house. Only the clocks have continued keeping time because I've always wound them up as something to do. And they strike the quarters and hours without fail and keep exact time, to fill in the void that can't be filled, however hard I try."

"As long as there's life, there's hope. Time will start up again in this house when you decide, Arturu."

"If it was up to me, it would start from tomorrow."

"Well then, that's what will happen. Right from tomorrow it will begin."

"This was a vow I took in front of you for my mother, in her last moments – to find a young woman who is suitable for me and whom I can love and marry and with whom I can keep house. These were her words, do you remember?"

"And she had gathered all her strength in her voice to ask you to make that vow. How could I forget? That woman gave you everything."

"I always called her 'Mother', and she wasn't called Lady in vain. There wasn't a beggar who didn't know her by this name, because none came away empty-handed from her. She used to keep by a few coins for that purpose."

"She used to help all the people she could. I know, I know."

"I heard that the villagers put up a great feast in your honour. You wouldn't guess who told me all about it, in great detail! A beggar! He came knocking at the door, and I opened it and as soon as he saw me he began to talk nineteen to the dozen all about it and wouldn't stop. I understood that he was expecting more money than usual in return. Because he told me a story! And that's what I did. I can't begin to tell you how overjoyed he was, and how much he praised me and how much he praised you! He was going to embark on another tale!"

Fr. Grejbel smiled. "If you gladdened someone's heart, you've planted a tree in heaven, Arturu."

"You were the one to cast the seed. Today more than ever I understand that everything you touch turns to gold."

"Turns to gold? I don't know about that," Fr. Grejbel said, amused. "All I know for certain is that a thing has to pass through fire, Arturu."

"You passed through fire, Fr. Grejbel."

"And you too passed through fire. It's one of life's rules. It's a hard rule, but not without any sense. If it was senseless, nothing would have any meaning because everything is linked to it. That's how it always was and that's how it always will be. But no sad tears should be wasted; finally they become tears of joy. Only time can show that this is so. Aren't you convinced of this, Arturu? Today you look more convinced than ever before."

"Today, I seem to see everything from afar, and can see it better. Even the loss of the baby posed a big question mark. Susanna was carrying another burden, and everything was putting pressure on her to give in. But today I can understand that she did not give up. She drew on enormous reserves of strength. Was she born like that perhaps? With a strength that was uniquely hers? Or did she inherit it? And if she inherited it, from where and from whom?"

"Life in a village provides its own kind of strength, Arturu, and it comes, primarily, through tradition, through the bond with its roots that are old and mature and strong. Just like the tall trees, densely leaved, watered by no one but which stand fast, rain or shine, as if they were a palace of certitude. They are churches too, in their own way...Maybe that's where all this strength comes from."

Arturu accompanied him to the front door. He said goodbye and waited on the doorstep till the priest had gone a fair distance. But before he closed the door he gave a look at his surroundings and observed the peace and tranquillity of the place. Then he raised his head to the sky and saw that it was a cloudless blue, a sky that was happy and content. He went inside and felt glad that the silence in there was soon to be broken. He went into his father's library and sat down in his father's favourite place, the armchair, where he had passed away. This is where everything stopped but it is also where everything began, he thought. At first, Susanna had not been allowed inside that room, but then she had entered and had browsed through books, and the two of them began having long discussions. Sometimes, hearing her put forward arguments, he had asked himself, "Where are all these thoughts she has coming from?"

He recalled their first kiss, and then their last fight. Now it all seemed far away in the past and he realized that he still loved her in the way he had come to love her in the beginning, when she had opened the closed windows of this large house for him.

Lady used to warn him, "Don't let the village take a foothold in here. We're not the same. We're different."

"Is she right or is she wrong?" he frequently used to ask himself.

When he used to peer out of the window overlooking the interior courtyard, he used to breathe in the air of their large garden, enclosed within high walls that were beautifully built, skilfully raised with one stone over another, each stone in a different shape and size. That air, he used to think, is the air of the village. It entered the house from the surrounding fields, and with it wafted the fragrance of fruit, the smell of manure, smiles and sobs, the screaming cries of hawkers, the songs of women at their window, the hubbub of children at play, the church bells, the beliefs and prejudices of those people who were different. But if all that air was entering into their garden and keeping the trees in good health, it was good air.

"Who knows? Maybe this is the air Susanna brought in with her," he wondered as he closed the last window on his evening round, to lock up the entire house.

"This is my air, the scent of my people, Arturu. The remembrance of all that came before us. The dreams of the two of us, they are one and the same, whether in a farmhouse or a mansion. Let me show you how true this is, and you'll see it's real," he imagined Susanna telling him.

"Where are you, Susanna?" he shouted in his solitude, as if to fill the silence in that house.

"I'm here, next to you though you can't see me. Wait just a little bit more, and you'll see," he imagined her telling him. "Everything has its own season. Soon, very soon it will be fine, fair weather is on its way and I'll come home...Just a bit more, you'll see." He remained there imagining all this, wishing it would all come true.

Chapter 15

It was their custom to wake up early, after also having gone to bed early the night before. That day, Katarina, Susanna and Wistin woke up much earlier than usual. There was still perfect silence but after a little while, the unbroken stillness of the night was slowly stirred, and gradually but continuously, the daily noises began to fill every corner of the house. The cockerels crowing, the banging of doors of houses and shops, the cries of the market sellers, the ringing of the church bells – everything was coming awake once more. In their simplicity, the villagers saw every day as different, monotonous but special too. They knew how to use their imagination and be happy.

"How very early we're getting up today, Granny!" Wistin protested as soon as Katarina went to his bed, knelt down and gently tapped his cheek to signal that it was time to wake up. She had a habit of waking him up like this, almost hurting him, and smiling when he gave a cry – "Ahh!" It was a complaint from someone who was spoilt. He knew that the woman in front of his eyes knew nothing except how to love.

He stretched a little, opened his eyes, closed them again and turned round on his other side.

Katarina put her hand on her knee and stood up straight, still looking at him fondly. "He's like Baby Jesus!" she exclaimed in her heart. She remembered her mother telling her that you should only show your love to children when they are fast asleep, otherwise you would spoil them. You need to approach them softly, on the tips of your toes, without making any noise, in secret, and praise them and look fondly upon them without them hearing or seeing you. She remembered the old saying that spoiling ruined children. "Oh no, that's going too far!" she thought now, contradicting herself quietly. "Maybe not all the things and sayings we were brought up with were unquestionably right!"

Wistin was still fast asleep.

Katarina tiptoed back a step and then turned and left the room. She put her hands on her hips, raised her eyebrows and shook her head, like one who has given in to something and is talking to herself noiselessly. She spent a good part of the day talking to herself, or else singing in the way she knew how.

"Didn't you wake him up after all, Mother?" Susanna asked her from the room next door. "It will be time soon. Or don't you want me to go, after all? I can understand what you're feeling today. At the end of the day, this event had to happen, and you prayed hard for it to come about, and here we finally are. But, after all, what can I teach you about life?"

Katarina did not answer.

"Wistin had better get up, Mother. Please, go and wake him up. You know what he does, the lazybones! He keeps stalling for time, luxuriating in bed, even though he'd be wide-awake already. He likes to play-act even in bed. And today even more so. He tricked you today, again. He knows he can pull the wool over your eyes any time he wishes. When are you going to learn?"

"Let him sleep on a bit longer. There's nothing better than that last snooze. And today's will be the last one, for sure. When we're ready, we'll quickly wake him up. And he'll just have to be a bit more quick about it than usual. He's not a disobedient child."

A few large bundles took up the central part of the room, bulging with objects trussed together, because they contained more than they could really hold. Katarina had chosen a few sheets from those she had put away and bundled everything in, tying each bundle with a large knot and then with another knot. "Everything fitted in those bundles. I calculated well. I didn't think I'd manage!" she preened.

"Thank you very much, Mother! You managed to cram everything in, the way you wanted. I've always known you like that, after all, you wait, have patience, and when the right moment comes, you do what you have to do. Mother, your patience can even be seen in the knots you tie. I only hope that I'll be able to untie them! Not all knots can be untied, usually."

"They will, you'll manage to untie them, you'll see, daughter! Your words make me very happy. I can look back on all these years and satisfy myself that I've done all my duty as a mother. I've prepared everything you might need. I never gave you a dowry on the day you got married. I couldn't. I wasn't the one who held the reins of command. But today, yes, and I'm giving it to you today. It's never too late, that's what I've learnt. I've never thrown away or put aside all the things that were meant for you, in all these years. I stored them all away for when the right moment came to give them all to you. In life, you must learn to wait. All that was yours that day is still here now. And if your father was here, that's what he'd think, too, and that's what he'd tell you what's more. Take my word for it. At least, that's what I think. A father's heart always remains a father's heart. Today, you'll be taking everything, never fear, at least to be able to make a start. And when you'll need more things in the future, I'll bring them to you as well. And then, finally you'll take everything." Katarina said to Susanna. "When the time comes for me to pass on as well, all that would be left would be for you. A gust of wind may then carry everything away."

Susanna looked at the bundles and smiled at her mother, rubbing her hands together. "I can hardly believe it!"

"The one who waits, has faith, daughter. This is all yours. I know that in the meantime you won't need the little I'm giving you. Your husband is too rich for me to match him when it comes to worldly goods. His pockets are deep! Mine are too, because that's how our skirts are made, but my pockets have holes in them," she said, putting her hands in her skirt pockets. "All these are mere nothings next to the wealth he has. But I want to show him my heart in this, all the same. And it's a generous heart. Isn't that what they say? I'm going to give him the little I have," she paused, "and, more than anything else, I'm going to give him you and that little angel who's asleep, lazy boy that he is. A lazy angel. With angels like that Heaven won't improve much! He doesn't want to lose out on the very last edge of sleep. That last snooze is too sweet for words, and today even more so."

"How well you've learnt to speak, Mother!" Susanna teased her.

"I'm making up for all those long years of silence, daughter. But what's past is past. God forgive him."

"Mother, you'd better go and come back here with Wistin. This time don't come alone. He still needs to wash his face and get dressed, and time flies. You'll see how suddenly it will be time to go! I don't want to be late. Since we agreed to be there at a certain time, we have to be punctual. I don't remember you procrastinating, usually. I know you like to be early, even too early at times! You could have been the sacristan, such a one for punctuality and preciseness, but you're a woman. A woman as sacristan? No!"

"But today, today I'm not the usual Katarina...Haven't you realized yet, daughter? How eager you are to leave me, Susanna! Ahh! Life is full of pain and grief!" she replied half-jokingly but in a serious tone. "No, no," she went on quickly. "I'm only joking. I wish you well and I can't not wish you to go where your life is calling you. I was the one urging you to take this step, after all. But a mother's heart always beats quickly, faster than it should, and feels many sentiments, that are strong and different, sometimes even contradictory. A mother's heart is like a pot on the boil. But, my dearest, why am I telling you all this? You know what I mean."

"Sometimes you forget Mother, that I've also grown up, and my son is in there," Susanna teased her. "I'm no longer that little girl playing with beads and *Pizzi Pizzi Kanna* and hopscotch with the other girls."

"And with a rope! How you loved skipping, Susanna! And you never missed a step and fell down! And you used to play with beads, pushing a bead with your thumb and then by a strong flick, letting it fly from where it was pressed behind your forefinger. And the bead would fly straight into the hole, a little hollow scratched out of the ground, in the middle of the street or in the fields, wherever you were playing. You would mark the ground with lines some distance away from the hole, and play for two or for four beads. So many happy girls, like the butterflies flitting around you, running and jumping about, carefree."

Susanna was on tenterhooks to leave and felt like cutting her mother short, but she remained silent, paying attention to her.

"You used to collect the beads, and every bead with an unusual colour was worth as much as a lot of beads in a common colour. And as you were playing, all you girls in the street would chant a ditty by heart pointing to each girl in turn, and when the last bit of the ditty came, the girl at whom you were all pointing at that moment would have to start the game...If I close my eyes, at this very minute, I can see you in front of me, as if it was yesterday. How strange it is, isn't it, that you can close your eyes and see everything, one vision after another? I don't forget, Susanna, nothing at all. Sometimes I feel that I'd like you to be a child still, the way you were once...in the time of butterflies."

"But I'm not any longer, Mother, and I never can be again. What's past is past. Forget it now, just forget it all, it will do you good," Susanna urged her mother.

"Forget? I can't forget, and let me tell you, I don't even wish to forget!" her mother exclaimed. After a pause she went on, "What would be left if memories fade and vanish? You were once a child, playing with paper boats floating in the stream, and you'd push them along, calm and tranquil, in the water. The stream was shallow with clear running water. Frogs and tadpoles, that's all there was in it. You're all of you grown up now, you and your playmates. You used to go down there and play for hours on end, summer and winter, and play and chase each other without getting tired. You've become a mother. I've become a grandmother. Only the Valley has remained the same. The Valley never grows old. The Valley is obstinate – it's male. Susanna, don't forget these words. There will come a time when you'll have need of them. What little I know I've passed on to you. Even what's stored in my head is all for you!"

"Mummy, Mummy!" Wistin bellowed from his bed.

Katarina ran quickly to his room, caught him up and brought him along. "Here he is at last! I caught him! And now that I've caught him he'll have to stay here."

"I'm still sleepy! How early we got up today!" Wistin groused, rubbing the sleep from his eyes.

Susanna heard a sound in the street, went to the window, opened the slatted shutters wide and peered out. "I heard right!"

The coachman stopped his horse in front of the house, shifted the brake handle on the seat next to him, and the *karozzin* stopped with a jolt. The horse gave a long neigh, shook its head vigorously and fell silent. The coachman got down slowly from his seat and began patting the horse and saying a few words into its ears.

Susanna remained at the window, not speaking, and smiled at him.

"I'm here, Madame, I've come."

"Who's come?" Katarina wanted to know from inside.

"We'll be coming out soon. Please wait just a few moments," Susanna addressed the coachman.

"There's no hurry, Madame. The day is just beginning. And it will be long enough. I'll wait, I'll be waiting here, that's my job," he responded without raising his head.

Susanna pulled the shutters closed and shut the window. "Who should come at this hour, Mother? The *karozzin* is waiting for us. I told you it's time. We'd better hurry now."

"Where are we going, Mummy?" Wistin wanted to know.

Katarina silently looked at her daughter as if she was asking her permission to speak or at least make some sort of gesture.

"And what are all these bundles, Mummy?" the boy asked.

Katarina held her tongue once more.

"Today, Wistin, we're going to a very large house, far, far away from here," Susanna answered her son.

"Mummy, tell me where we're going to," the boy insisted, almost annoyed.

"I told you, Wistin. We're going to a very large house..."

"We're going to a very large house, far, far away from here..." he repeated her words in a teasing drawl.

"How clever Wistin is! How well he talks!" Katarina burst in but fell silent immediately and winced, as if she'd bitten her lips.

"That's not true, that's not true. Mummy, that's just a story. There's one that begins just like that. I remember it. But it's not a tale I want you to tell me, now. I'm sleepy. Where are we going?"

"Wistin, have I ever lied to you?" Susanna told him.

Wistin was silent.

Susanna looked at him. "Come now, look, there's Baby Jesus listening to you. Baby Jesus sees everything, hears everything, and understands everything...And here's Granny too. And here's yourself too, hearing yourself speak, and I'm here as well. Did I ever once tell you a lie?"

Wistin seemed to withdraw within himself; he collected his thoughts and in a changed tone of voice holding respect, told her, "No, Mother, you've always told me the truth. That's what I think, at least."

"And Baby Jesus sees all that's hidden in our hearts as well. Isn't that true?"

"True," he replied solemnly. "Baby Jesus sees everything."

"So if I lie..."

"If you lie, Mummy, Baby Jesus will know."

"Well then, it's true, just as I was saying, today we're going to a very large house, far, far away from here...And we're taking those bundles with us as well," Susanna started telling him again. "In that house there's lots of space for them. We won't fill it up with them, but at least..."

"Oh very well, Mummy...You feel like storytelling this morning. It's too early for stories. That's what you usually say. But today, no. But now that you've started it, you might as well go on with it..."

"But not now!"

"When then?"

"When we get up on the *karozzin*!"

"See, it is a story! I've been wanting to ride a *karozzin* for ages, Mummy! I've never been on one."

Susanna told him, "I've taken you up on a *karozzin*, Wistin, but it was a very long time ago. So long ago that you don't remember. It was a different journey, and you were deep in sleep, and you were dreaming wonderful dreams, about Heaven, and you were waiting to come to the village...You had been dreaming for nine months. And I was waiting for you to wake up, but you were too sleepy, just like today." She remembered the time when her labour had started, and Fr. Grejbel had brought her back to her parents' house in a *karozzin*. The coachman had noticed that she was pregnant and had made sure that his horse went slowly, and the journey was a calm and peaceful one, though the roads were rough and rutted.

Katarina realized what Susanna meant and gave her a quick glance, a very serious cast to her features, and she bit her lower lip and was about to intervene but she lowered her gaze to the ground so that Wistin would not notice and wonder.

"I'd like to ride on a *karozzin*, Mummy! But not on the one in your story, on a real one! On a real *karozzin*!"

"You don't believe me, Wistin? Didn't you just tell me you always believe what I tell you? Do you have to see with your own eyes to believe me? The *karozzin* is waiting for us at the door. That's why I told you that today you must get up early and hurry."

Wistin ran out of the room to the door. Overcome with shyness he stood gazing at the *karozzin*, the horse and the coachman. "It's true," he whispered in delight to himself, "it's true!" Full of wonder he approached them, but then drew back, as if afraid of the least movement that the horse made. His hands went to his face, as if expressing his marvel and fear. But he was contented.

The coachman gestured kindly to him to approach, telling him, "Don't be frightened, don't be frightened! The horse is our friend. He's been a friend of mine for many years. He'll make friends with you too, very quickly. Don't be afraid, son! Do you want to ride on the *karozzin*?"

Wistin was dumbfounded and stood rooted to the spot but gave the coachman a slight nod of assent.

"Have you often ridden on a *karozzin*?"

Wistin shook his head.

"You've never ridden one?"

"My mother told me that I rode it once, but I don't remember. If I don't remember, then I've never been. I remember everything."

"Well then, today you're going to enjoy yourself mightily. And do you know where we're going? Far, far away from here. At least, that's what your mother told me. She asked me to take you both somewhere far away."

Wistin was full of curiosity. "Then Mummy really told me the truth," he said in his heart.

"And to make this long journey today, do you know what I had to do? I had to get the horse to sleep early, yesterday evening. He was very tired, poor thing, very tired, because he and I work together all day long. Come rain or shine, and these two aren't our friends. And we live on what we earn together. I drive and he ambles on, and that's how we live. From one village to another. We'll soon get going, I'll ride up on my seat and lead him on holding the reins and he goes where I direct him to go. We never go where we like, except to the stable in the evening. We only go where people ask us to go."

Wistin listened with great attention, almost in awe.

"And do you know where we're going? We're going where your mother would like to go. She told me we're going to a very big house and we'll be taking some bundles with us too..."

"Then Mummy told me the exact truth," Wistin said in his heart again. "When I'm grown up I want to be a coachman!" he shouted with joy, and ran inside.

In a little while, Katarina and Susanna appeared in the doorway.

"Here they are! I'm ready, ladies! As soon as you give me the word, I'll say 'Hi, hi!' to our friend here and we'll be off!" the coachman cried as soon as he saw them.

Susanna was holding a bundle and so was Katarina.

"Leave them in my hands, leave them to me," he told them, and promptly went to take their load. "Carrying stuff is for us men to do. That's our job. And then, come to that, my line of work is to carry things. And my colleague takes the weight. Every person carries his own particular load in life, each to his own, isn't that so?" the coachman went on saying as if he was talking loudly to himself. His job had made him get used to talking on his own, and it had made him imagine that there was someone listening to him and silently agreeing with whatever he said. His mates also spent their daily life being alone. He loaded everything and waited for Katarina and Susanna to lock the door and come to the *karozzin*. Wistin walked a little in front of them. Then, the coachman helped them up onto the footboard and informed them that they could draw the curtains or have them open, as they wished.

Wistin felt so happy he felt he could fly. Occasionally he drew the curtain closed on his side and then sidled across the seat to draw the curtain closed on the other side. And then he wanted both of them open. Up there, held above the ground on four wheels, Wistin felt as if he was flying, in the same way as when he was flying his kite and imagined himself carried up with it. All at once, everything appeared different in his eyes, sitting in the *karozzin*. Everything seemed to be moving slowly, in step with the horse, walking straight ahead with measured steps, through the winding paths in the fields and sometimes through a huddle of tiny dwellings, in the narrow streets or in the middle of the countryside. The world seemed to be stirring in front of his eyes, and he wanted to savour every moment of that protracted motion, so long wished for. He fantasized about going up there, on the coachman's seat and holding the reins...

"I'd like to go up next to the coachman, Mummy, and lead the horse on. Tell him, Mummy, I'd like to lead the horse too."

Katarina smiled at him, wordlessly telling him he could not do that. She was afraid that it was a dangerous place for him to sit.

He did not give up and looked at his mother.

"You're still too young to lead the horse, Wistin. The horse and coachman are friends, long-standing friends. That's why they know each other well," Susanna told him.

Even Wistin realized he was far too young, and besides, he also felt a measure of fear.

"Do you see now, Wistin, that I told you the truth?"

"Have you often ridden on a *karozzin*, Mummy?" he asked her.

"Yes, of course. Though not all that often, because we hardly ever leave the village, but often enough."

"And were you alone when you were in the *karozzin*, Mummy?"

"No, I wasn't alone, Wistin."

Katarina was looking fondly at him. But at the same time she was wishing he would change the subject. She knew she had done her best as a mother, but she was afraid that without wanting to, she might interfere. Now, during this journey, she began feeling this more than ever. She was also feeling rather shy. "Truly, the time when my daughter was skipping and playing hopscotch and with beads has long passed on," she thought. "Even the time of the Valley has passed...I wish it hadn't."

"What are you thinking, Mother?" Susanna asked her. "How quiet you are! You too haven't been on a *karozzin* often."

Katarina gazed back at her from between her lashes, a long, sweet look. "Only out of necessity daughter, and very rarely at that. The *karozzin* takes you far away, and I didn't need to. That's why I haven't ridden on it often. Those bundles now, they're your dowry, and some other things besides, some clothes, but all in all, that's your fortune. I don't have much wealth to give you. You must get that from your husband, now."

"Why are you saying that, Mother? Don't you have faith in my husband?"

"Yes, I do, of course I do. But I know nature very well. I may not know how to read but I've got used to life very well indeed. You must make it up to him with your love since the dowry I can give you is insignificant. My pockets are not so deep after all! You also need to buy your marriage, my dear daughter, like everything else. Life doesn't give you anything for nothing. Not even love comes for free. First you must give and then wait to receive. Love, too, is a contract."

The *karozzin*'s motion still held Wistin spellbound. He kept looking out from between the curtains, and felt glad to see everything moving while he remained there...right behind them, sitting down...in the same fixed place. He did not quite understand what was happening, and frequently felt like peeking out to see the wheels turning, but neither Katarina nor Susanna allowed him to peer out. He looked about in every direction, not wanting to miss a thing. He saw fields on fields, with low rubble walls separating them. Small houses and farmhouses and *giren*, the typical circular stone-huts, and tracks and paths, and small ancient chapels in the middle of nowhere. A windmill here and there. Flocks of sheep and herds of goats, each with their own shepherd flanking them holding a long staff in his hand and with a watchdog lolloping around making sure none of the animals strayed. Farmers ploughing their fields toiling behind an ox or donkey. Women sitting outside making silk lace on their *trajbu*, the traditional bolster-shaped lace pillow. Vegetable sellers walking alongside their cart, drawn by a horse or a donkey.

Suddenly, Wistin turned to his mother, tugging at her skirt to gain her attention, and began telling her, "Once upon a time, Mummy, there was a very large house, far, far away..." and then he stopped.

Susanna waited for him to continue.

"You go on with it, Mummy. But start from the beginning."

"From the beginning? But if I do that it will take a long time."

"Oh alright, Mummy, you can start it from where you began this morning before we left."

"Once upon a time, there was a very large house, and this house was far, far away. And to get there you needed to..."

"Ride on a *karozzin*!" Wistin burst in excitedly.

"How did you know? Yes! You needed to ride on a *karozzin*. And that's what those people did, the ones who wanted to get to that house. They had been waiting for that day for a long time, and after they woke up very early, and after someone, a little lazy boy who did not want to get up from his bed early..."

"I know who you mean!" he interrupted her, smiling happily.

"They'd been waiting a long time, as I was saying before that naughty boy of the story didn't let me speak further...They'd been waiting a long time for a *karozzin* to come and get them. And one fine day it did. And these people...Do you know how many persons there were, Wistin?"

"Three, Mummy!" he immediately replied, raising his right hand and leaving his first three fingers out and closing his fourth and little finger whilst with the index finger of his left hand he counted each extended finger.

Katarina, deeply ensconced in the corner with her arms crossed, gazed still at the boy, always smiling.

"And these three people," Susanna went on, "were called..."

"They were called Granny, Mummy and Wistin..."

"How do you know what they were called?"

A huge smile was spread all over his face but his curiosity to hear more was greater and he did not answer her question, saying instead, "Go on, Mummy."

"And these three people went on with their journey, riding on a *karozzin*...drawn by a beautiful horse...on and on to get to a very large house full of lovely things. And there were gold and silver ornaments, and high-ceilinged rooms, and wide windows, and portraits and paintings...and furniture...It had something of everything. But most of all, it had a gorgeous garden in which many flowers grew."

"And who lived in this house, Mummy? You said it was a large house. Well then, did many people live there?"

Katarina looked at Susanna and bowed her head.

"In this large house there was only one man living there, all alone. It had many rooms, but only he lived there."

"He didn't have anyone to stay with him?"

"A long time before he had some other people there. But a long time before...And then he ended up alone."

"Why did he end up alone, Mummy?"

"Because one day storm clouds began to gather and a great storm broke out, and all that bad weather carried off all he had with it. But he stayed there, waiting, alone...alone...Always waiting for the people to come back to him..."

"He was waiting for three people, who had climbed into a *karozzin* far, far away, and they were Granny, Mummy, and Wistin," the boy took up the tale.

"That's right, Wistin," Susanna confirmed. "And in this story there was also another man, and he too was waiting for these three people to arrive there. And this man used to be in black clothes from head to toe, standing straight. He too had once come from very far away..."

"Wearing black, always wearing black?" the boy asked.

"Always in black, son."

"But why?"

"Because he was a man of God. I was telling you, he too had come from far away..."

"He came in a *karozzin*, Mummy?"

"No, son, he didn't come in a *karozzin*. He had come by ship. And he had been on a long voyage. Very long. On the seas. And he came for the very purpose of meeting these three persons."

"He must have loved these people very much, Mummy."

"He loved everybody. He had a kind and generous heart, and there was a large space in it that could fit in everyone, even those who did not love him."

"There were even people who did not love him, Mummy?"

"Because he was an extremely good man, son."

"But if he was such a good man, how come some people didn't love him, Mummy?"

"Because that's life for you, Wistin. Life's like that."

"Really, Mummy?" he questioned her, looking thoughtful and disappointed. "I don't really understand."

"If that's so, so much the better. It means it's too soon for you to know about such things."

Wistin was silent for a few moments but then spoke up again, as if his mind had started turning over different thoughts. "Mummy, I've never climbed aboard a ship. Today is my first time in a *karozzin*. Will you take me on a ship, sometime? Who comes by ship?"

"Adults come by ship, Wistin. Children do come...but even adults come by ship. The ship can fit in everybody, all those who need to go from one place to another...whether they want to or not. The ship is like a *karozzin* on the sea, and the *karozzin* is like a ship on land. Do you like that?"

"Do we also go to Heaven by ship, Mummy? How did Grandpa go to Heaven? If Heaven is up there, then how...?"

"Maybe he went there with the kite, Wistin!" Susanna looked at her mother and said, "I think it won't be too long before we get there. If I remember the way correctly, we'll be there soon. Are you tired? Tonight you'll sleep better, because you'll have spent a strenuous day."

Katarina drew a long breath and opened her hands as if she was about to start praying. "Yes, tonight I'll sleep better, of course, of course I will."

The regular pace of the horse was like a clock measuring every minute of the journey. Whenever there was a lull in their conversation, they heard it more clearly, more strongly. The clatter of the horseshoes on the ground reminded them of the four legs stepping forward, on and on, because of them.

"We could have kept going to Heaven then, last time, Mummy. Do you remember? But then you told me that the weather had changed and we had to come back down as quickly as possible."

"The time wasn't right, yet. Everything in good time, in its own time and place."

"And what was that man's name, the one always in black, Mummy?"

Susanna hesitated, looking at her mother as if to ask her permission to speak. "He was called Fr. Grejbel."

"And that man who waited alone in that large house, what was his name?"

"He was called Daddy," Katarina interposed quickly, in the manner of one interfering strongly. She almost shot out the four words, in the tone of voice a woman makes when she is declaring something very important and would brook no contradiction. "He was called Daddy." She was still with her arms akimbo, as before.

Susanna gazed back at her mother, rather startled, and at once her eyes filled with tears.

"Daddy?" Wistin asked eagerly. "Daddy?"

"From the day that those three persons arrived at his house onwards, that man came to be called 'Daddy'," Susanna replied. "Just like Granny has told you."

"And is he still called that, now?"

"He's still called that, now. He's your Daddy, son."

"That's what he's still called, and what he'll be forever called, Wistin," Katarina butted into their conversation once more, her eyes downcast, stricken, gazing blindly out of the *karozzin*.

"And how does this story go on, Mummy?"

The coachman made a slow turn round a corner and entered the street where they were to stop.

"We've arrived, Mother," Susanna said.

"And how does the story go on, Mummy? Aren't you going to tell me how it goes on?" Wistin asked.

"You'll soon find out, son!" Susanna answered him happily.

With a sharp tug at the handle of the brake that was beside him on the seat, the coachman halted the *karozzin*. "Here we are, we've arrived!" he cried in a tone which the horse understood and which was heard by the others too. He descended and went to help them get down from the footboard.

Arturu and Fr. Grejbel were waiting on the doorstep. They both had a tremulous smile on their lips, enough to reveal their excitement and show that this happiness need not be expressed in everyday words. The two of them approached and warmly welcomed the three. The double door stood wide open behind them, proof that this was a rare occasion indeed. Since his childhood, Arturu had become used to making sure the door was kept closed, or at least only opened on one side or kept ajar. The inner glass door was barely visible. On this occasion it was wide open too, and the hallway looked inviting.

The coachman brought down all the bundles and for a few moments they remained in the middle of the road, in front of the door.

"That's all my daughter's dowry, well maybe not all, but most of it!" Katarina explained rather shyly, lifting her head slightly to look at Arturu.

"No it's not! The dowry you brought on behalf of Susanna is Susanna herself!" Arturu replied in a tone showing his contentment.

Katarina was overjoyed but still felt shy.

"And do you know what's the dowry Susanna brought?" Arturu asked with a smile, looking at Wistin.

"It's a little boy who never wants to get up from his bed in the morning," Katarina said with a slight smile. "He's a good, obedient boy, but in the morning he seems to be sleepier than in the evening. That's all."

"Not always, but today yes, because today we woke up so very early!" Wistin defended himself.

"And do you know why? Because today is not a day like any other," Fr. Grejbel told him, his open palms urging Arturu and Susanna to walk inside.

Wistin walked in front of them, almost dumbstruck, beginning to look here and there all around him. He imagined he was hearing a story about a beautiful house that was far, far away.

As soon as he realized that Katarina was hanging back, Arturu was prompt in turning to her and courteously holding her forearm he urged her to walk inside. "This is my father's house and my...mother's. This is where my father and mother lived, Susanna. And now it belongs to us all..." he declared, looking at each person in turn directly in the face. He went to Wistin and taking hold of his hand made him walk slowly forward, pointing out objects. They continued walking like this, step by step, and the others followed in silence, captivated in their turn.

All of them felt as if they were going inside that house for the first time. Even Fr. Grejbel and Susanna felt that.

When he was at the foot of the staircase, Arturu stopped and looked at Susanna from beneath his brows, telling the boy, "Look, Wistin, something wonderful happened here, once..."

"When did it happen?"

"A long time ago, a very, very long time ago," Arturu replied.

"How long ago?"

"Just imagine, the village didn't even exist."

It was the time when Susanna was pregnant with Wistin. Her eyes and those of Katarina's met, and they both immediately changed their expression and continued to look at Wistin.

"There was a young woman," Arturu was continuing, "and she came down these stairs and went out there, look, in the courtyard, to bring down the clothes that were hanging on the line to dry in the sun. And she lifted her arms to reach the washing line that was stretched taut, and at a little distance away there was a young man, reading a book..."

"And this young man was sitting down all alone on an old stone bench in the courtyard..." Wistin quickly added.

All of them stared at Wistin in astonishment, then smiled and looked at each other, wordlessly.

"Now the young man no longer felt like reading that book," Arturu went on with the story. "He knew that the young woman was about to bring down the clothes from the washing line and he smiled at her, and she..."

"She smiled back at him," Wistin burst in excitedly wanting to join in the storytelling. He spoke clearly, enunciating every word in a clear high voice, basking in the attention being accorded to him. "Except for the twittering of the house-sparrows, there was no sound. The birds flew around following each other, sometimes coming down onto the ground..."

"Pecking at the breadcrumbs they found on the floor..." Arturu continued and then paused.

"The breadcrumbs which the lady used to throw on the path for them every day," Wistin went on.

"The lady?" Arturu asked him instantly, with a changed tone of voice, full of curiosity, turning to look at the others to show his amazement. "Did you say 'lady'?"

"Yes, Lady."

"And who was Lady, Wistin? Who was this woman? How do you know about her?" Arturu pressed him, more curious than ever.

"She was a very kind and good woman who loved everybody, and who helped all those in need. She had a young woman to look after her in her house, and to keep it clean. Lady was very kind to the beggars who used to come to her door..." Wistin went on. Then he paused, as if he was trying to dredge something out of his memory and he raised his right hand, pressing it to his forehead.

"And then?"

"Then the young man got up from his seat and closed his book, because he didn't feel like reading anymore, and he went up to the young woman to help her. She was carrying a large tin bath full of clothes. He took it from her and followed her, carrying it. As soon as they got to the laundry room, he went to the spirit stove where the iron was warming up and brought it to the ironing table for her..."

"And then?" Arturu eagerly asked him, more fervently than before.

"Then they started imagining, dreaming up many wonderful dreams..."

"Dreaming up many wonderful dreams? Are you sure?"

"Yes, I'm sure, truly. Baby Jesus knows it's true."

"And what else, Wistin?"

"That's all, that's all I know..."

"A lovely story! It's really lovely, this story! But how do you know it, Wistin?" Arturu wanted to know.

There was a moment's silence and they all looked at each other.

Wistin paused to consider his words but a quick glance from Susanna emboldened him to speak and he continued. "Mummy told me the story. She told it to me, and not just once or twice, and she always said that one day she'll continue it till the end...she used to say that she would like it to finish with a happy ending, not with a sad one, but she herself did not yet know how it would end."

"And where were you that day when the story was happening, Wistin?" Susanna asked him.

"I was still with Baby Jesus, and I was waiting for a ship to bring me...That's what you told me, Mummy."

"And where was the ship bringing you, Wistin?" Katarina asked him.

"Here, Granny!"

They continued walking together through the various rooms. Katarina looked at every object and at every corner, shyly but also with admiration and wonder. It was a rare occasion for her to enter such a house. She was amazed that all her life she had remained seeing the village as a world of closed doors, locked-up houses that had a completely different atmosphere inside, totally different from the streets, alleys and fields.

The house where she had lived her married life with Saverju had nothing like this, and the few village houses she had entered were all like hers and Saverju's. This time, everything was different and new, because of Susanna. Susanna was not only her daughter; she was also the woman who was able to bring her into this world of experiences that she, like her husband, would never have been able to imagine. Since she loved Susanna, she had no choice but to follow her. After all, Saverju was now dead.

As she was looking all around her, Katarina observed a number of framed photographs, all showing the same face. They were photos of the same man, scattered all around the room. She went on gazing at them and expressed her wonder in the same words of praise, repeated in the manner of reciting a litany. Suddenly, she saw that there was a large portrait hanging in the middle of the wall. It was of the same man who graced the small photographs she had just noted. It was a rather large framed portrait with a thick frame, the colour of faded gold. It was placed where the rays of the sun would reach it, coming through the large window that overlooked the garden. She looked at it once, and then looked again, respect and shyness more pronounced than ever on her face.

Arturu observed that the portrait had caught her eye.

Involuntarily, Katarina remained staring intently at that portrait. Both her eyes and hands, moved by her simple naturalness, expressed her astonished reaction on seeing that portrait. It seemed to her that she had seen that face before, somewhere, at some point. She bowed her head and made to pass from in front of it. The portrait showed a serious face, wearing spectacles with small round lenses and with eyes that had a fixed, intent look in them, gazing straight at whoever passed and stopped to take a look. The man had a thick, bushy moustache with rounded tips that came down to his jawline and a little further beyond, too. He had a full head of hair, peppered with white hairs here and there, and it was curly in parts. His waistcoat could be seen clearly underneath the open jacket. It was a dark coloured waistcoat and it stood out because it was the darkest coloured object in the whole portrait. The portrait depicted the man down to his waist, and below that it was all blurred and indecipherable, looking for all the world like a bank of clouds, as if the man was resting on them or even emerging from them.

Katarina realized that the man himself had probably passed away and suddenly she raised her right hand to her forehead to make the Sign of the Cross and say a prayer for his departed soul. Photographs were uncommon objects in her life and nearly always signified pictures of people who were already dead. She felt she should say a prayer in front of every photograph she came across, a prayer known by heart, ever since she was a girl. This portrait reminded her of the stone sculptures depicting souls in Purgatory that were scattered along paths in the middle of fields – statues of figures praying with crossed arms, their head inclined to one side, their sad gaze directed upwards, figures sculpted up to their waist emerging from flames. Such sculptures were also placed high up on square stone columns at the entrance to a cemetery. She was in the habit of stopping in front of each statue to say prayers for their soul. And she had taught Susanna to do the same. It was the custom, going back countless generations, and she felt duty-bound to continue it.

Arturu was still looking at her. "Do you know him?" he asked with a grave smile. "Did you know him, I mean to say. God forgive him. That's my father."

"Your father?" she replied in astonishment. "Your father?" she asked once more, and then repeating the word to herself in hushed tones.

"Did you know him?" Arturu asked her again.

Katarina smiled tremulously, shyly, and remained with downcast eyes. She remained silent to avoid answering but then said to him, "It's a lovely picture, even the gold frame is beautiful. But that's not what counts. What counts is the person himself...the face. What a handsome man he was!"

"Thank you, Madam Katarina!"

"Madam Katarina...Me? What's all this? That man is a gentleman. He knew how to dress smartly and look groomed as befits a gentleman." Katarina paused a little and then continued, as if she had just made a discovery. "And I must tell you that that face resembles yours greatly. He has your face, exactly. Or rather, you have his, I should say. Blood will tell...that's what my mother used to say."

"You're right; I have my father's face. I resemble him a lot."

"Yes, you do resemble him, so much. His eyes, his nose, his cheeks, they're like yours. You can't deny he's your father." As she was speaking, she lifted her face to the portrait again and studied it for a long time.

"True, true. That's what people who knew him say. And you would have remarked on it even more had you seen him face to face..."

Katarina was silent. "I saw him, I saw him," she said in her heart.

"It appeared as if you knew that face," Arturu questioned her closer. "Do you recall? Try to remember. He began to forget everything, poor man. Do you remember?"

Katarina kept her head bowed with a smile on her face, but remained silent.

~ 0~

It was a day like any other. For Katarina it was as if it had happened that same day. She had an excellent memory, and never forgot anything except what she wished to forget. Mass had just finished and people were coming out of the church and spilling out into the square. The men put on their cap again, and the women took off their veil and folded it calmly. Some people went straight home but some lingered for a chat and others made for the market where the hawkers were already waiting for them, inviting people to go and buy with their loud cry.

A man stood up straight, right in the middle of the square, alone, looking at people, as if he was waiting for something or looking for somebody. He was wearing a pair of spectacles with small round lenses, and had a thick bushy moustache curling down to his chin. He had a waistcoat on, but it was open and his jacket was aslant, while his tie was loose around his neck and at an angle, as if it was about to be hidden under the jacket.

The villagers' curiosity was roused and they approached him. He continued to stare at them, without saying a word.

"This man isn't from these parts," someone said.

"Who's he? Where did he come from? How did he get here?" someone else asked.

"He's not one of us," they all had the same thought.

The man kept up his glazed look at the people, then, as if afraid of them, he slowly began to walk away, without knowing where he was headed, seeming to want to avoid the crowd. He did not walk more than a few paces.

The people followed him at a distance, slowly, full of curiosity.

Katarina was in the crowd. And she could see everything.

A few moments later someone suggested calling the parish priest to address him. Someone went running back to the church and it was not long before the priest came. He asked the crowd to give the man some space, so as not to bother him unduly.

"We don't know who this man is. We've never seen him before. He's not one of us for sure. He's not from this village," someone told the parish priest, as if he was the villagers' mouthpiece.

"It doesn't matter, it doesn't matter," the priest said encouragingly. "We'll ask him and he'll tell us." He stopped talking and approached the man, asking him in a lowered tone almost as if he did not want to be overheard, "Where are you from?"

"Me? I'm not from a village. I'm from nowhere!" the man cried.

Some people began to laugh but the priest shushed them at once.

"And what's your name? Come now, tell me your name."

"What's my name? I don't have one."

"But, are you sure you don't have a name? Just a name, mind. Come now, try to remember. You'll see. You have a name, everyone has a name..."

"But I don't have one. I never knew me having one. No, no, I don't."

"You too have a name. Try to remember. If you had to tell yourself, 'this is my name', come now, what would you say? You would say, 'my name is...' What?"

"Someone calls me 'Father'."

"Father? Good, good, and what's your son called?"

"What son? No, it can't be."

"Well then what's your name? You are someone. Look at all these people here, everyone is someone. Even you, then. Come now, tell me, who are you?"

"Someone?"

"Yes, and so, what's your name?"

"I'm called Someone."

"Mr...Look," the priest tried to explain, "I am called Grejbel, and I am a priest, and so people call me Fr. Grejbel. And you, they call you Mr..."

"Mr. Someone. I am Someone. That's my name."

"And who's your wife?"

"My wife? I don't have a wife. I have nothing that belongs to me."

"Can't you remember anything? At least you remember that you don't have a wife..."

"I remember all this because I've forgotten everything," the man said to the priest. "Someone. I know that I've forgotten things but I can't remember exactly what. One of these days I need to remember."

"And where do you live? How is your front door? From which other village are you?"

"My house, my house is here."

The people gathered around looked at each other, shaking their heads in denial.

"No, your house isn't here," the priest told him gently.

"Not here? Well then, it's not here. If it's not here, it's not here. You're right."

"Well then, where is it?"

"Nowhere."

"And who are you?"

"I am Someone. Mr. Someone."

"Do you remember your name well?..."

"Yes, I remember my name well, because I repeat the same word to myself all the time. But now I want to go home. Home, home, somewhere there's my home," he said, beginning to search in the distance through cupped hands as if through binoculars.

"Very well. We'll go home now. You and me, the two of us together. Do you want to?"

"Yes, I want to. But, who are you?" the man wanted to know, as if suddenly he wanted to understand what was going on.

"I'm a priest."

"What's a priest?"

"A priest is a man who tries to do everything he can to love others, whatever the cost. That's what a priest is, someone who loves others in every situation and under any circumstances."

"Love? So you love others?"

"Yes, I love people, even you, I love you."

"Even me, who's nobody," the man declared, beginning to laugh.

"Yes, even you. Even you, though you still haven't told me your name."

"Someone, that's my name. Don't you believe me? I don't lie, because I can't remember anything. You love somebody who's nobody."

"But now, both of us need to go home, you and me together. But where's your home?"

"Home, home, it's far away from here." The man spoke these words with his gaze fixed ahead, as if he was seeing someplace but in the far distance.

"Your home is far away from here?"

"Yes, it's far away. Lady's house."

"The lady, you said?"

"No, no, not the lady."

The priest took hold of him from his forearms and made him walk up the street that led out of the square, that would bring them to the edge of the village. He thought that the man would at least remember the way he had come on entering their village. But the man did not even remember the way he had come to be there. Some of the villagers followed in their wake. Katarina was still in their midst.

A few moments later a *karozzin* appeared, reducing its speed as it drew closer to them. It stopped and a woman, advanced in years, descended from it. Her hair was drawn back in a bun and she was wearing a long dark dress that came to her ankles and nearly hid her feet.

The priest looked at her, standing straight, waiting for her to speak.

The woman bowed her head and drew the man to her from his forearms, making him keep up with her firm decisive pace, all the while rearranging his jacket and tie.

"Who are you?" the man asked her, in a calm and quiet voice, like someone resigned to his fate.

"I'm Lady," she replied firmly, annoyed but low voiced so as not to be overheard. "How did you get out of the house? Didn't I tell you that you shouldn't?"

"I don't know you," the man said to her.

"You don't know me? You'll soon remember as soon as we get home." She lowered her voice even more and whispered, "We'll speak about it then, but not here."

The priest drew back a little and kept looking at them without saying a word.

Lady gave the priest a knowing look, giving him to understand that she was that man's wife. She helped her husband up into the *karozzin* and signalled to the coachman to drive off. "Drive on...Drive on out of here...As fast as you can!" she ordered. And within the space of a few moments the *karozzin* had left the village.

Katarina stayed there till the end. She had never seen such a scene. Without wanting to, she felt a strong wish to tell Saverju all about it as soon as she got home.

~ 0~

A few days later, Arturu asked Susanna, "This time, I would like us to have a feast, as if we're having a wedding celebration. And it will be a feast for all of us. Whom shall we invite?"

Susanna did not know what to tell him. "Whom can I invite? Who knows me in all the village? Except for my mother and Fr. Grejbel I know nobody."

"Shall we talk to Fr. Grejbel and see what he thinks? No one knows people better than he. It will be a feast in his honour, too," Arturu declared.

"He had taken care to arrange our wedding...if you can call it that," Susanna answered him with a soft moan.

"Let the past be, now. What you were wishing for at that time, will come about today."

"Father hadn't come that day, and he won't come today...That time he didn't come because he didn't want to, and this time he won't come because he can't. My father was always fated to be far away."

"But he'll be able to see everything from Heaven."

"You mean to say that my father always chose to see things from a distance, in secret. He never let anything escape his eagle eyes, and I don't think he'll hold back just because he's in Heaven. Over there he'll imagine he can see things even better. And without the need for spectacles. Father never wanted to wear a pair of spectacles. It seemed like some sort of disgrace to him. Two round glasses, in front of your eyes and hanging from your ears, that's how he referred to them. He used to laugh at people who wore them. And now that he's in Heaven, I wonder?"

"In Heaven no one needs spectacles."

"Is that what you think?"

"Haven't you forgiven him yet, Susanna?"

"Yes, I forgave him, a long time ago. If I hadn't, it would mean that I hadn't understood a thing from all the words Fr. Grejbel spoke. I would have made him out a liar, too. It wasn't just my duty to forgive my father, Arturu. I also needed to, most especially when he wouldn't say another word on his deathbed, and then fell silent forever, and that was the end of it. His silence was a signal showing how certain he was of his actions. In his heart there was no room for any doubt. When I finally understood this, a long time later, I could tell myself that I too had done all I could. Everyone needs forgiveness, Arturu."

"From that day onwards, your father changed his mind. You can be certain of that. In Heaven we change our mind...We can't think in the same way we are used to thinking in the village. There we wear a special dress, a long gown, for a special occasion. A dress for a feast day – every day!" He paused and then went on in a different tone, "And your mother, this time, will be with us too. Aren't you happy and content?"

"It could have been like this from the start, Arturu."

"From the start? Do you mean before you entered this house and we got to know each other? If that had happened, maybe we two wouldn't be together today. We would never have met, for sure."

"No, no, that's not what I meant, Arturu. Today I know for sure, more than ever before, that I've only ever loved you. And do you know why?"

"Let me try and guess! This can be a very hard question to answer or else a very easy one. You know all about the winds, and every one of them can be right. I don't know why. It depends what you have in mind. Tell me!"

"You can't guess, Arturu, because you can never begin to imagine what it means to me that I entered this house as a servant and ended up as your wife. All our squabbles arose out of the fact that I couldn't believe that such a dream was real and no dream at all. I was ironing some clothes with that old iron once..."

"I remember that iron, Susanna, as black as coal, kept somewhere in this house ever since I was a boy..."

Susanna picked up the thread of her thoughts from where she had left off, "And then you suddenly came into my life and changed it completely. Without you yourself knowing it, you ordered me to start living anew. It's your fault! And your life changed as well in the meantime. Did I change it for you? How should I know? I didn't do anything more than any other young woman would have done. It wasn't me who led you on. You know it well."

"I do know it. It was I who approached you."

"The baby wasn't yours, and at the time I had all those troubles. And in spite of everything, it was as if you took no notice at all. Today I know it was all my own fault."

"I was to blame, too."

"We were both to blame for not realizing that we'd found what we'd been looking for in each other. It was both our fault, which means it was no-one's!" Susanna declared looking him straight in the eye. Her face had come alive, expecting his praise for the manner of her speech.

"Well done, well done indeed! See how well you've learnt to talk! That's why I'm so proud of you, too!"

"You taught me to read, and open books, and walk along as they unfold till my mind awakes and spreads open. Do you remember when you wanted me to start reading and you chose a book for me from the many your father had collected, and at first I thought that it was something out of my reach, and difficult? At first I supposed reading to be something frivolous and superfluous. I read a book when I knew that you only need a pair of hands to work in the fields Arturu, you taught me to think in a better way. You taught me to understand the fields themselves, better."

"And you taught me to love in a better way, showing me how my heart, too, could open up."

"Maybe that time was a time of folly. For everyone. The folly of an entire village." With downcast eyes and bowed head she patted her skirts. She paused to choose her words with care and then said, "I want to tell you that in all this time I kept reading books, all the same. I used to tell myself, 'This is the best way to appear once more in front of Arturu when the storm has passed.' That's what I used to say. Fair weather comes to gladden fields as well."

"And why was this the best way?"

"Because it was the way I could learn to wait, wait without having a change of heart. All that I went through urged me to hurry on. That's the basic rule of the agricultural seasons, everything in its own time, week by week and day by day, almost by the precise hour...the weather forecasts. That's how my father was brought up, and that's how he brought me up and even my mother, because he also brought her up in his own manner with the hold he had over her. Nothing in our house moved, Arturu, if it wasn't in the way he wanted, with the least look, and even more with the command in his voice. He even commanded with silence, perhaps more so."

"I know, I know," Arturu said, to cut her short.

"I want to tell you everything. All that I went through was because of my son, because of Fr. Grejbel, and because of you. I had no one who was truly mine except my son, wherever he was, without whom I had to live. My mother kept her distance, too. I could confide in no one, trust nobody, except Fr. Grejbel, and I did not know where he was. I had no one for a husband, except you Arturu, wherever you were! Where were you?" she cried bursting into tears.

Without a word, Arturu took her into his arms. He patted her on the back with one hand and with his other caressed her cheeks.

"You all kept your distance, but you were all I had," Susanna said raggedly, trying to overcome her sobbing. "Now that you're all here, gathered around me, I don't know, I don't know, I can hardly believe it. It seems like another story, one of the fairy tales I tell Wistin." She disengaged herself a little from his embrace and put her hand in her pocket to bring out a handkerchief.

Arturu placed a finger on her lips and told her, "Where is that weeping coming from, Susanna? Crying helps to ease oneself. Do you know where it's all coming from?"

Susanna slowly turned her gaze to his. The armchair was roomy enough to allow her to turn and look at him directly without having to get up.

"It's coming from these rooms," he told her. "I used to call out to you from here when you were far away from me. This is where I scorned you, and this helped to purge me of all feelings and sentiments. And this is where I missed you and cried for you and desired you. It was in here that I grew proud of myself seeing you return from where you had come. But do you know what all this served to teach me? I realized that I was waiting for you to come back, and this time it would be once and for all. There was only one thing I was afraid of – that I would not keep remembering you. The scorn I felt for you was in itself part of the way in which I waited for you."

"You were waiting for this to happen? Truly?"

"I was waiting for it all – whether you'd manage to find your son, and whether Fr. Grejbel would return. It all depended on this. If one day two ships were to enter harbour...Isn't that what you used to like saying? Someone was waiting on the Quay."

Susanna smiled and went back into his arms.

"Well then, shall we see what Fr. Grejbel thinks? And we'll see what your mother wants, too," he reminded her.

"Let's see what Fr. Grejbel thinks, this time too," Susanna agreed with him.

They all met Fr. Grejbel. There was a long discussion. This time, Arturu thought, it must be a feast for all of them, in their honour.

"I would like to hold a celebration for Susanna, one that I couldn't hold for her when she got married," Katarina volunteered. "That day, my husband and I didn't attend the wedding. Today, Susanna and Arturu deserve all that they missed out on years ago. Fr. Grejbel, you know all too well what a very stern man my Saverju was, and he would not budge an inch from what he had decided. 'No, no, and for the last time, no!' he had declared. But he was only human after all. I was the only one who knew but he did not even want to show that he felt it keenly. A man is always a man, he liked to tell me, and if he softens his attitude he's no longer a man! He didn't mind showing his anger in front of everybody, but he never allowed anybody to see him cry. He almost did not dare to smile in front of people. Let alone cry! 'Tears are for women,' he used to say. But once he broke down and cried before me, but I won't say when. He wept only once in my presence and he appeared just like a little boy to me."

Fr. Grejbel urged her to change the conversation saying, "Come now, Katarina, try to forget all this."

"I do try hard to forget, Fr. Grejbel, but I don't always succeed. Anyway, I would like to provide the meal that I didn't offer her when she got married. The money we'd saved up for her wedding is still there, and Saverju won't say anything either way, wherever he is. He saved up the money with me, though I don't know whether I should tell you where he hid it..." Katarina came to a stop and raised her eyes to the priest, and with a bantering gaze lifted her index finger, straight up, below her nose and across her mouth.

Fr. Grejbel encouraged her to continue speaking her mind, and with a smile showed her they were all ready to listen to what she had to say. "Today, Katarina, who can deny you your dear wish?"

"I would like, if Arturu agrees to it, to hold the celebration in our village," she spoke up, emboldened to speak. "Today, Arturu, you're one of us."

"And you're one of us, Madam Katarina!"

"Madam Katarina! You are too good, Sir! Can you just imagine Saverju hearing me addressed as Madam? Thank the Good Lord he's not here. Me, Madam Katarina!"

"Of course we'll hold the celebration in your village," Arturu was only too happy to agree. "It's only natural, it's Susanna's village."

"Well then, we'll hold a feast for all the villagers who would like to attend, and we'll hold it in front of the parish church," Fr. Grejbel concluded. "You can leave the rest in my hands. Set your mind at rest, all of you, I'll take care of all the necessary arrangements. We'll hold a feast for all the villagers. It's right and fitting for everyone to be happy and celebrate with us."

Many people gathered round for the celebration in the village square that day. They dressed up for the occasion, putting on their best clothes which they only took out of the wardrobe a few times in a year for some such special occasion. At one point, a few beggars arrived as a group, men and women together, and they stopped all of a sudden, reluctant to keep on walking, feeling too shy to mix with the crowd. They had all come from the hidden corners of the village, forgotten places within the village and the surrounding neighbourhood. They walked on as one, prudently, up to Fr. Grejbel to greet him.

Susanna and Arturu approached them and found them places among the rest of the villagers. At first the villagers were loath to mingle with them, but slowly, slowly, after a warning look sent from beneath a brow, or a wink, they did not say anything and no longer looked askance at them, gazing with the same long contemptuous look as before. The beggars could be identified by their pinched and grimy faces, but they spent all their life in the hidden margins of the locality, or just beyond it, where solitude could watch over them by day and where darkness sought to hide them during the night.

After some time had passed, people expected something to happen. They had gone there to eat, too. Out of the sacristy, on the left hand side of the church, a stream of food flowed out. And then hazelnuts were handed out followed by almonds. Children, especially boys, came running out full of energy to snatch up as much as they could grab in their hands and cram in their pockets. There were also the traditional village *biskuttini*, oval-shaped biscuits, and almond ones, and macaroons with a cherry on the top.

After some time had passed, Fr. Grejbel made his way to the centre and gestured to the crowd, meaning to make a speech. He waited till people stopped their conversations. He directed his gaze in all directions, gathered his hands together, and then opened his palms. "My dear brothers and sisters of this village, this day has finally come round. We've awaited it for long," he said, "and perhaps had given up that it would ever come. But this day, too, had to pay a visit to our village. God be praised, and we are blessed, all of us, for we're His children. The path we followed was long, but as you can see it was not in vain, and we were never alone on the journey. We have all walked down this path, even those amongst us here who think they weren't with us on this journey. Everyone walked at his own pace, and all of us had only this one path to follow..." He paused briefly and then went on, "My dear brothers and sisters of this village, Arturu and Susanna and Wistin are here amongst us, united together. And Grandma Katarina is here as well."

People turned their face and craned their head to see where they were. Arturu and Susanna were in the centre of the crowd while Wistin had met up with some other boys his own age, some of whom were wearing a cap while others sported tangled tufts and locks, and they were all oblivious to anything but their games. Sometimes they played Hide and Seek, searching for those in hiding. They also played *Daqqa Xejn, Qabża, Gwerra Franċiża, and Kukkużejt.* Their shouts blended in with the hum of the adults' conversation, but their shrill voices were louder. Each scream echoed over and above any other noise. The girls were gathered in another area, playing hopscotch or skipping a rope. Some of them were happily dangling a doll from their arms. They were ragdolls and so were rather chubby, as if they were little overfed children. These ragdolls were stuffed with straw and had sheep's wool for hair. Each dress was multi-coloured and none was the same as another's. The children's mothers knew no bounds to their fantasy, because every mother, as she set to making her daughter a doll, brought to mind the doll belonging to all the other girls.

The children continued making a racket. Some people tried to hush them.

"Let them be, let them be, my friends," Fr. Grejbel waved to those adults to desist. "The children are enjoying themselves just as we used to when we were little children. Now that we've grown up, we choose other ways to enjoy ourselves, and we're noisy in a different way, as well. Everything in its own time. And this is our time, now, and it is a wonderful time. And the time of forgiveness is more wonderful because it's the time when love will have ripened and will be producing its fruit. With a little help from us all, brothers and sisters of this village, this small village, old and peaceful, seemingly cut off from the rest of the world, and none so beautiful! When we set foot on our path, we walked together, and when we put a foot wrong, we set it to rights together and rose to go on our way. Who can boast of greater freedom than us? Which is freer? The large town holding many, many people, and where distances are so great they seem never-ending? Or a village like this one, where the air is fresh, and the seasons regulate our whole year without any fits and starts? Our pace is calm and we walk slowly. It doesn't matter. When we fall, we get up and brush ourselves down. And when we manage to walk firmly on with steady feet, why, then we're happy at making some progress! The way is long, that's true. But from here, from the middle of the fields, as well as from the bottom of the Valley, the sky can be seen clearly, and it's a clear cerulean blue! Look up at it, my friends. From our village we can see the entire world clearly, as through a small ventilator. And we see well."

"Without spectacles," Susanna spoke in a humorous tone to Arturu.

"Your father was right, then," Arturu replied, sharing the joke.

The crowd applauded Fr. Grejbel, and the few musicians who had been engaged for the occasion, played a few notes to swell the applause.

"There are musicians here, too!" someone exclaimed in excitement, and everyone looked around, seeking the musicians.

"Yes, we have some musicians too. Whoever could come came today. Just look at them! We have someone on the tambourine, a bagpipe player, the one who plays the *żavżava*, another on the cymbals, and another on the drum and also the fife player. And we also have a guitarist!" Fr. Grejbel announced, his happiness spread all over his face, for all the world to see.

The tambourine player took centre stage and gripping the tambourine with his fingers, he raised it above his head and gently tapped it against his crown, then clashed it on his elbow and in one swift flowing motion, struck one knee and then the other. The crowd stood watching him happily, their mouths round circles of surprise. The bagpipe player took the opportunity to join in and the two of them began to play a tune.

Susanna and Arturu took each other's hand and going to the middle of the square they began to dance. They went round and round and swayed to every note that was played, and people broke the silence that had held them in its grip and made it apparent how much they were enjoying themselves. As soon as he observed this, the player of the *żavżava* joined the other musicians and the festive atmosphere visibly increased. Arturu began to wave, greeting the crowd and Susanna slowly lowered her head down and tucked her face in his shoulder, but he instantly raised it, to give her courage, and she spread her smile to encompass every corner of the square.

"In honour of Susanna, Arturu and Wistin!" Fr. Grejbel shouted, inviting the crowd to join in the greeting.

"I've never felt as happy as today, Arturu! I'm not the same woman I was before! How could I ever begin to imagine that I would end up dancing with you, in front of all these villagers? This isn't the same village I grew up in."

"You've certainly never learnt this dance from books! It was in you, innate, from long before! It must have been! I too don't know how to dance, but every natural rhythm seems good enough. At least, I haven't stepped on your toes, yet!" Arturu laughed cheerily.

"Can you just imagine my father's face if he could see me dancing here today!" Susanna whispered half-guiltily in Arturu's ear.

"He's changed his mind by now. I've already told you. In Heaven we experience a change of heart. We don't think in the same way we used to. We put on new clothes, special ones, like those we're wearing today."

"Who told you this? Is it true?"

"I told you all this once before..."

"But who told you?" she insisted, reassured that the music and hubbub around them were loud enough to drown her words to Arturu and so would not be overheard over the noise. She made an enormous effort to overcome her shyness.

"Guess! Lady did!" he answered her with a smile.

"Your mother," she gasped, and lovingly reiterated, "your mother, that's who she'll always be for me."

"Lady, Mother. That's right. And if she had told me this, who do you think had taught her this idea?"

"Who else can it be but Fr. Grejbel?"

"How do you know that?" he asked her in a teasing tone.

"That's the easiest question you've ever asked me, dear heart. Fr. Grejbel raised his hand as far as he could into the sky, and managed to bring a piece of Heaven down into this village..."

"I never knew the villagers loved him so much. I had to see it with my own eyes before I could believe it, and afterwards I can only remain amazed," he told her. "But to them, this love for him seems the most natural thing in the world."

Arturu and Susanna waited for the musicians' melody to stop, and then they disengaged from each other's arms and mingled once more with the crowd.

"And now I would like to announce that amongst us there are four people who are going to appear in front of us for the first time today," Fr. Grejbel told the expectant crowd. "Lately, they've set up a new theatrical company and they're going to play-act for us. They've formed the Village Theatrical Company. Here they are, my friends. Baskal, Ġwakkin, Kieli and Ġamri."

The four of them came out in the cleared centre, one after the other, and they welcomed the crowd's greetings.

"We're going to perform a short play which we haven't written down, yet," Baskal began to say. "We don't know how to write, but we make do in another way..."

"We keep everything in our mind, up here. We remember and invent things that very moment...We're memory actors! Our memory doesn't let us down and we always get to the point where it leads us. We've always given it a good workout because we don't have anything else, and it has continued serving us well. We hope that this evening it won't let us down and make us lose face," Kieli elaborated.

"We take stock of circumstances and make up a story out of the situation, the way we see it, from afar..." Ġamri added his bit.

"From our side of things, we see the situation in one way. But from where you are, you probably see it in another light," Ġwakkin said, not to be outdone and left out.

"And now we'll begin our little performance. We thought of it together in my wine tavern, and we kept the door closed and made it up as we went along, each one inventing a part of it, and then we joined it all together. Four different parts and we'll go through the performance as we imagined it that day. It pleased us then and today we hope you'll like it," Baskal announced, somewhat pompously. "Today it should come out better. And do you know why? Because today we're got up as actors, and no one recognized us as the usual persons they know."

"Give them a big hand, my friends! Applause to put heart into them before they begin!" Fr. Grejbel urged the gathered crowd of people.

"And at the end, as soon as we finish, clap again. That's all!" Baskal added, arranging his costume. "Anyway, in brief, all you have to do is clap, always clap. When we make a mistake – clap to console us. When we don't make mistakes – clap to encourage us."

At this feast there were the village *għannejja*, the singers who sang traditional folk songs or impromptu ditties according to a traditional chant. Other *għannejja* from villages nearby had also come. They had arrived hours before, riding their own horse, and displayed the satisfaction of people who had made a long journey. The feast was an important occasion for them, proof of how much they were sought after and respected for their sweet melodious voices and for the words that they expressed which moved hearts and made people shed a tear or two. During the year, these folk singers sang in the midst of fields, while they were at work or during the break they took, to rest from the hot sun at midday. They would lounge on a thick branch of an old tree or on a low rubble wall, keeping an eye on their hoe and singing a few verses about love. Some of them made up the lyrics there and then, according to the mood they happened to be in, an impromptu song, touching on the piques and little squabbles they had with others and about the dreams and desires that were sown and would sprout like the seeds in the fields which they themselves worked and toiled in, from dawn to dusk. They would greet each dawn with a song on their lips and break out into song again at midday and at sunset, when they would stop to say a prayer and thereafter sing no more till bedtime.

Some of them favoured the type of *għana* that used shrill high notes, sung almost hoarsely, where the words could hardly be understood. They would bring up each word with difficulty, from somewhere closed up deep within them.

All eyes were now on one special singer whom everyone had known about for a long time because he only sang the *Għana tal-Fatt*. He would take a story that had really happened and sing about it in rhyme in his own words. He would not invent the lyrics there and then like those who sang *spirtu pront*. He would have studied the story well, finding out all the details he could. His words would have been stored away in his memory for a long time and he would learn the song by heart. His voice would change according to the sentiments being expressed and he frequently moved people to tears as they listened to him, enthralled. He knew many such songs by heart, and he would sing them on demand, when people gathered around him in the square or in some wine tavern.

People waited till the *Għannej tal-Fatt* approached Fr. Grejbel, in the centre of the village square, and began to speak. Before he sang his song, the singer had the habit of saying a few words about it.

"What shall I sing for you, today?" asked the *Għannej tal-Fatt.*

The crowd was silent for no one could pluck up courage to reply.

"You don't want me to sing anything?"

The hubbub that arose all of a sudden testified to the crowd's eagerness to hear him sing.

"I can sing many songs for you, perhaps the song of 'The Two Orphans', recounting a very sad tale indeed, or 'The Bride of Mosta'. This story happened in the time of the Turks. Or I can sing 'Marija, the Maltese fisherman's daughter,' or 'The Young Woman of the Cliffs' or perhaps 'The Story of Joseph sold by his Brothers'. I can tell you all these tales from beginning to end, word for word, without stopping. At this very moment! All you have to do is tell me, 'Sing us that, or this one, or the other!' Just give me a minute to tune my voice accordingly and that's all! Do you want to see if this is true?"

But the people again stayed silent, not expressing which song they wanted him to sing for them.

The *għannej*, halfway between feeling proud and feeling astonished that he still could not get them to choose one, looked at Fr. Grejbel as if telling him that he had done his best and fulfilled his part, or nearly so.

Fr. Grejbel smiled back at him and his glance indicated that the *għannej* should continue mentioning other stories he could sing for them.

The *Għannej tal-Fatt* raised his eyebrows slightly, looked up skywards, and after a little while said, "I can also sing for you the story of 'Judith, an exemplary widow', or 'Toni Bajjada', a story of the time during The Great Seige, or 'Genevieve'..."

Everyone kept listening and waiting.

"But what else do these blessed people expect from me?" the *Għannej tal-Fatt* said in exasperation in his heart. Then he realized that they might have got confused with all the names he had spouted at them. So he raised his voice and went on with his litany, "Or, if you want, I can sing you a love song..."

"Yes, yes," some persons shouted.

"Well, I can sing you the story of 'The unfortunate Pia' then. This story will break your hearts, for sure. I know what I'm saying, my friends! I can't tell you how many people I made cry with this one! And then, to get over it quickly and stop crying, I know some comic songs, as well. Something sweet after tasting bitterness. Or perhaps I'll sing "Emily and Richard' for you, a story full of happiness and also sorrow. Or 'Falaride', a heart-breaking tale! And I remember now there's also 'Armand on Margaret's Grave'. Is it tears you want? Then it's tears I'll give you! Tell me which and I'll begin. Tears on tears and yet more tears! But afterwards don't complain that I made you cry! Don't blame the *Għannej tal-Fatt*! I will do my part, move your heart, with a word, with a break in my voice, with a cadence, but then your hearts are in your own hands, not in mine! You can take care of your own heart! Decide which one then, my friends, decide!"

No one answered him.

The children too were captivated listening to him, even though they did not always understand each word he spoke in that loud voice of his.

"Aren't these enough to choose from?" the singer went on, somewhat taken aback. "Are there more nooks and crannies in your heart that I haven't managed to stir? How big is your heart, then? My goodness, it must be really deep, high, wide, this heart of yours! I have other love stories up my sleeve. Ahh! How many tales of love I can tell you! How many loves! Stories that began but stopped mid-way! Stories that ended before they began! Maybe you'll tell me, 'But how can that be?' It can happen, oh yes, it can happen, in stories everything is possible. These things happen in fairy tales, not in reality. Well, in reality much more than that can happen!" he told them with a smile. "Let me tell you about one of them, the best one mind, the one like no other before it...and like no other that can ever be made up. And do you know why? Because this is everyone's story. Then, all the other stories are like it! Listen to it, my friends, it's 'The story of Romeo and Juliet'. This happened a very long time ago, very far away from here, but it happens in every corner everywhere, I think, in this village and also in every other village. As I sing to people, I've come to realize that every village leads into the other villages, and the villages then lead into the towns. And then, only the Good Lord knows what lies beyond the towns. He sees everything from up there, and from His window left ajar, He can peek out and see the towns that we can't see. From behind the slatted shutters. I don't know what lies beyond." The *Għannej tal-Fatt* paused again, looking at Fr. Grejbel to see his reaction.

The people remained silent.

"Decide, folks, decide! Tears or laughter? Perhaps you'd like to laugh a good belly laugh tonight? I know comic songs too," he coaxed them again.

"No," someone spoke up. Many others repeated it after him, and the word seemed to become everyone's verdict.

"At last, at least you've said something! I still don't know what you want. I only know what you don't want. You don't want to laugh!" he addressed the crowd. "Well then, I won't make you laugh! But tell me what song you want me to sing for you...your heart. A story that has a happy ending or one that ends with tears?"

"With a happy ending!" many of them told him.

"But can a story with a happy ending not have a few tears? In the beginning, at least? Well then, which story shall I tell you?"

"The Story of Fr. Grejbel!" shouted Susanna in the middle of that throng.

The people turned their head towards her, all at once, and their eyes searched for Fr. Grejbel somewhere in the crowd, waiting for her to continue speaking.

"But I don't know Fr. Grejbel's story well enough," the *Għannej tal-Fatt* told her, full of astonishment.

"Don't worry. I'll tell it to you in my own words..." Susanna decreed. "Hear me out carefully, word for word, and remember it all, and then make up the verses from the top of your head."

"Now, just like that, all of a sudden?" he asked her.

"Yes, as if you're going to sing *spirtu pront!*" she said firmly.

"*Għanja tal-fatt,* or *għanja spirtu pront?*"

"The two of them, together," Susanna responded in a decisive tone.

"The two of them together? How can that be? And how many characters appear in this story?"

"Besides Fr. Grejbel there are some others, somewhere between a little and a lot, because whoever wanted had a share in his story."

"Are there many characters?"

"There's an entire village...The story begins in the Valley a long time ago...And it goes on till it comes to the part in the village square, in front of the church," she said, her voice still firm. "Listen and remember! Once upon a time, there was a village, nestling among hills, far, far away, where nothing much ever happened except for people being born there and living there and dying there. There was no other place in the world except this village. It lacked for nothing because the villagers were able to understand life, all of it, by using their mind. All that they heard from their forebears, they willingly passed on to their descendants. In this way, generation after generation, the village came to the point where this story begins. It was evening. All the villagers were safely gathered in their own homes, and it was getting late..."

Suddenly, the largest church bell was heard ringing out with its loud and booming stroke. The echo eddied round high up above and people looked up, startled and bewildered, as if they expected to see the noise tangibly turning and turning above their head. The largest bell in the belfry was their pride and joy, one of their cherished glories, and they had dug deep in their pockets to acquire it. Its tone accompanied all their joys and sorrows during each year, from the time when they were newborn babies till they grew old and infirm. As soon as the echo died down, another one was heard and yet another hard on its heels, till in the space of a few heartbeats, all the bells in the belfry were pealing out together and producing a single mote. Everyone fell silent, their eyes fixed upwards or staring intently into one another's.

It was completely unexpected to have the church bells ring out at that moment. With his back resting against the outer wall of the belfry, the sacristan could be seen ringing all four bells at once, two with a rope tied to his legs and the two others with the rope in his hands. The four lengths of rope were coming and going with a measured rhythm, regular and poised, that only a person with his skill was able to maintain. He shook his head slightly in the same manner all the time, and he kept staring at the clappers coming and going from one side of each bell to the other side. The sacristan's joy and pride could be discerned in the least gesture he made.

Susanna, astounded like the rest, was instantly brought up short. The loud reverberations of the bells continued to resonate around the entire square. None of her words could be heard above the din any longer. She could not understand what had happened all of a sudden.

The mote continued, maintaining its rhythm.

Without more ado, Fr. Grejbel walked to the church and entered it from the little door that led to the stone spiral staircase, the narrow circular stairwell in the steeple that reached up to the belfry. He went straight up, in haste. He held up his soutane slightly with his right hand to avoid tripping over it on those narrow winding stairs, and to prevent it from gathering up dust, the loose powdered stone that flaked and fell off from the stone walls and stairs which, in spite of all the years they had been standing there without a lick of paint or plaster, retained their natural colour. The villagers' due care and attention paid off and their skills and crafts took care of everything and were made to last.

As soon as the sacristan saw the priest appear before him, he smiled, gestured with his mouth and continued to ring the bells. Every bell had its name and year of manufacture engraved on it, though the villagers knew each one by its nickname, in the same way they recognized most people. Fr. Grejbel stood staring back at him expecting him to stop, and gesticulating with his hands to show he did not understand what was happening. The sacristan smiled again at him, this time with a more pronounced movement of his cheeks, to reassure him that he was still in full control though it seemed it did not depend on him when he should stop.

Fr. Grejbel brought his hand up to his forehead, like one who has given up trying to understand, and turned to leave the belfry and go back down the stairs.

The people in the square were still expecting the bells to cease pealing out, but it did not seem as if that mote was about to be silenced.

"This is the moment! This is the moment!" Katarina kept repeating to herself as she hurried to her house as fast as she could. "The third floor slab in the courtyard, on the left. I don't have far to go, but at this moment I'm seeing every step as endless. And I'm no spring chicken either. Help me, Holy Mary, make me arrive safely home to be back in good time. You know that whatever help I get is never in vain. The third stone slab, the one that's in a straight line to the projecting stone in the wall. I've always done my best, and if I did something wrong, it wasn't by intention. I don't know what else I can do to have lived in the way my mother and father brought me up. Even from up above, they're witness to the fact that I've never forgotten their words, when it was to my advantage and when it wasn't. The third slab in the courtyard, on the left, in a straight line to the projecting stone, where I have my pot palm. There's no need to get confused and make a mistake. It's only this haste that has me all in a fluster."

Katarina held the large key of her door in her hand, in readiness. As soon as she arrived at her door, she opened it and went straight to the courtyard, knelt down in front of one of the stone floor slabs, prised it up gently, and from the cavity beneath withdrew a small pouch, and then she replaced the slab. She stood up, passed her right foot over the slab to check it was firmly in place, made the Sign of the Cross, quickly went to the front door and went out, pulling the door shut behind her. She went straight back to the church, entered from the side door to avoid being seen, and came to a stop in front of St. Joseph's niche, going down on her knees and drawing a long deep breath. "Thank the Lord!" she whispered.

The bells were still pealing forth and the people were still gathered in the square.

"Here's what I've been vowing to give you for so long," she told the statue of St. Joseph with downcast eyes. "I've come before you once more. I am Katarina, Saverju's wife, Susanna's mother, Wistin's grandmother, a villager like any other but one of those who keep their word, as well as men do, and perhaps even better. You've come to know me well by now, and now, the moment that I've been praying for to you, for so long, has finally arrived and you've granted me the good fortune to be still alive to see it come to pass. Now I know that you've granted all my wishes, to the very end. And here I am now, with all that I have left. This is the pouch I vowed to give you. I hid it for many, many years under a stone slab. Everyday, I guarded it with my eyes, continuously. I used to say, 'There it is, that's not mine, nor is it my daughter's, nor her son's. I don't even want to touch it.' That's what my mother and father taught me, 'What's yours is yours, and what isn't, isn't yours.' This has been yours for a very long time. Today you have granted me my dearest wish, and it's a worthy wish, and I have come to fulfil my part of the bargain and give you what is yours. For me, now, the story has come to an end, and it has a happy ending. And here I am, look," she went on, opening the pouch with trembling hands. "We didn't have anything more valuable than this, Saverju and I. I've never even handled it. It's not meant for women. But I used to see everything that went on. My husband used to wear it and keep it close to him, day and night, and without wanting to, I used to feel proud of it just as much as he did. The *polka* of the pocket watch. A long curb link chain made of silver. The pocket watch is silver too and is attached to one end of the chain. Look at it, see, I'm not lying," she addressed the statue of St. Joseph, lifting the heavy chain upwards and displaying it. "Saverju was quite vain about wearing it, passing the chain from one of the waistcoat's top buttonholes. And on the other end, look, he had a tiny box, made of silver too, and in it he held a few gold coins." She stopped there. She made the Sign of the Cross and with her eyes brimming with tears went on to say, "St. Joseph, this is all yours. Today you have granted me contentment, and I am completely content. Now I've finally walked all the way down my allotted path. There's nothing more I can expect in this world. When it pleases you, call me to you. Over there I can continue my story. If you can, please save me a place next to Saverju in Heaven...so that I won't be alone."

A few paces away from her there was a crowd of people that had entered the church from the square. They were all staring intently at her in total silence. Fr. Grejbel was slightly closer to her than the others, but he did not approach her too closely.

Katarina remained on her knees, with her wide skirt spread all around her like a carpet. When she slowly turned her head and looked at the people gathered there, she saw them all smiling the same sweet smile at her. She ducked her head shyly, but happiness overcame her and she smiled as well.

The bells were still ringing with the same rhythmic flourish, and there did not appear to be the least hint that the sacristan felt like stopping.